INTRODUCTION TO
RELIGIOUS PHILOSOPHY

INTRODUCTION TO
RELIGIOUS PHILOSOPHY

Y. Masih

MOTILAL BANARSIDASS PUBLISHERS
PRIVATE LIMITED • DELHI

8th Reprint: Delhi, 2013
Second Revised Edition: Delhi, 1991
First Edition: Varanasi, 1971

ISBN: 978-81-208-0853-9 (Cloth)
ISBN: 978-81-208-0854-6 (Paper)

MOTILAL BANARSIDASS
41 U.A. Bungalow Road, Jawahar Nagar, Delhi 110 007
8 Mahalaxmi Chamber, 22 Bhulabhai Desai Road, Mumbai 400 026
203 Royapettah High Road, Mylapore, Chennai 600 004
236, 9th Main III Block, Jayanagar, Bengaluru 560 011
Sanas Plaza, 1302 Baji Rao Road, Pune 411 002
8 Camac Street, Kolkata 700 017
Ashok Rajpath, Patna 800 004
Chowk, Varanasi 221 001

Printed in India
by RP Jain at NAB Printing Unit,
A-44, Naraina Industrial Area, Phase I, New Delhi–110028
and published by JP Jain for Motilal Banarsidass Publishers (P) Ltd,
41 U.A. Bungalow Road, Jawahar Nagar, Delhi-110007

PREFACE

RELIGION COMES out of life and can never be divorced from it. The root meaning of religion is that which binds men together and which binds the loose ends of impulses, desires and various processes of each individual. Hence, it is an integrative experience of men collectively and individually. There are many forms of religion, but there is one underlying factor in all of them. They are all occupied with the task of living and adjustment to the various demands of life and society. The need for a successful adjustment requires an understanding of the world in which an individual lives. He lives in a physical and a social environment and the social environment consists of his fellowmen with their histories and prophecies that have evolved as a result of competitive and co-operative enterprise of numerous generations. Here the various strands of science, ethics, economics, history, traditions and myths are all intermingled and each has an important claim on the individual and the society. But a general plan has to be drawn up first in which each individual and his impulses may be assigned a rightful place. From the time immemorial the master plan or the blue-print of life includes philosophy, ethics and religion. In any philosophical construction logic has to be used as its most reliable technique. But logic no matter however important is not the whole of philosophy. But what is philosophy?

Philosophy draws up a conceptual framework of the world in which we live and quite naturally for constructing it, it has to rely on the information supplied by the science of the age. Hence, philosophy has to keep on revising its conceptual framework in the light of scientific advance from age to age. The present age with rapid rise in scientific advance, in theory and technology in numerous departments, makes the task of philosophers extremely difficult. As the task of building a framework of thought is becoming difficult, so philosophers are trying first to assimilate a large number of concepts which have gained currency in science and every day life. Here also there is the painful realisation o' the fact that we think correctly *with* concepts but not so clearly and precisely *about* concepts (G. Ryle). Hence, philosophers are more worried about the clarification of concepts than about building up of a blue-print of life.

No matter how much philosophy may lean on science, it is not science. Its aim is not to understand, control and predict the events of the world as a whole. It aims at understanding the hang of the world with a view to carrying out the task of living, maturing and becoming. Man has to carry out not only conscious adjustment, but also an adjustment to his Unconscious; not only has he to change the world outside of him, but also to effect a change within him; not only a change *of* will, but also a change *in* will, as John Dewey puts it. This understanding of the world is better called wisdom than knowledge: this wisdom is less concerned with the actualities and histories of men than with their hopes and aspirations. Nay, more.

Philosophy is not merely daring speculation: it has to issue out into actions, even though it may mean action for the sake of inaction, the example of which is found in some sectors of Indian thought and practices. Hence, ethics forms a natural corollary of philosophy. Here as a philosophical discipline ethics is less concerned with specific problems and is more concerned with general standards and norms of conduct. Just as in its intellectual construction philosophy draws upon the fund of information given out by sciences, so ethics too not only relies on the general conceptual framework of philosophy, but also on the various codes of conduct in the multitudinous walks of life. At the moment ethics does not try to establish any one standard as the absolute norm. It recognizes the plurality and relativity of ethical norms. Now norms may differ, but they have relevance with regard to intentions to act. At this stage a practical difficulty is experienced. The performance of one's duty is a difficult thing: temptations and natural inclinations play havoc with our ethical intention to carry out the duty. Here, from the time of the Vedas, the Gita and the Bible, from the time of Kant up to Matthew Arnold, R. B. Braithwaite, philosophers recognize that religions are a great help to a moral man. His energies are boosted up and the inclinations standing in the way as obstacles in the performance of duties are brushed aside, if the moral man looks upon his duties as divine commands. Religion may be a myth, but is indispensable for any morality, open or closed, as Henri Bergson has so graphically brought out in '*The two sources of morality and religion*'. But the question is: What is a religious myth?

A myth tries to integrate a man with the supernatural with the help of interrelated symbols. A symbol tries to express the inexpressible and deals with what the individual considers as his ultimate concern. Hence, religion deals with symbols which serve as so many windows to what is concerned as the ultimate reality. Quite naturally the 'ultimate concern' is very much akin to the pervasive features of the world with which philosophy is concerned. But the ultimate concern of religion is not merely conceptual: it deals with the inexpressible and the decisions of gifted men all down the ages with regard to what they have considered to be the ultimate destiny of men. Religion is not a purely intellectual affair for it is not limited to the conscious psyche of the individual, but is largely influenced by the stirrings in the depth of the unconscious. The unconscious is found in every human enterprise, even in his philosophical construction, ethical decisions and scientific pursuits. Not only the metaphysician of the past was dictated by his repressed-suppressed impulses in the unconscious, but the anti-metaphysician of contemporary times is no less guided by his unconscious. As I have already dealt with this topic in some other place,[1] so I shall pass on to the next point.

Religion is not merely an unconscious reaction, but is rather a response and adjustment to the unconscious along with the adjustment to the world and society. A religious symbol dawns as a result of much thinking about one's *why* and *whence*. It is wrung out of the individual in the context of the intellectual reaches of the man with his lodgement in a socio-economic environment. Naturally with the change in the intellectual equipment of the individual, the symbol too changes and the old ones may entirely fade away. A symbol is not true or false: it is either authentic or inauthentic, living or dead and so on.

But why should there be any symbol at all? Well, one reason which has been stated is that religion, to a large extent if not exclusively, is a matter of the Unconscious and the language of the

---

1. Y. Masih, **The Psychology of Philosophers**, Rabindranath Tagore Birth Centenary Celebrations, Vol. III, Visva-Bharati, 1963.

Unconscious is symbolical. However, there is another deeper reason. In the existential literature one hears a good deal of the power of Being and the threat of non-Being and the consequent states of dread, anguish, despair and self-alienation, on the one hand, and also the states of salvation, resignation, meaningfulness and authentic existence, on the other hand. One may try to escape from dread, anguish and the other allied states by self-alienation. However, one cannot always succeed in escaping from one's own self. The threat of non-being, of being annihilated and of death will force a man to be aware of his existential problem, that is, the problem of living in a hostile world which keeps on threatening his existence all the time. How can man establish himself, that is, can have a meaningful existence in the face of physical, moral and metaphysical threats? This problem refers to the Ultimate Concern of man with which he is ultimately concerned. In popular language of theism this Ultimate Concern is known as God. If it is so, then it means that man cannot live without religion. If a person acknowledges God as his ultimate concern then he is said to have an authentic existence. However, if a person follows a tradition sheepishly or slavishly by participating in a collective norm, then he is said to be having an inauthentic existence. In either case man is said to be religious. This is known as the doctrine of religion *a priori*, i.e., man cannot live without religion, the religion may be genuine or faked, but there cannot be an absence of religion *in toto*. Some important thinkers in the west in the wake of God-is-dead movement, are challenging this assumption of 'religion *a priori*'. In this book it has been assumed that man can live without accepting any of the traditional form of religion. To this extent it is true to hold that there cannot be religion *a priori*. But along with this it is also maintained that man cannot live up to his highest potential without some focal orientation in relation to an object of devotion. And this state of mind is said to be religious. So in the final analysis it has been assumed that man cannot live without religion—without some object of devotion, whether this object be concrete or abstract.

However, the modern man has tasted of the tree of knowledge. He is an heir to the human experiences of ages. He knows that there were many gods and they ruled absolutely as long as they were in vogue. But now they have been consigned to the limbo of oblivion. In their times they formed the Ultimate Concern of man and yet many of them, one by one, came to be discarded with the advance in knowledge, with the widening of the intellectual horizon of man. He has become deeply aware of the impending death of his own God who embodies his deepest ideals and meanings of his life. He stands in dread and fear. One natural conclusion which follows from the researches of J.G. Frazer, S. Freud and others is that 'God is dead'. If man takes this lesson to heart then he has no other option left to him but to bow down fully resigned to the inevitable, as certainly Freud did and before him Spinoza and the Stoics preached and practised. But is this Philosophy of resignation inescapable?

Traditional form of God may be dead, but if 'religion *a priori*' is correct, then some modern God is already there enthroned preaching his own gospel of salvation to man. This God may be humanity itself, or may it be the brotherhood of man in a classless society or who knows some vaguer form of God whom we see only darkly. Whatever may be the modern 'God', one thing appears certain that man must have an image whom he worships in order to have some meaningful existence in the face of all kinds of hostile forces and their threats. As long as a god answers to the needs of man, he lives and acts in the lives of men and their history. He ceases to exist the moment he fails to inspire his worshippers. The modern man does not confess his death only, but also of his god. The way out of this dread is that he should further confess that god cannot die. In this lies his salvation.

Man cannot help becoming aware of his Ultimate Concern whom he tries to understand, conceptualise and pin down to precise points. He has thrown out many symbols in his attempt to understand the Ultimate Concern. None of the attempts have succeeded so far, but through the symbols alone man can know that which engages him. 'Knowing' here means 'being energised in his efforts of establishing himself in his meaningful existence as a teacher, preacher, lawyer or any such station in his life'. 'Knowing' is not merely confined to the cognitive activities of man, but includes every fibre of the man as a whole as he participates in the genius of the race of which he is a link. If philosophers demand more precision here then the whole matter can be stated thus. The Ultimate Concern haunts man as soon as he becomes aware of his existential concern. It is his Being, as the power by which he lives. He is more aware of this than of anything else. But in the face of the conceptual challenge all that he can say about it is that it is neti, neti (not this, not this), a pure nescience, about which he can say at most what It is not, or can speak about It only analogically or symbolically. It is a pure colourless canvas on which man projects his symbols. To be successful the coloured symbol must show transparently the colourless canvas below it. Is it paradoxical to say that man tries to know the colourless through the coloured glasses? Well, the seeing of the colourless through the coloured glasses may be paradoxical, but the fact is undeniable that such coloured (symbolical) seeing has enriched life. The teachings of Buddha, Christ and Upanishadic teachers have certainly contributed to the meaningful existence of man. Life lived and death died alone form the 'truth' of religious statements.

Now I take this as an opportunity of thanking the publisher Sri Jainendra Prakash of Motilal Banarsidass for bringing out this volume.

Y. MASIH

PREFACE TO THE SECOND EDITION

The book was out of print for a long time and during this period many changes have taken place. In this edition much attention has been paid to religious language in the light of Wittgenstein's view of religion.

Many topics in Chapter II, a new Chapter III (Foundation of Religious Belief), Chapter V (A General View of Religion and Language) have been added. Meantime the author has adopted the Advaitic Philosophy of Religion, in the light of the teachings of Sant Kabir and Sri Ramakrishna, as the absolute principle for unifying all rival claims of different religions. Further newer topics of Secularism, Proselytization, Conversion and the political use of religion have been added.

However, the chapters *The Psychology of Religion* and *The Truth of Religious Statements* have been omitted.

It is hoped that the present revised edition of the book will meet the needs of the general readers and the students of religious philosophy.

Christian Colony, Lodipur, Patna　　　　　　　　Y. MASIH
June 1st 1990

CONTENTS

ABBREVIATIONS

APR	Approaches to the Philosophy of Religion, ed. D. J. Bronstein/H. M. Schulweis
B.U. or Br. U.	Bṛhadāraṇyaka Upanishad
Chh. U.	Chhāndogya Upanishad
EA	Existence and Analogy, E.L. Mascall
EG	The Existence of God, ed. John Hick
FK	Faith and Knowledge, John Hick
FL	Faith and Logic, ed. B. Mitchell
M.	The Gospel of Sri Ramakrishna, Mahendranath Gupta
NEPT	New Essays in Philosophical Theology, ed. A. Flew/ A. Macintyre
RET	Religious Experience and Truth, ed. S. Hook
RK	Sri Ramakrishna
Sayings	Ramakrishna, F. Max Muller
SBE	Sacred Books of the East, Delhi
U or UP	Upanishads
UT	Unconditioned Transcendent
Vs	Vedārtha-Sūtras of Shankara, tr. George Thibaut

CHAPTER I

DEFINITION OF RELIGION

GALLOWAY AND MARTINEAU

Indian thinkers largely follow the West and they do so also with regard to the definition of religion. As the western mind is largely theistic in its approach to religion, so it usually regards religion as some form of theism. Here the western theologian tacitly maintains the view of Flint[1] according to which anything more than theism is not possible and anything less than theism is no religion at all. In like manner William James has remarked:

"Anything short of God is not rational,
anything more than God is not possible".[2]

Following this hint Galloway (some fifty years ago) defined religion as a

"Man's faith in a power beyond himself
whereby he seeks to satisfy emotional
needs and gains stability of life, and
which he expresses in acts of worship
and service".[3]

Few theologians in the West would totally accept this definition. But before giving the reasons for its non-acceptance, its good points have to be mentioned.

This definition is definitely applicable to theism inasmuch as faith in *a power beyond man* is regarded here as the essential feature of religion. Further, this power is such that it induces the emotional satisfaction of man. In other words, this power responds to man, his prayers of thanks-giving or help in his hours of trouble. Naturally unless this power be personal in some sense of the

---

1. Flint, R. 'Theism'—Lecture II, Sec. III.
2. The Will to Believe and Other Essays, p. 116, also p. 134.
3. Galloway, G., '*The Philosophy of Religion*, p. 184.

term, it cannot satisfy the emotional needs of man. In this sense, the definition given by Galloway is not as bold as that which was given by Martineau:

> "Religion is a belief in an Ever-living God, that is a Divine Mind and Will ruling the Universe and holding Moral relations with mankind".[4]

The second point about Galloway's definition is that it regards religion as the response of the whole man involving his intellect, feeling and will. In the first instance, it is held that religion is a matter of 'faith' or 'belief'. At this stage it is not possible to clarify the concept of 'faith'. But it will be conceded by most theologians that it does imply some sort of cognition. Of course, they would add that a fully understood God is no God at all. They would, however add that *God* or 'a power beyond man' cannot be all-mystery. The worshipper should be able to apprehend at least this much that such a being is worthy of worship,—a being to whom all allegiance is due. This knowledge might be very meagre, and might be intermixed with many other elements drawn from feeling and will, and again might be both conscious and unconscious. Hence a religious man needs only this much of assurance that 'the power beyond man' or 'an Ever-living God' is an actual entity.

Again, few theologians would deny that religion involves an element of feeling, even when they may not agree with Schleiermacher in defining religion as *a feeling of absolute dependence*. The feeling to which Galloway refers is 'emotional satisfaction' and the feeling of stability or security. This point has been greatly emphasized by Freud. In his book 'Civilization and its Discontents' he tells us that a belief in God subserves the purpose of giving us a feeling of security in the face of helplessness caused by the pitiless and dark workings of nature and by the hostile acts of fellow men. Formerly, in "Totem and Tabu" he had pointed out that a belief in God tends to assuage our sense of guilt caused by the Oedipus-situation. Similarly, Jung also would hold that religion gives us *'peace and pistis'*. Thus, the state of *'sthitaprajña'* or *'Nirvāṇa'* is certainly a state of stability in which

---

4. Martineau, James, 'A Study of Religion', Vol. I, pp. 1, 15.

an individual remains unmoved by the vicissitudes of life. This is what the Stoics, Epicureans and Spinoza emphasized as the ripened fruit of the tree of wisdom. In theism this state may assume the form of 'creatureliness' or a state of being abased or a feeling of being dust and ashes before one's creator, or simply the feeling of being an unclean being before the sacredness of God. In current literature this State is being talked of as pure subjectivity, inwardness or a state of commitment.[5] According to Bultmann the life of faith delivers a man from the insecurities and anxieties of this world. Similarly N.F.S. Ferre states that religion is a search for power to overcome the evil side of life even more than its concern for understanding what life at its centre or depth means.[6] Hence, we can agree with Galloway in holding that religion has an element of feeling with its rich overtones.

Further, there is a conative element in every religion. Even in the most primitive forms of religion there are taboos to be observed and in many cases the whole tribe has to take part in magico-religious dances and feasting on the occasion of sacrifice. Later on, when religions become more organised prayers, hymn-singing, keeping of fast many rituals are prescribed as so many religious acts. With the deepening of ethical consciousness social acts of charity, of alleviating human sufferings, forgiveness, sympathy, care of widows and orphans and so on, are also religious if they are taken as divine commands. Even missionary enterprise is a religious act of a high order. Hence, James Martineau, Matthew Arnold and, at the present time Prof. R.B. Braithwaite, regard religion as a matter of morality. Most probably they are right in interpreting religious acts as ethical so far as this observation pertains to higher theistic religions exclusively. However, there are many religious acts which are mostly ritual without any moral principles involved in them. Hence, here also we agree that Galloway is essentially right in holding that religion does consist in acts of worship and social service.

That religion is a matter of the whole man will be conceded

---

5. Beardslee, W. A., '*Truth in the Study of Religion*', in 'Truth, Myth and Symbol', A Spectrumo Book, Edited by T.J.J. Altizer, W.A. Beardslee and J.H. Young, 1962. H.H. Price, 'Faith and Belief' in 'Faith and the Philosophers' Edited by J. Hick, Macmillan, 1964.
6. Reason in Religion, p. 21.

by a majority of religious thinkers. And this fact has been included in the definition given by Galloway. Most probably two things stand out with regard to religious phenomena in their traditional forms, namely, a concern with the supernatural agency and a life of commitment issuing into some pervasive patterns of behaviour. Both these elements have been included in the definition of religion given by Galloway. Any yet this definition would not suffice for us.

JAINISM AND BUDDHISM AS FORMS OF RELIGION
In the Hīnayāna form of Buddhism and in the orthodox kind of Jainism and even in the Śaṁkarite type of non-dualistic Vedānta there is ultimately no room for 'a power beyond man' or 'an Ever-living God'. But it might be pointed out that Jainism and Buddhism are not forms of religion, but are really ethical systems. We reject the contention that they are so many forms of ethical systems. True, Westerners so define religion as to exclude the claims of Jainism, Hīnayāna form of Buddhism and Śaṁkarite Vedāntism. For them Jainism and atheistic Buddhism are forms of ethical systems and Śaṁkarite Vedāntism is taken as a form of either superreligion or as a form of philosophical speculation. If the contention of Dr. A. Schweitzer is sound that a true ethic consists in regarding this world as a thing of value and in service to fellow beings with a view to attaining to the realisation and knowledge of the World Spirit[7], then Jainism and Hīnayānism cannot be regarded as ethical since both of them renounce the world as essentially illusory. Again, both Jainism and Buddhism aim at self-culture or perfection which does not appear to be essentially attainable through service to fellow beings. The most important means is said to be *Samādhi* which consists in total withdrawal from the world. Hence, it would be wrong to treat Jainism and Buddhism as forms of ethical system. But why has this misconception arisen?

Both Jainism in its doctrine of pañca-mahāvrata (the five vows of Satya, Ahimsā etc.,) and Buddhism do include much that is certainly ethical. But the ethical precepts and practices are preparatory disciplines. Thus ethics remains subordinate to

---

7. A. Schweitzer, 'Indian Thought and its Development', chapters I and XVI.

their spiritual aims. We regard Jainism and non-theistic Buddhism as religion because they emphasize the spiritual goal as the real end of life and its activities. They are to be called religion because of their commitment to a life of spiritual culture, issuing into an all-pervasive pattern of behaviour. If our contention is correct then Jainism, Hīnayānism and Śaṁkarite Vedāntism are also forms of religion. If so then religion has to be interpreted by taking cognizance of them also. A few important implications follow from such an attitude. We now know that in the light of analytic philosophy theistic statements have not been shown to be fully intelligible. If theism be the only form of religion, then religious statements too tend to be regarded as meaningless, self-contradictory or absurd. On the contrary we want to hold two things: First, theistic statements are not cognitive; they are existential, convictional and paradoxical. Hence, the conclusion of analytic philosophy with regard to theistic statements is not relevant. Secondly, we hold that there are non-theistic statements in religion. We may call them *Nirvāṇist* statements. They do not describe any object, but are largely autobiographical reports of the religious man himself, or, are expressive of a life of ascesis or are indicative of commitment to an axiological way of life. Hence, even if theistic statements are not intelligible, this would not mean that all religious statements are equally meaningless. We shall show that ultimately all theistic statements are existential and *Nirvāṇist*. Further, the most ancient form of religion is *Nirvāṇist* and linguistic attack as yet has not touched it. Even if theism becomes impossible, religion does not become impossible on that account.

But another objection may arise. We have defined religion in terms of commitment to an object of devotion. We have also hinted that even Communism, Scientism and Humanism may be called religion if the main point of this definition be sufficiently emphasized. For example, Paul Tillich has defined religion as the ultimate concern of man, which determines his ultimate destiny beyond all preliminary necessities and accidents.[8]

"The infinite passion as faith has been
described, is the passion for the infinite,

---

8. S.T., Vol. I, p. 17.

or, to use our first term, the ultimate
concern about what is experienced as ultimate".[9]

Naturally the communist regards classless society as the ultimate and the humanist holds humanity itself his god. If this observation be granted, then even those people who deny religion become religious. This is the variant of the well-known paradox of
the fool who knowing the full implication of what God is cannot
meaningfully say that there is no god. But atheism and irreligion
are too patent facts. They cannot be explained away by our arbitrary definition of religion. So we have to avoid 'conversion by
definition'. Besides, a definition which cannot distinguish between
what is and what is not a religion forfeits its right to be a proper
definition of religion.

Of course, man cannot live without some object of devotion
and to that extent every man is religious. But there is a distinction
between the religious and irreligious. A truly religious person is
not only concerned with what he considers to be the ultimate and
through it seeks his fulfilment, but tries to search for the ultimate
with passion, vigour and with all his soul and strength. In contrast a non-religious person unknowingly accepts his god in an
unconcerned way: he does not acknowledge the ultimate and lives
an inauthentic existence. This point has been expressed thus by
Prof. J. E. Smith:

> "Every one has a god or gods; not
> every one acknowledges God".[10]

And even a seemingly religious man may be an idolater. God
is not of the dead but of the living.

> "Not every one that saith unto me,
> Lord, Lord, shall enter into the
> Kingdom of heaven; but he that
> doeth the will of my father which
> is in heaven".[11]

So, though every one is religious, yet he need not be so in earnestness, in passion, by his choice and free decision and earnestness

9. *Dynamics of Faith*, p. 9.
10. J.E. Smith, *Ultimate Concern and the Really Ultimate*, RET, p. 68.
11. Mt. 7: 21.

which distinguishes between religion and irreligion. If so, then we need not so define religion as to exclude some of the most important types of living religions. It should be conceded that any belief and practices which aim at evoking-invoking an all-pervasive attitude, leading to a culture of the soul should also be regarded as religious.

WORSHIP AND COMMITMENT

Now if Hīnayānist Buddhism, Jainism and Śaṁkarite Vedāntism be regarded as religions, then we have to make a decision with regard to that which can be taken as the essence of religion. On the one hand, there is an object of *worship* and all religious thoughts, feelings and acts are supposed to issue from this worshipful attitude to that object; and on the other hand, there is the element of all all-out staking of the whole personality for realising an ideal state of perfection. Should we take the reference to some sort of supernatural agency as the essence of religion, either with or without the element of all-out commitment to it, or, should we take the existential commitment of the whole man as the essential feature of religion? The more we are concerned with the Judaeo-Christian and Islamic tradition, the greater will be the need for regarding the supernatural reference as the defining element of religion. However, if we take the Eastern and Spinozistic type of religion, then the total and absolute commitment to a certain life of value, as an object of supreme devotion, will appear as the most dominating character of religion. Further, any phenomenon of an enduring kind, has to be judged not in terms of its past history alone, but also in terms of its present and future promise and possibilities. If religious yearnings of man are not supposed to be dying, then we have to regard Communism, Democracy and Humanism as some forms of religion in its modern garb. Now, any total commitment to any pursuit of life as something of an infinite value has to be termed religious[12]. This is exactly the view which was also held by J. Dewey. According to him any activity pursued on behalf of an ideal issuing from conviction of its general and enduring value is religious in quality. A scientist who devotes his life consecrated to the search of truth is no less religious. And the same

12. J. Dewey, A Common Faith, Yale paperbound, 1960, p. 27, first printed in 1934.

is true for the meanest citizen of any state if he performs his duties with the singleness of his heart and purpose. The total effacement of one's likes and dislikes, emotions and wishes for the discovery of scientific truth appears to me akin to the state of Nirvāṇa itself. It differs from the state of Nirvāṇa inasmuch as it is mediated through whole social backing and is not an individual enterprise. Hence, most probably *total commitment* to an object of devotion will be considered to be the most essential feature of a religious life. 'Commitment' is such an important thing that a theist now defines religion thus:

> "Religion is commitment to a kind or quality of life that purports to recognize a source beyond itself (usually but not necessarily called God), and that issues in recognizable fruits in human conduct (e.g., law, morality), culture (e.g., art, poetry) and thought (e.g., philosophy)".[13]

We would not accept this definition of religion given by MacGregor because the recognition of a 'source beyond life itself' is not an essential feature of religion. Secondly, the morality, art, culture and philosophy need not be merely by-products of religious commitment. A great many times they serve as the source of religious experience itself. In other words, morality, culture and philosophy of a certain type may follow from religious conviction. But in their turn they may also serve the purpose of inducing conviction in persons who without such aids might have lacked it. So they may not be 'recognizable fruits', but also may be the roots of religious conviction. However, in this definition the key-notion is 'commitment', which stands in need of elucidation.

The notion of commitment has been largely derived from existential theology and philosophy, where it means encountering a problematic situation, a situation which is ambiguous, multi-forked and yet is a live issue, demanding a solution. Once a decision is reached, a solemn or an all-out pledge is made to follow it up to the end,—to the last ounce of one's energy, then this decision and pledge may be termed 'commitment'. For

---

13. MacGregor, G., 'Introduction To Religious Philosophy', Houghton Mifflin Co., 1959, p. 2.

example, Lord Buddha must have felt a great deal of difficulties in reaching his decision to renounce his wife, son, parent and the kingdom. However, once a decision was reached he followed it out by staking his total personality. Similarly, when the neophytes after tending the cows were thoroughly bored with this life used to decide for a life which is away and different from mundane existence, then the Guru used to recognize in them a commitment for a life of value,—a life which may be called eternal. Again, when one of the thieves hung from the cross, on either side of the Master, decided to confess his sins and seek forgiveness, then he may be said to have encountered his God by whom he was overawed, subdued and conquered. There is the analogous word 'conviction' which has been used by the late W. F. Zuurdeeg. 'Conviction' means to be subdued by the weight of argument or evidence in favour of a persuasion for the meaning of life, which persuasion has certitude for action involving the whole man and his total psychological environment. The whole man has much reference to the inwardness of life. It is not so much cognitive as it is conative-affective. Hence conviction is a matter of permanent and strong disposition. In the language of James, it is 'live', 'forced' and 'momentous'. Most probably conviction, has an overtone of a referent beyond the 'convicted'. Here there is a tacit implication of a convictor who is a quasi-transcendent source of inducing conviction in a worshipper who is convicted by the over-powering majesty of his convictor. Of course, Zuurdeeg does not say this. His use of the term is pretty wide. The convictor for him, as also for us, may be an ideal, a quality of existence itself or a personal Being whose service is felt to be the highest freedom. Hence, here we may say that 'conviction' is neutral with regard to a transcendent 'convictor'.

Why is a worshipper convicted by a life of value or a Jesus or a Rāma? Why is he not equally convicted by all? Of course, consistently no one worshipper can worship both God and mammon. But the real reason does not appear to be wholly intellectual. In some sense all gods are equally worshipful and yet only one or a few alone can be the object of worship. It appears that in the final analysis no reason can be given. When pressed hard a worshipper would say that not he, but his god has chosen him. This point is very much emphasized in the so-called prophetic religions of Judaism, Christianity and Islam. But even Hinduism is not bereft of it, for on many occasions gods are stated to appear in a vision. Hence, in the light of modern psychology we can say that the choice of a God or an ideal or ideal state of society is a matter of one's unconscious. According to the Indian tradition it is due to the past saṁskāras that a person is born with proclivities for a certain choice of his object of devotion. The moderner would say that this choice depends on the typology of the individual and the kind of mentality with which he is born. A *Freud* would say that this choice depends on the infantile fatalities of one's upbringing. An existentialist, on the other hand, would maintain that it is a matter of free choice of the individual.

An object of choice to which all devotion is due or which demands an absolute commitment cannot be an object whose existence can be demonstrated by means of public verification. This therefore has been variously called a symbol, a myth, an archetype, an ultimate concern and so on. Unless this peculiar nature of the object of religious commitment be recognized, we shall commit nothing but errors. One consequence of this language of commitment is that religious statements should not be confused with scientific statements. The latter have the value of truth and falsity or even meaninglessness. In contrast, religious statements are either authentic or inauthentic, genuine or fake, live or dead, forced or trifling. Secondly, they are akin to aesthetic statements. Naturally any demand for the elucidation of religious concepts in terms of the precise formulations of logic or science is foredoomed.

Further, a religious commitment always issues in some acts, thoughts and feelings. Are these acts and feelings individualistic or social? Well, religious experience has both the poles and a satisfactory religious life must balance both the strains. We find that in all the three definitions given by Galloway, Martineau and MacGregor social aspect has been included. Galloway mentions that religious belief issues into 'acts of worship and service' which are certainly social. Similarly, 'the moral relations' of Martineau have social implications for morality without society is not possible. Finally, the 'law, morality, culture and philosophy' which issue out of religion, according to MacGregor are all social in essence. And this is also supported from what we know about the great religious personalities. A Jesus or a Buddha would not only pray in solitariness or meditate, but also would come out into the public life preaching to the poor, healing the sick, comforting the widows and so on. In primitive forms of society religious fervour could be induced only through the medium of social rituals, dance and acts. But in advanced forms of religion, religious acts assume moral earnestness where social service and individual feelings are equally matched and delicately balanced. Then we find that in some forms of higher religions either inwardness or the social service is one-sidedly emphasized. Mysticism would favour the former, Vivekananda and others would emphasize the role of social service and the alleviation of human suffering. Most probably we would say that traditional forms of religion, (even when they contained the germs and even the programme of social evolution as the ethics of Jesus, Buddha and the prophet Mohamad would amply testify,) cared more for individuals' perfection than social perfection. Hence, Whitehead speaking on behalf of the traditional form of religions *rightly* maintains his point:

"The great religious conceptions which haunt the imaginations of civilized mankind are scenes of solitariness: Prometheus chained to his rock, Mahomet brooding in the desert, the Meditations of the Buddha, the solitary man on the cross".[14]

Hence, for Whitehead, religion is what a man does with his own 'solitariness'. And this is an essentially correct observation. As noted earlier, the social changes envisaged by Christianity, Islam or Buddhism were secondary by-products. Their teaching in essentials was: 'What shall profit a man if he gains the whole world and loses his own soul?' The moderners do not think much of the traditional ideal of self-prefection. For them religion is essentially an opiate for the masses. They would say that centuries

---

14. A.N. Whitehead, '*Religion in the Making*', in *APPROACHES TO THE PHILOSOPHY OF RELIGION*, ed. by D.J. Bronstein and H.M. Schulweis, Prentice Hall, 1960, p. 67. Similarly, Prof. H.H. Price has stated the inwardness of religion: "To this I can only answer that if there is no inner life, there is no religion either. Religion *is* a matter of the inner life". Faith and Philosophers, Edited by J. Hick, Macmillan 1964, p. 7. See also pp. 16-17.

of religious teachings have not improved matters. They would urge therefore for the direct concern with the society. The moderners hold that social change through improved technology and science alone hold the key to human progress and individuals' happiness. Communism, scientific socialism of Nehru, Democracy are so many forms of humanism with the goal of social improvement. In India there is hardly any contemporary thinker of note who does not favour social service as the necessary consequence of a religious life. Radhakrishnan, Tagore and Swami Vivekananda have spoken with one breath in favour of social service or amelioration.

Therefore, we need today most urgently a religious philosophy which shall balance the *rival* claims of individuals' self-culture and collectivism. Whether such a philosophy can be consistently presented or not will remain a programme for the persent and future thinkers, but in any adequate definition of religion these points have to be kept in view. Hence, in the light of the above-mentioned observation we can define religion thus:

"Religious beliefs are those that provide an all-pervasive frame of reference or a focal attitude of orientation to life, through a total commitment to an object of devotion".[15]

OBJECT OF DEVOTION IS DISTINCT FROM
    AN OBJECT OF COGNITION

The central thing, according to this definition of religion, is an object. But this object is an *object of devotion* which has to be sharply distinguished from the *object of pure faith or belief.* Faith or belief is some sort of cognition and so there should be some sort of descriptive statement concerning an object of faith or belief. In contrast, the object of devotion need not be a public object. It may be simply an ideal or self-culture, or one's country or profession or simply the pursuit of science or art. Of course, the object of devotion can certainly also be a god. Naturally this kind of definition includes both the theistic type and Nirvāṇ-ist kind of religion. Again, according to this definition, religion is

---

15. This definition is largely indebted to W.T. Blackstone, '*The Problem of Religious Knowledge*', A Spectrum book, Prentice Hall 1963, Chapter—IV (Defining religious beliefs).

a matter of *commitment* to an object of devotion or is an *attitude* to life. Now neither commitment nor attitude can be said to be wholly cognitive, though both of them have to be cognitively supported. At the outset the definition rules out that religious statements are primarily cognitive. Consequently, religious statements strictly speaking need not be true or false. They may have a different kind of value like authentic or inauthentic.

RELIGIOUS BELIEF IS NON-RATIONAL

Here an objection may arise. The definition takes religion as some sort of belief. Is not belief cognitive? This has been taken as such, but it need not be so as the following analysis of belief will show. According to Prof. Paul Schmidt[16] and Prof. H. H. Price[17] a religious belief can be profitably analysed into 'believe-in' and 'believe-that'. A believe-that has a propositional sense in which context a demand can be made for evidence. For example, if a person believes that God is love, then one may request such a believer for the justification of his statement. According to the nature of evidence, therefore, believe-that can be divided into four classes: rational, a-rational, irrational and non-rational. A rational believe-that has sufficient evidence in its favour. Prof. Paul Schmidt defines an irrational believe-that as superstition because it is held against evidence.[18] For a non-rational believe-that it would be inappropriate to ask for evidence, because in the ultimate analysis, for Prof. Paul Schmidt, this is not a proposition at all.

A believe-in, says Prof. Paul Schmidt, consists in the affirmation by a person of an object rather than of a statement.[19] And there are many kinds of objects: a person, a people, a cause, a policy, socialism, totalitarianism, welfare state and so on. A belief-in, for Prof. H. H. Price,[20] is not a propositional attitude. If the object of a belief-in is a God, then for Prof. H.H. Price, belief-in here would mean an attitude of loving adherence to a person.

---

16. Religious Knowledge, Chap. VI (The Free Press of Glencoe, 1961).
17. *Faith and Belief* in *FAITH AND THE PHILOSOPHERS*, Edited by J. Hick, Macmillan 1964.
18. Ibid, p. 79.
19. Ibid, p. 81.
20. Ibid, p. 14.

"The term 'belief-in' emphasizes the trust which is an essential part of the faith attitude."

Now a belief-in usually rests on some type of believe-that. Prof. H. H. Price illustrates this well. For him, before one gets the real experience of God, one should accept theistic propositions, i.e. one should believe that there is a God, or, that there is valid or trustworthy testimony of religious persons concerning them. Similarly, before there is *nididhyāsana*, one should come to hear about and think over the truth of the Vedānta as an object of believe-that. In the same strain, a person willing to have Nirvāṇa should *believe that* there is suffering, that there is its cessation, that it has its cause and that there is a way out of it. For this reason we pointed out in connection with MacGregor's definition that the so-called fruits of commitment may in turn be the very basis of commitment itself. Hence, the relation between belief-in and belief-that is very close. But the two need not be equated. One may believe that there is an omnipotent God and yet may not believe-in him. For example, a devil is supposed to believe that there is an omnipotent God and this belief-that may also make him afraid. But he does not believe in him, for to believe-in means to trust him, and to love him. In other words, to believe-in God is to praise him, worship him and live him in one's life. A belief-in therefore implies an attitude, a commitment or a disposition to act or behave or feel in accordance with its object. Hence, to believe in God and yet not to praise or trust or worship him will be a contradiction. However, one can believe that there is an omnipotent God and yet there is no contradiction in remaining indifferent to him or in not worshipping him.[21] There-

---

21. This will not be perhaps accepted by Malcolm; vide 'Is it a religious belief that' God exists? by Norman Malcolm in Faith and Philosophy, Edited by John Hick; Macmillan 1964, pp. 108-110. Malcolm subscribes to the validity of ontological argument for the existence of God. So according to him for a believer to believe that there is a God is to have belief *in* him. "If one conceived of God as the almighty creator of the world and judge of mankind how could one believe that he exists, but not be touched *at all* by awe or dismay or fear?" (Faith and Philosophers, p. 107). The condition is that it is so for a believer. However, for a non-believer a belief-that need not be accompanied with a belief-in, as in the case of a devil. The devil believes that there is a God but he does not believe *in such* a God, he does not worship Him and is not loyal to Him.

fore, for A. N. Whitehead religion transforms character when it is sincerely held and vividly apprehended.[22] Similarly, Prof. H. H. Price holds that a believe-that has power to change a man's whole life when it is ruminated upon, and vividly pictured mentally.[23]

As usually a belief-in rests on a believe-that, so a belief-in depending on the kind of believe-that may also be called rational, a-rational, irrational and non-rational. Our contention is that a religious belief-in is supported by a non-rational believe-that. Hence, it has an object which induces a worshipper of having a commitment for a certain kind of life. A religious belief has some transforming effect on the life of the individual. Hence, belief-in is supported by a believe-that, and if the believe-that be non-rational, then the religious belief also comes to be non-rational. But even this non-rational belief requires some objects for its support. Even wishes and emotions are directed to some objects. There is an object of which one is afraid or else there are some *sweets* or sounds which give the feeling of pleasure. Hence, non-rational religious beliefs 'have a thought-factor built into them'.[24] Thus a religious belief need not be cognitive, though seemingly it may be defended, supported and helped through rational arguments. In the long run all arguments and all cognitive statements in religion are mere pleas in the interest of belief-in, which for us is the same thing as 'faith'. Cognitive elements are mere means for persuading others or evoking in others and invoking in the worshipper or the mystic himself the numinous experience.

HOLISTIC NATURE OF RELIGIOUS RESPONSE

As we noted earlier, religious experience is of the whole man which means that it includes his cognition, conation and affection, conscious and unconscious, in their totality. But this holistic response, is also directed to the universe, society and everything within the psychological sphere of the individual. This is clear from the etymological meaning of 'religion' itself. This has been derived from *religare* which means to 'bind together'. Hence,

---

22. *Religion in the Making* in *Approaches to the Philosophy of Religion*, edited by D.J. Bronstein and H.M. Schulweis, p. 65.
23. Ibid, p. 17ff.
24. Ibid, p. 15.

religion integrates all intra-individualistic impulses, giving rise to a unified personality, and binds together all fellowmen, and the whole universe under one religious notion. These elements of a religion have been indicated by the terms 'all-pervasive frame of reference', 'orientation to life' and 'commitment'. The terms 'commitment' and 'orientation to life' are more indicative of the integrative approach of the individual and the phrase "all-pervasive frame of reference' refers more to the reality as a whole. For Paul Tillich religious concern is ultimate and unconditional. The unconditional concern is total; no part of ourselves or of our world is excluded from it, there is no 'place to *flee* from it'. The total interpretation, according to Hick, includes one's *en bloc* interpretation of one's entire experience of the universe as a whole. It means a comprehensive world-view, relating the individual to his entire universe. The total concern is infinite: no moment of relaxation and rest is possible, in the face of a religious concern which is ultimate, total, and infinite.[25] Further, as was noted earlier, even something most subjective, like our wishes or feelings of satisfaction-dissatisfaction, requires its appropriate objective substrate. Therefore, there can be hardly any religious integration of all the impulses and processes within the psyche of the individual without some objective reference or significance. Hence, there is always an object, either concrete or abstract. Socialism, welfare state, science itself, classess, society are so many abstract objects. On the other hand, God, Christ, Lord Buddha are concrete objects of religious devotion. But the hard lesson to learn is that the objective referent in a religious experience can never be totally separated from the experience itself. The objective here is not that which is free from the subjective involvement of the scientist. In some sense of the term the objective here is that which is most subjective. The truth of religion is not one which is *found* or discovered at the end of seeking, but is precisely that which is exhibited in the process of seeking itself. The whole life lived, as it comes to be appreciated or evaluated, is the truth of religious quest. Religious truth is

25. Paul Tillich, *Systematic Theology* in *READINGS IN TWENTIETH, CENTURY PHILOSOPHY*, Edited by W.P. Alston & George Nakhnian, Free Press of Glencoe, 1963..., p. 729. See also J. Hick, 'Faith and Knowledge, Cornell University Press, 1957, pp. 127-133.

made true. The life of Jesus, as leading to a life of sacrificial death on the cròss, is the truth of Christian experience.

AUTHENTICITY OF RELIGIOUS LIFE

When religion includes the reality as a whole, then naturally it is social as well. This aspect has been included not only in the phrase 'all-pervasive frame of reference', but more particularly in the phrase 'focal attitude of orientation to life'. The focal attitude not only determines the direction in which religious acts of service and worship take place, but also the spirit or the enthusiasm or grace with which they are performed. Hence, MacGregor regards religion as a commitment 'to a kind or quality of life'. Religious beliefs are held in earnestness or passion. Now commitment implies this concern of man for what is considered to be the ultimate thing for him. Besides, the term 'attitude' or 'commitment' implies readiness to act in a particular way. Hence, religious attitude or commitment need prior preparation and exercises often called spiritual practices, so that a kind of character may be formed or a type of action may readily issue forth from the worshipper. Therefore, it is said that faith without its appropriate works is dead. In the last analysis then, a life of commitment to an object of devotion reflects that object. Here belief-in and belief-that coincide. A knower of Brahma or Brahamvid becomes Brahma himself.

ब्रह्मविद् ब्रह्मैव भवति

or

लाली मेरे लाल की जित देखों तित लाल ।
लाली देखन मैं गयी, मैं भी हो गयी लाल ॥

Similarly, a Buddhist does not worship a Buddha towards the end of his meditative acts, but attains Buddhahood. This is what is known now in existential theology as an authentic life.

Chapter II

RELIGION AND OTHER DISCIPLINES

RELIGION AND THEOLOGY

Religion is a system of lived experiences. This therefore includes the first order language in which we communicate our feelings, thoughts and acts in relation to an object of devotion and commitment. For example, a theist prays *to* God, talks *to* him and uses Him in hours of his distress, elation and gratitude. With his belief in Him he never doubts the existence of God and does not feel any need of *proving* His existence. But no religious believer can remain in this state of receptivity all the time. He has to take into account his non-religious activities also. He has to earn his livelihood, maintain his social life and hás to undertake many other social, political, cultural and intellectual activities. Well, very few people can maintain a water-tight compartment between their religious life and non-religious experiences. Hence, the demand for an integrated life makes the believer unify the diverse and competing experiences. He has to use the intellectual categories of his time in order to integrate his religious and secular experiences into a system. This making use of intellectual categories is another name of philosophising. Again, this use of the conceptual framework of one's age with a view to clarification, elucidation and systematisation of one's religious beliefs and practices is known as theology. 'Theology' literally means 'discourse about God'. So in theology we do not talk *to* God, but *about* God.

Theology is the philosophy of any one religion. There are as many theologies as there are religions, and, at times within the fold of the same religion there can be various theologies. For example, Buddhism, Christianity and Islam have various kinds of theologies. Theology is not simply concerned with the elucidation of concepts in use in any one religion, but very often it has to defend itself against the objections of sceptics, agnostics and the attacks of other religions on it. Therefore theology is not a disinterested study. It participates in the commitment of the religion to which it belongs. However, theology is not the first-order thinking: it is a second-order thinking. It is thinking about religious thinking. This peculiarity of theology has its dangers. Because of its commitment, it may remain too much tied up with its traditional conceptual framework. However, it must be conceded that theologies have been changing with the change in the intellectual climate from age to age. For example, the early Christian thinkers took the help of the logos-philosophy of the Greek. Later on St. Thomas embodied a good deal of Aristotelian philosophy. Only fifty years ago a number of theologians were Hegelians and in contemporary times they tend to be existentialists.

THEOLOGY AND PHILOSOPHY

But no matter what theologians may do with philosophy, they are not primarily philosophers. They make use of philosophical technique for elucidating, interpreting and even for apologetic defence of their specific religious beliefs and practices. The task of philosophy is much wider. It has to reach a conceptual framework of the largest number of experiences of mankind. As the most reliable and progressive experiences of man are included in science, so philosophy at present is much more concerned with scientific discourse than with any other type of talking and thinking. This peculiar development of current philosophy, specially analytic philosophy, poses special difficulty for theologians. Science is a disinterested pursuit of knowledge and its subject-matter is sought to be depersonalised. In contrast, religious thinking requires a good deal of self-involvement and passion and a full commitment. Naturally a philosophy which takes science seriously as the very model of knowledge proper is ill-suited to serve as the vehicle of theological thinking. On the other hand, there is another current of philosophy known as existentialism which takes individuals in their creative moments, in the hour of crisis and personal decision as root-metaphor or its key-notion. This kind of philosophy is farthest removed from physical sciences, but is suitable for theology. Naturally the theology of Karl Barth, Rudolf Bultmann and Paul Tillich can hardly be made intelligible in terms of analytic philosophy which is predominant current of thought in the English-speaking world. Nonetheless a theologian has to take the help of current philosophy of the age with a view to making his religious thinking compatible with the largest possible segments of life. Unless he does so he will be religious on Sundays and will be secular on all other days. This disintegration of personality is neither possible nor is conducive to healthy living. So a theologian has to build up a conceptual framework in which he can harmoniously lodge all his experiences, secular and religious.

There is another reason too. There are many theologies and each theology fairly well seeks to become a world theology. And this gives rise to encounter of religions. Hence, there is a need of a philosophical theology. A philosophical theology is meta-theology which tries to elucidate the concepts of various theologies. If the task be successful then as a result of the clarification of the concepts, mutual dialogue and understanding between thinkers of various faiths may result in a vast ecumenical movement. For example, 'God' is used by many forms of theistic religions, but the term is not used in the same sense. The God of the Gītā is more monistic than theistic and that of Spinoza is more pantheistic than deistic or theistic. Even the term 'religion' is full of ambiguities. Is it necessary for religion to have belief in some ontological entities higher than man, or, does it consist in some all-out orientation towards some object of devotion? Theists in the west would accept the first alternative. Indian thinkers need not accept the necessity of any being higher than man as an object of worship, but they assume some kind of metaphysical commitment for religion. Only the modern secular humanist does not make any metaphysical commitment for this type of religion. These ambiguities with regard to 'religion' have to be clarified and their implications have to be carefully worked out for any kind of religious philosophy. Thus religious philosophy, as distinguished from theology, consists in the application of the discipline and technique of any current philosophy with a view to analysis, elucidation and clarification of religious and theological concepts and beliefs.

True, religious philosophy is a branch of philosophy and it differs from philosophy proper only in regard to the nature of its specialised subject-matter. The scope of religious philosophy is much narrower than that of general philosophy. But it is neither religion nor theology. In religion the believer uses religious concepts and beliefs in their customary meanings without subjecting them to any critical analysis. Broadly speaking, the believer cares more for the end result which may be said to be the culture of the soul. Theology, in relation to religion, is much more intellectual, though the whole web of thought is woven round its realm of commitment and self-involvement. Karl Barth, Rudolf Bultmann, Paul Tillich and Dietrich Bonheffer are great theologians of the present century and yet they are all *christian* thinkers par excellence. In contrast, religious philosophy tends to be purely objective and disinterested enquiry into the concepts and beliefs of various religions and their theologies. Thus, the mutual understanding and dialogue between theologians of different camps brought about by religious philosophy would be purely intellectual. Hence, a religious philosopher need not be religious though he should not be without sympathies for religion. But even as a philosopher he has his non-religious commitment and self-involvement.

A religious philosopher need not be a theist or even a humanist, though the task of remaining fully neutral may prove too difficult. However, as a philosopher he must be committed to finding truth and to a rigorous analysis of religious situations, beliefs and practices. He must throw all his energies in the task of understanding religious phenomena and thought. Again, a theologian too has to practise detached objectivity if he wants to bring out the universal validity of what he considers to be the ultimate concern of mankind. Thus, both the philosopher and the theologian have to practise self-involvement and detachment in turn. A philosopher gets involved in his enquiry with regard to religious phenomena. Unless he pursues his enquiry with passion, seriousness and courage, the philosopher will not be able to achieve excellence in his performance. In the same way a theologian has to practise detachment if he has to universalise what he considers to be his ultimate concern. Further both the philosopher and the theologian have to oscillate between detachment and involvement in the inquiry of their subject-matter. Even a philosopher has to enter into the spirit of religious phenomena and for doing this he has to put on the spectacle of a believer to see things as a theologian sees them. So commitment, even though induced and transitory, is necessary for a religious philosopher. In the same way, a theologian has to put himself aside for a while from the ground which he considers to be holy and has to adjudge the ground for its holiness. Thus, a philosopher of religion and a theologian have to be on talking terms and must start a dialogue between them in their mutual interest and to their mutual benefit.

We can summarise the relation between religion, theology and religious philosophy in the following way:

RELIGION	THEOLOGY	RELIGIOUS PHILO-SOPHY
1. Religion is a system of lived experiences in terms of self-involvement and full commitment for the object of religious devotion and focal orientation.	Theology is an interpretation of religious experiences in terms of current concepts. However, the intellectual clarification is made in the interest of one's religious commitment.	Religious philosophy analyses and elucidates religious concepts in terms of general conceptual framework with detached objectivity.
2. There is no one essential religion in general, but there are religions.	Corresponding to various religions there are a number of theologies, with their different assumptions.	Religious philosophy is metatheology which examines the various claims and uses of theological concepts.
3. Religious statements may be termed as first-order statements.	Theological statements are second-order statements with religious statements as their subject-matter.	Philosophical statements are third-order statements as they deal with second-order statements as their subject-matter.
4. A theist talks *to* God.	A theistic theologian talks about God with reverence and piety.	A philosopher talks *about* God with disinterestedness and detachment.

RELIGION AND MORALITY

Religion is a holistic response of man to what he considers as his ultimate concern. As such, religion contains all the three aspects of human life, namely, cognition, conation and affection. Cognition is most prominent in scientific pursuits; conation is well expressed in morality, and the effective aspect is most clearly manifested in the artistic pursuits of man As all these three mental aspects are found inseparably together, so religion too is found together with morality and art and also science. In the early stage of civilization religion, art and science were found inextricably together. But with the development of thought, they became relatively independent of one another. At the present time they tend to become autonomous disciplines with the cry 'Art for the sake of art', and 'Morality for the sake of morality'. This requires a careful study of the relation between religion and morality, religion and art, and so on.

RELIGION AND MORALITY

Different views have been taken with regard to the relation of religion to morality.

1. Religion and morality are inseparable and interdependent.
2. Religion is independent of morality.
3. Morality is independent of religion as an autonomous discipline.

In contemporary thinking, morality is taken to be an autonomous discipline. But at one point the involvement of God in morality is widely discussed. 'Free will' is said to be an important postulate of morality. Some contemporarv philosophical analysts like A. Flew and J.L. Mackie hold that God could have created man with free will and yet could have so fully determined his free act that he might not have fallen into any moral lapse. However, Alvin Plantinga challenges this claim of A. Flew and J.L. Mackie. According to Alvin Plantinga, the very linguistic convention maintains that no free act can be totally determined. Hence, God the creator could not have granted free will to man and at the same time could not have totally determined free acts so as to preclude his moral lapse.

INTERDEPENDENCE OF RELIGION AND MORALITY

Higher religions have remained inseparably related to morality. For example, Judaism and Christianity have accepted the Ten Commandments. Yahwe gave the following ten commands:

1. I am the Lord your God. You shall have no other God before me.
2. You shall not have any image of me.
3. You shall not misuse the name of the Lord, your God.
4. Observe the Sabbath day as holy.
5. Honour your father and mother ....*Pañca Mahāvrata*.
6. You shall not murder. ....   *Ahimsa.*
7. You shall not commit adultery ....*Brahmacarya.*
8. You shall not steal ....   *Asteya.*
9. You shall not give false witness.........*Satya.*
10. You shall not covet ....   *Aparigraha.*

The last five commandments are virtually the same as the *pañca mahāvrata* of Jainism which five moral vows have been accepted by all the Indian religions. Thus, religion and morality are inseparable and interdependent at least in the traditional higher religions of the world. By 'interdependence' is meant that religion helps morality and morality, in turn, keeps on refining religious demands. In general, according to Freud, man has been able to give up many cruel and aggressive impulses within him in the name of God. This is seen in the case of the head-hunters of Garo and Khasi hills after their embracing Christianity. Now they respect their neighbours. Thus, religion does help in cultivating the life of morality. The very religious necessity of the ten commandments and *pañca mahāvrata* shows that religion helps the growth of morality. Even when morality is regarded as independent of religion and wholly autonomous, religion does not remain wholly discarded. Both Kant and R.B. Braithwaite bring in God as the psychological booster of morality. The performance of one's duty is not an easy task. Therefore, Kant recommends that duties should be regarded as 'divine Commands'.

Further, religious development has been greatly helped by the deepening of moral insight. For example the later growth of Judaism did not emphasize the cruel rite of animal-sacrifice. The

Lord was said to be better pleased with the practice of justice, mercy and with a contrite heart. In the same way the R̥gvedic Āryans were persuaded to give up animal-sacrifice and accept the doctrine of Brahman which taught the conquest of one's own animal desires.

Religion with its derivative of *re* and *legere* means to bind its adherents together and also to bind the loose ends of lower impulses within each man himself. Hence morality includes both the external and interiorized rules of conduct. The more morality is interiorized, the purer it becomes. Both in Christianity and Hinduism the emphasis is laid on the interiorization of morality in the direction of self-conquest and the self-culture of the soul. For example in Christianity it is not enough to refrain from adultery, for whosoever looks at a woman to lust for her has already committed adultery with her in his heart. Similarly, in Indian religious thought people are taught to overcome desires like sexual passion, anger, infatuation, greed etc. Hence, higher the religion the stricter is the demand for higher morality. In general morality is the purifier of religion and religion is said to be the perfection of morality, for God is said to be the conservator of all values, specially morality. In other words, God is the embodiment of morality and its chief guardian. However, at times religion is said to be independent of morality.

RELIGION AS INDEPENDENT OF MORALITY

In primitive religions there is more of magic than morality. In early forms of religion there is more of *tabu* than moral code. Even in totem-cult cannibalism was practised without any moral considerations. Even children were sacrificed, a trace of which is visible in Abraham's willingness to sacrifice his only son Isaac to please Yahwe.

Again, Ājivikism and other heretical sects mentioned in *Brahma-Jāla-Sutta*, practised and believed in *antinomianism* which is opposed to the obligation of observing morality. For example, Pūraṇa Kassapa is an *akriyāvādi* (inactionist) who held that any action has no effect on the soul. *Samañña-phala-sutta* thus mentions the doctrine of antinomianism :

"He who performs an act or causes an act to be performed,

........he who destroys life, the house breaker, the plun-
derer......the adulterer and the liar.....commits no sin"
"In generosity, in self-mastery, in control of senses, in speaking truth, there is neither merit nor increase of merit".[1]

Here the religious belief in Karma theory was independent of
morality.
In later times, both in Christianity and Indian thought, there
is the teaching of being saved by the Grace of God alone.

"This Soul (Atman) is not to be obtained by instruction, Nor
by intellect, nor by much learning. He is to be obtained only
by one whom he (Atman) chooses; To such a one that Soul
(Atman) reveals his own person (*Kaṭh*, 2.33; *Muṇḍaka* 3.23).

In the same manner Calvin taught that men are saved by the grace
of God. This can be traced even to Pauline teaching. In the same
vein, Karl Barth has taught that God's word can be understood
only through the divine grace. In these religious teachings,
moral excellence is discounted, for no man can be counted righteous before God.
    In both Advaitism and *Bhakti* cult of the Āḷvārs, it is taught
that after the final attainment of spiritual ascent, the seeker goes
beyond 'good and evil'. This has several nuances of meanings.
In the first instance, the actions whether good or evil belong to
Prakṛti. Once this illumination dawns on the seeker that Prakṛti
alone is the doer, then this knowledge releases a man from all
actions, good or bad.
    Secondly, it also means that in reaching the state of *prapatti*,
it is realized that not the *prapanna* works but God alone. Thus
the *prapanna* is not the doer of any work whether good or bad.
According to Sri Ramakrishna, the released soul feels,

"I am the machine, and Thou, O Lord, art the Operator.
I am the house and Thou art the Indweller. I am the chariot
and Thou art the Driver".[2]

---

1. A.L. Basham, *History and Doctrines of the Ajivikas*, p. 13.
2. The Gospel, p. 211; *Vide, Ibid.* p. 209, Teachings 70, 71.

Again,

> 'He is truly free, even in this life, who knows that God does all and he does nothing'.[3]

It may also mean that the devotee becomes so holy that he can commit no sin. Only holy acts flow from him.

Thirdly, the phrase 'Beyond good and evil' means that morality remains valid at the dualistic stage. When, however, one becomes one with Brahman, then action ceases, for there is none to whom one can do either good or bad.

Thus, there are religious thoughts where morality is either not invoked as in certain primitive forms of religion, or, where one goes beyond the stage of morality.

AUTONOMY OF MORALITY

Kant has powerfully advocated the case of the autonomy of morals. According to this way of thinking morality is good not because God wills it, but God wills it because it is good. The memorable words of Kant are that Good Will is good, not because of the consequences which can be frustrated by the niggardly provision of a stepmotherly nature, but good will is good in itself. Nothing in the world, nay, even beyond the world is good categorically as is good will. Health, wealth, honour, learning and so on, all can be misused, but not the good will. Hence, it is a jewel which shines by its own light.

Since the time of Kant the autonomy of morals has become an accepted creed for the philosophers. They have been regarding religion as a set of moral principles, either with emotion (Matthew Arnold), or, backed by stories (R.B. Braithwaite). For Braithwaite, a religious assertion is a statement of an intention to carry out a certain behaviour policy, subsumable under a sufficiently general policy to be a moral one, together with a story as a psychological energiser. There is hardly any analytic philosopher at present who studies morality with any reference to religion. Even the ideologies of Communism and democracy denounce religion. The Communists have always been critical of religion, but even a philosopher like John Dewey denounces religion and

---

3. *Teachings*, 86.

teaches the self-sufficiency of democracy. The words of John Dewey are remarkable:

"The ideal ends to which we attach our faith are not shadowy and wavering. They assume concrete form in understanding of our relations with one another and the values contained in these relations. We who now live are parts of a humanity that extends into the remote past, a humanity that has reacted with nature. The things in civilization we most prize are not of ourselves. They exist by the grace of the doings and sufferings of the continuous human community in which we are a link. Ours is the responsibility of conserving, transmitting, rectifying and expanding the heritage of values we have received that those who come after us may receive it more solid and secure, more widely accessible and more generously shared than we have received it. Here are all the elements for a religious faith that shall not be confined to sect, class, or race. Such a faith has always been implicitly the common faith of mankind. It remains to make it explicit and militant".[4]

In spite of the good which religion has done in the past, even at persent to the development of morality, according to Freud, morality must be made independent of religion now. Why? Because religion is largely mythological and myths are bound to disappear in the white light of science. If, therefore, religion and morality are kept together, then with the disappearance of religion, morality will stand in danger of disappearance. But can man live without religion?

We have maintained the doctrine of religion *a priori*. Much of the scaffolding of mythology in religion is bound to disappear, but a purified and refined form of religion along the path of Advaitism of Shankara, Kabir, Sri Ramakrishna and Vivekananda will continue to guide men towards the higher goal of struggling humanity in which caste and communal riots and international cold wars will become things of the past. But morals without religion remain a hoax. Even Kant, the father of the doctrine of the autonomy of religion, recommended the psychological

---

4. John Dewey, *A Common Faith*, p. 87, Yale 1960.

booster of the religious myth. He recommended that duties should be performed as divine commands, because Kant felt that the performance of duties is difficult for men without such a booster.

Hence religion and morality have to go together by refining, criticizing and sublimation of one with another.

RELIGION AND ART

Religion is a holistic response of man to Absolute Reality. Hence, it includes all the three mental processes of cognition, conation and affection. As these three are inseparable, they remain together in every human pursuit. In science there is the element of cognition which dominates over conation and feeling. But without the conative trend of curiosity and affective drive of simplicity, science cannot run. Similarly, in religion all the three aspects of mind are found inseparably together. For example, God is said to be omniscient (cognitive aspect), omnipotent (conative element), benevolent (cognitive-conative aspect) and bliss (feeling or affective aspect). Again, God is said to be the embodiment of Truth, Beauty and Goodness. Hence, art in which the aspect of beauty dominates, can also be pressed in the service of religion. For example, music, poetry, architecture, painting are all used in religion in its performance. In general, religion becomes attractive and popular in the masses when it is combined with art; and, art becomes sanctified and sublimated when pressed in the service of religion. However, the following relations may be found between religion and art:

1. Religion may remain relatively independent of art.
2. Art may be pursued independently of religion.
3. Religion and art may remain inter-dependent.

I. Religion can never be completely independent of art, for art includes a great many cultural expressions without which no civilized life is possible. Art includes music, poetry, dance, literature, sculpture, architecture and so on. Not to speak of religion, even the most primitive life is not possible without art. But when it is said that religion may remain independent of art, then it simply means some sort of iconoclasm of artistic products. For example, sculpture has remained closely associated with religion. But Judaism, Puritanical Christianity and Islam have always remained highly critical of image-worship. So whenever these tendencies against image-worship have been in force, the destruction of images has been practised. Even dance and music have been banned. Even now mosques and Protestant Churches have hardly any image. But religion cannot continue without some sort of art. Even a mosque is built with its own beautiful domes, minarets and lattice work. Similarly, churches in Vienna under the influence of Puritanism have developed artistic window-panes even when they are bereft of any human images. But can art flourish without religion?

II. There have been artistic creations in primitive society without reference to religion. For example, artistic drawings of animals in the cave-dwellings of primitive men are more for the magical success of hunting than for totemistic worship. Similarly, much of dancing and music of primitive men are for the sake of food-production and the abandonment of joyous living rather than for appeasing gods or jungle-spirits.

Not only in the past, but also in modern times art is pursued for the sake of art. Many T.V. shows tend to promote secular interests largely for pushing the sale of industrial products. In modern times, much of poetry, music, architecture, dancing and all such pursuits have no religious end. For example, pop music does not appear to have any religious end. Much of Western painting has nothing to do with religion. Everywhere there is activity of secular interests with efficiency as their sole end. But can art flourish without religion?

III. Undoubtedly religion goes with morality. Hence, art without religion means art bereft of moral and spiritual values. Much of dancing shown in *Chitrahar* is bereft of religious values. And the result? Vulgarization of art. In general art is sanctified and sublimated when it is combined with religion. Even now the most beautiful temples of South India are the examples of the best Indian archaeology. Similarly the most impressive churhes in Europe, of Gothis structure have been prompted by religious motivation. Some pieces of music both in India and Europe have been dedicated to spiritual pursuits. Bach and Beethoven even now cast their spell on the Western audience. Further, some pieces of poetry from the ancient times up to the mediaeval age were dedicated to religious ends.

Some of the most inspiring pieces of poetry, sculpture, archaeo-logial remains have been sanctified by religion. Hence, the following lines from '*The Testament of Beauty*' by Bridges:

Beauty is the highest of all these occult influences.
The quality of appearances that thru' the sense
Waketh spiritual emotion in the mind of man:
And Art, as it createth new forms of beauty.
Awakeneth new ideas that advance the spirit in the life of
Reason to the wisdom of God.[5]

In *Kumārasaṁbhavam*, Kalidasa has expressed the view that the beautiful can do no wrong. Similarly, Ramanuja credits Ish-vara with infinite beauty manifested in his idols:

He (God) has captivated the eyes and hearts of all by his surpassingly sublime beauty—His eternal and inconceivable youthfulness is infinitely marvellous. He has the delicate fresh-ness of smiling blossom.[6]

But religion and art have to be distinguished from one another. Art cannot be restricted to religion. Religion is largely mythological and myths tend to disappear with the spread of science and technology. Hence art cannot remain confined to the singing of praises of gods and their representation in plastic arts and poetry. For this reason in recent times there is the cry 'art for the sake of art'.

However, art without the sobering effect of religion tends to be vulgarised. The reason is that art works through sensuous forms, which tend to restrict the advance of man towards his higher spiritual pursuits. In Indian tradition in *yoga*, *dhyāna* or *samādhi*, the seeker starts with gross images, which get subtle with further progress. But in the end all images, whether gross or subtle have to be left behind in the final realization of *Brah-man*. Otherwise according to Kabir one remains condemned into idolatry.

---

5. Quoted by Atkinson Lee on page 66 of his book, *The Philosophy of Religion*.
6. *Vedārtha Saṁgraha*, pada 220.

RELIGION AND SCIENCE

At the dawn of religion, science, art, morality all were found intermingled together. Science was present in religion in the form of magic. It was believed that given the spell of magical incantation the result will follow inexorably. However, man slowly and gradually realized the insufficiency of magic. Even its association with religion was dropped because magic was used often to harm people and for obtaining evil ends. In due course religion condemned sorcery. However, both religion and magic have their roots in the supernatural. However, science is concerned with the natural. But science and magic both cherish the ideal of predictability of future events and their control. With this introduction let us detail the relation of science and religion.

1. Science is concerned with the natural and the traditional religions with the supernatural. Religion is pre-occupied with the supersensible and science is limited to the sensible. Science is rooted in data which can be repeated and varied at will according to the requirements of the scientists all over the world. Of course mere collection of data is not science. The data have to be organized under some hypothesis in quantitative terms and when the hypothesis is sufficiently verified then it becomes a scientific law. Even the laws are subsumed under some theory. But even the theory in the end has reference to the data. Besides the laws and theories are framed with a view to regulating, controlling and predicting the future. It is this control and unerring prediction of future events that has made science most acceptable to the civilized people of the world. In contrast, religion in the end remains a personal achievement and an autobiographical account of what the mystic reports about the supernatural. The mystic account is not amenable to public check. Hence, Whitehead regards religion as what one does with his solitariness.

The great religious conceptions which haunt the imaginations of civilized mankind are scenes of solitariness: Prometheus chained to his rock, Mahomet brooding in the desert, the Meditations of the Buddha, the solitary man on the cross.[7]

---

7. A.N. Whitehead, *Religion in the Making*, quoted in *Approaches to the Philosophy of Religion*, p. 67.

However, the religious insight is won by an individual, but it is also a gain for the whole society and even for the whole world. For example, the insight of the solitary man in the cave, or away in the forest, or under a banyan tree is what the people of that era and place are fervently seeking to know. For example, Lord Buddha found what the Ājivikas, 262 heretical sects at that time and the Brahmins were trying to find out. And when it was known and preached by the Buddha then many wise men of the time gratefully accepted his teaching. Even the cave-dweller meditator has an ideal community in his mind when he is meditating alone. Jesus hanged on the cross had the vision of the angels and archangels who were sharing his suffering on the cross. Besides he had the vision of a future community who would follow him and would acknowledge him as the Master and the Lord. Hence, even a solitary meditator thinks with the whole community and has an ideal society in his mind. Thus, religion is as much social and has social significance, perhaps more in India than in the Western world, because Indian democracy is sustained by caste and communal considerations. However in contrast, in the modern developed State it is science which is supported and sustained by the resources of the State in preference to religion. Religion has become a personal matter for the citizens of the State. Why is this favouritism for science ? For science alone has given us conquest over nature, over many diseases and has taught us to fight successfully against droughts, floods and many other such natural calamities of nature. And its promises for the future have no known limits. But has religion nothing to say at this juncture of the triumph of science?

According to religion, science no doubt has conquered nature, but it has not conquered the inner core of man himself. Without the still small voice of religion the beast in man may use science and technology to destroy man and life itself. Indeed the weapons of destruction are many times more powerful to destroy the whole life on this planet. The lust of power and money has grown so much in the politicians of India and the world over that religion has become a toy in their hands. This has given birth to caste and communal riots in India and cold war over the whole globe. However, the real believers do not favour the political use of religion. According to them, religion rightly used can do much to conquer the evil in man. At least this was the case in ancient India, as was recorded by the Greeks. But there is also danger in religion itself.

2. Science has been able to clip the events of nature with the help of laws. But these laws are always tentative. At the most, they can enjoy high probability, but can never be true beyond all possibility of doubt in the light of future investigation of nature. This is perhaps a very healthy attitude in science. In contrast, religionists tend to be highly dogmatic due to their psychological conviction. The felt certainty in religion is purely subjective and wholly psychological. The very nature of religion is that it excludes any doubt. No theist would say, 'If I secure a first position in the examination, or a job, then I will accept the reality of God. In religion a believer cannot assume a hypothetical attitude to God. On the contrary, a theist has to accept God with all his heart, with all his soul, with all his mind and with all his strength. He remains so much committed that he says, 'Even though He slay me, I will cling to Him still'. It is so unfortunate that this attitude breeds fundamentalism which is the cause of so much of hate amongst the followers of various religions. This same attitude of dogmatic conviction causes conflict between science and religion. But more.

3. There is another difference between religion and science. Religion is emotionally neutral. A scientific truth is established irrespective of the wishes of the scientist. For example, Charles Darwin was a devout Christian, and according to Christianity of his time it was believed that God had created man in His own image. However against this theory of creation, Darwin had to accept the evidence of facts and accordingly he accepted the doctrine of Organic Evolution.

In religion on the contrary, the mystic sees the vision of what he wishes to see most ardently. A Christian mystic will report the seeing of Christ, and, a Ramakrishna will report seeing of Ma Kali or other *Paurāṇika* gods. Not only there is no unanimity of mystic reports, there is no newness of fresh observed data. The mystics report what has already been maintained in the past. However, science extends the field of observation and keeps on observing fresh data in every field of investigation.

4. However, thinking people, including the scientists have

maintained that there is no conflict between science and religion because their spheres are different. Religion deals with *value* and science with *facts*.

True, religious judgements have reference to values, traditionally known as Truth, Beauty and Goodness. But one should be careful in saying that 'Truth is God'. 'Truth' has several nuances of meaning. 'Truth' may mean moral truthfulness; it may mean the value of being true or false with regard to propositions; and, it may mean metaphysical Reality. The value of truth and falsity is legitimately applied to factual propositions only. In this analysis it is clear that religious statements are not true or false. For instance, it cannot be validly said that God is true or false. But religious statements are largely mythic, and, a mythic statement may be authentic if it is held as living and momentous for the believer. If it is not so, then it is fake or inauthentic. This point will come again in relation to religious language game.

No doubt science is firmly established in the world of facts. What cannot be sensed does not come under science. But the facts are orderly and connected by the string of uniform happenings known as laws. These laws when they are confirmed through repeated public verification, are known as true; otherwise they are false. Hence a scientist is given to utter sincerity in relation to facts and this sincerity counts as his moral virtue. Again, a scientist prefers a simpler explanation to a complex one. Hence his laws are neat and tidy, and, this is counted as an aesthetic value. Therefore, a scientist is also an artist. But it must be conceded that morality and aesthetic value in science are incidental in scientific pursuits and they are not directly pursued in it. But there is another point in relation to value and fact.

5. A scientific statement has to be disinterested, highly reasonable and predictable. For this reason the language of science is *quantitative*. Whatever exists, exists in number, according to science. Why? Because 2 and 2 together equal to 4, for any one anywhere irrespective of the likes and dislikes of the people. Hence a scientific statement is *exact*. In contrast, religious statements are valuative and qualitative, e.g. God is love, Brahman is without any difference within or without, and so on.

6. For the moderners science has produced wonderful results. Man flies in the sky and one person can talk to another from

afar and can even see his face on the phone. Computers have developed skills which any man can hardly perform himself. Hence the moderners hold that there is no knowledge anywhere else except in the sciences. Scientific pursuits are so thrilling and so rewarding that science has been raised to the status of religion itself. Science raised to the status of religion is known as *scientism* which accepts the methodology and results of science as absolute. At present any discipline to gain any adherence has to put on the garb of science.

Yogic and mystic disciplines are regarded as fully scientific for they have to undergo mental and physical exercises and they also maintain specific stages of development with their uniform results. But can religious discipline be regarded as trustworthy as the sciences?

No matter how rigorously religious discipline be enforced and no matter how precisely the steps and stages of meditation be maintained as in the case of eightfold *samādhi* and the fourteen stages of *Guṇasthāna*, the result of such discipline can never be as reliable as in science. The reason is that a scientist remains faithful to facts by maintaining strict neutrality with regard to his feeling and wishes. Nothing of the personality of the scientist is allowed to enter into his game. In contrast in religion our whole personality enters in noting and reporting our religious experience as in mystic experience. Hence, Martin Buber has correctly observed that in science we maintain the relationship of I-It concerning the facts. However we commune with God in I-Thou relationship. In science our *mind* alone works, but in religion our whole personality works most intensely. Are they opposed? No. In science we try to find pearls of facts, but in religion a seeker wants to become a thing of value, a pearl of great price. In religion *knowing* is subordinated to the supreme task of *becoming* gold, fit for heaven. After all cognition has an instrumental value for subserving the biological and spiritual end of life. Hence, knowing and becoming are complementary, and, so religion and science are complementary and are not opposed.

RELIGION AND PSYCHOLOGY

Religion is a holistic response of man. But it is more concerned with the inwardness of feeling and emotion than with outward behaviour. Now psychology is the newest science which studies the experience and behaviour of man in their depth. The term 'experience' includes all the three phases of mental life, namely, conscious, subconscious and unconscious processes. Hence there is hardly any human experience which cannot be studied in psychology, specially the unconscious urges and complexes at work. Hence, psychology has become important in the study of religion where unconscious complexes are most involved. But psychology is concerned with the subjective *origin* and mental processes at work, but not with the end-result of such activities. For example, the repressed urethral erotism motivates an engineer in making tunnels and bridges. Similarly, according to Freud, the repressed love of the mother determined the artistic creations of Leonardo Da Vinci. But from this it does not follow that psychology can evaluate engineering constructions of tunnels and bridges, and, that a psychologist as a psychologist can evaluate a work of art. The task of evaluation of any work of art can be done by only the art critics. Again, whether religion is a normal or abnormal activity of man has to be determined by the criteria of normality as established by social sciences. This distinction between the *origin* and the *evaluation of product* as a result of human activity should not be lost sight of, in any psychology of religion. For example, lotus has its origin in mud, but the lotus flower itself is not muddy. Similarly, some repressed impulses may enter into religious activity, but from this it does not follow that religion itself is a neurotic phenomenon.

2. Secondly, religious language may not be amenable to clear and precise analysis. From this it does not follow that religion is a meaningless or absurd phenomenon. According to Cardinal Newman so many subconscious and half-articulated processes enter into religious thinking that even psychological study of all of them is extremely difficult. Hence, religion is hard to analyse even by psychology.

Further, Rudolf Otto by his careful study of Eastern and Western religions has established that religion is essentially non-rational. He calls religious experience *mysterium tremendum et fascinans*. Clearly if religious experience is non-rational, then it cannot be rationally explained even by psychology. However, the greater the careful study of religion by psychology, the greater will be the helpfulness in explaining and understanding the complex processes involved in religion. In general, a study of religion by the psychologists has contributed to the understanding of the role of religion in the process of civilizing the beast in man, both ontologically and phylogenetically.

3. Even Freud, the arch enemy of religion, has granted that in the past religion has been valuable as a force of education and progress.[8] Similarly, another follower of Freud, namely, O. Pfister has beautifully pointed out that God as father has been man's greatest help in his fight against the father as God.[9] Even the totemistic religion, according to Freud, has laid down the following two moral principles, namely,

1. Not to kill the father, and
2. Not to marry the woman belonging to the same totem.

This custom of exogamy has resulted in many useful biological consequences.

Again, in due course, these moral prohibitions were generalized and interiorized in the course of civilizing human beings. In *Moses and Monotheism*, Freud has laid down that God as father has helped the Jews in sublimating their animal impulses.[10] Besides the command of not worshipping any graven image has helped the Jews in the development of their intellectual and spiritual capacities.[11] Further, Freud has conceded that

". . . . .the civilized world of today will admit that so long as they were (religious illusions) in force they offered those who were bound by them the most powerful protection against the danger of neuroses".[12]

4. A psychological study of religion by Freud and Freudians has helped the believers in understanding the dangers of abnormal types of religion. Such a study has helped the believers in refining and purifying religion and eradicating cruder ideas of religion. This kind of study will be helpful in getting rid of gros-

---

8. T. Reik, *From Thirty Years With Freud*, p. 126.
9. O. Pfister, *Some Applications of Psychoanalysis*, p. 345.
10. Freud, S., *Moses and Monotheism*, pp. 187-88.
11. *Ibid.*, pp. 138, 178.
12. *Ibid.*, p. 180.

sest forms of dogmas still preserved in the forms of myths. For example, the talk of hell cannot be consistently maintained in relation to the loving and forgiving God of Christianity. It is also hoped that in the interest of the unity of religions, the believers will rise above the narrowness of fanaticism and will support the movement for establishing a universal brotherhood of man, bereft of mutual hate. This was the hope of Sigmund Freud himself. His final words referred to the stage when man released from his inner complexes will work for the brotherhood of man and resignation to the inevitable.

Hence, psychology can be useful to religion both in its theory and beliefs and practices.

CHAPTER III

METAPHYSICAL THEORIES OF RELIGION

We are giving philosophical analysis of religious concepts and finally we are interpreting them in the existential mode of thinking. And, both of these modern currents of thought are anti-metaphysical. However, the long tradition of religious philosophy in the west has been predominantly metaphysical. So we shall give here a very brief account of a few metaphysical theories of theism which is the special if not the exclusive subject-matter of this book. We shall classify religion in our own way. We have made a sharp distinction between *worship* and *meditation* (samādhi). Indian religions make use of samādhi predominantly with Nirvāṇa as their goal. However, in western theism worship is the dominant means for achieving salvation. We find that Śaṁkarite Vedāntism strikes an intermediate ground between these two poles. In Śaṁkarite Vedāntism the worship of a god or goddess is prescribed as a preparatory means for achieving the final goal of absolute mokṣa or mukti (release from the chain of endless births and deaths) through knowledge. With this introduction we can classify religions in the Table on page 42.

Deism, pantheism and theism assume the existence of one God as an adequate object of worship. However, they differ from one another with regard to the relation in which God stands to the world. We shall now deal briefly with each one of these theories.

DEISM
Deism was the predominant religious philosophy of British thinkers. It was introduced by Herbert of Cherbury (1583-1648) and was greatly popularised by Sir Isaac Newton (1642-1727) and was accepted by Charles Darwin (1809-1882). In general, according to deism, God is perfect, infinite, eternal, omnipotent, om-

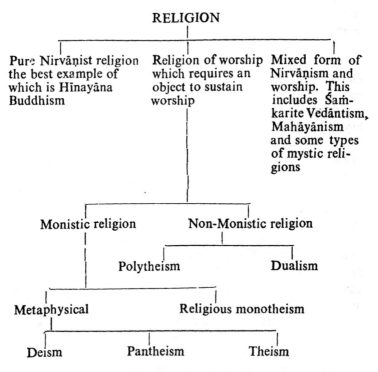

RELIGION

| Pure Nirvānist religion the best example of which is Hīnayāna Buddhism | Religion of worship which requires an object to sustain worship | Mixed form of Nirvāṇism and worship. This includes Śaṁkarite Vedāntism, Mahāyānism and some types of mystic religions |

Monistic religion   Non-Monistic religion

Polytheism   Dualism

Metaphysical   Religious monotheism

Deism   Pantheism   Theism

niscient, personal and the absolute reality. As God is perfect, so He has created this world as a perfect machine. As the machine being perfect requires no supervision, so God has retired from the world as an absentee landlord. God has created man with freewill and has endowed him with the natural light of reason by virtue of which he can determine his moral duties. Later on, the doctrine of evolution was assimilated into the theory, specially by Charles Darwin. According to Darwin, God breathed life into a few living cells and imbued them with full potency and powers for their future evolution into myriad forms through millions of years.[1] Deism maintains the following points:

(*a*) God is *transcendent* to the world and as such has no logical relations with the on-goings of the world. This perfect

---

1. Darwin, C., 'Origin of Species', concluding passage.

machine called the world,[2] being created by a perfect mechanic called God, does not require any divine supervision and interference. So consistently speaking 'miracles' cannot be allowed.

(*b*) God has been pictured as an absentee landlord.

(*c*) Being transcendent, God and world become mutually exclusive which led to two main implications. (*i*) God being transcendent and having no concern with men and their affairs, remains essentially a 'hidden' God. This renders God an object beyond worship and knowledge of man. (*ii*) Ultimately, God and world become two realities in which the world in the sense of being created, is dependent on God. This kind of dualism is found in Descartes. The notion of transcendence is fairly important in Christian theology. St. Thomas Aquinas (1225-1274), Karl Barth (1866-1968) and Paul Tillich (1886-1966) have specially emphasized the transcendence of God in their theologies.

(*d*) The transcendence of God makes him unworshipful, so to remove this anomaly deism ascribes personality to God. But the very nature of personality is that it tends to make God finite and not infinite. This introduces the inner struggle between the infinitude of God and his personality.

(*e*) The great force of deism lies in its acceptance of a natural light in man which alone is taken as the sole authority for deciding things in morality and religion. It, therefore, denies the place of revelation in religion. Hence, it is a religious theory of Enlightenment.

But here lies the internal tension. Once we emphasize transcendence, the need of revelation comes by the back door. If God be transcendent, then he by implication becomes unknowable. How else can he be known, if not through revelation? For this reason Karl Barth and Paul Tillich who fully accept the transcendence of God, have laid great stress on revelation. But can this expedience of revelation solve the issue? If God by nature be unknowable, then how can revelation make the unknowable God intelligible? Not even the Grace of God can make the unknowable intelligible. Thus deism has raised a good deal of im-

---

2. Though Newton required God to interfere with the workings of the world from time to time to check deviations, yet his scientific theory of universal mechanism made God unnecessary in the goings-on of the world, since for Newton this world was a perfect machine (Vide, W.T. Stace, *Religion and the Modern Mind*, Macmillan, 1953).

portant theological issues and they have not been solved even now.

One thing is certain that insistence on the light of reason as the final court of appeal in matters of God and morality in due course has paved the way for rationalism, scientism and humanism. As the transcendence of God logically excluded the possibility of worship, so some modifications have been introduced in it in order to make room for worship.[3]

1. The doctrine of the absentee landlord came to be questioned and the modification was introduced that God occasionally interferes with the workings of the world and some deists began to regard God as the sustaining power of the universe.

2. God came to be further emphasized as essentially a moral being and so the world as the creation of this Moral Agent came to be regarded to have some moral purpose.

3. Lastly, deism began to emphasize the duties of man towards God Who in turn came to be regarded as the final Judge for rewarding virtuous acts and punishing evil deeds.

Deism proved fruitful in many ways. Its insistence on the human light of reason purified religion by banishing many superstitions which had crept into religious beliefs. It also succeeded in holding a truce between religion and science by allowing science unfettered freedom in its rational pursuits. According to deism, the whole universe has been created by an infinite intellect and as such the whole universe is fully intelligible to human reason and what it reveals is sacred. The deist granted the following charter to science:

1. Nature can be explained in terms of natural causes only and there is no room for supernatural agency and miracles.

2. Each natural event is determined by its own causes. Hence, prayers for warding off natural calamities or inducing beneficial effects of rains or harvest are useless.

3. There is hardly any inner law in the heart of nature which can be styled as moral. Therefore, organic evolution, as was taught by Darwin, is guided by mechanical selection of the fittest in the race of survival for food and mate.

---

3. W.R. Sorley, Moral Values and the Idea of God, Cambridge University Press 1921, pp. 450-51; also Encyclopaedia of Religion and Ethics, Vol. 4.

It appears now that deism won its truce with science at the cost of religion. Emphasis on the transcendence of God robbed the possibility of encounter with and the worship of God Who had no concern with man. Further, deism accepts that God created the world and this problem of creation which is difficult for any form of theism, becomes insoluble for deism. Why did a *perfect* God create the world? How did he create? Out of himself or out of some pre-existing matter? Again, did God create the world in void time or did he create time along with the world? Further, if God is perfect, then is this world of no value to him? If so, then is this creation a mere incidence in the life of God? Again, if God is infinitely good and omnipotent then why is there evil at all?

All these problems raised here are almost insoluble for any rational form of religious philosophy (vide Chapters IX, X). And deism certainly claims to be wholly rationalistic. But a purely rational system errs in another direction. A God fully understood is no God at all. A fully understood God becomes a mere concept of human intellect. God can be apprehended only through symbols. However, deism totally disregards the language of the heart, the demands of the Unconscious and working of the psyche at its depth. For these reasons deism lost its hold on the masses and in due course invited its opposite, namely, pantheism.

PANTHEISM

Literally pantheism means seeing all things in God and God in all (pan=all, theos = God). This is well illustrated in the following verse of the Gītā:

यो मां पश्यति सर्वत्र सर्वं च मयि पश्यति, तस्याहं न प्रणश्यामि स च मे न प्रणश्यति ।

(He who sees Me everywhere and he who sees all in Me, I am never lost to him, and he is never lost to me.)
The same thought has been expressed in Īśāvāsyopaniṣad:

यस्तु सर्वाणि भूतान्यात्मन्येवानुपश्यति, सर्वभूतेषु चात्मानं ततो न विजुगुप्सते ।

(He who sees all the animate in God and sees God in everything living, can hate none.)
The very opening verse of the same Upaniṣad says:

ईशावास्यमिदं सर्वं यत्किञ्च जगत्यां जगत् ।

(Whatever all is in this universe is possible indeed through God.)

Unlike deism, pantheism is a much older system of thought and is clearly stated in both east and west. It is closely related to mystic experience and as such should not be treated as a mere intellectual system. This statement does not rule out the fact that some of the pantheists have been highly intellectual philosophers. Śaṁkara, Spinoza, Upaniṣadic seers and Buddhistic thinkers have to be classed among world intellectuals. And yet they are pantheists. Indian thought is not predominantly theistic, and, so Indian pantheism does not accord personality to the all-pervasive reality. But pantheism need not be impersonal, as some thinkers in the west seem to maintain. Historically speaking pantheism has been impersonal (Spinozism, Wordsworth's naturalism, Śaṁkarite Vedāntism), super-personal (F.H. Bradley, Radhakrishnan and other idealists) and also personal (as in some forms of Sufism and Christian mysticism).

Just as transcendence is the key-concept in deism, so in like manner immanence is the key-concept in explaining pantheism. The term 'immanence' that which occupies every fibre of the thing in which it is immanent. In pantheism God is said to be immanent in the world in the sense that God pervades the whole universe as its indwelling spirit. Negatively it means that an immanent God cannot exist outside the universe at the same time. Samuel Alexander reminds us that immanence does not mean omnipresence[4] (as is the case with the Big Brother). If immanence means indwellingness and all-pervasiveness without being transcendent at the same time, then it may mean at least these two things.

(*i*) The immanent God may be the vitalising, sustaining, moulding and indwelling power of the world in the same sense in which the indwelling vital impetus in the egg is the hormic principle within it by virtue of which the egg is transformed into a chick. Bergson's elān vital, or Bosanquet's spirit of totality or Spinoza's notion of *natura naturans* or the nisus of Samuel Alexander may be cited as so many cases of this form of immanentism.

(*ii*) Immanence of God also means that God is the primordial stuff of which everything is the modification. Samuel Alexander's notion of the Space-Time continuum is the best example

---

4. S. Alexander, *Philosophical and Literary Pieces*, Macmillan, 1939, p. 322.

of this. But he appears to have derived his notion from Spinoza's notion of *Natura Naturata*. According to Spinoza the sum total of all that exists is God and so he equated the world with God and God with the world. As a matter of fact the non-dualistic Vedānta also speaks of everything as the projectional modification of the one reality in the same way in which the earth is the one underlying reality behind all pots of clay. In this sense it is held that everything being divested of its name and form is nothing but Brahman.

This form of immanence of being one primordial stuff may also include the doctrine of emanation, according to which the reality diminishes as it gradually proceeds from the subtle to the gross, from the proximate to the remote. Emanationism is most pronounced in neo-Platonism and in other oriental forms of pantheism.

It is contended sometimes that by equating the world with God and God with the world, there can be oscillation between Acosmicism (in which the world is engulfed in God) or Naturalism (in which God is swallowed in the world). However, in the religious form of pantheism there is hardly any room for naturalism. No doubt Spinoza equated nature with God, but in his case nature ceases to be nature and appears divine, an object of *amor intellectualis dei*. Religiously speaking, acosmicism is the logical and consistent conclusion of Spinozism and Śaṁkarite Vedāntism. Things of the world with their names and forms are illusory, according to Śaṁkara; and they are said to be mere modes which are just like the ever-vanishing waves that never are, according to Spinoza. For both Spinoza and Śaṁkara, the absolute reality is beyond the category of personality. Now if God has no personality, then how can there be any intellectual love of God? Well, the intellectual love of God, for Spinoza, is neither selfish nor unselfish, but is totally selfless. It is much more than the unconscious and the instinctive love of the moth for the fire: it is the love which does not require to be reciprocated and recompensed. It is that love which continues to be the animating principle of life even when it is rebuked, rebuffed and ignored. It is that love which hate cannot quench, evils of the wicked cannot turn away and even the complete indifference of the supreme object cannot destroy. Therefore, such a love is fully compatible with the impersonal nature of the absolute reality. It may be likened to the Budd-histic compassion for the whole world. The all-pervasive abso-lute reality of the world may be impersonal, but it is calculated to inspire and imbue the pantheist with the spirit of commit-ment for a life of universal, unreciprocated love. For this reason Spinoza was justly called 'God-intoxicated mystic'. The in-built structure of Spinoza's pantheism is wholly religious even tho-ugh it is supported by abstruse intellectual arguments mostly of the *a priori* kind.

For Śaṁkara too Brahman is much more than what appears on the surface. It consists in reaching a state of mind in which the narrow boundary of one's ego is lost and dissolved in the process of expansion and the stretching forth of the whole per-sonality. The imagery of the dissolution of the drops of water in the ocean flow or of absorption has been interpreted as the doctrine of extinction. Rightly understood the Śaṁkarite pan-theism asks us to go beyond customary morality of good and evil and to make this life a thing of supreme value through the process of expansion. Intellectually interpreted the whole system appears arid and impossible. According to this intellectual inter-pretation the whole world is to be taken as a meaningless play of Brahman or an ultimate mystery. However, the system is not a philosophical system. The system is wholly religious even when it is sustained by abstruse logical and hair-splitting arguments. These arguments are designed to create an attitude of utter de-tachment in man. With this attitude man will not regard even the state of heavenly bliss as of much value. The aim is to reach a perfect life beyond which nothing higher can be conceived or thought. True, the ideal aimed at may be mere illusion. But it is the conviction of the Vedāntins that Brahmanhood alone is wor-thy of realisation and it is this conviction which fills him with absolute concern and total self-involvement.

OBJECTION AGAINST PANTHEISM

What is maintained here is that religious philosophers have gravely erred in interpreting pantheism as an intellectual system of bloodless categories. So far the interpretation of pantheism is that all is God and God is all. In holding this it is contended: If God is all, then this world (all) becomes illusory. But this world is our starting premise. If the starting premise is illusory, then the conclusion (either concerning Brahman or Substance of Spinoza) is equally illusory. If, on the other hand, the world is real, then the impersonal world of vast forces becomes the only object of devotion. But who would like to merge and be lost in this ocean of meaningless forces? So it is contended that pantheism is not capable of sustaining the fire of religious devotion and experience.

Again, it is maintained that pantheism cannot be consistent religious philosophy, for it cannot have any room for worship. In order to worship a deity, the deity has to be distinct from the worshipper, that is, it should be transcendent to the worshipper. However, in pantheism the deity is the immanent principle of the worshipper: the deity and the worshipper coalesce. So no worship is possible.

There is yet another objection. It is said that without the freedom of will there can be no morality. But in pantheism there is no room for individual's freedom of will. God is taken to be the indwelling spirit which rolls through all things and moves even the inmost desires of man. So God is the real agent and man becomes only an instrument in the hands of God. If it is so, then man is not responsible for his acts. Thus, if there is no real freedom, then there can be no true morality. So it is contended that pantheism does not sustain the moral life of man.

The objections made against pantheism are pointless, but are not valueless. They serve to deepen and clarify our notion of religion. Theism is not the only form of religion. For a theistic system God must be transcendent in order to be worshipful. But we have already seen with regard to deism that the transcendence of God ultimately leads to his unknowableness and even his unworshipfulness, unless one is prepared to worship a Being incapable of responding to his worshipper. But worshipfulness is not the only form of becoming religious. In the Nirvāṇist form of religion one tries to realise the immanent and indwelling reality through meditation or samādhi. So here meditation takes the place of worship. In the same way theism cannot but preach 'closed morality', no matter however enlightened it may be. The distinction of the goat and the sheep, says John Dewey, is essential for any supernatural form of theism. As against this pantheism teaches 'open morality' which taught duties and obligations not only to human beings, but also to the Sun and the Moon and to all things. The absolute compassion and absolute love through total participation in all existences is the supreme aim of a pantheist. In attaining this his mind is purged of lower passions and selfish desires. Such a morality may be difficult of attainment. However, as Spinoza observes, all excellent things are not only difficult, but are also rare. Hence, in pantheism morality is not denied: it is purged of its grosser elements and narrowness. The emphasis is on the purification of the whole man in his participation in the world, the best example of which is contained in the doctrine of Bodhisattvas. Again, the realisation of omniscience (sarvajñatā) or Brahmanhood is not an empirical fact. But what it aims at clarifying is that life lived with infinite passion for the infinite, results in a state of mind, which however much may defy description and analysis, is worth achieving. If this *ascesis* is not bliss: it is not less than bliss.

SUPER-PERSONAL PANTHEISM

Pantheism need not be impersonal: it may be personal and also super-personal. According to personal pantheism the absolute reality is personal in nature. This type of pantheism is found among the sufists and also among the Christian mystics. In contrast to this, some neo-Hegelians, for example F. H. Bradley, would not hold that the all-inclusive, all-harmonious sentient self is impersonal or personal. According to F. H. Bradley, the absolute reality being all-inclusive cannot be less than its appearances. Now the dead nature and also mind are appearances and the Reality is much more than appearances. It cannot be, therefore, impersonal for matter is an appearance of low degree. Now the Reality is not personal because it is much richer and higher than person. So the Reality is better described super-personal. However, the term 'super-personal' is very vague. The Absolute is not itself self-conscious, but attains to self-consciousness in the thoughts, aspirations and value-consciousness in man. Again, the best of individuals will not be preserved. They only serve to articulate the potentialities of the absolute and when their mortal centres are no longer needed by the Absolute, then they have to quit the stage for ever, allowing others to further actualise the nature of the absolute. Thus the term 'super-personality' does not permit any kind of conscious reciprocity on the part of the Absolute in relation to its votaries. In contrast, personal pantheism is religiously important.

PERSONALISTIC PANTHEISM

Consistently speaking pantheism can only be impersonal, since no personal God can be said to be the indwelling spirit of the world. Nor can God be said to be the ultimate stuff which underlies all things. But pantheism is closely allied to mysticism which contains religious experience in its concentrated form. In the mystic trance all things may appear permeated and pervaded by a personal God.[5] This is not a matter of intellectual apprehension so much as it is a matter of one's feeling called God-consciousness. Under the spell of this mystic experience St. Paul declared: 'I live, yet not I but Christ liveth in me'. In the same strain St. Tulsidas sees the whole world impregnated with Rāma and Sītā. Both St. Paul and St. Tulsidas were certainly theists, but both of them felt the all-pervasiveness of their respective deities. As in the case of St. Paul, so in like manner other theistic mystics (Muslim and Christian) have declared that in mystic trance only God is experienced as the only one essence of everything. Now what happens to the individuality of the mystic himself? Here both W.T. Stace[6] and R.C. Zaehner[7] hold that theist mystic remains existentially distinct from God. Is the language of absorption or fana (annihilation) misleading? No, it is not misleading provided we interpret correctly the meaning of absorption. When the mystic reports that he sees God only and naught else besides Him, then he becomes so much lost and absorbed in God and becomes so much forgetful of himself that he has nothing to report anything about himself. In the words of Ghazali, the mystic becomes so much engrossed in the beloved that he perceives nothing else.[8] Similarly, R.C. Zaehner quoting from Ghazali holds that the mystic theist does not gain identity with God Most High. However, in the mystic trance, the theist experiences the presence of God so overwhelmingly, so

---

5. Cp. W.T. Stace, *Mysticism and Philosophy*, Chap. III, sec. 6, pp. 178-82.
6. *Mysticism and Philosophy*, Chap. IV, Sec. 2.
7. *Mysticism*: Sacred and Profane, Oxford Paperbacks 1961 (First published 1957), Chap. VIII-IX.
8. W.T. Stace, *Mysticism and Philosophy*, p. 228.

overpoweringly that the personality of theist is completely sub-merged and dwarfed (but not lost or annihilated). And this state of being thoroughly abased and dwarfed may be called absorption or fana:

> The mystics, after their ascent to the heavens of Reality, agree that they saw nothing in existence except God the One...... They were drowned in pure solitude: their reason was lost in it, and they became as if dazed in it, they no longer had the capacity to recollect aught but God, nor could they in any wise remember themselves. Nothing was left to them but God. They became drunk with a drunkenness in which their reason collapsed.[9]

Thus, the state of self-absorption is more psychological than ontological. The mystic is conscious of God only: his own personality becomes so much benumbed and insignificant that it can be styled as lost and absorbed. So fana means the experiencing of the 'oceanic feeling' as Freud would term it. It is a state in which the personality of the mystic is overwhelmed and overcome by the Majesty of the Most High, but is not annihilated. As a matter of fact this kind of absorption in the ocean flow of God makes the personality of the theist richer and fuller.

R.C. Zaehner, a Catholic orientalist, claims the superiority of theistic mysticism over Vedāntic monism. He holds with Blessed Jan Ruysbroeck that Vedāntic emptiness is a prelude to or stepping-stone to God-consciousness in which Holiness is attained.[10] Here we need not enter into the controversy, but one thing is there to remember. Before claiming the superiority of theistic mysticism, any theist must be able to answer the objections which empirical analysis has brought against theism.[11] He should also be in a position to make the theistic symbols acceptable to modernity. Now without accepting the contention of R.C. Zaehner, we can outline the merits of personalistic pantheism.

1. In impersonal pantheism one often hears of going beyond 'good and evil'. Such a state of perfection is attained all by the

9. R.C. Zaehner, Ibid., p. 157 (Ghazali quoted).
10. R.C. Zaehner, Ibid., pp. 173, 174, 182.
11. Vide Chapter III.

efforts of the yogi or the mystic himself. The ultimate reality
which is finally realised is indescribable, *śūnyatā* (emptiness) or
unity without duality. So the realisation of this state does not
encourage ordinary morality for there is nothing to whom any
obligation is due. However, in contrast, in personalistic pantheism, the theist reaches all his excellences through the Grace of
God. And for him God is infinitely good. So a mystic theist
continues to be fully moral and he practises all virtues.

2. Albert Schweitzer has brought the charge of world and
life negation against Indian Thought which, according to him,
preaches perfection. And perfection which is attained by systematic emptying of one's mind of all sensations and images, certainly gives one peace and joy. However, according to A. Schweitzer, real morality consists in promoting well being and alleviation of sufferings of one's fellow beings. This humanistic ethic
of ameliorism and service to suffering humanity, according to
A. Schweitzer, is possible through theism. On the other hand,
impersonal pantheism promotes quietism. Thus, mystic theism
does help the growth of holiness.

3. R.C. Zaehner holds that fana and baqa (survival) both
have to be maintained.[12] Impersonal pantheism, according to
him, would be incomplete because it encourages emptiness and
absorption only. However, personalistic pantheism teaches the
enrichment of the individual after he survives the preliminary
step of emptiness experienced in impersonal pantheism.

Whatever may be the merit of R.C. Zaehner's claims for mystic theism, he clearly states that religious statements are convictional. The Jñāna of non-dualistic Vedānta, according to
him, really means conviction.[13] So all mystic and pantheistic
statements are really convictional. This will be taken up in the
next chapter. However, A. Schweitzer and R.C. Zaehner support humanistic ethic because both of them are confirmed theists.
And it is their kind of theism which is the main target of attack.
So let us turn now to western monotheism which is the main
subject-matter of this book.

---

12. Ibid., pp. 194-96.
13. Ibid., pp. 176-77.

MONOTHEISM

Theism is that form of religious belief in which God is taken to be a supernatural person and the creator of a value-evolving world. He is transcendent to the world as well as its immanent principle. There is a subtle distinction between theism and monotheism. According to theism there is a supreme personal God, but he may not be absolute. For example, in Indian system of thought, Íśvara is the supreme God who created this value-evolving world, but He is not the absolute. Above Íśvara there is a higher reality of Nirguṇa Brahman. Further, according to Indian theism, the worship of a supreme God need not exclude the worship of any lesser god. If men worship a god of finite stature, then they would get smaller merit of less enduring kind.

Arjuna, even the devotees who, endowed with faith, worship other gods, they too worship Me alone, though not in accordance with rules. For I am the enjoyer and also the Lord of all sacrifices. ...(*B.G.* IX: 23-24)

However, in the west theism assumes the form of monotheism in which the worship of any other gods except one is considered aberrant.

"Thou shalt have no other gods befor me" (Exodus 20: 3). From this notion of one exclusive God follows the doctrine of the monopolistic cult of God, breeding hate and intolerance. From this also follows the strange doctrine of the objective truth of God, for, according to it, only one God is true and all others are false. For monotheism God is both a Person and is also an Infinite Being Who necessarily exists. We are more concerned with monotheism than with theism. It is the claim of monotheism which is most at stake and the following weighty problems have been raised with regard to it:

1. Worship demands the surrender of one's total personality. This total surrender is logically possible only in relation to an Infinite Being who not only happens to exist, but must exist necessarily. However, it has been held that the concept of a *Necessary Being* is as self-contradictory as a square circle. (Chapters III and IV)

2. Again, God is said to be a Person, but this is said to be an unintelligible concept with regard to an Infinite Being. Secondly,

personality implies limitation, and an Infinite Being, therefore, cannot be regarded as a Person. (Chapter IX)

3. Not only God to be worshipful must be a Person, but He should also be omnipotent, omniscient and infinitely good. However, the attributes of omnipotence and infinite goodness of God are untenable in relation to the presence of evil in the world. (Chapter X) Further, it is contended that the very notion of omnipotence with regard to a continuing entity is self-contradictory. (Chapter X)

4. For monotheism God is the creator of a value-centred and value-evolving world. This notion raises a number of very knotty problems concerning the purpose of creation and the relation of God to the world. If God is perfect, then does this world make any difference to him? If it does, then God's perfection admits of change and degrees and this means that there is no real perfection at all. If, on the other hand, the world makes no difference to Him, then man (belonging to the world) is no concern of God. So God ceases to be worshipful. Again, if God has created the world out of pre-existing matter, then besides God there is also another entity called matter. So under the circumstance God will cease to be an absolute reality. If, on the other hand, it is maintained that God creates the world out of Himself, then it means that world follows from God either logically or emanationally. In either case God becomes the immanent principle of the world, leading to pantheism and not to monotheism. Further, God is related to the world either as its transcendent cause or as its immanent principle or both. The former alternative leads to deism and the latter to pantheism. And it is maintained that God cannot be logically said to be both transcendent and immanent. (Chapter IX)

Thus we find that monotheism is the most popular doctrine in the west and yet it is bristled with difficulties. In the following pages we shall take the problems of monotheism one by one.

CHAPTER IV

FOUNDATION OF RELIGIOUS BELIEF

It has been accepted by religious thinkers that there is *religion a priori*. This means that there is something in human structure which prompts man heavenward. In prophetic religions it is maintained that there is the *breath* of God in man which prompts him to find his rest in Him. In Greek and Indian thought there is the doctrine of fall of the pure spirit into the miserable worldly existence. However, either the *reminiscence* in him (Plato) of his pristine existence goads him towards spiritual pursuits, or, his essentially spiritual nature makes him restless to regain his former glorious nature (Jainism, Vedāntism and even others). In general it might be laid down that man is endowed with a strong predisposition towards his spiritual quest (St. Paul, St. Augustine, Paul Tillich, Sri Ramakrishna, and so on). This spiritual pursuit in man gives rise to religious belief. But 'belief' is a vague term and requires analysis. Here the analysis of 'belief' by H.H. Price[1] will be followed, for it has been considered to be valuable in this context.

In the first instance it is pointed out that belief-in is an attitude to a person, whether human or divine. In contrast, *believe-that* refers to a proposition, that is, a proposition for which some reason can be demanded and presented (143). However, Price tells us that there is also an element of factuality in belief-in with the result that in many cases *belief-in* can be reduced to *believe-that*.

1. Both in *belief-in* and *believe-that* there is an element of trust. However, in *belief-in* this trust is very strong so much so that even life can be risked (149-150).

---

1. H.H. Price, *Belief 'In' and Belief 'that'* in B. Mitchell, *The Philosophy of Religion*, pp. 143-67. Page reference is being made to this book.

2. Belief-in in an evaluative sense means *good at*, implying efficient skill or effective in producing a certain good result, at all times (155, 159). However, this kind of confidence appears to be interested, and, as such cannot be always distinguished from believe-that (160-161).

3. But belief in a friend is quite different from any kind of belief-that. This belief-in need not imply any efficiency for any job or effectiveness for producing any result.

> It is something which I believe for its own sake. In this res-
> pect, then, my belief in him is disinterested. More than that,
> I value *him* for his own sake. (162)

Here we trust a friend as a unique human being. Here our whole heart enters into the transaction.

Believers believe in God with their whole heart and this can-not be reduced to believe-that. This is like believing in a friend.

> It is perhaps significant that some theistic mystics have refer-
> red to God as 'The Friend'. (167)

But certainly God is not an equal of man. He is much more, as Abraham knew Him. But belief in God is both interested and distinterested. There is interestedness, for God is our refuge at all times and a tower of strength in times of all sound gloom. But when human beings give Him thanks for all His favours, then they do so in a disinterested way. At this moment of gratitude

> We are beginning to value him for his own sake, and to believe
> that it is a good thing, intrinsically good, that he exists and
> is what he is. (167)

This belief in God is highly evaluative and not merely factual, that is, the acceptance of an existential proposition. (167) In other words, the Ontological Argument for the existence of God is not enough. This means that religious belief is not merely cognitive and cannot be assimilated to factual or scientific know-ledge. It has an element of heart, of affectiveness and warmth of feeling. Thus the foundation of religious belief rests on Reason, Revelation, Faith and Mystic Experience.

Now according to H.H. Price, the nearest analogue of belief

in God would be our belief in a friend. Hence, it is a matter of absolute trust in God who is "the fundamental 'good thing' without which there would be no others". (167) Is it a rational attitude?

THE PLACE OF REASON

The function of reason is to control and guide the conative trends in man. Religion too is a matter of a holistic tendency in man which drives a man in search of his ideal self. True, very often this ideal Self is posited in one's religious upbringing. But the nature of the deity which embodies this ideal self gets exposed to increasing knowledge and ever-deepening sensitiveness to what one considers to be his highest concern. Hence, it is for reason in man to get him well established in his belief of the kind of deity whom he worships.

Man derives his deity from religious books and teachings. But he soon finds that there are various kinds of deities and scriptures. Naturally he has to use his reason, as far as it can carry him, to make a decision about his deity. This clash between different religions may give rise to various possible results.

1. Out of the clash may result cross-fertilization of ideas concerning one's own religious beliefs and practices. Christian theologians like Paul Tillich learnt a lot from Advaitism, and, in like manner Brahmo Samaj incorporated much of Christianity. Similarly, Sufis also incorporated a lot from Advaitic mysticism.

2. Clash may lead to the rejection of other deities. Then there may be forced conversions.

3. Clash may lead to wholesale mass conversion, as in ancient India. Here many foreigners like the Greeks, Huns, Parthians etc., were converted to Hinduism.

Thus, reason serves as solvent of many religious issues. However, reason remains at most merely a regulative force in all possible sources of religious beliefs. Mystic experience, revelation and faith, all in one way or other are responsible for religious beliefs, and, reason remains as a helpful guide in every one of them. For example, the mystical experience of God or Brahman is very transitory, even when it is highly momentous. This momentary experience has to be made permanent, either for one's own future use, or, for communication to others. How is this possible? This momentary glimpse of God is conceptualized in words, and, their meaning has to be fixed. As the experience is extraordinary, so words can never be precise. We shall find that religious language is evocative and exhortative. The expressions containing ordinary words are used in an extraordinary way. Sometimes silence, at times paradoxes. At another times reversal of the ordinary order of things known as *ulaṭabāṅsi* are used to convey to others what cannot be directly talked about. But even these expressions found in the Upaniṣads have been useful to mankind by the reasoning of Śaṅkara, Rāmānuja, Kabir and Sri Ramakrishna.

As a result of what was heard (*Śruti*), the Upaniṣads and Gītā have come down to us as 'holy Scripture'. But the scriptural statements have to be interpreted and reason has to be advanced in favour of one's interpretation. In this regard, the views of Śaṅkara and Rāmānuja are worth mentioning.

Śaṅkara holds that Brahman, being devoid of form cannot be an object of perception and inference (*Vedāntasūtra* II.1.6). But Śaṅkara quoting (*B.U.* 2.4.5. and *Chh. U.* 6.14.2) holds that *inference* has to be used as a means of understanding Scripture. (Vs. 1.1.2) Similarly, Rāmānuja holds that Brahman is supersensuous and it cannot rest exclusively on arguments. (*Śribhāṣya* 2.1.12.) Scripture alone is authoritative in this regard, 'and that reasoning is to be applied only to support of Scripture'.

Hence, reason is subservient, though necessary for interpreting religious scriptures.

The place of reason in Faith is not always prominent, as we shall soon find for ourselves. But reason has been greatly advocated by Jainism, Buddhism and the Thomists. An important Jaina thinker called Ratna Shekhara in the opening lines of *Sambadha Sattari* states the following:

No matter, whether he is a Shvetambara or Digambara, a Buddha or a follower of any other creed one who has realised himself the self-sameness of the soul, i.e. one who looks on all creatures alike his own Self, is sure to attain Salvation.[3]

---

2. P.C. Nahar and Krishna Chandra Ghose, '*An Epitome of Jainism*',

In the same vein, Lord Buddha recommends his teachings

......not because it is a report, not because it is a tradition, not because it is said in the past......nor because it appears to be suitable, nor because your preceptor is a recluse, but if you yourself understand that this is so meritorious and blameless, and when accepted, is for benefit and happiness, then you may accept it.[3]

Roman Catholic thinkers still believe that God's existence can be proved. St. Thomas Aquinas presented 'Five Ways' of proving God. Even now they are defended by the Thomists. However, from the time of Kant onward, religious philosophers hold that the so-called arguments for proving God are mere pleas. These proofs are neither deductive nor inductive. There might be arguments, and much appeal to facts, but they are all persuasive appeals for tipping the scale of decision either for a religious attitude, or, for a disbelieving attitude.[4]

Hence, reason by itself cannot *originate* faith, though it can be used either to strengthen it or weaken it. This is best seen in what is termed as Revelation.

REVELATION

Revelation means bringing into light what was hidden before. Now God is said to be a hidden entity, according to the Bible. Again, Brahman (or God) is essentially unknown and unknowable, according to the Upaniṣads. Hence, God remains a supersensuous entity. He can neither be known through perception nor inference, according to Śaṅkara and Rāmānuja. Then how can He be known? Through *revelation*.

God is essentially a transcendent Being, beyond the ordinary means of knowing ordinary things. But man has an inner urge to know God. Therefore, man stands in need of some sort of promptings through God, according to prophetic religions of the Semites. According to this tradition God reveals Himself through

---

Calcutta 1917, p. 12. The Jainas based their religious philosophy on Saptabhaṅginaya and *Syādavāda*, the two interrelated logical principles.
3. *Anguttara Nikāya*, Part 1, 3.65, p. 192, also repeated on p. 196.
4. John Wisdom, 'The Gods', p. 420 in *Classical and Contemporary Readings in the Philosophy of Religion*, ed. J. Hick.

1. Revealed religious Scriptures, known as the Torah and
Talmund (Judaism), the Bible (Christians), the Koran (Islam)
and the Vedas (Hinduism), and so on.
2. Through His angels in Judaism and Christianity and
Islam. Gabriel was responsible for God's revelation to Prophet
Mohammad.
3. Also in dreams and visions, God is revealed to His prophets and other holy men.
4. Prophets in Semitic religions and Parsiism are the special
messengers of God for revealing Him to the people.
5. Christianity accepts the mediation of the Holy Spirit for
revealing the message of God. God, however, may be revealed
in a trance.
6. Both the Bible and Koran hold that God can be known
through His creation.

Most Christian theologians think that the Holy Scriptures
are inspired writings, but a few fundamentalists in Semitic religions take their Scriptures as eternal, and, a copy of which is
said to be in Heaven.

The Indian religious tradition also supports the doctrine of
Revelation, and the points relating to it can be thus laid down.

1. Brahman or God is revealed through Nature. Gītā 14.3
puts down that Nature is the womb through which God creates
all things. Similarly, Śaṅkara gives a teleological argument in
favour of the existence of Iśvara. According to him, the entire
world has been so constituted that it enables the souls or jivas to
enjoy the fruits of their various acts.

> We rather must assume that just as clay and similar subs-
> tances are seen to fashion themselves into various forms, if
> worked upon by potters and the like, so the pradhana (*Pra-
> kṛti*) also is ruled by some intelligent principle. (*Vs.* 2.2.1)

2. However, the Indian lays very great emphasis on the Scripture as the source of knowledge of supersensuous Brahman.
This view is supported both by Śaṅkara (*Vs.* 1.1.2) and by
Rāmānuja (*Śribhāṣya* 2.1.12). Of course, there are two important views about *the Vedas* which form the most sacred Scripture
of the Hindus. According to the Mimāṁsakas, the Vedas are

eternal. But the Naiyāyikas hold the Vedas to be inspired revelation, though they are wholly reliable, and authoritative about our knowledge of God.

3. Through His incarnation, God reveals Himself to the people. The well-known Gītā IV. 7 can be put down here.

Whenever there is a decline of righteousness and rise of unrighteousness, then I incarnate myself.

Commenting on this verse. Radhakrishnan holds that by his teaching and example, the *avatāra* shows how a human being can raise himself to his higher being.

4. *Brahmasākṣātkāra*. Śaṅkara accepts the doctrine of *jivanmukti* (release in this very life). Such released souls are there to teach about the reality of Brahman and the Advaitic teaching about Brahman. Rāmānuja does not accept the doctrine of *jivanmukti*. (*Śribhāṣya* 1.1.4) But he also grants the possibility of direct knowledge of God in this very earthly frame.

In my view Scripture produces knowledge in the mind purified by works . . . . . and a clear mind gives rise to direct knowledge of Brahman. (*SBH* 1.1.4)

Sri Ramakrishna had the most favoured vision of MA KALI and even Brahma-realization. The Bible too holds that the pure in heart shall see God.

5. There is also the remarkable doctrine of Grace, according to which God reveals Himself to His devotees, according to His inscrutable will.

This Soul (*Ātman*) is not to be obtained by instruction.
Nor by intellect, nor by much learning.
He is to be obtained only by the one whom he chooses;
To such a one that Soul (Ātman) reveals his own person.
(*Kath. Up.* 2.23; *Muṇḍaka* 3.2.3)

This has been similarly expressed by Kabir.

तुम्हारे चरन कवल मन राता, गुन निरगुन के तुम निज दाता,
जहुंवा प्रगटि बजावहु जैसा, जस श्रनभैं कथिया तिनि तंसा ।5

5. *Kabira-Granthavali*, Ramaini 12.

(O Lord, my mind is rooted in your lotus feet. You are the bestower of both, that with form and without form. You appear to him in a form most suitable for him, who describes you as he sees you.)

FAITH

If revelation is the work of God, then faith is the receptivity of man to acknowledge this revelation. Hence, revelation and faith are correlative. The Bible tells us that faith is the substance of things hoped for, the evidence of things not seen.[6] 'The substance of things hoped for' simply means that the beginning of having faith is almost the certainty of having attained the end. But what kind of certainty can one have in faith. Of course, this certainty is not born of scientific knowledge, because it pertains to things, not seen or perceptible. Therefore, for Kant, faith has subjective certainty sufficient for action, but insufficient for objective knowledge. As such a proper relation has to be established between faith and knowledge.

Prof. A. J. Ayer states three conditions of knowledge, namely[7]

1. Sufficient condition for knowing that something is the case what one is said to know.
2. Second, that one is sure of it.
3. One has the right to be sure of it.

In the light of what Kant has stated about faith, it can be said that in the case of faith there is not sufficient evidence for reasonable certainty, but there felt certainty for action is felt, or, commitment for action. For this reason Kant has stated,

I have therefore found it necessary to deny *knowledge*, in order to make room for *faith*.[8]

And for Kant, faith has to do with *Practical* reason. But it must be conceded that even full commitment for action, which is the

---

6. Hebrews 11.1.
7. *The Problem of knowledge*, p. 35.
8. I. Kant, *Critique of Pure Reason*, tr. by N.K. Smith, abridged edition, p. 22.

soul of religion must be reasonable. Yes, it is reasonable, but it cannot be clearly and distinctly stated as Cardinal Newman states. Why?

Because in faith not a *mind*, but a *person* reasons[9] and faith is the result of a 'global impression'.[10] This can be better clarified through the statement of Newman himself:

> It is by the strength, variety, or multiplicity of premises, which are only probable, not by invincible syllogisms—by objections overcome, by adverse theories neutralised, by difficulties gradually clearing up, by exceptions proving the rule, by unlooked for correlations found for received truths, by suspense and delay in the process issuing in triumphant reactions—by all these ways and many others, it is that the practised and experienced mind is able to make a sure divination that a conclusion is inevitable, of which his lines of reasoning do not actually put him in possession.[11]

In other words, faith is the product of the whole man and naturally it cannot be analysed into clear and precise steps of cognition alone. This is what is known as the illative sense* and John Hick states it thus:

> Our capacity to see a large field of evidence as a whole and to divine its significance is what Newman calls the illative sense.[12]

Here in faith reasoning is cumulative and much of it is unconscious. Hence, it is a matter of maturational process. If the account of faith, presented here of Cardinal Newman is correct, then any demand for its analysis in clear and precise statements is wholly unreasonable. However, a few characteristics of faith can be noted down:

(a) The object of faith in the religious sense is the ultimate concern of man, or, what man considers to be his object of worship, devotion and the like.

---

9. John Hick, *Faith and Knowledge*, p. 99.
10. *Ibid.*, p. 105.
11. *Ibid.*, p. 94.
12. *Ibid.*, p. 96.
Illative means pertaining to or introducing an inference.

(b) Faith cannot be reduced to ordinary or scientific knowledge.

(c) Faith means the whole man at work and means all-pervasive attitude to the whole reality, society and his total
or global relationship.

(d) It is a matter of a man's total self-involvement and full
commitment to a certain field of actions. Hence, faith is
the response of the whole man to his whole lived reality.

Though faith defies any clear analysis, yet usually two elements
of believe-that and belief-in are said to constitute it. As stated
earlier, belief-that refers to a proposition and this part has some
cognitive content. But belief-in in the last resort refers to trust
and loyalty to the Supreme Being who is considered to be the
most fundamental good intrinsically. This trust is likely to be
weakened or strengthened in relation to believe-that involved in
belief-in which constitutes the core of faith.

Prof. Paul Schmidt has subdivided belief-that into four kinds,
namely, rational, arational, irrational and non-rational.[13]

Rational beliefs have some evidence in their favour, e.g. the
historicity of Lord Buddha, Christ etc. Irrational beliefs do not
have sufficient evidence. Prof. P. Schmidt does not illustrate
their kinds. But irrational beliefs may contain the postulates of
religious beliefs, e.g. the doctrine of transmigration, the creatorship of God, and so on. Irrational beliefs have evidence against
them. Once again Prof. P. Schmidt does not give any example,
but we can list here the many myths that are found in any religion, e.g. the virgin birth of Jesus. The myths are not superstitions, but they may be living or dead. Non-rational beliefs
do not require any evidence. We may list here the theory of
Karl Barth, according to which the truth of Christianity is a
gift of God and it is doubtful whether there can be any dialogue
between the believers and non-believers.

The function of faith is *not to know* so much as it has to do
with the *becoming of man*. Through one's faith man wants to
become the very deity whom he worships, or, whose teachings
he wants to follow. A Christian wants to become Christ him-

---

13. *Religious Knowledge*, p. 79.

self, and, a follower of Buddha aims at becoming Buddha himself.

THE MYSTIC EXPERIENCE

Mysticism is said to be religious experience in the purest and concentrated form. Both in the East and the West there have been important mystics. In the West, the most celebrated name is of Plotinus (208-270 A.D.) whose mysticism was largely influenced by the East. In the West, W. R. Inge, E. Underhill, Rufus Jones (1863-1948) and Henri Bergson (1859-1941) have favoured mysticism in their philosophy. William James (1842-1910) in his *The Varieties of Religious Experience* and W.T. Stace in *Mysticism and Philosophy* have presented an admirable account of mysticism.

However, mysticism is the most distinctive feature of Indian religion. It is found in the most undiluted form in the Upaniṣads, Advaitism, Bhakti Cult, Kabirism and Sri Ramakrishna. The Sufis subscribe to mysticism. Al-Hallaj, El-Ghazali, Omar Khayyam, Ibn El-Arabi, Saadi of Shiraz and Jalaludin Rumi have been very notable figures. But the mystics have also been subjected to criticism and very often they have been deemed as psycho-neurotic persons.

For Bergson, ' . . . the ultimate end of mysticism is the establishment of a contact, consequently of a partial coincidence, with the creative effort of which life is the manifestation'.[14] Bergson speaks of partial identification with the creative source of Life, but in Indian tradition, in the last analysis, the seeker identifies himself completely with Brahman. And this tradition of Indian mysticism has been fully maintained in Kabir in medieval times, and in Sri Ramakrishna and Vivekananda.

The Sufis do not talk of identification so much with God as they talk of vision and communion with God. For the Muslims God is transcendent and no mortal man can dare identify himself with God. The Jews too believe in the holy, transcendent God, and, Jesus Christ was crucified, for he identified himself with God. In Islam too Al-Hallaj was stoned to death because he dared to identify himself with God.

---

14. *Two Sources of Morality and Religion*, p. 182; Otto also tells us that there are different degrees of completeness of identification with the Transcendental Reality, *The Idea of the Holy*, p. 22.

Whatever be the view of the mystics, either one of complete or partial identification with the supreme object of worship, they have talked about this object with a good deal of warmth born of actual acquaintance. This is certainly an abnormal state, but not a neurotic state. In a neurotic state two elements of social adjustment and mental integration are lacking, and, both these elements are found in supreme abundance in the mystics. Now Bergson talks about two kinds of mysticism, namely, partial or incomplete and complete mysticism. In incomplete form, the mystics remain in absorption and ecstasy and this kind of experience was greatly valued in Indian tradition. But Sri Ramakrishna, himself a man of ecstasy, asked his disciple Sri Vivekananda to practise works, for the alleviation of human sufferings. Bergson highly values social service and works for mitigating human suffering. In complete mysticism, according to Bergson, contemplation gives rise to boundless action. Here there is action, creation and love.[15]

....they burst a dam; they were then swept back into a vast current of life; from their increased vitality there radiated an extraordinary energy, daring, power of conception and realization.[16]

St. Paul, St. Teresa, Joan of Arc, St. Francis in the past and Mother Teresa at present in India are so many examples of complete mysticism.

Vivekananda too interpreted the words of his Master 'jiva is Shiva', as the commissioning his fellows to work for the upliftment of the toiling masses of India.

The poor and the miserable are for our salvation, so that we may serve the Lord, coming in the shape of the diseased, coming in the shape of the lunatic, the leper, and the sinner.[17]

Again, the memorable words of Vivekananda are:

---

15. *Two Sources*, pp. 188, 195, 275.
16. *Ibid.*, p. 194.
17. *Selections from Works of Vivekananda*, p. 230.

What our country now wants are muscles of iron and nerves of steel, gigantic wills which nothing can resist,....[18]

Can a neurotic mystic accomplish this kind of social service? But there is also the second mark of a normal person which is to have clear ideas and the most lucid presentation of his experience. Hence, for Bergson after vague disquietitude, there,

> comes a boundless joy, an all-absorbing ecstasy or an enthralling rapture: God is there, and the soul is in God. Mystery is no more. Problems vanish, darkness is dispelled; everything is flooded with light.[19]

Further, in a true mystic his whole personality gets integrated, and, this point has been emphasized by R.M. Jones.

> It is a notable fact that their (mystics') experiences, and their stabilized faith through what they believe to be their contacts with God, in many cases, in fact usually, result in a unification of personality, in a great increase of dynamic quality—a power to stand the universe—and in a recovery of health and normality.....Hysteria does not unify and construct life as mystical experience indubitably does.[20]

Thus, the mystics enjoy the three criteria of *happiness, mental efficiency* and a *friendly relationship* to one's fellows. Hence, the mystic experience is quite normal and the religious believers have accepted the testimony of the mystics with regard to religion.

CHARACTERISTICS OF MYSTIC EXPERIENCE

William James thinks that personal religious experience has its roots and centre in mystical states of consciousness and has described four marks of mystic experience, namely, ineffability, noetic quality, transiency, and purity. Let us describe each of these marks.

---

18. *Selections,* p. 206.
19. *Two Sources,* p. 196.
20. R.M. Jones, *The Testimony of Mystical Experience* in *Approaches to the Philosophy of Religion,* ed. D.J. Bronstein and H.M. Schulweis. p. 192.

INEFFABILITY

By this, W. James simply means that mystical experience defies expression, for no adequate report of its contents can be given in words.[21] Others have given reasons for the ineffability of mystic experience. For Rudolf Otto, mysticism is essentially the non-rational element in religion.[22] This numinous experience is unique and *sui generis* and cannot be assimilated to any other experience. Hence, it defies the use of any category of thought. Cardinal Newman has also stated that there is so much of coalescence of all the mental states that they cannot be separately described.

However, Indian mysticism means the complete identification of the seeker with Brahman. There is no knower and the known, for both of them become one. According to Sri Ramakrishna, it is like a doll of salt trying to fathom the depth of the ocean. When it approaches the ocean, it is lost in the ocean and so nothing returns to tell us about the ocean. The moment the seeker knows Brahman, he becomes Brahman. There is no longer any knower and the known.

> For where there is a duality, as it were, there one sees another......But where everything has become just one's own self, then whereby and whom would one see?[23]

NOETIC QUALITY

William James mentions that mystic experience has a noetic quality, because here there is an insight into 'depths of truth unplumbed by the discursive intellect'. It is some sort of illumination, revelation and significance for man.[24]

> Mystical experience states, when well-developed, usually are, and have the right to be, absolutely authoritative over the individuals to whom they come.[25]

But immediately after this William James adds:

---

21. *The Varieties of Religious Experience*, p. 380.
22. *The Idea of the Holy*, pp. 3, 22; *Vide*, the analysis of '*Mysticism*', *Ibid.*, p. 26.
23. *Bṛhadāraṇyaka Up.* 4.5.15.
24. *The Varieties*, pp. 380-81.
25. *Ibid.*, p. 422.

No authority emanates from them (mystical States) which should make it a duty for those who stand outside of them to accept their revelations uncritically.[26]

This means that the verdict of mysticism has no public truth or scientific truth. At the most it can be said that it is a highly valuable experience for the mystics. The reason is that mystic experience is quite opposed to what is known as scientific truth. Mystic experience occurs to people who most ardently look forward to having it. Hence, there is an element of auto-suggestion and self-hypnotism. In contrast, scientific truth is established irrespective of the wishes and feelings of the seeker or the scientist. Later on, it would also be shown that there is a good deal of unanimity amongst the scientists with regard to a certain conclusions. The result in science can be repeated at will all over the world in terms of public check. However, the unanimity of mystic report is not true. Each mystic more or less reports what he has been taught in his own professed religion. St. Paul confirmed his Pharisaic beliefs and Sri Ramakrishna spoke eloquently about his Vedāntic training. However, more about this later.

TRANCIENCY

The third characteristic of mystic experience, according to James is that it is transient for it cannot be sustained for long.[27] But certainly the experience may recur from time to time.

In the case of Sri Ramakrishna, the mystic states lasted for long periods and even for several days together. His mystic trance took place most frequently, and he could induce it in others as well, notably in his pupil Vivekananda.

PURITY

The last characteristic is *passivity*, i.e. the mystic feels that his will is in abeyance and a superior will wholly grasps him in power.[28] Rudolf Otto also reports that numinous experience appears to come from something wholly 'Other'.[29] Hence, mystic experience is a great source of religion.

26. *The Varieties*, p. 422.
27. *Ibid.*, p. 381.
28. *Ibid.*, p. 381.
29. *The Idea of the Holy*, p. 29.

CHAPTER V

RELIGIOUS KNOWLEDGE AND LANGUAGE

The history of Positivism is old, but it was most clearly stated by Hume:

> If we take in our hand any volume of divinity or school metaphysics, for instance, let us ask, 'Does it contain any abstract reasoning concerning quantity or number? No. Does it contain any experimental reasoning concerning matter of fact and existence? No. Commit it then to the flames; for it can contain nothing but sophistry and illusion.'

Hence, according to Hume, a statement to be meaningful should be either analytic or synthetic as we now understand them. Any empirical or synthetic statement to be meaningful should be amenable to the two principles of verifiability and falsification. A proposition which even in principle is neither verifiable nor falsifiable is factually empty, absurd and nonsense (meaningless). But is a religious statement analytic, i.e. a statement where there is a consistent use of terms in their stipulated meanings? No. Is God, the principal concept used in religious discourses, a sensible event? No. Quite obviously God-talk cannot be reduced to empirical statements. Is God-talk nonsense? A. Flew, J. Mackie, J.N. Findlay at least in his article on 'Ontological Atheism' do maintain that God-talk is nonsense.

The so-called logical positivists enjoyed celebrity for at least a decade. However, a fresh look at Wittgenstein's *Philosophical Investigations* showed that instead of putting emphasis on 'meaning', we should attend to the use of language and its rules of usage. According to it, language is used in a variety of ways, and not for conveying information only. Religious language is used not to convey any information about any fact, but is used to tell people to live with a picture, which picture is not a picture of any state of affairs. However, the logical positivists treated God-talk as if it was an empirical statement, conveying some information about a fact called God. God is certainly a picture, but not a picture of something which can be sensed. Hence, the logical positivists were killing a horse of straw. They never correctly understood the nature of religious statements, which are not factual, but are mythological (Mircea Eliade, R. Bultmann), symbolical (Paul Tillich), analogical (St. Thomas Aquinas), evocative, or exhortative (as has been maintained in Chapter V).

As some of the essays have become classical, so they have been given a place in this chapter.

Section I

THE ONTOLOGICAL ATHEISM OF J.N. FINDLAY

According to J.N. Findlay, by 'God' is meant an 'adequate object of religious attitude'. And a religious attitude is one in which we tend to abase ourselves before its appropriate object, to defer to it wholly, to commit ourselves to it with unquestioning enthusiasm and to bend our knee before it whether literally or metaphorically.[1] In relation to one's God, the worshipper feels to be absolutely dependent, creaturely and to be nothing but ashes; and, in contrast, God appears to be overpowering, mighty and the creator of the whole universe and of all things therein.

The religious attitude may be either justified or unjustified, appropriate or inappropriate. For example, a state of anger is appropriate in relation to a frustrating situation, and inappropriate in relation to an amusing scene. Now an appropriate attitude demands that its object, namely God, should have the three characteristics of all-comprehensiveness, necessary being and of having all his attributes in a necessary manner.

1. The religious object must possess superiority of such a nature that in relation to it the worshipper may feel his utter insignificance or nothingness. It must be surpassingly superior to everything in order that a worshipper may surrender himself

---

1. J. N. Findlay, 'Can God's existence be disproved?' NEPT, p. 49.

to it completely and absolutely. In other words, the object of worship must be without *limit* in any thinkable manner. For all other superiorities in comparison are relative and can be dwarfed in thought by still mightier superiorities.

And hence we are led on irresistibly to demand that our religious object should have an *unsurpassable* supremacy along all avenues, that it should tower *infinitely* above all other objects.[2]

It should also be a source of any and every excellence in any object whatsoever. Hence, it should be all-comprehensive.

2. Secondly, the object of worship must not simply *happen* to exist. It not only includes all that exists and but also everything possible.

And not only must the existence of other things be unthinkable without him, but his own non-existence must be wholly unthinkable in any circumstance.[3]

In him essence and existence must be found inseparably.

3. Lastly, all the attributes which the object of religious attitude possesses, must not simply happen to have them *as a mere matter of fact*, but must have them in some necessary manner. If the object comes to acquire even the highest excellences contingently, then it may possibly lose them too, or, at least we can conceive this possible state of affairs. In that case the object may deserve the *douleia* canonically accorded to the saints, but not the *latreia* that we properly owe to God.

That the object to be an appropriate object should be all-comprehensive, must necessarily exist and have all its attributes in some inescapable manner, according to Findlay is either senseless or impossible.[4] 'Necessity' is not applicable to things but to propositions. If the proposition, 'God cannot be conceived not to non-exist' be necessary, then it reflects our conventional use of the term 'God' and says nothing about any actual state of affairs. If the religious frame of mind "desires the

---

2. NEPT, p. 51.
3. NEPT, p. 52.
4. NEPT, p. 54.

Divine Existence both to have that inescapable character which can, on modern views only be found where truth reflects an arbitrary convention and also the character of 'making a real difference' which is only possible where truth doesn't have this merely linguistic basis".[5]

In other words, religious people who try to think hard want both to eat the cake and at the same time have it. They *doublethink* the contradictory things about God, his *existence* which can only be expressed in contingent propositions and also his *necessity* which has no application to an actual state of affairs. Hence, the object of worship to be an appropriate object, being self-contradictory is senseless.

From the arguments of Findlay it follows that the object of religious attitude is either self-contradictory or absurd. Hence, for Findlay religious attitude is not justified, because it refers to an object which is logically impossible. In showing ontological atheism Findlay confines himself to the two characteristics of the worshipful God, namely, his necessary being and his possessing all the attributes in a necessary manner. He does not make use of the divine characteristic of being all-comprehensive. A. Flew takes up the thread of the argument for atheism just at this point. For A. Flew, if God is infinite and all-inclusive, then there can be no event outside God which can count against the assertion concerning God. If the existence of God cannot be falsified by any actual state of affairs, then any statement concerning God can be vacuous only. A. Flew was obviously influenced by the article 'Gods' which John Wisdom had written in 1944.[6] He makes a simplified version of the parable of John Wisdom.

Suppose two persons return to their long-neglected garden. They find a few of the old plants surprisingly vigorous. One explains this with the help of an invisible gardener; the other denies this. Both of them examine the garden carefully; at times

---

5. NEPT, p. 55.
6. It was first printed in *Proceedings of Aristotelian Society*, 1944-45. Since then it has been reprinted in a number of the books of *Readings*. References here have been made from '*Classical and Contemporary Readings in the Philosophy of Religion*', Edited by John Hick, Prentice Hall, 1964, abbreviated here as CCRPR.

a few facts support the hypothesis of an invisible gardener. However, a few other facts falsify such a supposition. Later, they put electrified barbed wires and even put blood-hounds to smell the presence of any being. But these contrivances make no difference to the believer in existence of the invisible gardener. The believer even adds that this gardener remains unsmelt and unheard. Here Flew and Wisdom differ in the implication of the belief in an invisible gardener. Wisdom agrees that our belief in God is not experimental and therefore does not relate to the facts.[7] For Wisdom, theological statements are not nonsensical on this account. They may evince an attitude to the familiar[8] and often are expressive of feeling[9] and even may help the 'recognition of pattern in time easily missed'.

Things are revealed to us not only by the scientists with microscopes, but also by the poets, the prophets, and the painters.[10]

Flew does not subscribe to this view of John Wisdom. According to Flew theological statements are wholly vacuous and empty because they are not falsifiable by any actual events.

A. Flew's Disproof of God's Existence

Flew's argument has two steps:

1. "Religious utterances may indeed express false or even bogus assertions; but I simply do not believe that they are not both intended and interpreted to be or at any rate to presuppose assertions, at least in the context of religious practice; whatever shifts may be demanded, in another context, by the exigencies of theological apologetic."[11]
2. Again, to assert that such and such is the case is necessarily equivalent to denying that such and such is not the case.
   "And to know the meaning of the negation of an assertion, is as near as makes no matter, to know the meaning

7. CCRPR, Gods, p. 421.
8. *Ibid.*, p. 417.
9. *Ibid.*, p. 421.
10. *Ibid.*, p. 417.
11. A.G.N. Flew, Theology and falsification, NEPT, p. 108.

of that assertion. And if there is nothing which a putative assertion denies then there is nothing which it asserts either: and so it is not really an assertion.[12]

Of course, theologians can deny both the steps: many theologians do not treat religious utterances to be assertions at all. And if they are not assertions, then they need not be empirical statements. It is to be noted here that Flew has used the criterion of Karl Popper for demarcating empirical statements from those of logic, mathematics and metaphysics. For him the empirical content of a statement increases with its degree of falsifiability: the more a statement denies the actual states of affairs, and the more it says about the world of experience. By amending and generalising a remark of Einstein, Karl Popper writes:

> Insofar as a scientific statement speaks about reality, it must be falsifiable: and insofar as it is not falsifiable, it does not speak about reality.[13]

Further, he adds that it is almost a contradiction to say that an empirical statement is not falsifiable. Hence, if it could be said that religious assertions are empirical and yet are not falsifiable, then it would be as self-contradictory as the concept of 'Necessary Being' which has been shown to be so by J.N. Findlay.

Now why are theological statements not falsifiable? Three main reasons have been advanced; namely,

(i) The attributes that are ascribed to God are killed by a thousand qualifications and this admits of innumerable occasions of shifting the argument.

(ii) A theist is so much committed to his belief in God that he would not accept anything to count against theistic assertions concerning the divine attributes of love or wisdom.

(iii) A theologian takes a metaphysical plea. He says that his knowledge is very partial, but God's ways deal with the whole universe. Unless one knows about the whole uni-

---

12. NEPT, p. 98.
13. Karl R. Popper, *The logic of Scientific Discovery*, Hutchinson, 1952, p. 314.

verse one cannot take any instance to count against religious assertions.

All these three reasons either severally or together may contribute towards the non-falsifiability of theistic statements. We shall illustrate the device of shifting ground first.

Let us take such theistic statements as 'God is love', 'God has created the world', 'God has a plan for the universe' and so on. When it is said that 'God is love' then people ordinarily mean that God's love is akin to human love. But human love is certainly falsifiable. There are instances which can count against the assertion that X loves Y.

But can the death of a young promising man, pestilence which kills a million people, a hurricane which destroys a whole city be cited as instances to falsify the statement 'God is love?' No. Some qualifications are added. It would be pointed out that God's love is not like the human love or that God's love is to be judged in relation to the total picture of the universe, past, present and future, or that God's ways are too mysterious to be judged.

> And there lies the danger of that death by a thousand qualifications, which would, I agree, constitute 'a failure in faith as well as in logic'.[12]

The result is that the statement 'God is love' remains unfalsifiable by anything which may happen in the universe.

> Who shall separate us from the love of Christ? *Shall* tribulation, or distress, or persecution, or famine, or nakedness, or peril, or sword?[15]

This shows that 'God is love' is intended to be an assertion and being unfalsifiable is not an assertion. Therefore, Flew maintains that religious intellectuals indulge in double thinking.

The kind of assertion-criterion to which Flew refers is not possible in theistic religion. No theist can point to a thing and say this is God. This would reduce God into an idol and theism

---

14. NEPT, p. 107.
15. Romans 8: 35.

into idolatry. But anybody who still accepts the factuality of theological statement will have to reply to Flew. Basil Mitchell and I.M. Crombie undertake to defend theism in the face of the difficulties raised by ontological disproof of the existence of God.

BASIL MITCHELL'S REPLY TO FLEW

Basil Mitchell would not straightaway declare theological statements to be factual, because the attitude of a religious thinker is not of the detached observer, but of the believer.[16] Now a theological statement like 'God loves men' may be interpreted in three ways:

1. As a provisional hypothesis which can be refuted if there are instances against them.
2. As a significant article of faith.
3. As a vacuous formula which makes no difference to the actual state of affairs.

According to Mitchell, no theological statements can be taken provisionally, otherwise we shall be tempting the Lord. He also fears that at times such statements are likely to slip into vacuous formulae. He, therefore, would take theological statements to be significant articles of faith. But as articles of faith they are assertions, even when they cannot be decisively falsifiable with regard to the statement 'God loves men'. Mitchell admits that the fact of pain does count against it, but cannot *decisively* count against it.[17] Because disaster, human suffering and moral evils count against divine love and providence, therefore, the theist experiences the full force of the conflict. His faith is put on trial and his light-hearted belief in God is put to a great strain. Hence, pain *does count* against the statement 'God loves men'. But a theist would not succumb to such falsifying statements concerning pain. He would say,

> Naked came I out of my mother's womb, and naked shall I return thither; the Lord gave, and the Lord hath taken away; blessed be the name of Lord.[18]

---

16. NEPT, p. 103.
17. NEPT, p. 103.
18. Job 1: 21.

Most probably the brief defence of Mitchell has something of very great value, but is he right in calling theological statements to be factual? If the statements are made convictionally, as significant articles of faith, then can they be regarded factual in the public language of Flew? Hence, his view falls into an easy refutation by D.R. Duff-Forbes.[19] According to Duff-Forbes, if instances cannot *decisively* count against the statement 'God loves men', then they only *appear* to count against and do not really count against the theological statement in the required sense of Flew. Most probably Mitchell would accept the criticism of Duff-Forbes, but he would add that by a factual content of theological statements, he means that they have *empirical application*.[20] For example, the concept of 'Grace of God' is said to have a factual content in the sense that it must be perceptible or discernible in some genuine religious experience. But how can we recognize the genuineness of the experience? Here Mitchell falls back on the religious tradition, which according to him has been largely influenced by the inspired scriptures.[21] According to the tradition the marks of saintliness are: Felicity, purity, charity, patience, self-severity. These excellent characteristics have been described by W. James in *The Varieties of Religious Experience* thus.[22] A saint, by having a convictional experience of an Ideal Power, feels a certain widening of his personality and an inner elation and freedom. The saint is an *ascetic* for he finds positive pleasure in sacrifice. Again, the sense of enlargement of his personality is so elevating that he enjoys a certain *bliss*, undisturbed by any fears and anxieties. The contact with *the Holy* creates in the saint the character of purity. The saint enjoys the cleansing from all beastly and sensual desires. Lastly, there is *charity* and tenderness for his fellow-creatures in so marked a degree that a saint loves his enemies and embraces even loathsome beggars as his brothers, and these may be the marks of the workings of the

---

19. D. R. Duff-Forbes, 'Theology and falsification again', *The Australian Journal of Philosophy*, Vol. 39, 1961, p. 149.
20. FL, p. 152.
21. FL, p. 161.
22. 38th Impression, Longmans, 1935, pp. 272-74; 370.

Grace of God. But here the whole thing becomes circular, for we may as well ask for the 'truth' of the tradition itself. Here we will be told that the 'truth' is tested on the interpretation as guided by the Grace of God. Thus the truth of the tradition depends on the Grace of God and the workings of the Grace in its turn are tested by the tradition. Mitchell himself notes this, but he tells us that the argument is not *viciously* circular, if one of the beliefs did conform to the test of falsifiability. But can we really accept any one of these beliefs to be independently open to falsifiability? Mitchell himself sees the point:

> Belief in the grace of God cannot be established by empirical evidence but once accepted, it can be seen to have empirical application.[23]

Besides, can we say that a proposition is empirical because it has an empirical application? If the applicability were the test, then even the statements of mathematics and logic will become empirical since they are also applicable to facts. Most probably this was the sense of Kant's contention, according to which even *a priori* precepts and concepts have application to facts. However, applicability to facts is not the criterion of the factuality of statements. If the meaning of a statement is derived from experience, then alone it will be said to be empirical. And Basil Mitchell has not shown that the content of 'God loves men' has been derived from repeatable, communicable and sharable experience. Thus, we fear that Mitchell has not faced the difficulty raised by Flew. However, Mitchell's defence is not without its protest against the handling of the theological statements by Flew. Mitchell wants to hold the view that falsifiability-test is applicable to theological statements, but such tests have their own logic. The logic applicable here is to be derived from convictional language and it would be improper to apply here the logic of scientific language. It is the empiricist who will be said to be committing the category mistake and not the theologian. Here it might be pointed out that theological statements are made true by believers who have been convicted of their sins by a saviour (in this case Jesus Christ) and by per-

---

23. FL, p. 174.

sons whose whole personality is greatly involved in the religious experience. Theological statements have both content and sense within a religious tradition. Within faith they are both verifiable and falsifiable. Of course such a defence is not without its own difficulty, But before discussing it we have to turn to I.M. Crombie and John Hick who have taken up Mitchell's defence at great length.

I.M. CROMBIE'S AND JOHN HICK'S DEFENCE OF THEISTIC ASSERTIONS

According to John Hick religious facts can be established through *post mortem* experience.

In the same way John Hick whilst trying to establish religious facts through *post mortem* verification writes:

> It may then be a condition of *post mortem* verification that we be already in some degree conscious of God by an uncompelled response to his modes of revelation in this world. It may be that such a voluntary consciousness of God is an essential element in the fulfilment of the divine purpose for human nature, so that the verification of theism which consists in an experience of the final fulfilment of that purpose can only be experienced by those who have already entered upon an awareness of God by the religious mode of apperception which we call faith.[24]

If this proviso be not kept in mind then misconceived criticisms will be directed against the theory of theological falsifiability. Most probably I.M. Crombie and John Hick themselves are not unequivocal in their stand. They tend to think, because theistic statements are theologically falsifiable and verifiable, therefore, they also in some sense embody scientific facts.

Both I.M. Crombie and John Hick think that in principle theological statements are falsifiable through *post mortem* experience. I.M. Crombie states that 'God is love' is certainly falsifiable by the presence of suffering.

"Does anything count decisively against it? No, we reply,

---

24. John Hick, 'Religious statements as factually significant', EG.

because it is true. Could anything count decisively against it? Yes, suffering which was utterly, eternally and irredeemably pointless.[25] Can we then design a crucial experiment? No, because we can never see all of the picture. Two things at least are hidden from us; what goes on in the recess of the personality of the sufferer, and what shall happen hereafter.[26]

Crombie does not elaborate the first point, namely, the experience of the sufferer in the very depth of his personality. Most probably he implies that suffering is never pointless because it might have redemptive function to perform even in the case of apparently futile sufferings. However, his emphasis is on the theistic belief in eschatological existence. There is some difference between Crombie and Hick concerning eschatological existence. Crombie and Hick both agree that the picture concerning God's design and so also consequently concerning religious facts will become much clearer, fuller and even crucial through the resurrected life of the dead. But how do we know that there is going to be the survival of the dead? Hick clearly states that there can be conclusive evidence for the truth of the *survival-claim*, but no conclusive evidence against it if it be untrue.

> For if we survive bodily death we shall (presumably) know that we have survived it, but if we do not survive death we shall not know that we have not survived it. The verification situation is thus asymmetrical. However, the religious doctrine at least is open to verification and is accordingly meaningful. Its eschatological prediction assures its status as an assertion.[27]

Is eschatological prediction the same as scientific predictability? If survival claim is not falsifiable even in principle, is it a factual claim? John Hick ought to have pondered a little over the non-falsifiability of non-survival-claim. He would have discovered that the silence of death extinguishes both the claims

25. I.M. Crombie, FL, p. 78.
26. I.M. Crombie, NEPT, pp. 124-25.
27. John Hick, FK, p. 150.

of survival and non-survival after death. 'Death' means the 'end of this earthly existence' and any extension of this earthly experience in *post mortem* existence is self-contradictory.[28] But even on perusing this point, he writes:

> I am, however, still of the opinion that the notion of es-chatological verification is sound; and further, that no viable alternative to it has been offered to establish the factual character of theism.[29]

Hick ought to have made clear the nature of factual claim of theistic statements. As noted earlier, we unnecessarily assimilate scientific factuality to the convictional factuality of religious entities. By doing this nothing but confusion will arise. Here the stand of Crombie is much clearer. For Crombie the hope of immortality is an article of faith. A Christian, for Crombie,

> admits that if this hope be vain then we are of all men the most miserable.[30]

Of course, within Christian language eschatological verification or falsification has sense, but this kind of verification-falsification can lay no claim to scientific truth and factual meaningfulness. If John Hick and John Wilson[31] still think that eschatological falsifiability can yield scientific factuality, then they should be able to answer the following objections. The objection pertinent to the problem of falsifiability is that eschatological experience in the sense of John Hick is not intelligible. 'Death' means the extinction of 'me' or 'my', and any talk of continuance of experience after death means 'my' living and not 'death'. Apart from this linguistic difficulty, can eschatological experience be treated as factual? If it be so, then even *post mortem* experience is open to the same difficulty to which the experience of this life in this earthly frame is exposed. If the finite experience cannot establish the scientific knowledge of

---

28. John Passmore, *Christianity and positivism*, in *Australian Journal of Philosophy*, Vol. 35, No. 2, p. 135.
29. NEPT, p. 129.
30. EG, p. 259.
31. Philosophy and Religion, Chap. III (Ox. U.P.), 1961.

the Infinite God whom Crombie[32] calls 'mystery', the *post mortem* experience can fare no better, for it will continue to be finite. Of course, Crombie takes recourse to the language of parable and analogy. However, he is candid enough to confess that theology is not a science; it is a sort of art of enlightened ignorance.[33] He is fully aware of the agnostic nature of the analogical statement. The point is either *post mortem* experience is a continuation of this life or it is entirely different from it. If it is the former, then the limitations of this life will cling even to the *post mortem* experience and one will not be able to gain much. If, on the other hand, *post mortem* experience is quite different from this present mundane existence, then it can have no relevance for our problems of this life. As a matter of fact, Kai Nielson correctly observes that 'no conceivable *post mortem* experiences could *falsify* or *disconfirm* the existence of God'.[34] The reason is if we survive bodily death, then God's existence will get verified and *not falsified*; and if we do not survive bodily death, then God's existence can neither be confirmed nor disconfirmed. But if by means of even *post mortem* experience God's existence remains unfalsifiable, then certainly it is not an empirical statement.

The truth has to be conceded that eschatological experience cannot be communicated, even if there be one. Any one remembering the parable of Miss Betty knows that the man risen from the dead cannot return to report what he experiences there. People should know the answer which Jesus gave in his parable of the rich man and Lazarus.[35] Feeling the torments of hell the rich man requested father Abraham to send a man from the heaven to the earth to report the eschatological experience. Father Abraham said:

If they (People) hear not Moses and the Prophets, neither will they be persuaded, though one rose from the dead.[36]

The meaning is plain. The eschatological experience is religious

---

32. FL, p. 73.
33. NEPT, p. 128.
34. RET, p. 270; also Paul Edwards, RET, p. 246.
35. St. Like 16: 31.

and convictional. This experience is strange from the scientific standpoint.

> Verily, verily, I say unto thee, we speak that we do know, and testify that we have seen; and ye receive not our witness.[37]

Facts about the heaven are not the same as facts of the earth: and, even earthly things spoken in heavenly terms do not form plain factual statements in the language of science.

The very fact that eschatological experience is not open to verification-falsification of our ordinary earthly experience rules it out as the kind of experience in which we are said to cash factual statements. When we talk about the falsifiability of any statement, then we mean this in terms of our ordinary sense-experience. Any claim to factuality of religious statements in terms of eschatological verification is a gross violation of linguistic use of the term 'falsification'. But of course, we can talk of theological falsifiability in terms of religious experience and language. Only in this sense, Crombie can meaningfully be said to have written that no fact can decisively count against 'God is merciful' or 'God loves men', because *it is true*. By saying that a statement 'A' is true, we really mean that it is what it is. Hence, when we say that the statement 'God loves men' is true, we merely assert it, and add nothing more. The word 'true' does not add anything to it. So cognitively speaking Crombie stating 'because it is true' means no more than mere repetition of the statement 'God loves men'. However, from the religious stand it means the affirmation and one's conviction of the Christian article of faith.[38]

Though Hick and Crombie do not distinguish convictional language from the language of science, yet they do tacitly mean that the theological factuality can be made in the convictional language only. Hick tells us that eschatological verification is possible in the context of 'actually operative religious concept of God'.

In the language of Christian faith, the word 'God' stands

---

37. St. John, 3:11.
38. W.T. Blackstone, 'The Problem of Religious Knowledge', pp. 123-24.

at the centre of a system of terms, such as spirit, grace, Logos, incarnation, kingdom of God, and many more; and the distinctly Christian conception of God can only be fully grasped in its connection with these related terms.[39]

And Hick approvingly accepts the view of Ninian Smart,[40] according to which theological statements have meaning 'in the doctrinal scheme from which it is extrapolated'. Crombie states that theistic statements of Christianity are made in terms of authoritative and authorised images concerning God used by Jesus Christ. Further, he tells us that by the practice of Christian precepts for life the mind is 'stretched and suppled for the grasp of the divine truth'.[41] This means that religious statements have sense within the doctrinal scheme or the grammar of the respective religious language.

Therefore, it is clear that eschatological statement is one of the religious utterances in question and it can have no direct relevance to the factuality of religious statements.[42] It appears then that Flew is victorious with regard to his stand. Judged as factual statements religious utterances are self-contradictory, (J.J.C. Smart, J.N. Findlay) and vacuous (A.G.N. Flew). Religious statements are not factual in the language of science. They have convictional factuality, whatever that phrase may mean. Religious utterances can be both verified and falsified within the doctrinal scheme of a religion. But this kind of verification-falsification does not directly establish the factual meaningfulness and truth of theological statements in the language of science. Scientifically speaking, theological statements can neither be verified nor falsified. As soon as we say that nothing can conclusively count against theological statements, either on the basis of commitment, trust, all-comprehensiveness of God, or on the basis of eschatological experiences, we throw away the claim to the factuality of science.

IN DEFENCE OF 'NECESSARY BEING'

The ontological atheism of Findlay relies on two main points.

---

39. John Hick, EG, p. 259.
40. Ninian Smart, *Reasons and Faiths*, Routledge, 1958, p. 12.
41. FL, p. 76.
42. D.R. Duff-Forbes, *op. cit.*, p. 152.

1. First, the concept of 'Necessary Being' is self-contradictory and that the statement concerning God's Being is vacuous.
2. Again, God to be worshipful must be a *necessary being*, and not a contingent being.

The first point has been taken up by G.E. Hughes, A.C.A. Rainer, A. Kenny, N. Malcolm and others. Again, P.A.E. Hutchings has tried to meet the grounds of J.N. Findlay most clearly in his article *Necessary Being and some types of theology* in *Philosophy*.[43] The second point too has been very well commented upon by W. D. Hudson in the same issue of *Philosophy*.[44] Let us take the problem of 'Necessary Being' first.

G.E. Hughes and A.C.A. Rainer have suggested that there can be existential propositions which can yet be necessary. According to them the current dogma that existential propositions are necessarily contingent and that necessary propositions are necessarily non-existential is too arbitrary. According to G.E. Hughes 'God exists' is a necessary existential proposition.[45] In the same way A.C.A. Rainer holds that the necessity of God's existence relates to a property of God and to the property of an assertion concerning God's existence.[46] Let us analyse the notion of 'existential necessity'.

POSSIBILITY OF NECESSARY EXISTENTIAL PROPOSITIONS
Here the view of Prof. A.N. Prior is useful in throwing light on *necessary existential propositions*. A.N. Prior has elaborated a remark of G.E. Moore. According to G.E. Moore, some concepts are exemplified and some are not. For the purpose of showing that the concept of 'lionhood' is exemplified we say 'Lions exist' and of showing the concept of unicorn to be unexemplified we say 'Unicorns do not exist'. In the same manner we can illustrate the cases of contingent and necessary non-exemplifications. It is contingent that unicornhood is unexemplified: in contrast, the concept of 'square circularity' is necessarily unexemplified. Can we not in like manner think of neces-

43. P.A.E. Hutchings, *Necessary being and some type of Tautology*, *Philosophy* Vol. XXXIX, January, 1964.
44. W.D. Hudson, An attempt to defend theism, *Philosophy*, 1964.
45. NEPT, pp. 64-66.
46. NEPT, p. 68.

sary and contingent exemplification? Can there not be concepts which get exemplified by virtue of certain properties inherent in them? When Anselm states that God is a Being who cannot non-exist, then he really means that God exists by virtue of his own properties, and, this contention underlies the argument from contingency in favour of a Necessary Being. Here Anthony Kenny further comments on the. possibility of a necessary existential proposition in the light of Aristotelian logic.[47]

Of course, Aristotle talked of sentences and not of propositions. But if his views be taken up in relation to propositions, then some interesting results follow. According to the current view, no proposition can be true at one time and false at another time. For example, the proposition 'Socrates is sitting' is true then it does not become false, if Socrates afterwards begins to walk. Each proposition is true or false timelessly. If 'Socrates is sitting' is true, then it is true timelessly, and, if it is false, then it is false timelessly. However, according to Aristotle, a proposition is significantly tensed. It is true to say 'Socrates is sitting' if Socrates is actually sitting and becomes false the moment he begins to walk. Now if this view concerning the tensed significance of statements be accepted, then 'God exists necessarily' may become logically possible. According to the theory of tensed significance of propositions, a statement is contingent when it is true at one time, but need not be so at another time. However, a statement is necessary which is true at all times. The key-notion here is of a Being which is true everlastingly or always. This notion of a Being that endures for all times is to be distinguished from the notion of that which is timelessly true. *Logical* necessity is timelessly true: in contrast, existential necessity is always true. Now God is, God has always existed and will always exist. Yahweh, the God of the Jews, declared 'I am that I am'. So 'God exists' is a. necessary existential proposition, according to the theory of tensed significance of statements. In the same way God is said to possess His attributes of wisdom, love, power and goodness through all moments of time. So He can be said to be having His attributes *necessarily.*

47. Anthony Kenny, God and necessity, in *British Analytical Philosophy* Edited by B. Williams and Alan Montefiore, Routledge, 1966.

Thus the notion of a Necessary Being and of His possessing all His attributes in a necessary manner need not be absurd or impossible. Hence, in the light of the tensed significance of propositions the following statement of P. Hutchings can be easily understood:

> 'God exists' must be true as long as God exists; 'God exists' must *necessarily* be true as long as God exists. Nevertheless the necessity of God's existence is what, if anything, will guarantee the 'necessity' or the being always true, of the proposition that He exists, and unless this point is understood, argument can only proceed at cross-purposes.[48]

Further, for P. Hutchings 'God exists' is also not vacuous as it is falsifiable. Resting his case on the argument from contingency, P. Hutchings succinctly remarks, 'If God did not exist, we and the world would not exist either'.[49]

> ......The description of God as necessary is distinguishable from another description, and does not evaporate the possible distinctions between 'a state of affairs in which God does not exist'.[50]

Thus, according to P. Hutchings and A. Kenny, after all God as 'Necessary Being' is not as absurd and impossible as J.N. Findlay and A. Flew have us believe and that the statement about God's existence and his necessary attributes need not be vacuous.

WORSHIPFULNESS OF NECESSARY BEING
Before commenting on the defence of A. Kenny and P. Hutchings, let us take up another question which has been already raised. According to J.N. Findlay, God in order to be worshipful 'must in some manner be *all-comprehensive*'[51] and the object of worship 'must possess its various qualities *in some neces-*

48. P. Hutchings, *op. cit.*, p. 6.
49. *Ibid.*, p. 12.
50. *Ibid.*, p. 14.
51. NEPT, p. 52.

sary manner'.[52] Now W.D. Hudson analyses the meaning of this 'must'.[53] In order to be worshipful, should God be Necessary Being? Does 'must' mean that 'we can't help feeling'?[54] If this is a psychological necessity, then quite obviously *Necessary* Being does not become self-contradictory or absurd. Only when 'necessary' is logically necessary, then being cannot be logically necessary. Again, if the believer can't help feeling God to be infinite and to be having all His attributes necessarily, then the infinitude of God is just a matter of the intensity of subjective feeling and cannot be said to be an objective property of God. At the time a deity is worshipped, it is felt to be infinite and all-comprehensive. This is a phenomenon which has been called henotheism by Maxmuller in relation to Vedic Gods. Each of the important Vedic Gods at the time of being worshipped was called infinite. But there were many such Gods who were called so in their turn of being worshipped. Thus, empirically considered, a God of worship need not be infinite: very often he is just finite. Even Yahweh was just a finite God by the side of other Gods. However, the whole basis of J.N. Findlay's argument is that logic of worship logically *implies* that God must be infinite and must have all His attributes in a necessary manner. In other words, he means to say 'I worship X' logically means 'I worship Necessary Being', that is, 'I worship Necessary Being' is an analytic proposition. But does the analyticity of the above-mentioned proposition follow from the linguistic convention of the concept of 'worship'? Of course, there is no such convention. Hence, 'worship' and 'necessary being' are not necessarily connected. As an anthropological fact any deity, even a finite god has been an object of worship. However, Western theologians ordinarily have taken God as an object of worship as Necessary Being. If so, then what does 'must' or 'can't help feeling' mean? It is significant to note that for J.N. Findlay religious attitude is largely a thing of feeling; it is an attitude in which 'we feel disposed to bend the knee before some object, to defer to it wholly, and the like, . . .'[55] J.N. Findlay thus describes the religious attitude:

---

52. NEPT, p. 53.
53. W.D. Hudson, *Philosophy* 1964, p. 26.
54. NEPT, p. 52.
55. NEPT, p. 51.

Here, as elsewhere, we find ourselves indicating the *felt* character of our attitudes, by treating their inward character as, in some sense, a concentrated and condensed substitute for appropriate lines of action, a way of speaking that accords curiously with the functional significance of the inward.[56]

This 'concentrated and condensed' feeling or inwardness is really another name for commitment with one's total involvement. It is this commitment with one's total involvement which does not allow falsifiability of theistic statements.[57] We have already seen the difficulty of falsifiability of theistic statements because of one's commitment to God. But there is one more point which requires to be mentioned here.

Has commitment to God any logic? Is it verifiable-falsifiable? Well, the belief in God means the acceptance of a certain attitude to all possible experiences of life, an attitude of fortitude in the presence of rebuffs and rebukes which life may throw out for a believer and also an attitude of trust and courage. Naturally such an attitude remains unruffled by any fortune or mishap. Naturally within a wide range of facts faith in God remains compatible with all kinds of events. But such a faith-statement is neither vacuous nor dies the death of a thousand qualifications. Such a faith helps the believer live with courage for a certain meaningful life. Only when this meaning is lost then faith becomes impossible. Therefore, life affirmed and lived and death faced and accepted do bear witness to the 'truth' of a religious attitude. Hence, there is room for acceptance-rejection of a certain religious attitude, and, the phenomenon of conversion testifies to this. Under the circumstances, W.D. Hudson correctly writes:

It may, of course, be objected that a faith held in spite of empirical circumstances is vacuous; it dies by a thousand qualifications. Against that, I think it should be recognised that the theist's position is that no circumstance which he has so far encountered has made him abandon his faith, not that

---

56. NEPT, p. 49.
57. P. Hutchings, *Philosophy*, 1964, p. 27.

no circumstance which he could conceivably encounter would make him abandon it.[58]

COMMENT OF THE NOTION OF NECESSARY BEING

Whatever may be the possibility of necessary existential propositions, this is not free from certain objections. First, the whole notion of a necessary existential proposition concerning God is based on the possibility of exemplification of certain concepts and these concepts and their exemplifications are both logically contingent. Even if God be taken to be an entity who endures all the moments of time, then how can we not logically think of God to be non-existing? Can we not imagine the whole series of time to be ending? Only by defining time as that which can never be imagined to be ceasing and only by defining God as one who never ceases to endure all the moments of time that we can analytically define God as necessary existential being. But under the circumstance God becomes necessary linguistically and the term 'existential' is brought into being by definition. If, on the other hand, God *happens* to be enduring all the time, then we simply cannot say that God *must* happen to be enduring all the time. The distinction between logical and existential necessities cannot be blurred. And as long as we can distinguish between existential and logical necessities, the point of J.N. Findlay remains sound and secure. J.N. Findlay means by 'necessary' that which is logically necessary and with that clarification 'Necessary Being' is certainly self-contradictory.

Let us summarise the position:

1. First, the analysis of 'worship' by J.N. Findlay is faulty. 'Worship' is an empirical fact of life. It is contingent, and as such cannot imply 'necessary being' in the sense of Findlay. A finite God has been worshipped throughout the whole course of human history. In the Advaitic version of worship according to Sri Ramakrishna, one worship at the start a finite god (saguṇa Brahma) for one's spiritual attainment. And finally through this kind of worship one is helped to reach the final stage of Brahman realisation.

Again, 'Worshipping' simply means an attitude to life, according to R.B. Braithwaite and John Wisdom. It is living with

58. W.D. Hudson, *Philosophy*, 1964, p. 27.

a picture of what one considers to be one's ultimate concern (Paul Tillich, L. Wittgenstein). This attitude to life does not depend on rational arguments decisively. Arguments are mere pleas in the service of religious attitude (Kant, John Wisdom). Hence, Findlay is not correct in holding that 'worship' is a matter of logical implication.

Further, if God endures through all times, as the Aristotelian theory of tensed propositions holds, then God is not logically necessary, but is factually necessary. This is a distinction which has been drawn up by Terence Penelhum.[59]

A thing is necessary if it is indispensable. For want of a better phrase I call it necessity in this sense 'factual necessity'. To be a theist is to believe that there is a being, God, who is factually necessary, all other beings being dependent, contingent, upon him.

Hence, if 'worship' means psychological necessity of bowing down before God for one's peace of mind, then 'worship' means *contingent* indispensability of God. An indispensable God is *so* for a believer only, not for an atheist or a non-believer. A believer or a non-believer does not dispute God as a fact, for religion is a matter of an attitude to facts of life. A believer has a picture of what he considers to be divine. A non-believer has no such picture to live with. Where is the room for dispute?

Thus, we conclude that in the light of the empirical analysis by J.N. Findlay, A. Flew and others that the cognitiveness of theistic statements cannot be consistently held. Now, if theistic statements can no longer be cognitive, then what is their real nature? Are they quasi-cognitive or wholly non-cognitive? One very old view is that theistic statements are quasi-cognitive; they are said to be analogical in nature. Besides the analogical theory, there are a number of theories according to which theistic statements are non-cognitive. For our purposes we shall take up only three of them which may be regarded as fairly representative views concerning theistic statements to be non-cognitive. We can put all the views in the form of a Table.

---

59. Divine Necessity, in 'The Philosophy of Religion', by B. Mitchell, p. 189.

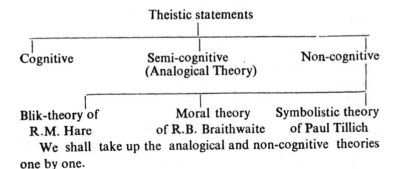

Theistic statements

Cognitive   Semi-cognitive   Non-cognitive
(Analogical Theory)

Blik-theory of   Moral theory   Symbolistic theory
R.M. Hare   of R.B. Braithwaite   of Paul Tillich

We shall take up the analogical and non-cognitive theories one by one.

Bibliography (*Ontological Antheism*)

1. Findlay, J. N., *Can God's existence be disproved*? NEPT.
2. Flew, A., *Theology and falsification*, NEPT.
3. Somart, J. J. C., *The existence of God*, NEPT.
4. Martin, C. B., *A religious way of knowing*, NEPT.
5. Edwards, Paul, *Some notes on Anthropomorphic theology*, RET.
6. Nielsen Kai, *Is God so powerful that he doesn't even have not to exist*? RET.
7. Richardson, C., *Do the gods exist*? RET.
8. Schmidt, Paul F., *Frustrating strategies in religious discussion*, RET.
9. *Religious knowledge*, Free Press of Glencoe, 1961.

Section II

RELIGIOUS ASSERTIONS AS ANALOGICAL STATEMENTS

A good many western theologians do not regard theistic statements to be literally applicable to God. They have variously called these statements, namely, parabolical, mythic, symbolical and even paradoxical. Theologians had to take recourse to these theories on account of their certain presuppositions. They hold God to be the creator of the world. True, but how is he to be related to the world? God may be conceived to be wholly transcendent to the world (deism), or, to be immanent in the world (pantheism), or, to be both immanent and transcendent to the world (Christian theism). If God be wholly transcendent to the world, then there will be hardly any relationship between the world and God. This would mean that no words applicable to finite things of the world would be legitimately applicable to God. If, on the other hand, God be immanent in the world, then God and world would become co-extensive and indistinguishable from each other. This would imply that God and man become indistinguishable and there will be no room for worship, praise and prayers. Under this relationship of immanence, theism itself will become impossible. Hence, in order to avoid the difficulties arising from deistic transcendence and pantheistic immanence theologians hold that God is both immanent and transcendent. Most probably this theistic stand is also riddled with philosophical difficulties, but from the viewpoint of epistemology it has one advantage. If God is both immanent and transcendent, then he is partly unknowable (being transcendent) and partly knowable (being immanent), the question therefore is: what is the nature and status of theistic knowledge?

When we use statements concerning God then either they apply to him univocally or negatively or analogically. For instance, we use the words like wisdom, love, omnipotence, infinite goodness concerning God. If these terms mean the same as they do with regard to human beings, then God comes to be regarded as a superman and we are said to commit idolatry, anthropomorphism and even blasphemy. If, on the other hand, we hold that no words can describe God and we resort to negation, i.e. neti, neti (not this, not this), then we are landed up in scepticism and agnosticism. To steer through the difficulties of univocacy and negation, the doctrine of analogy has been advanced by St. Thomas Aquinas (1224-74). The term 'Analogy' consists of two Greek words *ana* (according to) and *logos* (ratio, proportion) meaning similitude in relationship in proportion to their respective being or essence. It is used here in the more familiar sense of a direct comparison between *terms* which somehow are similar and have somehow like *relations*. The qualification 'somehow' betrays the danger involved in the doctrine of *analogia entis*. And Aquinas was fully aware of it. For Aquinas, God is wholly transcendent and is perfect, i.e. in whom essence and existence are wholly united as a unitary thing. As God is wholly transcendent, human beings cannot know anything about his essence: they can know only his existence.

But if we accept the doctrine of transcendence, as does Karl Barth, then, consistently speaking we become committed to negation only. We have to agree with Spinoza that every determination is negation and that words and thoughts recoil whilst describing the supreme reality of God (Vācho nivarttante manasā saha). To some extent Aquinas does accept the negative way. He also maintains that we know what God is not rather than what he is.[1] This admission would be tantamount to agnosticism. Aquinas always maintained a kind of reverent agnosticism. However, for Aquinas the negative way is not final: it is only a means of purifying our concepts concerning God. For example by successively denying that God's love is not the love of the father for the child, or of the lover for the beloved, or of the mother for her son, we increase in some sense our knowledge of God.[2] Aquinas could not successfully solve the difficulty with regard to our knowledge of God for the simple reason that he widened the gulf between man and God too much. God was taken to be radically different from everything we know. For this reason with no amount of logic he could bridge the gulf again through his doctrine of Analogy. The following considerations would make this contention plain.

According to Aquinas, Being is prior to essence or idea. For this reason Aquinas rejected the ontological argument, according to which the existence of God follows from the idea of a Perfect Being. However, for Aquinas the existence of God is prior to any idea. Further, the existence of God means complete actuality and not mere possibility. Hence, God is pure actuality at all times and can never be thought to be non-existing at any time. This is expressed by saying that God is a *necessary being*. In contrast, all created things are contingent, for they all can be imagined not to be existing at any moment of time. If God is necessary and created things are contingent, then how can contingent creatures know the necessary being?

Further, God is said to be infinite and created things are finite. Does the term 'infinite' mean 'that which is not finite'? No, it means that God is infinite absolutely in the sense that he has no limit at all. The implication is that God and creatures

---

1. F.C. Copleston, *Aquinas*, Pelican Book, 1955, pp. 126-27, 131.
2. *Ibid.*, p. 127.

are at the opposite poles. If God and created things are poles apart, then how can terms taken from finite things be applied to God? In a sense God being wholly undifferentiated, God as a simple Being is indeterminate and as such is completely indescribable. To mitigate this situation Aquinas advances the theory of transcendentals. He holds that there are certain pervasive features of every thing called *transcendentals*. Being, thing, unity, distinction, true and good are six transcendentals. These transcendentals are said to be univocally applicable to both finite creatures and the infinite Being. But do these transcendentals throw any light on the nature of God? It might give one the impression that 'true' or 'good' is applicable to God in an ethical sense. The hope is at once belied. 'Good' is used here in the Aristotelian sense, according to which a thing is good if it realises its own end. Hence, God is good because he realises the end of his own Being. In simple language it means God is his own being which is the repetition of the Biblical statement of Yahweh about himself, namely, 'I am that I am'.[3]

Later on, Paul Tillich repeats the same thing when he says that beyond the statement, 'God is being itself' nothing more can be asserted literally of God. Here Aquinas holds that we know *that* God is, but we have to take the help of analogy when we want to know *what* he is.

The doctrine of analogy derives its force from the assumption that cause and effect are similar in nature, at least to some degree. Men and other finite things have been created by God. So finite creatures reflect the nature of their creator, namely, God.

Terms signify God to the extent that our intellect knows Him. And since our intellect knows God from creatures it knows Him to the extent that creatures represent him.[4]

The doctrine of analogy comprises the analogy of attribution and the analogy of proportionality. The analogy of attribution requires that one of the terms be 'prime analogate' of

---

3. According to E.L. Mascall, as matter of fact, this was the real concern of St. Thomas, pp. 12f, 52f.

4. F.C. Copleston, quotes, this in his book 'Acquinas', p. 129.

which the analogous property is predicated 'formally' or intrinsically, while the other analogate receives it derivatively or secondarily by virtue of its relevant relation to the prime analogate. For example, 'healthy' is an attribute which man possesses formally or properly. Thus man is the prime analogate here. But we also apply the attribute 'healthy' to medicine and to urine analogously on account of their causal relation to the healthy man. When we say that medicine is healthy, then really it means that it promotes the health of man; or when we say 'urine is healthy', we mean that it is a sign of health in man. Hence, on account of causal relation the term 'healthy' comes to be analogously attributed to widely dissimilar analogates. We can contrast this analogy of attribution with the analogy of proportionality. Take the predicate 'intelligent'. When we say 'Dog is intelligent' and 'Man is intelligent', then we are applying the attribute of intelligence to both dog and man univocally. But the attribution is in strict proportion to the essence of dog and man. The intelligence of dog is in proportion to his being and the intelligence of man is in proportion to his being. This is known as the analogy of proportionality. Strictly speaking, the analogy of proportionality implies that the analogous property is found formally in each of the analogates but in a mode that is determined by the essence of the analogates themselves. Thus, the two kinds of analogy are not really separate and distinct from one another. Let us take up each case of analogical predication.

The Analogy of Proportionality

According to the analogy of proportionality the properties of anything are related proportionately to its being. For instance, the properties of man and stone are related proportionately to their respective being. Hence, there is a proportion between the ratios of properties and being, throughout the whole range and grades of being, e.g.

$$\frac{\text{Man's properties}}{\text{Man's being}} \quad : \quad \frac{\text{A stone's property}}{\text{A stone's being}}$$

Similarly,

$$\frac{\text{Properties of created beings}}{\text{Being of creatures}} \quad : \quad \frac{\text{Properties of uncreated Being}}{\text{Being of ens Realissimum}}$$

All creatures are derived from the Absolute Being. Hence, the excellences of created beings are also derived from the Absolute Being in whom all excellences are actualised perfectly. This means that relative excellences belonging to created beings can only be analogically though not univocally applied to Absolute Being. The whole hierarchy of creatures, from the dead matter to the highest spirit, may be quite near to God. But no one creature, not even at the highest rung of the ladder, can rise to the nature and status of the perfect Being. So no relative perfection can ever be, except analogically applied to God. Goodness or wisdom belongs to God infinitely and we can never understand what infinite Goodness can ever mean. The disparity between mans' Goodness and God's Goodness remains irreducible. As we cannot give any adequate and positive account of divine Goodness or wisdom, so we try to approximate our knowledge of God by purifying these concepts through negation. We can say that God has no external end, does not employ any external means and has no need of foreseeing things, since all past, present and future moments of time are given to him in one ever-present now. Even the negative way of describing God is not valueless. It is a safeguard against idolatry and is certainly an advance over the way of silence.[5] If we take the negative way seriously, then it would mean that after all Aquinas was not wholly agnostic. The purifying through negation would mean that our knowledge of God is very imperfect and inadequate. Indeed this appears to be the conclusion of Aquinas himself:

"The first cause surpasses human understanding and speech. He knows God best who acknowledges that whatever he thinks and says falls short of what God really is".[6] But lisping is also talking and seeing darkly in the mirror is also seeing. Hence, most probably analogical knowledge was not understood by Aquinas as a case of agnosticism. But after all it depends on the temperament of the critic himself either to treat analogical thinking as a case of scepticism or a case of reverent agnosticism. When we do not know the being of God, then the statement that the property of Goodness is in proportion to the being of God is

---

5. J. Macquarrie, *God-talk*, pp. 25, 213.
6. F.C. Copleston quotes in 'Aquinas' on pp. 131-32.

equally unintelligible to us. To remove this negative conclusion, the analogy of attribution has been advanced.

THE ANALOGY OF ATTRIBUTION

This is a weaker form of the analogy of proportionality. Here an attempt is made to say something positively about God with the help of terms derived from creaturely relation. Now Goodness or love, properly speaking, is applicable to man alone, but in a derivative sense is attributed to God.[7] When we attribute 'love' to God, we use it as a floor-concept 'and not as a ceiling-concept'. By ceiling-concept is meant that divine love is not literally speaking human love. By saying that we use 'love' as a floor-concept, W. Norris Clarke means that it connotes the positive value which the term 'love' has.[8] But the term 'love' is not to be used anthropomorphically nor expressively. If the term be used anthropomorphically then there will be the danger of idolatry or even blasphemy. If, on the other hand, we use the term 'love' as our imaginative expressions of feeling then it is tantamount to subjectivism and even agnosticism with regard to the real attribute of God.

The analogy of attribution in a certain respect helps us to attribute an analogous property to God. Just as on the basis of causality we analogically attribute 'healthy' to urine and place, so on similar grounds we attribute wisdom, love or goodness to God because God is the first cause (creator) and man is the creature. True, the Goodness of God is radically different from that of man, but in some way this is reflected in his creatures. Of course, here too we know that the property and essence of man are quite distinct and in God all his properties are identical with his existence. But the contingent existence of creatures implies causal dependence on God. Hence, the possibility of applying to the Infinite Being terms that are formally derived from the finite creatures arises from the fact that the finite order is dependent for its existence on the Infinite and self-existent Being. Whenever

---

7. D. Baillie holds that we know the Goodness, Wisdom and other attributes of God, directly and non-analogically. (The sense of the presence of God, O.U.P., 1962 pp. 116-21.) But unless we resort to mysticism, there is no verification of this direct knowledge.

8. W. Norris Clarke, RET, p. 230.

we talk about God we can hardly exclude the creative act of God in relation to finite beings. Hence, the terms derived from the created finite beings can be analogically applied to the creator God. Of course, the creative act of God is not easily intelligible to us, but his basis of creative act does give us some justification of applying analogy with regard to God.

COMMENTS

According to the analogy of proportionality we hold

$$\frac{\text{The Goodness of man}}{\text{Essence of man}} = \frac{\text{The Goodness of God}}{\text{Essence of God}}.$$

But the infinite essence of God remains unknowable and formally speaking God's essence and existence are identical. If essence is unintelligible, then this Goodness too is unintelligible. So we can make no sense of 'God's. Goodness'. Even if we grant that formally speaking man's Goodness is proportionate to his being and God's Goodness is in proportion to his Being, we make no progress with regard to the knowledge of God's Goodness.

Again, many critics have raised objection with regard to the sign of '='. If 'Goodness of man/essence of man' is really equal to 'God's Goodness/essence of God', then there is univocality and the case for analogy is destroyed. And if there is univocality then God's uniqueness and transcendence are also effaced. If, on the other hand, there is no identity or equality between the cases of proportionality then the sign of '=' really means nothing.

At this stage it might be accepted that the analogy of proportionality might lead to agnosticism. But it would be maintained that the forms of analogical predication should be combined. In order to remove the defect of agnosticism arising from the analogy of proportionality, we should take the help of the analogy of attribution.[9] But does it improve the matter? Even when both forms of analogy are combined, we cannot *conceive* God's Goodness as identical with his essence, but can at most *affirm* that God's Goodness is identical with his existence. In the final analysis, even according to its most sympathetic interpreter E.L. Mascall, all assertions about God are grossly

9. E.L. Mascall, EA, p. 113.

inadequate in so far as they apply concepts to him.[10] In other words, assertions about God are non-conceptual and non-cognitive. As a matter of fact God is simple and no relation, not even of resemblance or likeness or equality can be ascribed to him. Likeness or resemblance can be maintained between two entities of the same kind. But God and creatures are radically different from one another. So God being simple has no relation within it and for this reason essence and existence are said to be identical in God. Again, God being transcendent has no external relation to anything beyond him.

But if there are no relations in God, then the relation of attribution is also ruled out. Or is the relation of attribution itself to be viewed analogically? If so, the theologian is left in uncomfortable position of attributing unknowable properties to an unknowable being, using an unknowable relation of attribution. The 'cloud of unknowing' is a complete overcast.[11]

Again, either the attributes of infinite goodness, wisdom, love and so on, belong to God extrinsically or intrinsically. By extrinsic quality is meant that quality which God causes without any necessity on his part for doing so. By intrinsic quality is meant that quality which formally belongs to God as its primary analogate. If the attributes of infinite goodness, wisdom or love be extrinsic to God, then they do not describe him at all, since they do not really belong to him. Further, why should we name a few qualities only like wisdom or love? Why should we not attribute *all* qualities including evil ones to God since they are all caused by him?

On the other hand, if the qualities be intrinsic to God, then it means that God is the primary analogate of infinite wisdom, Goodness and love; and, man's Goodness and wisdom are said to be applied to him only derivatively. This admission would imply that we have direct knowledge of the divine attributes and

---

10. E.L. Mascall, EA, p. 120.
11. W.T. Blackstone, *The Problem of Religious Knowledge*, Prentice-Hall, 1963, p. 67.

D. Baillie admits this.[12] If we have direct or non-analogical cognition of the divine attributes, then what is the necessity of analogical prediction? But this is not the view of Thomas Aquinas and the Thomists. So far as the Thomists are concerned, we shall not be in a position to know even the human qualities of Goodness and wisdom if these qualities be found formally in God and only derivatively in man.

God's Goodness and wisdom are in proportion to his mode of existence and we can never know this proportion at all. So the divine Goodness and wisdom remain unknown to us and in the same proportion they cannot be directly applied to human beings too.

The doctrine of analogy rests on the principle that cause and effect are similar. God is the first cause and the finite creatures depend on him. But can we now hold that cause and effect are similar? Prof. D.M. Emmet observes that the resemblance between cause and its effects can no longer be held to be the essential characteristic of causality. Where is the resemblance between the pressing of button and the electric light? It is far more appropriate, according to her, to talk of functional dependence or concomitant variation between the cause and its effects than of resemblance between them.[13]

But Thomists do not really mean by causality temporal causality: they really mean the relation of ground and consequent. Hence, it is said that finite things depend on God as their first cause. But what is the meaning of this *dependence*? Does it mean logical relationship? No, this is a unique kind of dependence produced by the creative act. Hence, first cause is really used here not literally, but analogically. But if 'cause', or, 'ground-consequent relationship', or, 'unmoved mover' etc., be used analogically then can such relations be the basis of analogies between God and his creatures?[14] Analogy in order to be effective and

12. D. Baillie, *The Sense of the Presence of God*, O.U.P. 1962, pp. 116-21. But unless the meaningfulness of human knowledge about God be ascertained the view of D. Baillie will be simply a dogmatic assertion.

15. D.M. Emmet, '*The Nature of Metaphysical Thinking*', Macmillan, 1949, p. 183.

14. *Ibid.*, pp. 181-82.

intelligible ultimately has to rest on some non-analogical relationship.

Ultimately it may be assumed that there are some basic structural patterns or ontological structural similarities underlying all beings which may serve as a prop of the theological doctrine of analogical prediction concerning God. Unfortunately in the current thinking no intelligible meaning can be ascribed to ontological structure of fundamental pattern underlying all entities, creatures and God.

The doctrine of analogical predication has failed because God is taken to be a non-symbolic, Ontological Being. E.L. Mascall tells us that according to the realist philosophy of Thomas Aquinas, words and ideas ultimately relate to things.[15] However, all the Thomists regard God as a unique being,—radically different from creatures. Naturally no finite segment can literally describe God. It was left for Paul Tillich to show that much of God of the Christians is only a symbol. So the full meaning of analogical predication has been elaborated into the symbolic statements concerning God. Paul Tillich himself thinks his theory of symbolical statement as a modern version of *analogia entis*,[16] and this has been accepted by the Catholic theologian Gustave Weigl and by John Baillie.[17] But before taking up the nature of symbolical statement, we have to present the case of Faith-statements because, religious statements have been traditionally taken as faith-statements.

Section III

HARE'S 'BLIK'-THEORY

R.M. Hare does admit that falsifiability is a good test of determining the meaningfulness of factual statements. But he also accepts the observation of L. Wittgenstein that language is a kind of game with many possible rules for playing it. Naturally, according to this view, there is a very large number of different things that we do with words: scientific use is one of the many ways in which we use words; moral language is another, and, so

---

15. E.L. Mascall, EA, p. 96.
16. P. Tillich, ST, Vol. I, p. 239.
17. *Ibid.*, Chap. VI.

is likely to be the case with religious language.[1] Most probably it is a sound principle to hold that a factual statement in order to have empirical meaning should be *in principle* either verifiable or falsifiable. However, this principle of factual meaningfulness cannot be maintained for moral statements. The same is the case with theistic statements, because theistic statements are neither merely factual nor purely moral.

If we take religious language as a whole, it is too factual to be called specifically moral, and yet too closely bound up with our conduct to be called in the ordinary sense factual.[2]

Hare thinks that a religious statement involves both a factual belief and a certain principle of conduct. Religious statements express 'our whole way of living':

they have for us value, relevance, importance, which they would not have if we were atheists.[3]

Hence, religious statements are both prescriptive and descriptive.[4] Religious statements, for Hare, do not describe facts, but express our *attitude to facts*. A statement expressive of an attitude to facts may be called a 'blik' statement. By a 'blik' is meant the mode or manner in which things appear to a perceiver in the light of his deep-seated disposition. Bliks, according to Hare, are neither true nor false: they determine as to what is to be taken as a fact or an illusion.[5]

But it is nevertheless true to say that, as Hume said, without a *blik* there can be no explanation; for it is by our bliks that we decide what is and what is not an explanation.[6]

Now let us try to illustrate by a parable what Hare means by holding that religious assertions, are not factual assertions, but are blik-statements.

---

1. R.M. Hare, Religion and Morals, FL, pp. 176-79.
2. *Ibid.*, p. 189.
3. *Ibid.*, pp. 189-90.
4. *Ibid.*, p. 90.
5. *Ibid.*, pp. 190, 192.
6. R.M. Hare, Theology and Falsification, NEPT, p. 101.

A certain lunatic is convinced that all dons at Oxford plot to murder him. No matter however kind and considerate a don is shown to him, he yet interprets his acts of kindness as so many instances of his diabolical cunning. Thus no act, however, kind can count against his conviction concerning the dons as his enemies. Similarly, religious conviction is a kind of blik. A theist has a blik concerning the universe. He thinks that this world has been created by a loving God and no matter whichever facts of evil be cited, he yet thinks that God is love.

Now Flew or an empiricist can show that a *blik* does not consist in an assertion, but says Hare, blik is an important thing to have. One may have a right blik or a wrong blik, e.g. the sane under-graduates are said to have a right blik; and, the insane one is said to have a wrong blik; but we cannot think without some blik. Even in our ordinary walks of life we resort to all kinds of blik. We trust to our steering-wheel of the car, to the safe travel by trains and so on. And yet one may develop an insane blik, namely, travel-phobia by car or train.

It was Hume who taught us that our whole commerce with the world depends upon our *blik* about the world; and that differences between *bliks* about the world cannot be settled by observation of what happens in the world.[7]

Similarly, says Hare, Kant has taught that the so-called factual *objectivity* of scientific statements is uneradicably *modal* (a reference to causal necessity). Hence for Hare, even the distinction between fact and illusion is a matter of a certain attitude to the world. For example, for one who believes in spirits and ghosts, charms and spells are facts: but, for the modern man of science they are just superstitions.

Certainly it is salutary to recognize that *even* our belief in so-called hard facts rest in the end on a faith, a commitment, which is not in or to facts, but in that without which there would not be any facts.[8]

Now just as Kant regarded causal necessity to be *a priori* or

---

7. NEPT, p. 101.
8. FL, p. 192.

non-empirical *blik* of the scientist of his day or just as Hume regarded our belief in the existence of the outer world and causality as a matter of natural or instinctive belief, so Hare holds that bliks are matters of commitment to facts or non-empirical dispositions to the world of facts. Just as Kant held that *a priori* forms of sensibility and the twelve concepts of the understanding cannot be settled by observation or cannot be derived from sense-experience and yet without them no objects or facts can be *known* as facts, so in the same manner God is not himself a being, but is the source and cause of beings. Here Hare quotes a passage from Plato to make himself understood.

> In the case of those things which we see by the light of the sun, the sun is the source, not merely of the possibility of our seeing them, but also of their very coming to be, their growth and their sustenance. But it is not itself a coming to be. And in the same way in the case of those things which we know by the light of the Idea of the Good, it is the source, not merely of the possibility of our knowing them but also of their very being—for from it their being comes.[9]

The blik-theory of Hare seeks to emphasize two things. First, belief or disbelief in God may not have any predictive value concerning facts, yet it does make a good deal of difference to the world in which a theist or an atheist lives. The Hindus and Muslims live in the same world of facts in India, but, according to R.M. Hare, their religious bliks or attitudes do make a good deal of difference to their ideologies, political activities, family planning, dress, food and other behavioural patterns. Blik-theory rejects the view that religion is a matter of mere cognitiveness or inquisitiveness, a view which Wisdom's parable concerning the dispute between two explorers with regard to an invisible gardener suggests. The two explorers appear to dispute the existence of God in an unconcerned manner, as if the existence of God is a scientific hypothesis. They discuss with interest but not with *concern*. However, the example of the lunatic blik brings out this concern of the religious man.[10] This point

9. FL, p. 193.
10. NEPT, p. 103.

has also been emphasized by Paul Tillich, W.F. Zuurdeeg and has been included in our convictional theory of religious assertions.

Secondly, Hare holds that religious statements are not factual assertions.[11] He thinks that the mistake of Flew is that he assumes that religious statements are some sort of scientific explanation.[12] Yet a religious belief is never bereft of factual reference.

> The person who worships is bound to govern his conduct (or let it be governed) in a certain way; and he is bound to believe in the truth of certain factual statements (empirical ones about what has actually happened in the world, and, what is likely to happen).[13]

A blik is an attitude but an attitude to *facts*. The preoccupation of Hare prevents him from holding the view that religious conviction makes the believer see new facts, a *new* Jerusalem. He does not, but does not emphasize the fact that seeing of religious values in old facts dawns as a result of a change in the believer himself. This is a point which he has noted with regard to the conversion of St. Paul.[14] But can such an inner change be austively described by the fact of 'blik'?

CRITICAL COMMENTS

'Blik' is a metaphorical word and need not be interpreted too literally. Hare himself has likened it to the 'instinctive belief' of Hume or the modal element in knowledge, according to Kant. At times he calls it 'prescription', 'faith' and 'commitment'. However, he does admit that a religious blik does change the mentality of the worshipper as in cases of 'conversion'. Further, he says that the difference between men is largely due to their religion.

After all, man has not changed biologically since primitive

---

11. FL, p. 189.
12. NEPT, p. 101.
13. FL, p. 189.
14. FL, p. 188.

times; it is his religion that has changed, and it can easily change again.[15]

For Hare the formation of 'blik' is a very complex affair: it may involve beliefs about matters of fact or moral principles or some other kind of value-principles or the attitude to this or that thing. In the formation of 'blik' almost everything of the man is involved.[16] Though Hare does not give the rationale of blik-formation, he yet holds that bliks need not be fixed and that bliks may be sane-insane or right-wrong. But, is it true to say with Mitchell[17] that Hare's lunatic who has a blik against dons doesn't admit anything that counts against his *blik*?

Well, if we literally interpret the *blik* of the lunatic, then it is impervious to facts on account of its being an abnormal phenomenon. However, for Hare, a religious blik is sane and right. A *blik* is said to be sane or normal precisely because facts do count for or against it.[18] If it is so, then a sane blik, which religious belief is, becomes open to facts. Hence, facts do count with regard to a blik. But even if we grant that facts do count in the formation of a blik, how are we going to distinguish between right and wrong bliks? If no state of affairs can count against the bliks, then, according to Blackstone, this deprives Hare of the right to distinguish between right and wrong bliks.[19] These remarks of Blackstone and of Mitchell suffer from the over-simplification of Hare's view.

First, if a person works under the influence of a *blik*, then all facts become compatible with that *blik*. For instance, according to Kant, anything to be perceptible at all must appear under the form of space and time. If *blik* be the very condition of their being any observation at all, then it cannot be falsified by any observable fact. Thus all facts should be compatible with religious beliefs. But of course there must be some facts, some moral principles, some attitudes to a number of things which do account both for the formation and changes in the *blik* and, we

---

15. NEPT, p. 102.
16. FL, p. 188.
17. NEPT, p. 105.
18. W.T. Blackstone, 'The Problem of Religious Knowledge', p. 77.
19. *Ibid.*, p. 78.

have already seen that Hare does admit so.[20] But should we not say, as John Wisdom does seem to state, that facts are marshalled together to tip one's attitude to facts as a whole? The taking up an attitude to facts is a matter of faith, commitment and a decision.

> It has its own sort of logic and its own sort of end—the solution of the question at issue is a decision, a ruling by the judge. But it is not an arbitrary decision, though the rational connections are neither quite like those in vertical deductions nor like those in inductions.[21]

The decision manifests itself in the giving of a name.

> With the judges' choice of a name for the facts goes an attitude, and the declaration, the ruling, is an exclamation evincing that attitude. But *it is an exclamation which not only has a purpose but also has a logic*, a logic surprisingly like that of 'futile', 'deplorable', 'graceful', 'grand', 'divine'.[22]

Now the view of Hare is akin to that of John Wisdom even though he does not detail the place of facts in the formation of religious *blik*. Hare maintains that empirical component in religious statements is not very important, and, yet, he says, even advanced religions require *some* empirical expectations.[23] Further, he does admit that religious *blik* going with the word 'good' is both evaluative and descriptive.

> In virtue of its descriptive meaning statements containing it may be said to be verifiable and falsifiable by those who accept the same standards of evaluation as the speaker (and this does not necessarily involve accepting the *whole* of his religious beliefs).[24]

---

20. NEPT, p. 102; FL, p. 188.
21. John Wisdom, *Gods* (1944-45) reproduced in 'Classifical and contemporary Readings in the philosophy of religion,' Edited by John Hick, Prentice-Hall, 1964, p. 420.
22. *Ibid.*, p. 240.
23. FL, p. 187.
24. FL, pp. 187-88.

Thus, we conclude that the blik-theory maintains that statements made under a religious blik are not falsifiable, and, yet they are not wholly irrational, since the formation of *blik* is not totally instinctive or what Blackstone thinks that according to Hume may be called 'non-positivistic sensitive beliefs'.[25] Hence, there are reasons both for determining and ascertaining one kind of *blik* in relation to other kinds of blik. But once it is formed it works in its own way, irrespectively of the reason which has given birth to it or the fact which has induced or evoked it. Therefore, religious *blik* is changeable and is open to the pressure of facts; but the openness to facts is not decidable by rational arguments alone.

If the formation of a *blik* is not a matter of reason alone or of facts alone but also of attitudes to facts, moral principles and even of the whole man, then not only facts but other attitudes, principles etc., do count against a blik. Hence, a blik is right when it harmonises with facts, moral principles and the other attitudes to life in general. A blik is wrong when it is narrow in scope and clashes with the accredited moral decisions of mankind and so on.

Thus it is not fair to Hare's doctrine of blik to hold that *facts alone* can distinguish between *right and wrong* bliks, as does Blackstone.[26] It was the very purpose of Hare's paper to show that religious assertions are not assertions at all: they are blik-statements which are neither true nor false. They may be right-wrong or better still sane-insane. Even though a *blik* is not true or false, it can be said to be appropriate-inappropriate or healthy-unhealthy. For example, according to William James, an attitude of optimism is appropriate, whereas of pessimism is inappropriate, provided one accepts the prescriptive value of risk, enterprise and adventure. So a religious *blik* is right or wrong in relation to a certain religious community, accepting a certain prescriptive religious value. If not, why should there be any dispute at all amongst Christian theologians concerning the manhood and godhood of Jesus Christ? Further, even believers belonging to different religious *bliks* do argue about the appropri-

25. W.T. Blackstone, *op. cit.*, pp. 80-81.
26. *Ibid.*, p. 81.

ateness and inappropriateness of certain religious claims. For example, for the Jews, Jesus is not the Messiah; for the Christian He is. So there can be arguments for justifying one's religious *blik*. But these arguments are not wholly rational. They have cumulative effect of factual truths, moral decisions and religious bliks of other persons in one's community and so on, to induce an attitude. This is so specially when the issues are live, momentous and forced and when there are no possible rational grounds to decide the issue.[27] Hence, even if *bliks* are not wholly rational, it does not follow that we cannot give arguments in justification. And if we can offer arguments in justification, then certainly we can distinguish between right and wrong *bliks*.

Finally, Hare talks of sane and insane *bliks* and the distinction is a matter of psychological health or normality. For determining the criteria of normality one refers to the behaviour-norm of the majority, relation to one's fellows, mental efficiency, happiness and so on.[28] So certainly one can distinguish between sane and insane *bliks*, even though the criteria are not merely factual or wholly cognitive.

Even though the blik-theory of Hare is not as vulnerable as Blackstone thinks, yet it one-sidedly emphasizes the fact of inner change, a becoming of 'a new creature,'[29] without referring to the disclosure which the religious bliks bring about. *Pari passu* with the formation of a blik, there is also the recognition of a pattern amongst facts. This is a point which has been correctly emphasized by John Wisdom and John Hick.[30] Though in one sense, a religious *blik* is not an experimental issue and so not wholly falsifiable by facts, yet says John Wisdom:

"......*We must not forthwith assume that there is no right and wrong about it*, no rationality, or irrationality, no appropriateness or inappropriateness, no procedure which tends to settle it, *nor even that this procedure is in no sense a discovery of new facts.*[31]

---

27. W. James, The will to believe and other Essays, p. 29.
28. Y. Masih, *Freudianism and Religion*, Thacker Spink, 1964, pp. 290-94.
29. FL, p. 188.
30. John Wisdom, op. cit., pp. 417, 421.
31. *Ibid.*, p. 421.

And yet discoveries are made not by the scientist alone, says Wisdom, but also by the poets, the prophets and the painters.[32] And this also has to be noted with regard to any theory of religious assertions.

R.M. Hare seems to suggest that we cannot do without bliks of some sort.[33] He does not state that religious bliks are indispensable, but he does say that religious bliks express 'our whole way of living'[34] and conversion from one religious blik to another means 'a new creature'.[35] Now we do accept that religious blik is a holistic response of the individual—is expressive of total life orientation, but we would also add, that every one has to deal with what one considers to be one's ultimate concern. Hence, religious blik is indispensable for choosing the kind of life we want to live. A religious blik ultimately is a matter of personal decision and commitment. In the end then a religious statement is convictional and existential. This is the conclusion to which the empiricist view of Prof. R.B. Braithwaite points. So we shall now take up the view advanced by R.B. Braithwaite.

Bibliography (Section III)

1. Mascall, E. L., *Existence and Analogy*, A Libra Book, 1966 (First published in 1949).
2. Mascall, E. L., *Words and Images*, Longmans, 1957.
3. Cardinal Cajetan, '*The analogy of names*', Duquesne University Press, 1959.
4. Paul Hayner, '*Analogical Predication*', Journal of Philosophy, 1958.
5. Emmet, D. M., '*The nature of metaphysical thinking*', Macmillan, 1949 (First published 1945).
6. The highly well-informed article of '*Analogy*' in *The Encyclopedia of Philosophy*, Edited by Paul Edwards, Macmillan, 1967, is recommended for reading.

---

32. J. Wisdom, *op. cit.*, p. 417.
33. NEPT, p. 101; FL, pp. 190-93.
34. FL, p. 189.
35. FL, p. 188.

Section IV

R.B. BRAITHWAITE'S EMPIRICAL THEORY OF RELIGIOUS ASSERTIONS

Prof. R.B. Braithwaite, unlike Flew, holds that theistic statements are not empirical assertions. Nonetheless, according to Braithwaite they have meaning. In his lecture, *An empiricist's View of the Nature of Religious Belief*, R.B. Braithwaite has been largely influenced by Matthew Arnold, and also to some extent by R.M. Hare and P.H. Nowell-Smith. His analysis of theistic statements is empirical. The meaning of a religious statement, according to him, is given by the way it is used.

A theistic statement is not an empirical assertion according to Braithwaite. Further, a statement having a literal meaning is either:

1. A statement about particular matters of observable facts, or
2. A statement about scientific hypothesis and other empirical statements, or
3. A logically necessary statement of logic and mathematics.

A theistic statement is not about empirical facts of direct observation, because God cannot be known by direct observation.[1] Again, a theistic statement is not about any scientific hypothesis, since it is not falsifiable by any fact.[2] Here R.B. Braithwaite appears to be influenced by Wisdom's article '*Gods*' (1944-45) and by *Theology and Falsification* (Flew and others) in NEPT. Lastly, a theistic statement cannot be a logically necessary proposition, for such a statement does not say anything about 'what is the case'. And God does belong to the world of reality[3], according to the theist.

True, a theistic statement may be empirically vacuous, but then it has meaning, for theists do talk and understand one another. So a theistic statement has a meaning which may be quite different from the empirical meanings mentioned previ-

---

1. EG, p. 231.
2. EG, pp. 232-33.
3. EG, p. 234.

ously. Now whatever be the meaning of a theistic statement, it can be tested both by observing what a theist does and what he reports about it.[4] Following the remark of Matthew Arnold that religion is morality touched by emotion, Braithwaite holds that a theistic statement is primarily a moral statement backed by stories. Here we have to analyse a moral statement and the notion of 'a story'.

Braithwaite favours a conative theory in preference to an emotive theory of a moral statement. He rejects, therefore, that a moral statement expresses a feeling of approval. For Braithwaite, the primary meaning of a moral statement lies in the intention to perform the action when the occasion arises for it, i.e. a moral statement primarily embodies a policy of action. But every policy of action is not moral. To be moral the policy should be general or should be subsumable under a general policy which can be advanced as the reason of the specifically moral intention.[5]

By assimilating a theistic to a moral statement, Braithwaite holds that a theistic statement embodies primarily 'declarations of adherence to a policy of action, declarations of commitment to a way of life.[6] Further, Braithwaite states that a theistic statement does not explicitly refer to a specific policy of action, as does a moral statement. He tells us that the policy can be ascertained only in relation to the whole system of theistic statements of a religion. In this aspect it is very akin to a scientific statement whose meaning can be determined only in relation to a whole system of hypotheses. The important point for Braithwaite is to see that every religion has some fundamental moral principles,—the resolution to follow a way of life is primary.[7] But of course religion is not mere morals. The two do differ.

MORAL AND THEISTIC STATEMENTS
The first point of difference has already been referred to. A moral statement in isolation usually successfully specifies the

---

4. EG, p. 237; The influence of R.M. Hare is most marked. See also 'The language of morals', p. 241.
5. EG, p. 237.
6. EG, p. 239.
7. EG, pp. 241, 249.

behaviour policy intended by it; in contrast, the policy of a theistic statement has to be determined in relation to the whole system of theistic statements, comprising a particular religion. Secondly, a moral statement is stated in abstract terms; whilst, a theistic statement is made by means of concrete examples, namely, parables, stories, fictions, myths and so on. Lastly, a theistic statement embodies not only external but also internal behaviour, a certain quality of personal life, as Hick would say. In other words, a theistic statement refers an intention to change not only the outer order, but also the inner life. Braithwaite holds that intention to feel in a certain way can be held to distinguish theistic declarations of policy from merely moral declarations.[8] However, it is the second point of difference, which not only distinguishes theistic from moral statements, but also religious statements of one religion from religious statements belonging to other religions and this requires some emphasis.

RELIGIOUS STATEMENTS BACKED BY STORIES

At this stage Braithwaite anticipates an objection. It will be contended that the same moral policy might be accepted by different religions, e.g., Christianity, Judaism and Buddhism. If both Christianity and Buddhism accept the agapeistic way then how can we distinguish one from the other? Of course, religions do differ with regard to rituals, but it cannot be said that the agapeistic way of Christianity is different from that of Buddhism on account of their ritual practices. The simple reason is that ritual practices are not taken to be the fundamental characteristics of a religion.[9] However Braithwaite states that religious behaviour-policies always remain associated with different stories or sets of stories. For example, Christian agapeistic way is associated with gospel, parables, life of Christ and other Christian myths. In the same way the Buddhistic agapeistic policy is backed by the stories in the Jātakas, and in other Buddhist scriptures. Now we can say that the behaviour policies of different religions can be distinguished from one another on account of different stories or sets of stories. Further, as was mentioned before, a religious statement differs from a moral statement on

---

8. EG, pp. 242-43.
9. EG, p. 244.

account of this characteristic in the former. A moral statement and a religious statement both contain an intention, but the latter in addition is backed by associated stories.

A religious assertion will, therefore, have a propositional element which is lacking in a purely moral assertion, in that it will refer to a story as well as to an intention.[10]

How are we going to understand the term 'story'?

The story should consist of a set of empirical propositions. It means that the characters of the stories may be human beings or mythological beings, that is, beings who might have never existed but who nevertheless would have heen empirically observable had they existed. The important point according to Braithwaite, is that the story should be entertained in thought, but it is not necessary that a religious asserter should believe in the truth of the story.[11] The story, according to Braithwaite, may be variously called a parable, a fairy tale, an allegory, a fable, a tale and a myth and so on. The fundamental contention is that every religious statement embodies a moral principle and that a religious believer associates his moral intention by entertaining appropriate stories.[12] Why should a story be associated with declarations of adherence to a policy of action, declarations of commitment to a way of life?

Well, the relation between the story and the religious behaviour policy is psychological and causal. A great many times the moral policy of action goes against one's natural desires and inclinations. But when it is associated with a story or a set of stories then the resolution to carry out a course of action is considerably strengthened. To illustrate his point, Braithwaite mentions the stories in Bunyan's *Pilgrim's Progress* and the novels of Dostoevsky. They are works of fiction and yet they have considerably influenced the moral tone of the whole generation of their time. Not only true, but all kinds of beliefs, according to Braithwaite, influence actions of men: these beliefs include their

---

10. EG, p. 244.
11. EG, p. 246.
12. EG, p. 246.

phantasies, imaginations and also propositions which they believe to be true.[13]

The relation between the story and moral policy is not intrinsic; it is causal. The story may be a fiction and even inconsistent and yet may be determinant of action. For example, according to Braithwaite, Christian stories hold both pantheism and the dualism of God and Satan and nonetheless they are efficacious. Pantheistic stories inspire confidence, and the dualistic stories spur Christians to action.

However, according to Braithwaite, there is one story which deserves special mention in this context. A religious man is very much helped in his resolve to carry out his religious behaviour policy if he believes the story that in doing so he is doing the will of God.

Though the story may psychologically support a course of behaviour policy, it does not logically justify it. However, the fundamental characteristic of a religious statement is that it includes the resolution to follow a way of life, and not the story with which it is invariably associated.[14] He concludes thus:

> A religious assertion, for me, is the assertion of an intention to carry out a certain behaviour policy, subsumable under a sufficiently general principle to be a moral one, together with the implicit or explicit statement, but not the assertion, of certain stories.[15]

If the behaviour policy is the primary thing in religion, then how can it be justified, how can this behaviour policy of believer be held to be reasonable for others? Stories do not justify; they at most support causally and psychologically. Braithwaite gives two reasons, first social and then ethical. We are social animals, says Braithwaite. What is profitable to one man may be so to other members. Hence, if a certain way of life is profitable for one then it might be approved by other members. If the basic needs of men are similar, then the inner change as a result of a religious way of life may have an influence on the life of

---

13. EG, p. 247.
14. EG, p. 241.
15. EG, p. 250

others.[16] Finally, however, Braithwaite adopts the view of R.M. Hare and P.H. Nowell-Smith. According to Hare and Nowell-Smith the adoption of a set of moral principles is a matter of personal decision. But this decision, according to them is not arbitrary. In making decisions, not only all the possible consequences but everything upon which they can be possibly based is taken into full account. In the same way religion is a personal affair, having commitment to a personal way of life and each man adopting it has to answer for himself. And this, according to Braithwaite, is the very essence of Christian religion.[17] In simple language it means this. A personal decision on the part of a believer to follow a way of life gives rise to some inner feeling. He finds that this inner feeling in carrying out a way of life is greatly helped by stories. He passes on his way of life together with the stories to his fellow men. If they have the same basic needs then they might find this communication useful to them also. But it can have no truth claim.

CRITICAL COMMENTS

Braithwaite has stated his reasons for not regarding religious statements to be empirical assertions. For him religious statements are not cognitive: but they have use. And they are used as moral assertions backed by stories. Should not stories be believed to be true in order that they might inspire policy behaviour or the resolution of the religious man to carry out actions? Braithwaite thinks that it is not necessary: John Hick thinks that it is necessary that stories be regarded as assertions of fact, and not merely as imaginary fictions.[18] Obviously it is an experimental issue and is a matter of psychology to decide: philosophy can only analyse the situation. But more importantly, God too for Braithwaite is a story. As such he may be just a fiction or a myth.[19] If God turns out to be a fiction, then what sense can a theistic statement like 'God exists' have? The real trouble of Braithwaite lies in not throwing sufficient light on the nature of

---

16. EG, p. 251.
17. EG, p. 252.
18. J. Hick, 'Philosophy of Religion', Prentice-Hall, 1963, p. 93. This is also the View of Prof. A.C. Ewing, 'Religious Assertions in the light of contemporary philosophy', *Philosophy*, 1957; H.J. B. Horsburgh, Australasian Journal, 1958.

'story'. He says that the story can be indifferently called a parable, a fairy-tale, a fable, a myth and so on.[20] But are such terms synonymous? A story which can be empirically told in intelligible concepts fails to be religiously useful. Even the primitive people make a distinction between a profane and a sacred story. Only sacred stories are religious. It must arouse awe, mystery and other elements to which Otto has drawn our attention. In other words, these stories should be symbolical. The stories are said to be psychological determinants, but then one has to determine their nature as such. How can a story inspire a religious believer to carry out his moral resolution? The story must be able to appeal to the Unconscious and tap the hidden resources of the repressed-suppressed ideas. Braithwaite did not analyse the nature of some of the religious stories sufficiently enough. Had he taken a few truly Christian stories, and had he not limited himself to Bunyan's allegories alone then he would have found that they cannot be stated in empirical terms. Now take stories 'God in Christ reconciles man to himself', or, 'Christ redeems the world of its sins'. Neither God nor redemption of sin can be reduced to empirical statements. And if God can be pictured as the Lord of Shaftesbury, then we commit the sin of idolatry. Every religious story must point to an essentially invisible and transcendent reality and only as such becomes efficacious psychologically in energising believers. Even Freud who was the arch-critic of monotheism regarded God as a symbol of the repressed image of the physical father of one's infancy. What is wrong in thinking of God as the Lord Shaftesbury? Because the story which can be clearly understood in empirical terms fails to inspire. A religious story, whether recited in religious meetings or screened in films invariably contains mystery and aims at inspiring awe and reverence, and it is never credited with empirical meaning only.

But apart from the superficial treatment of 'stories', Braithwaite considers the resolution to follow a way of life to be the primary meaning of a theistic statement and the story is said to be a secondary thing, purely as a psychological energiser. But

19. *Ibid.*, p. 91.
20. EG, p. 246.

can we separate the religious behaviour-policy from the stories? Can the agapeistic way of life be meaningfully entertained in thought without the life, teaching and death of Jesus? We trust that without the stories concerning Jesus there couldn't be the agapeistic way. The two are inseparable.

Yet the explanation of Braithwaite is not totally pointless. It brings out the close relationship between morality and religion. Many thinkers from time immemorial have held that the task of moral endeavour is fulfilled in religion. Moral consideration becomes religious only when it is not only intense but is actuated and supported by an inclusive end that unifies the self, according John Dewey. Further, he adds that this inclusiveness relates to both self and the universe.[21] Even Kant who had taught the autonomy of morality realised that duty no matter however rational is difficult to be performed without the aid of religion. So he recommended that duty be performed as if it were a divine command. Now God is a supernatural being and the statement 'God commands his children to obey him' is a mythic statement. A myth, says Prof. Leroy E. Loemker,[22] integrates an individual with the cosmos, consequently with his fellowmen in society. Hence, through God there is the integration of man with other men and this enables an individual to perform his duties. This means that God is not a mere character of a story, but a myth and a symbol. Then, again, religion is a holistic response of an individual. A man cannot be holistically active without being energised to carry out all kinds of resolutions, moral and non-moral. For this reason by holding duties as divine commands, the believer is strongly motivated for carrying out his moral resolutions. Further, Braithwaite himself has noticed that religious statements differ from moral statements in the fact that the former are accompanied with internal behaviour. For instance, *agape* includes not only external behaviour, but also 'an agapeistic frame of mind',[23] i.e. the orientation of the whole man towards the agapeistic policy of behaviour. Again, he says that

21. J. Dewey, *A Common faith*, Yale University Paperbound, 1960, pp. 22-23 (first printing 1934).
22. *Symbol and myth in philosophy* in 'Truth, Myth and Symbol' Edited by T.J.J. Altizer, W.A. Beardslee & others, p. 122.
23. EG, pp. 242-43.

ultimately the religious declaration of adherence to a policy of action is a matter of personal decision by each man.[24] Do not these confessions of Braithwaite show that religious statements are a matter of existential decision and commitment for a certain way of life and action? This would mean that religious statements are not merely moral: they are mythic, symbolic and existential.

Bibliography

1. R. B. Braithwaite, 'An empiricist view of the nature of religious belief', EG: First published in 1955.
2. A. C. Ewing, 'Religious assertions in the light of contemporary philosophy', in *Philosophy*, July 1957.
3. J. A. Passmore, Christianity and Positivism, Australasian Journal of Philosophy, August 1957.
4. H. J. N. Horsburgh, 'Professor Braithwaite and Billy Brown', Australasian Journal of Philosophy, December 1958.
5. E. L. Mascall, Words and Images, Chap. 3, Longmans, 1957.
6. John Hick, Philosophy of religion, Prentice-Hall, 1963, pp. 90-93.

Section V

RELIGIOUS ASSERTIONS AS CONVICTIONAL, MYTHIC AND SYMBOLICAL

The term 'conviction' was widely used by W.F. Zuurdeeg and it would be well to start our enquiry with his elucidation of this word.

According to W.F. Zuurdeeg[1] the word 'conviction' is composed of *Vinco* and *con*. *Vinco* means to conquer and *con* means 'with' and also 'thoroughly'. 'Conviction' is a popular word in law courts where it means that the criminal has been 'thoroughly overcome by the power of evidence, or the testimony of a witness'. In the religious context it means strong sentiment or atti-

---

24. EG, p. 252.
1. *An analytical philosophy of religion*, Allen, 1959.

tudes² induced by rational arguments. Hence, very often it has the adjective 'inner'.

We take the term 'Conviction' to mean all persuasions concerning the meaning of life; concerning good and bad; concerning gods and devils; concerning representations of the ideal man, the ideal state, the ideal society; concerning the meaning of history, of nature, and of the All.³

The term, W.F. Zuurdeeg tells us, is never purely intellectual. In conviction the certitude is felt so overwhelming that the believer will lay down his life for the sake of his conviction. Here his whole personality is involved;⁴ may be he *is* his convictions.⁵

The most important characteristic of 'conviction' is that it implies a change in the believer himself. A Saul the *persecutor* of the Christians becomes a Paul, the preacher of Christianity. Again, conviction also refers to a thing, a situation or a Being, which may be called 'the convictor'. W.F. Zuurdeeg tells us that a man has many convictors and often a hierarchy of them is arranged, the highest of them lies at the top.⁶

Our exposition is not yet complete, but even at this stage it has to be contrasted with scientific knowledge. In science a statement *describes* a fact and the description is said to be *objective* in the sense that nothing of the personality of the scientist enters into the description of a fact. The scientist is just like an impersonal instrument which reveals the various characteristics of the fact as soon as it is presented to him. Quite the reverse of this takes place in religious language. The whole personality of the believer is involved in describing the religious situation as he sees it. Scientifically speaking 'Bethel' for Jacob was just a rocky place. But later on as a result of his vision in a dream a change took place in him. He was full of the holy dread and found the place holy. A thing becomes religious only as a result of some

2. *An analytical philosophy of religion*, Allen, 1959, p. 24.
3. *Ibid.*, p. 26.
4. *Ibid.*, p. 27.
5. *Ibid.*, pp. 37, 57.
6. *Ibid.*, p. 40.

change in the man without which the divine will pass unnoticed. And this is what happens with Jacob.

Surely the Lord is in this place; and I knew *it* not. And he was afraid, and said, How dreadful *is* this place: this *is* none other but the house of God, and this is the gate of heaven.[7]

In other words, the believer *participates* in what is divine for him. Isaiah saw his God as Holy and also found himself an unclean man in the same moment.

Then said I, Woe *is* me: for I am undone; because I *am* a man of unclean lips, and I dwell in the midst of a people of unclean lips: for mine eyes have seen the King, the Lord of hosts.[8]

Here God and the believer cannot be divorced from one another. The objectivity of scientific knowledge is not to be found in religious experience. There can be no God without a believer and there can be no believer without a God.[9] Here we are trying to show that there is a language of participation as against the scientific or objective language of disinterestedness or depersonalisation concerning factual description. This is known as *mythic* language which we can introduce thus.

MYTHIC LANGUAGE

A myth integrates man with the cosmos and the sacred. This can be elaborated in the context of Prof. Leroy E. Loemker's remarks. According to him a myth is a story which primarily answers questions which are matters of life, not merely of understanding.[10] This meaning of life is realised through participation into what is sacred or supernatural. Myths of the primitive

7. Genesis, Chap. 23: 16-17.
8. Isaiah, Chap. VI, Verse 5.
9. S. Coval, *Worship, Superlatives and concept confusion* in *MIND*, April 1959, pp. 221-22. See also its rejection by Mark Fisher, *MIND*, 1960, p. 415.
10. *Symbol and myth in philosophy* in *'Truth and Symbol'*, Edited by T.J.J. Altizer, W.A. Beardslee & others, p. 122.

people describe the break-through of the sacred (i.e. the supernatural) with a view to *establishing* the world. The mythic story is *living* because it is 'true'. It is living because it deals with that which concerns the primitive man existentially. In contrast a profane story (i.e. a disinterested factual or historical account of persons and events) does not touch him existentially. In other words a profane story, even when historically true, is one which makes no difference to one's existence, emotions and feelings. A mythic story, however, tells about the creation of the *cosmos* specially those *aspects* of the *cosmos* which concern the *primitive* man, his existence and his meaning of life. It is existentially true for him because it *re-enacts* the original acts of the divine creation for him and he participates both in the act and the time of its happenings. Hence, according to Prof. Mircea Eliade, one 'lives' the myth.

In the sense that one is seized by the sacred, *exalting* power of the events recollected or re-enacted.[11]

For this reason a 'true' *myth* for the primitive man is one which is *edifying*. In contrast, the story of a deceiver for a trickster is false because, it does not exalt or edify. Again, a 'false' story can be told anywhere and at any time. But a true myth can be told only at *sacred* times.[12]

For the primitive man time is reversible, whereas for the man of science it is irreversible. Hence, the telling of the myth means for him the re-enacting the deeds of the supernatural with regard to the cosmos and the world. By reciting the myth he lives it and becomes the contemporary of the supernatural.[13] Hence, a living myth implies a genuinely religious experience for the archaic man, if by religion we mean communion with the sacred.

The 'religiousness' of this experience is due to the fact that one re-enacts fabulous, exalting, significant events, one again

---

11. Mircea Eliade, *Myth and Reality*, Allen & Unwin, 1964, p. 19; See also John Macquarrie, God-Talk, SCM Press, 1967, Chap. 8 (Mythology), p. 174.
12. *Ibid.*, pp. 9, 10.
13. *Ibid.*, pp. 13, 18.

witnesses the creative deeds of the Supernaturals; one ceases to exist in the everyday world and enters a transfigured, auroral world impregnated with the Supernaturals' presence. What is involved is not a commemoration of mythical events but a reiteration of them. The protagonists of the myth are made present, one becomes their contemporary. This also implies that one is no longer living in chronological time, but in the primordial time, the time when the event *first took place*.[14]

A myth therefore expresses, enhances, vivifies and codifies beliefs in the supernatural and the meaning of life for a mythic believer.

A myth does integrate the man with the sacred and the cosmos. But the modern man cannot easily accept the archaic myth. With the deepening of his intellectual horizon, the richer and the more complex meaning of life is disclosed to him in other kinds of modern myths. The cosmos for him is very much fuller and the origin of things can no longer be enacted for him. Further, human relations too have become far more complex and the moral tone has become differently coloured for him. No longer can he think of loving his friends only and killing the aliens. At least in his thought and ideas he feels that loving one's enemies is a worthy ideal for him, even when he falls short of it in his practice. Therefore, the myth of the modern man embraces the whole world, and all the races that inhabit it. Hence the primitive myths have faded out, giving way to newer myths through which the modern man participates in the unseen powers and draws vital energy by having communion with them. These myths are now better *known* as symbols.

It is so unfortunate that the terms 'metaphors', 'myths', 'signs' and 'symbols' have been used in various senses and sometimes even celebrated writers speak with the most discordant voices. For example, Prof. R. Bultmann uses the term 'myth' for that which is *historical* (historisch) and the existent (vorhanden). As against this, religious symbols for him may be called eschatological which have the sphere of *Dasein*. Dasein for him

---

14. Mircea Eliade, *Myth and Reality*, George Allen & Unwin, 1964, p. 19.,

refers to the life of a man as he freely decides and chooses. Whereas *Vorhanden* are impersonal existences which have no choice and decision to make for a life of commitment. Hence, his use of the term 'myth' is quite opposed to the meaning of 'myth' presented here. As a matter of fact we have used the term myth to stand for the category which Bultmann would call eschatological or *geschichtlich*.

Again, 'metaphor' is used ordinarily to exhibit points of similarity between very dissimilar object, e.g. when a ferocious man is called a tiger. As against this usage F.W. Dillistone tells us that a metaphor tries to hold the contrast with a view to reconciling them in a higher synthesis. However, the function of metaphor for him is to throw the mind into a creative tension for finding out something (a symbol) which would reconcile the two disparate aspects of reality. He insists on the dynamic role which a metaphor plays in the life of *individuals*. The story-teller, the prophet, the poet

> will link together words, events, situations, patterns of life in a way which has never been attempted before. The combination will startle, surprise and even repel. Men's first reaction is to cling to the familiar. Even if they are willing to advance a short distance into the unknown they prefer to be able to return to their base whenever the spirit moves them. But the man of faith and imagination insists on coupling together the immediate and the remote, the present and future, the material and the spiritual, the ugly and the beautiful, the evil and the good.[15]

Here the important point to note is that metaphor is a power-symbol for it helps the individual to leap beyond the ordinary and profane towards the supernatural, extraordinary, sacred or the holy. In this sense it becomes identical with myth or symbol. Here a metaphor becomes a myth, which is a power-thought, according to E. Brunner and Ernst Cassirer. Through the myth a new dimension of reality comes to view and the myth becomes

---

15. F.W. Dillistone, *The function of metaphor* in *Readings in religious philosophy*, Edited by MacGregor/Robb, Houghton Mifflin, 1962, pp. 389-90.

a new category in describing this existential situation. For Cassirer even the simplest myth lifts the ordinary, the everyday and profane impression to the level of the holy.

> This involves not merely a transference, but a real *metabasis eis allo genos*; in fact, it is not only a transition to another category, but actually the creation of the category itself.[16]

SYMBOLS

We are using the term 'myth' in the sense of Ernst Cassirer and of Mircea Eliade and the term 'symbol' largely though not quite in the sense of Paul Tillich. Paul Tillich makes a sharp distinction between 'sign' and 'symbol'. According to Paul Tillich, like a sign, a symbol points to something beyond itself. But a sign is an arbitrary connection. In contrast, a symbol *participates* in the reality of that to which it points. A symbol therefore, according to Tillich, as long as it effectively symbolises, cannot be replaced, but, a sign, being conventional can be. For example, 'red' is a sign of danger in most of the countries of the world. But the Chinese now want to reverse this conventional meaning of the sign 'red'. That the symbol participates in the reality of the symbolised is a very important point. However, this usage will be greatly disputed by the empiricist. According to the empiricist whenever one thing stands for another thing quite naturally without much of human convention, then the former is said to be the *sign* of the other. For example, a nimbus cloud is said to be sign of impending rains. In this sense a sign is an index of the other things. Whereas a 'symbol' is employed

> to refer only to those cases of standing—for in which one thing has been *made* to stand for another, by a decision of some human being or group of human beings.[17]

Similarly, according to C.W. Morris[18] when sign does not

---

16. Ernst Cassirer, 'The power of metaphor' in *Readings in Religions Philosophy*, Edited by MacGregor/Robb, p. 371.

17. John Hospers, 'An introduction to philosophical analysis', Routledge and Kegan Paul, 1963, p. 1.

18. *Foundations of the theory of signs* in *International Encyclopedia of United Science*, Vol. 1, No. 2, Chicago Press, 1938, pp. 23f.

incorporate the characteristics of the object denoted, then it is called a symbol, e.g. the word 'photograph' may be called a symbol. Well, the empiricist may be right in defining 'symbol' as it is formed in scientific language. Our concern is with convictional language. In convictional language a symbol is a power-- thought which derives its energy from what it symbolises. This may be called the language of the Unconscious. Both Freud and Jung use the term 'symbol' as that which participates in the symbolised. For Freud a symbol stands for and is a substitute of repressed (sex objects, organs, energy and act); for Jung it stands for the hitherto unrecognised unconscious, either racial or primordial. According to both of them, however, the symbol specially the religious symbol energises the worshipper or believer. However, Paul Tillich was the philosopher of the language of religious symbols, and we shall be using the term, more or less in the sense of Tillich.

According to Tillich, the first point is that a symbol participates in the symbolised,[19] e.g. a flag participates in the power and glory of the nation of which it is the flag. Hence, an attack on the flag is deemed to be an attack on the country represented. Therefore, there is something of the magical in regard to a symbol. In magical thinking a part symbolises the whole and participates in the whole. What happens to a part is supposed to happen to the whole of which it is a part. For instance, nails, hairs spittle, excrement and even the shadow are the parts of a man. Now in order to have magical power over the enemy one need procure only his pared nails or cut-off hair or even his effigy. What one does to his hair of effigy is said to be done to the enemy himself. In the same manner a symbol gives power of the god to the man who has the appropriate symbol of the god. A flag, a cross, a swastika are so many symbols.

Here, 'participation' for us means the identification of the symbol with the symbolised. For example, the 'cross' does become one with Christ, either partly or wholly. In contrast, a believer in using the symbol may be profoundly affected, but a symbol-user cannot be said to be identified with the symbolised.

---

19. Paul Tillich, The meaning and justification of religious symbols in RET, *Religious experience and truth*, Edited by S. Hook, NYU Press, 1961, p. 4.

A Paul in his moments of deep stirrings within his soul may utter that not he but Christ lives in him. However, this identification of the use of symbol with the symbolised will be called mysticism. Symbols may be used to induce mystic trance, however, the two uses of symbols should be kept distinct for our purpose. The use of symbols in a convictional language need not imply mysticism. Most probably convictional language is well-suited to analyse mystic situation, but it does not favour the mystic language of silence, *paradoxes* and indescribableness. By the 'language of participation' (which the symbolic language is) meant the personality-involvement of the user of the symbol and the efficaciousness of the symbol in working or shaking up of the whole personality of the believer. This is what John Macquarrie and Malcolm have also maintained. For John Macquarrie when we talk of God, we talk at the same time of ourselves. The word 'God' does not simply signify Being, but also implies, says J. Macquarrie, our evaluation of Being, and our commitment to Being.[20] In symbolic language two aspects are inseparably implied: a new dimension appears on the horizon *pari passu* with the newly created sensitiveness of the believer. If no change takes place in the person then he would not see his god; and the seeing of God implies an inner change, a transformation of the man. a having of the third eye (trinetra), a bodhi (enlightenment). A Christ hung on the cross was just a man, a bruised and despised man for one of the dacoits; not so for the other. The other dacoit saw in him a saviour. There was the leap towards faith in a god, a jump from the finite to the transcendent, infinite and the ultimate as a result of a triumphant repentance from past misdeeds. New dimension, wider horizons require fresh categories for the purpose of description. Hence, Cassirer tells us that a myth creates a new category which cannot be assimilated to the categories already extant. Symbols are the categories which are used to describe the new dimensions of reality.[21]

This opening of the hidden depths of our souls to the reality in unparalleled light gives rise to symbols. But symbols cannot be conjured up by one's will, nor can they pass away by one's mere wish. They seize the man and hold him fast.

---

20. God-Talk, p. 101.
21. Paul Tillich, RET, p. 5.

They (symbols) grow out of the individual or collective unconscious and cannot function without being accepted by the unconscious dimension of our being. Symbols which have an especially social function (e.g., political and religious symbols) are created or at least accepted by the collective unconscious of the group in which they appear.[22]

A symbol as such is born, lives and dies. It comes to birth when the situation is ripe for it; it fades way and becomes obsolete, when the situation becomes unfavourable for it, i.e. fails to be living, momentous and forced for the group of individuals amongst whom it once held its sway.[23]

Again, the symbol deals with the ultimate, because a symbol integrates the individual with the cosmos and the sacred, and, the cosmos and the sacred are the ultimate concerns of man.

The fundamental symbol of our ultimate concern is God. It is always persent in any act of faith, even if the act of faith includes the denial of God.[24]

An atheist in the true sense of the term, according to Paul Tillich, does not deny God, but ignores Him and remains unconcerned about his ultimate concern. As was stated before, God-concept can never be religiously speaking approached impersonally, disinterestedly and impartially.

The numinosity of the object makes it difficult to handle intellectually, since our affectivity is always involved. One always participates for or against, and 'absolute objectivity' is more rarely achieved here than anywhere else.[25]

Naturally when the whole personality is involved in becom-

22. Paul Tillich, 'Symbols of Faith' in *Philosophy and Religion*, Edited by Abernethy, George, L. and Langfor, Thomas A., Macmillan, 1962, p. 358.
23. Paul Tillich, *Ibid.*, p. 4.
24. *Ibid.*, p. 360.
25. C.G. Jung, *Answer to Job* in *Psychology and Religion*, Collected Works, Vol. 11, p. 452.

ing aware of God, then feeling and will are as much 'evoked' as our intellection. Hence, in believing God we take Him to be a person and our symbolic thinking verges more towards trust and love of Him than of cognitive apprehension of Him. But before this we have to mention one thing more.

According to Tillich, in the notion of God two elements can be distinguished: the element of ultimacy or the Being of God which is not a symbol, and the other element of concreteness which is borrowed from our profane experience and is symbolically applied. Yahweh or Christ or Ram or Krishna have both the elements: the ultimate concern and a concrete image of what concerns a believer ultimately.

> God as the ultimate in man's ultimate concern is more certain than any other certainty, even that of oneself. God as symbolized in a divine figure is a matter of daring faith, of courage and risk.[26]

The point is that the Unconditioned Transcendent (abbreviated as UT) is being-itself, which is beyond *essence* and existence. 'Essence' means a universal, a concept and also a norm, a value. But a norm or a concept is merely possible and the UT is actual. Again, 'existence' in general means the fact of concreteness and every concrete object is finite. So the UT is beyond essence and existence and so is beyond any description. Here Paul Tillich, Thomas Aquinas and Śaṁkara, all three agree that the Absolute Reality can be expressed only negatively. Why should we not remain silent? Why speak about UT when it is unsayable?

Well, because man cannot live without being ultimately concerned, without being concerned about the UT which is the Ultimate Concern. Hence, he has to grasp it. And he can grasp it only through a finite segment which can serve him as a symbol, something which points to UT and helps him to receive the supreme fulfilment of his life. God as a symbol of the UT is not out there.

> "It means that whatever concerns a man ultimately becomes god for him, and, conversely, it means that a man can be

---

26. Paul Tillich, *op. cit.*, p. 361.

concerned ultimately only about that which is god for him.[27]

But can a finite segment serve as a symbol? Yes, because the UT is being-itself and everything including any finite segment participates in Being-itself and so a finite segment can serve as a symbol.[28] However, no symbol can be literally applied to the UT.

The truth of a religious symbol has nothing to do with the truth of the empirical assertions involved in it, be they physical, psychological, or historical.[29]

Buddha and Christ no doubt are historical figures and they are also symbols of the UT. But these historical personalities, insofar as they are religious symbols, they have no place in the objective world. The historical, the factual can never be certain; it is problematic.[30] Peter and John found the tomb empty and since then the spade of the archaeologist confirms it. But the risen Christ can be known only through faith; the historical Jesus has to be raised to the status of a myth if he has to serve as a symbol, as a saviour of man reconciling man to the UT, by overcoming the insecurities and anxieties of becoming non-being through the infinitude and Being of the UT.[31] Here 'Being' does not mean the most general and emptiest of categories of Hegel: it means the whole of human reality, the structure, the meaning, and the aim of existence.[32] Thus a symbol arises as a result of man's ultimate concern about that which is considered to be his ultimate concern. This requires an analysis of 'ultimate concern'.

The 'Ultimate Concern', for Tillich is both a subjective process and the object of this process. It is an ontic category, to describe something beyond the distinctions of subject and object. As psychological process the ultimate concern in man is a sovereign drive within him to seek his ultimate being or destiny. Being

---

27. ST, p. 211.
28. ST, I, p. 239.
29. ST, I, p. 240.
30. RET, p. 317.
31. RET, p. 313.
32. ST, I, p. 14.

ultimate it excludes all other finite concerns for wealth, name or position. It is holistic and is well-expressed in the Biblical command of loving the Lord our God with all our heart, with all our soul, with all our mind and with all our strength.

> The unconditional concern is total: no part of ourselves or of our world is excluded from it; there is no 'place' to flee from it. The total concern is infinite: no moment of relaxation and rest is possible in the face of a religious concern which is ultimate, unconditional, total, and infinite.[33]

It is not an ordinary process as some of the critics of Tillich take it to be. The word 'concern', Paul Tillich tells us, points to the existential character of religious experience.

When we come to the object of our ultimate concern, then the first thing to be said about it is that it can never be given in 'detached objectivity'. Here there is *something* which, however, cannot be known or handled without concern.

> That which is ultimate gives itself only to the attitude of ultimate concern......It is the object of total surrender, demanding also the surrender of our subjectivity while we look at it. It is a matter of infinite passion and interest (Kierkegaard), making us its object whenever we try to make it our object.[34]

No finite thing can be the object of ultimate concern, otherwise we shall be taking up the finite for the infinite. And this is known as idolatry. However, a finite thing can serve as a medium, a vehicle, pointing to the UT beyond itself.

> Man is infinitely concerned about the infinity to which he belongs, from which he is separated, and for which he is longing. Man is totally concerned about the totality which is his true being and which is disrupted in time and space...... Man is ultimately concerned about that which determines his ultimate destiny beyond all preliminary necessities and accidents.[35]

---

33. ST, I, p. 12.
34. ST, I, p. 12.
35. ST, I, p. 14.

We are landed up in a paradox. The object of our ultimate concern is infinite, the Unconditioned Transcendent which we can know only through a finite symbol. Even God as a Supreme Being is only a symbol and figurative:

> The word 'God' produces a contradiction in the consciousness, it involves something figurative that is present in the consciousness and something not figurative that we really have in mind and that is represented by this idea. In the word 'God' is contained at the same time that which actually functions as a representation and also the idea that it is *only* a representation.[36]

Every symbol should be transparent and self-negating. This means that a symbol should be able to point to the UT without usurping the place of the UT. Again, it should negate itself so that through it the UT is grasped and clearly intuited.[37] No symbol should be treated as an existent thing. If a symbol is objectified and secularised in the form of a thing then it ceases to be a religious symbol.

> It is the religious function of atheism ever to remind us that the religious act has to do with the unconditioned transcendent, and that the representation of the Unconditioned are not objects concerning whose existence or non-existence a discussion would be possible.[38]

Hence for Tillich God is not an objective entity. Yet every symbol is double-edged. It points to the infinite which it symbolizes and the finite through which it symbolizes. It forces the infinite down to finite things and elevates and opens up the finite things for the divine.[39] The double meaning of the truth of a symbol has to be kept in mind:

> A symbol *has* truth: it is adequate to the revelation it

---

36. RET, p. 315.
37. RET, p. 10; PR, p. 398.
38. RET, p. 315.
39. ST, I, pp. 240-41.

expresses. A symbol *is* true: it is the expression of a true revelation.[40]

But what is the meaning of 'truth'?

CRITERION OF MEANING AND TRUTH OF SYMBOLS

Quite obviously no literal statement can be made about the UT. Again, a symbol is not a fact about which any discussion can be made.

> The criterion of the truth of a symbol naturally cannot be the comparison of it with the reality to which it refers, just because this reality is absolutely beyond human comprehension. The truth of a symbol depends on its inner necessity for the symbol-creating consciousness. Doubts concerning its truth show a change of mentality, a new attitude toward the unconditioned transcendent. The only criterion that is at all relevant is this: that the Unconditioned is clearly grasped in its unconditionedness.[41]

The above statement of Tillich may give one the impression that literal statement can be made about the UT, since Tillich allows the possibility of its being grasped in its unconditionedness. Further, Tillich also holds that a non-symbolic statement can be made about the UT itself.

> The statement that God is being-itself is a non-symbolic statement......However, after this has been said, nothing else can be said about God as God which is not symbolic.[42]

But does Tillich really mean it? I do not think so. The symbolic statement is existential and the adequacy of a symbol depends upon its success in evoking an ultimate concern.[43] The ultimate concern is both existential and ontological simultaneously. Our ultimate concern is that which determines our being or non-

---

40. ST, I, p. 240.
41. RET, p. 316.
42. ST, pp 238-39.
43. ST, p. 240, DF, p. 96.

being. Tillich holds that man becomes aware of his finitude and of the infinite implicitly involved in the finite. To the extent we are finite we are non-being and this awareness causes insecurity and anxiety. We have to be reconciled to the infinite and we can do so by participating in the power of the infinite being. A symbol takes us into the UT through our faith in it. A faith in a symbol as the representative of the UT is a matter of risk. The risk is that in future the symbol may cease to be a symbol. A personal God, sacramental activities, prophetico-political ideologies are all so many symbols through which a man seeks the fulfilment of his life. The risk is that what one takes to be a symbol, may turn out to be an idol.[44] Thus the 'true awareness' of the UT is existential certainty which an individual can claim by staking his total personality. 'The inner certainty' or 'immediate awareness' of the UT is the existential grasping of it. Thus, no symbolic statement can be impersonally, timelessly, literally or factually true. A symbolic statement about the UT is power thinking and one who makes it derives power from it and reaches security of his ultimate destiny beyond 'all preliminary necessities and accidents",[45] and gets his impulses integrated into a unified personality.[46] Hence, symbolic statements "are not true or false in the sense of cognitive judgements".

> But they are authentic or inauthentic with respect to their rise; they are adequate or inadequate with respect to their expressive power; they are divine or demonic with respect to their relation to the ultimate power of being.[47]

Thus, a symbolic statement has no logical certainty, not even factual reasonableness and certainly not subjective indubitableness. It is a statement which a believer makes with all his heart, with all his soul, with all his strength[48] and he does this with full risks. A symbolic statement is authentic when it evokes an ultimate concern of what is his ultimate destiny; it is authentic when it represents the UT with the full awareness that it is only a representa-

44. ST, pp. 297-398.
45. ST, p. 14.
46. RET, p. 5.
47. PR, p. 409.
48. ST, p. 115.

tion.[49] It becomes inauthentic, when instead of representing the UT, it takes an empirical fact or itself as the UT: it thus becomes idolatrous. It is inauthentic, when it becomes demonic, when instead of having an integrating influence it disintegrates the personality. For example, the symbol of Fuhrer with the swastika or the worship of Moloch requiring human sacrifice[50] is said to be demonic.

So far we have held that the question of 'truth' is irrelevant with regard to symbolic statements. However, there is analogous valuation of authenticity. Again, corresponding to 'falsity' there are the analogous concepts of 'inauthenticity', 'demoniac' and 'idolatry'. But let us further clarify this position.

Religious symbols represent that which is unconditionally beyond the conceptual sphere: the object of a religious symbol can never become an empirical object.

Religious symbols represent the transcendent but do not make the transcendent immanent.[51]

Here there is an echo of the Kantian doctrine of the unknowable. According to Tillich, we can know the UT only by symbolizing it, but we have no means of cognizing it without the symbols. If we have no means of cognizing it, then why should we not lighten the ship by throwing it overboard? Because we are aware of it in our paradoxical and existential situation in our moments of anxieties, insecurities, estrangements and in other analogously ambiguous situations; and also of course in the hour of reconciliation and triumph. The acknowledgement of the UT through the adequate and appropriate symbols contributes to the seriousness, reality and power in man's existential situation. But apart from this there is a mystical strain in Tillich's theology. Tillich at several places drops the hint that the UT can 'be grasped in its unconditionedness',[52] in true awareness through the symbols. Again,

---

49. RET, p. 315.
50. RET, p. 137.
51. RET, p. 303.
52. RET, p. 316.

The term 'truth' in this context means the degree to which it reaches the referent of all religious symbols.[53]

Then in another place, he observes that the criterion of every concrete expression is 'the degree to which the concreteness of the concern is in unity with its ultimacy".[54] This suggests the possibility of comparison of the symbol with the UT and the non-symbolic cognition of the UT for the purpose of comparison. Further, he hints that the referent of all religious symbols, that is the UT, can be reached both negatively and positively. Negatively, a symbol should not serve as an obstacle but should remain transparent, i.e. exhibiting the UT, perhaps in the same way as a lens by virtue of its transparency shows the object. For this reason W. Norris Clarke calls a symbol as 'pointer concept' of infinity or infinity-operator.[55] Positively, according to Tillich, the truth of a religious symbol lies in the value of the symbolic material used in it,[56] on 'the valuation in an ultimate perspective of the individual persons'.[57] However, the ambiguity of Tillich's expressions makes it difficult to insist on the possibility of the mystical intuition of the UT. His enigmatic statement, cited before is:

'A symbol is true: it is the expression of a true revelation'.[58] And revelation is not empirical intuition, apprehension or any such cognition. In any case, Tillich does seem to admit the cognition of the UT in its unconditionedness either through the transparency of the symbol or its pointer-function or in the breaking of the idolatrous symbol, or in the form of the colourless screen on which all symbols are projected. This question might become easier to answer if we raise a few more questions about the status of the symbol itself.

A symbol does not remain fixed. It keeps on changing with age, peoples and their paradoxical situations of inner tension and insecurities and with their existential decisions. Hence, no

---

53. RET,,p. 10.
54. PR, p. 398.
55. RET, p. 229.
56. RET, p. 10.
57. RET, p. 11.
58. ST, I, p. 240.

transitory and changing symbol can be objectively true of the infinite and the unconditioned transcendent. Are they subjective then? By 'subjectivity' we mean three things:

(a) A symbol is expressive of the mental state of the believer in the sense in which dancing is, or, even the expressive art of painting, out of sheer delight of form and colour. In this sense, a symbol is not a symbol of anything and does not represent anything beyond itself.

(b) Again, a symbol may be said to be subjective in the sense that it is created at will by individuals.

(c) There might be a third sense in which a symbol can be said to be subjective in the sense of Marx and Freud. In this sense a symbol is an expression of the psychological and social situations and apart from such an expression there is no reality which it represents.

Tillich rejects the subjectivity of symbols in all these three senses. As to the first point, Tillich holds that symbols do not refer to a world of objective facts.

Yet they intend to express a reality and not merely the subjective character of a religious individual.[59]

Again, Tillich denies that symbols can be created at will: they are born and they die as a result of the unconscious-conscious reaction of a group.[60] A symbol is a matter of the whole community.[61]

As for the third meaning of subjectivity, Tillich holds that psychological and sociological conditions explain the proclivities for emphasizing, receiving and *selecting* certain symbols in preference to other symbols. But the symbol-making power has to be posited *a priori* as an ultimate metaphysical structure of existence. For Tillich, the vital impulses which select the symbols are 'themselves the operation of a primordial shaping of life'.

---

59. RET, p. 304.
60. RET, p. 4.
61. RET, pp. 302-33.

Symbols are not merely expressive: they do have their root in reality.

> ....the possibility has not been taken into account that the vital impulses which induce the selection of the father symbol are themselves the operation of a primordial shaping of life, and therefore the intuition of the Unconditioned in this symbol ('father-symbol' of Freud) expresses a truth which, though limited, is yet an ultimate, and therefore a religious, truth.[62]

Again, Tillich notes that the symbols of creation and salvation are reflections of something real in the nature of the divine.

> "They are not merely different subjective ways of looking at the same thing. They have a *fundamentum* in *re*, a foundation in reality, however much the subjective side of man's experience may contribute.[63]

But a symbol is an amalgam of subject-object affair. The intuition of the UT can never present the UT in its non-symbolic or naked form. Ontologically speaking it becomes just a Being-itself,—it is a colourless canvas on which all symbols are projected. There are many gods in terms of which man has been trying to reach the ultimate object of his ultimate concern. But what is the basis of such projections? There is the ultimate concern which is subjectively felt by every man, but which goes beyond every preliminary finite and concrete concern. Then there is God, the object of man's ultimate concern. All projections result out of the tension between the ultimate concern and God as the object of the ultimate concern. Whatever psychological and sociological theories of symbols may be they should not confine to the subjective side only, ignoring the ontological objective side.

What these theories disregard is that projection always is projection *on* something—a wall, a screen, another being, another realm. Obviously, it is absurd to class that on which the projection is realized with the projection itself. A screen is not projected; it receives the projection.[64]

---

62. RET, p. 306; See also ST, I, p. 243.
63. ST, III, p. 283.
64. ST, I, p. 212.

If any critic presses the non-symbolic statement about the UT, then either he has to accept that it is Being-itself or if he prefers, he can say that it is the colourless screen which induces man to throw his projections of symbols on it.

Bibliography

1. Zuurdeeg, W. F., *An analytical philosophy of religion*, George Allen, 1959.
2. Mircea Eliade, *Myth and Reality*, Allen & Unwin, 1964.
3. Paul Tillich, *Systematic Theology*, 3 Vols. Nisbet & Co.
4. Do.   *Dynamics of faith*, Harper & Brothers, 1957.
5. *Classical and contemporary readings in the Philosophy of Religion*, Edited by J. Hick.
6. Do.   *Two types of philosophy of religion.*
7. Do.   *Existential analyses and religious symbols.*
8. *Religious Symbolism*, Edited by F. Ernest Johnson, Harper & Brothers, 1955.
9. *The theology of Paul Tillich*, Edited by C. W. Kegley & R. W. Bretall, Macmillan, 1956.
10. RET in which two articles of Paul Tillich and critical Comments on Tillich's theory of symbols have been given.

CHAPTER VI

A GENERAL VIEW OF RELIGION AND LANGUAGE

A comparative study of religions shows that religion is mythological, ontological, analogical and symbolical. But it means that being mythological or even symbolical, religion is not a purely cognitive enterprise of man. This is fully supported by the fact that all the proofs about the existence of God have been shown to be fallacious. Not much weight can be attached to the direct encounter with God in mystic experience. Even the numinous experience described by Otto is said to be too elusive to be called cognitive. Paul Tillich, after revising and modernizing the doctrine of *analogia entis*, presents his theory of symbolism. However, this doctrine of symbols ultimately comes to a conclusion in which 'God above God' is beyond all description and verbalisation.

Hence, at least theistic statements are not cognitive Any criticism of God-talk as cognitive is highly irrelevant. Both the defender of theism and its opponent beat the empty air. The most important statement of Christianity, Islam and the Upaniṣadic tradition in India is that the highest reality is unknown and unknowable, and indescribable.

Section A

THE UNKNOWABILITY OF GOD

I. Semitic Religions hold that God is invisible, and, all that we know that He *is*, but *not what He is*.

Semitic religions hold that God is essentially transcendent and as such He is beyond the human capacity to know Him. He is known by His revelation in Holy books through Prophets, Angels and even dreams. Let us come to Judaeo-Christian tradition.

(a) The book of Exodus states,

> 'And God said to Moses, I AM WHO I AM' (Exo. 3.14).

This utterance simply means that we know only this much that God *is*, but we do not know what He is, i.e. His attributes. This is how St. Thomas Aquinas and Paul Tillich have interpreted the meaning of Ex. 3.14.

Again, in the book of Job, there is the statement,

> Can you search out the deep things of God? Can you find out the limits of the Almighty? They are higher than heaven— what can you do? Deeper than sheol—what can you know?
> (11.7-8)

In the same spirit the New Testament declares,

> 'No one has seen God at any time' (John 1.18; 1 Jn. 4.12).

Further, St. Paul declares that God is essentially 'invisible' (Col. 1.15). Again, Jesus said, 'God is Spirit, and those who worship Him must worship in spirit and truth' (John 4.24). And Spirit is like the wind which blows where it wishes, and you hear the sound of it, but cannot tell where it comes from and where it goes (John 3.8).

If God is Spirit, then there can be no visible image of Him (Exo. 20.4).

(b) The Koran also holds that God is essentially invisible.

> 'No mortal eyes can see Him' (Surah 6.102,103).

Again, Caliph Abu Bakr is quoted to have said,

> Praise to God who hath given His creatures no way of attaining to the knowledge of Him except through inability to know Him.[1]

In the same manner Ibn-Al-Arabi has declared that no human

---

1. R.S. Bhatnagar, *Dimensions of Classical Sufi Thought*, p. 139.

intellect can know the absolute existence of God. God and God alone knows His own transcendence.[2] Again, Wahed Hossain has stated that in Islamic Philosophy it has been maintained that God's existence and attributes are beyond the human intellect.[3] Besides, Al-Junayd holds that God is apprehended only through gnosis,

> Gnosis involves the negation of whatever is reason......
> (R.S. Bhatnagar, *Ibid.*, p. 139)

II. The Indian tradition has upheld the unknowable character of the Supreme Reality, and the source of this comes from the Upaniṣads. Reality for the Upaniṣads is non-dual and is indescribable, unknowable and can be described only negatively. It (*Brahman*)

> is not this, it is not that (*neti, neti*). It is unseizable, for it cannot be seized (*Bṛhadāraṇyaka* Up. 4.2.4; See also, *BU* 2.3,6; III. 9.26).

Again,

> Where knowledge is of a dual nature, there, indeed, one hears, sees, smells, tastes—where knowledge is not of a dual nature, being devoid of action, cause, effect, unspeakable, incamparable, indescribable—what is that? It is impossible to say (*Maitri* 6.7; Cp. *BU* 2.4.14)

The *Śūnyatā* of Nāgārjuna is wholly indescribable.
III. Sant Kabir describes his ultimate reality as attributeless, invisible and beyond the senses.

> What you are nobody can know,
> Every one says what you are not (*Kabir-Granthāvali*, pada 47)
> Nobody can know the unknowable (*K.G.*, pada 49).

---

2. Dr. Tarachand, *Growth of Islamic Thought in India*, in *History of Philosophy, Eastern and Western*, p. 498.
3. W. Hossain, 'The Conception of Divine Being in Islamic Philosophy', *Visvabharati*, Quarterly, 1930, p. 379.

IV. In our modern times Sri Ramakrishna too has maintained that Brahman is essentially indescribable.

> Even when one has realized Brahman,
> One cannot describe It. If someone asks you what ghee is like, your answer will be 'Ghee is ghee.'[4]

> My child, you have understood a little of Brahman. What It is cannot be expressed in words.[5]

> God is formless, and is with form too, and He is that which transcends both form and formlessness. He alone can say what else He is.[6]

V. Even in the West, God has been said to be mystical. Here the words of the most modern philosopher Wittgenstein are worth quoting:

> There is indeed the inexpressible. This *shows* itself; it is the mystical (*Tractatus* 6.522).

> Whereof one cannot speak, thereof one must be silent (*Tractatus* 7).

Section B

REASONS FOR THE UNKNOWABILITY OF GOD

One cannot dogmatically state that God is unknowable. Some reasons have to be assigned. The *Bṛhadāraṇyaka* is most clear on this point.

The Upaniṣads hold that Brahman, the Supreme Reality is pure, objectless consciousness. The presence of this pure consciousness alone makes human thinking, remembering, recognizing possible. But this objectless consciousness cannot be made the object of any thought.

> You could not see the seer of seeing. You could not hear the hearer of hearing. You could not think the thinker of thinking. You could not understand the understander of understanding (*Bṛhadāraṇyaka Up.* 3.4.2).

---

4. *The Gospel of Sri Ramakrishna*, by M., p. 920.
5. *Ibid.*, p. 102.
6. F. Max Muller, *Ramakrishna*, sayings, 32.

In other words, the very nature of Brahman is that it can only be the *Knower* or subject. It therefore cannot be the *known* or object. This is essentially the same reason which has been advanced by Kant.

Kant has pointed out that *the synthetic unity of apperception* is at the basis of what we perceive, remember and think. But this presupposition of thinking cannot itself be an object of thought.

> Now it is, indeed, very evident that I cannot know as an object that which I must presuppose in order to know any object....[7]

In our own time, Wittgenstein has also maintained that God cannot be known. His reason is that God holds the key to the understanding of the world. It is said that God is the guarantor of the human values. If God be the meaning of the world, then God cannot be known.

> It is logically impossible for the sense of the world to be itself a part of the world, since the meaning of anything cannot be a part of that of which it is the meaning (*Tractatus* 6.41).

> God does not manifest Himself in the World (*Tractatus* 6.432).

Finally,

> The solution of the riddle of life in space and time lies outside of space and time (*Tractatus* 6.4312).

Kant had laid down that the category of causality can be legitimately applied to the sensible phenomena, but it cannot be meaningfully applied to noumena. Now the world as a whole is not a phenomenon, but is a noumenon. Hence, the cause of the world cannot be legitimately applied to the world as a whole or God. In modern logic, the principle has been stated thus:

> What is true of a member of a series, cannot be true of the series as a whole.

---

7. *Critique of Pure Reason*, Eng. tr. N.K. Smith, (abridged), p. 201.

Human beings can talk about the events of the world, but not about that which is prior to or beyond the world.

Section C

WHAT IS GOD OF WHOM MAN SHOULD BE SO MUCH MINDFUL?

If God were really unknown, then man would have remained unconcerned. Whether God is apprehended is a difficult thing to hold. But there must be some reason, perhaps some psychological constitution of man which impels man to think of Him. In the history of religions various reasons have been offered. This is called the doctrine of religion *a priori*, i.e. man has been so constituted that he cannot live without God. Apart from psychological reasons there are metaphysical, mythological and religious statements to support the doctrine of religion *a priori*. For example, *Chāṇdogya Up.* 6.8-16 states that which is in the sun, moon, rivers and mountains and in everything else is within each man. *Uddālaka Āruni* dinned into the ears of his son Svetaketu nine times in succession.

That which is the finest essence—this whole world has that as its soul. That is Reality. That is Atman (Soul). That art thou, Svetaketu.

Again, *Bṛhadāraṇyaka Up.* (3.2-23), i.e. twenty-two times stated that which is in the river, the earth, in atmosphere and sun is the indwelling Soul, the Inner Controller, the Immortal is in each man. This inner thread alone binds man to the Supreme Reality. Is it any wonder then that man seeks to know the unknowable Brahman within each man as his indwelling spirit?

In Judaeo-Christian and Islamic tradition,

the Lord God formed man of the dust of the ground, and breathed into his nostrils the breath of life, and man became a living being—(Genesis 2.7).

Earlier in Genesis 1.28 God made man in His own image, into His own likeness. It is the presence of this divine breath and His image which impel man to know His creator. St. Paul states that this divine spirit in man make him cry out, 'Father, my Father' (Gal. 4.6). For the same reason St. Augustine declares

> Thou hast created us for thyself and our heart knows no rest until it may repose in thee.

In our own time, Sri Ramakrishna supports the doctrine of religion *a priori*.

> As the lamp does not burn without oil, so man cannot live without God.[8]

Again,

> Man is born in the world to realize God.[9]

> You have been born in this world as a human being to worship God; therefore try to acquire love for His Lotus Feet.[10]

Similarly, Swami Vivekananda also stated:

> There is intuitive notion, ingrained in man that makes him believe in the existence of the Supreme Being.[11]

Again,

> It is my belief that religious thought is in man's very constitution, so much so that it is impossible for him to give up religion until he can give up his body and mind, until he can give up thought and life.[12]

In contemporary thought, Paul Tillich is the Christian theologian (1886-1966) who has championed the cause of religion *a*

---

8. F. Max Muller, *Ramakrishna. Sayings*, 19, 288.
9. The Gospel of Ramakrishna, M., 672.
10. *Ibid.*, p. 901; See also 331, 453, 671, 907; *The Great Master*, p. 892.
11. *Vivekananda in Indian Newspapers*, New Delhi, p. 194.
12. *Philosophical and Religious Lectures*, p. 117.

priori most loudly. According to him, there is an ultimate concern of man for the ultimate.[13]

> The ultimate concern is unconditional, independent of any conditions of character, desire or circumstance. The unconditional concern is total; no part of ourselves or of our world is excluded from it; there is no 'place' to flee from it.[14]

Again,

> The fundamental symbol of our ultimate concern is God. It is always present in any act of faith, even if the act of faith includes the denial of God. Where there is ultimate concern, God can be denied only in the name of God. One God can deny the other one. Ultimate concern cannot deny its own character as ultimate.[15]

According to Tillich, 'A God disappears, divinity remains'. A symbol of God and myth are the expressions of one's faith.

> One can replace one myth by another, but one cannot remove the myth from man's spiritual life.[16]

The grip of religion in man is very great. After years of indocrination in U.S.S.R., the Muslims in Azerbaijan and Christians in Russia and in the Eastern Europe are returning to the Church again. In the Punjab, Kashmir in India and Bangladesh religion has powerfully reacted. Even otherwise in India, Hinduism has definitely come up to the surface in Northern India. Hence, the claim of religion *a priori* cannot be easily set aside. Quite naturally the ultimate concern has its roots in the psychological constitution of man.

---

13. Paul Tillich, *Dynamics of Faith*, pp. 45, 50, 75, 77, 101, 106, 114.
14. Paul Tillich, *Systematic Theology*, Vol. I, p. 12.
15. Paul Tillich, *Dynamics of Faith*, p. 45.
16. *Ibid.*, p. 50.

Section D

THE PSYCHOLOGY OF RELIGION A PRIORI

It was Kant who has pointed out that religion* is based on natural disposition in man. According to him, *Transcendental Dialectic* deals with a *natural* and inevitable illusion. Even after its deceptiveness has been exposed, it will not cease to play tricks with reason.[17] The psychology of religion is powerfully supported by the holistic tendency in each organism and human psyche.

It was Aristotle who emphasized the place and importance of holism. He pointed out that there is a *hormic* tendency in each organism by virtue of which it tends to become a whole and complete. For example, by virtue of this holistic drive in each egg it in due course gives rise to a complete chick. However, it was Eduard Driesch (1897-1940) who emphasized the presence of holism, specially in the field of embryology. He found that if a part of the embryo is injured then the remaining part of the organism compensates for the injured part in the development of the full embryo. Later on K. Lashley demonstrated this presence of holism in the functioning of the brain. He found that the brain functions as a whole in relation to the learning process. He showed that the remaining part of the brain takes over the function of the parts removed from the brain. For a long time the German psychologists like Kurt Koffka, W. Kohler, Lewin and Kurt Goldstein demonstrated the principle of *Gestalt* formation in perception, learning and thinking. However, for our purpose, the principle of holism is most marked out in the study of human personality.

It was S. Freud who stated that each organism tends to maintain an equilibrium of certain potentials in *Beyond the Pleasure Principle* (1920). Any increase in excitement threatening this equilibrium is felt as pain. The restoring up of the equilibrium is known as pleasure. Hence, the wholeness of the psyche is maintained in man. This doctrine of wholeness has been pushed further by C.G. Jung.

---

* Transcendental Dialectic deals with Soul, God and the World and they are ultimately objects of faith according to Kant, therefore, are matters for religion.

17. I. Kant, *Kant's Critique of Pure Reason*, tr. N.K. Smith, abridged, pp. 36, 162.

C.G. Jung holds that there is a holistic tendency in each human psyche. The first half of life, according to Jung, is spent in making adjustment to the outer world, known as the life of a house-holder in Hindu world-view. When a successful adjustment is completed in the first half, then there is the call of the inner psyche in the second half of life. There are four successive stages in the ascending order for making an individual complete and whole. These stages are of *Shadow, Anima-Animus, Mana-Personality* and *Maṇḍala-experience*. The whole process of becoming a unified whole roughly corresponds to the culture of the soul, according to Advaitism and Buddhism. However, for the purpose of this book the doctrine of holism in the development of human personality is most important.

The Organismic theory in the building of personality has been emphasized by Kurt Goldstein, Andras Angyal, Abraham Maslow, Prescott Lecky, Carl Rogers and others. Like Jung, Goldstein emphasizes the presence of a central tendency in each individual in the task of self-actualization. This process is known as *autonomy*. Apart from autonomy, there is the process of *homonomy* by virtue of which an individual expands and enriches his personality by appropriating and incorporating things and values from the environment. At the higher level of his development, the individual forms an image of his whole personality which, according to Andras Angyal, may be termed 'Symbolic Self'. It is the symbolic Self which gives rise to the projection of one's deity as God or *Brahman*.

This symbolic self embodies the whole meaning of life in relation to his total lived sphere of an individual, as Lewin has termed it. This central drive behind the formation of one's own symbolic self makes an individual transcend his own narrow concern to become his spiritual self. It is the formation of one's own symbolic self which is at the basis of religion *a priori*. Thus, religion is concerned with *becoming* a thing of value, a pearl of great price. Here *knowing* is pressed in the service of *becoming*. A God is there, not to be known primarily, but an ultimate end into which an individual has to be transformed and changed. The same point has been made by the Metaphysician Samuel Alexander.

Indian religious thinkers (the Upaniṣadic seers, Rāmānuja,

Kabir, Sri Ramakrishna and many others) have pointed out that God (*Brahman*) is the indwelling spirit in each man. This has been powerfully emphasized by Samuel Alexander in his metaphysics* of Emergent Evolutionism.

Samuel Alexander holds that there is a creative current behind the push in the evolutionary scheme of things. He calls this push and pull '*nisus*'.

According to Samuel Alexander, there are two prominent tendencies in man, namely, *conatus* and *nisus*. By virtue of his *conatus*, following Spinoza, man perseveres in his own being. But by virtue of *nisus* within man, he is driven towards becoming higher than what he is. This drive is towards his deity. Therefore, the presence of *nisus* contributes to the doctrine of religion *a priori*.

Section E

THE PREDICAMENT OF MAN

Section (A) teaches that the highest reality is unknown and unknowable. Then again Section (D) maintains the doctrine of religion *a priori*. The psychological nature of man impels him to know the unknowable. This is the condemnation of man to remain imprisoned in his absurd position. The man has to listen to the Delphic Oracle, 'Man know thy Self', or, the Upaniṣadic injunction 'Ātmanaṁ Viddhi'. What is in man which condemns him to do the absured? This is much more difficult than the monotonous task of taking the stone to the mountain top. The repetitiveness may breed boredom, but the compulsiveness to know the unknowable is absurd and meaningless. However, the *nisus* is man, the holistic task in him to become his symbolic Self, the indwelling Brahman in man would make him restless till he finds a way out of the tangle. How can he achieve this absurd demand?

By taking recourse to imagination Man pictures his symbolic Self and superimposes this arch-image on the determiner of his

---

*By metaphysics is meant that it deals with the hitherto unexplored dimension of man. In the Kantian sense it *does not give* us *knowledge*, but is an imaginative construction encouraging thinkers to extend the sphere of knowledge. Hence, it is an imaginative thrust of man towards higher, deeper and wider dimension of man.

destiny. As men are different not only due to various types and functions of their psychological structure, so also they are due to their various kinds of upbringing called *saṁskāra*. The picture of the ideal self must differ from men to men, from races to races on account of the difference of culture and psychological constitution. When a picture grips us and shakes us from the very depth of our being, then it takes the form of deity. In the form of deity, the picture becomes living, and, even more real than other things of the world. This picture then is known as 'myth'. Why and how the myth of a god becomes so living and gripping? The reason is that the myth arises from the holistic tendency in man to become his own complete self. As soon as the symbolic self assumes a concrete form, then it appears to the man as a perfect self. By worshipping this Self, he feels to have become his own Ideal Self. In surrendering to this Self, man psychologically realizes to have become a whole, complete and entire.

Even Freud had to confess that religion is a great defence against neurosis. It is this fact of Self-realization through one's deity, that religion has such a powerful grip over man, and, determines his entire destiny.

This picture or the myth arises from the Unconscious of man and is collectively accepted as the worshipful deity. What has been maintained by Paul Tillich about 'symbols' is largely true of myth.

Religion can hardly do away with myth. This was well observed by Paul Tillich.[18] In the same way, Swami Vivekananda observes,

We are all born idolaters, and idolatry is good, because it is in the nature of man... [19]

Again,

Why is the face turned towards the sky in prayer? Why are there so many images in the Catholic Church? Why are there so many images in the minds of Protestants when they pray?

---

18. *Dynamics of Faith*, p. 50 (already quoted).
19. *The Philosophical and Religious Lectures*, p. 94.

My brethren, we can no more think about anything without a mental image than we can live without breathing.[20]

By 'image' is meant here not only concrete images of marble, stone and wood, but also verbal images. We do talk of God in words, at times in the most anthropomorphic way, and, even we dwell on the attributes of God, in our praise of Him. Here the observation of Sri Ramakrishna is worth stating. Sri Ramakrishna listened to the sermon of Sri Keshab Chandra Sen, and, then he remarked:

Images and other symbols are just as valid as your attributes. And these attributes are not different from idolatry, but are merely hard and petrified forms of it.[21]

Of course, there images are of the unknown and unknowable Reality. They are not, and, cannot be true or false pictures. They simply arise from the depth of the Unconscious. Even Jesus has been described as 'the visible image' of the invisible God. Hence, even the verbal images or so-called descriptions of God cannot be true-false, for they are not factual statements about any sensible reality. Any application of verifiability-falsifiability to determine their meaning is wholly irrelevant. This is the mistake of the positivists.

Even when religious images cannot be called true or false pictures, yet they may be described as authentic or inauthentic. When a religious image touches the heart of a devotee and shakes him from the depth of his being, then it is an authentic experience. And the deity is really a living being. However, when the deity leaves his worshipper cold then that deity is said to be dead. For about ten years, even the Christian priests and Bishops participated in what is known as 'God-is-dead' movement. Hence, any religion is always exposed to the growing scientific knowledge as the deity of the moderners, and, the traditional forms of religion

---

20. *Selections from the Complete Works*, p. 11. This is repeated in *Vedānta*, p. 104. Of course, there may be imageless thinking, according to Wurzburg school. But in general in religions there are myths and images.

21. Romain Rolland, *The Life of Ramakrishna*, 1930, p. 182; Please also see p. 152 of '*The Gospel of Sri Ramakrishna*, 1986.

have become unacceptable to them. But even this form of religion has become unacceptable to them; even this form of religion called *scientism* is becoming a suspect. The latest example comes from the breaking up of the monolithic structure of communism. And the people are returning to the older forms of traditional religions once again following the break-up of Communist hold in Eastern Europe.

Thus, religion is a matter of commitment to values enshrined in the myths and images, and self-involvent or existential acceptance of them. The language of religious statements is mythological, metaphysical, analogical and symbolical, but not at all cognitive or descriptive of any state of affairs. Hence, we have to turn to the nature of religious language. One point can be mentioned here.

Loss of faith means that the holistic tendency in man has failed in making him complete, whole and entire. And this is bound to end in despair, anguish and meaninglessness. This is very much illustrated in the writings of atheistic existentialism. Hence, according to C.G. Jung, restoration of the neurotic to a religious faith alone yields him *peace* and *pistis*.

THE NATURE OF RELIGIOUS LANGUAGE
What has been said about the nature of 'God' just now, shows that we can say that a God-statement cannot be said to be 'true or false'. But for the user of God-statements, they can be either authentic-inauthentic, genuine-fake. This conclusion can be maintained in the light of the analysis of religious statements for about fifty years now. Briefly speaking, numerous papers have been influenced by Wittgenstein's philosophical analysis. Wittgenstein was not a positivist, but there are some statements of his in *Tractatus Logico-Philosophicus* (1921) which were understood in the positivistic way by A.J. Ayer, A.G.N. Flew, and many others. In this form, specially God-talk was declared nonsense, for this could not be either verifiable or falsified. Even the defenders of theism like John Hick and I.M. Crombie accepted the criteria of verifiability-falsifiability for determining the meaning of God-statement. The criterion of verifiability is contained in the following statements of *Tractatus* (4.021-4.031).

> To understand a proposition means to know what is the case,
> if it is true.........One understands it if one understands its
> constituent parts (Simples') (*Tract*. 4.024).

Again, the criterion of falsifiability can be traced to *Tractatus*
5.5151.

> The positive *proposition* must presuppose the existence of
> the negative *proposition* and conversely.

Wittgenstein's thought however matured and in '*Philosophical
Investigations*' (posthumously published in 1953), he came to
teach that language indeed rules our thought. But he gave up
thinking that language is a picture of the world. He rather insisted that language is a kind of game like chess. What is important
is that one should know the rules of the game without caring to
know whether the items of chess refer to any facts at all. The
central thing is to know as to how these rules are observed by
users of a particular language. This view of the *Investigations*
has changed the nature of the analysis of religious language.

John Hick and I.M. Crombie still think that God is a Being
who could be encountered in *post mortem* existence. But the
difficulties of regarding God as existing in His own right are too
patent. I.M. Crombie himself mentions the anomalies in relation
to God.

> It (God) resembles a proper name like 'Tom' in that we are
> told that statements about God are direct statements about
> God and not oblique statements about something else, and
> yet it differs from ordinary proper names in that its use is not
> based fundamentally, as theirs is, on acquaintance with the
> being it denotes.[22]

In other words, God is an *Improper Proper name*. Secondly,
God is supposed to be 'love' or 'creator'. But the theist cannot
clearly state what 'love' or 'creatorship' means. It is 'killed by
inches, the death by a thousand qualifications', as Flew has put

---

22. B. Mitchell, *The Philosophy of Religion*, 1986, p. 30.

it. It is described by negations as it is not the husband's love for his wife, or the mother's love for her child, and so on. Hence, the divine love is neither definitely affirmed nor can it be falsified. The result is that the good word 'love' is emptied out of any meaning.

Again, by the analysis of the word 'worship', J.N. Findlay has come to conclude that God is a *necessary Being*. But the analysts also show that 'necessary Being' is as self-contradictory as 'a square circle'. No doubt 'necessary' may be understood as 'indispensable' in the sense that heating may be taken to be indispensable for cooking. This is called by Terence Penelhum as '*factual* necessity'.[23] But quite obviously one can imagine 'heat' not to cook, as was case with Shadrach, Meshach and Abed-Nego.[24] Hence, factual necessity is not the *logical* necessity implied in 'Necessary Being'.

The result of the Positivistic analysis of God-talk concluded that God-talk is meaningless. The result is too startling and shows that the positivistic investigation is highly irrelevant. Do not the theists pray, worship, sing hymns to praise God, become penitent before God, give Him thanks and so on? Are all these acts and the use of language involved in them meaningless? The positivist does not ask the right kind of questions in relation to religious language. A believer does not prove-disprove the existence of God. For Him God is living and real for whom he can even lay down his life. If some one asks, Is God real and living? Well, see what the Hindus and Muslims do in relation to *Ramajanmbhumi* or *Babri Masjid*; what the Christians and Muslims are doing in Lebanon? So God is either living or dead, or, is worshipped or not. Does anybody ask, 'Does Zesus exist'? It will be deemed an irrelevant issue. Such is also the case of God-talk.

Hence, so far no analysis of religious language-game has become acceptable either by the believers or the philosophers themselves. One thing has become established in the light of Wittegenstein's *Philosophical Investigations* that religious statements cannot be assimilated to factual statements. But what

---

23. B. Mitchell, *Divine Necessity*, p. 189.
24. *The book of Daniel*, O.T. Chap. 3.

more can be said about religious language? Here nothing appears to be clear. Why is this stalemate? The reason appears to me to be this. Philosophers have not thrown their nets wide to cover Advaitism, Jainism and Buddhism. Their sole pre-occupation has been with Christological statements which have been taken to be analogical (St. Thomas Aquinas), symbolical (Paul Tillich) and also mythological (R. Bultmann). In the eyes of competent authorities the doctrine of *analogia entis* ends in agnosticism. No doubt Paul Tillich tried to reformulate the doctrine of analogy into his theory of symbols. This doctrine of symbols, however, leans on Advaitic Ontology which is not very popular in the West.

According to R. Bultmann, much of Christology relating to Virgin birth of Jesus, Resurrection, Ascension and Advent is mythological which is not acceptable to the modern mind. For R. Bultmann, the real meaning of Christological statements is existential. This again is not quite popular for the analytical philosopher.

One thing appears quite clear that religion involves some sort of ontology and even mythology. But religious mythological ontology is related to the aphorism: 'Man! know thyself'. Here knowing means becoming one's own real Self. This is essentially the message of Advaitism. However, both Indian and Western scholars take Advaitism to be a form of philosophy. For them it is not religion. But both Ramakrishna and Vivekananda practised advaitism as a form of religion.

Advaitism is not only a religion, but a religion which underlies all other forms of theistic religions. In such a case the religious language-game of Advaitism is likely to throw some light on the nature and function of religious language.

In Advaitism God remains subservient to the task of *Brahma-jñāna* and Brahma—realisation. However, in Jainism and Buddhism there is no place for God. And yet they are also forms of religion. In these religions the function of religious language is not to describe something external to the believer existing in its own right, but to evoke and exhort the believers to become himself his own real Being. Let us take the case of Advaitism.

Advaitism, the most widely accepted religious philosophy of India, maintains that individuals are really the most real Brahman itself. It is only nescience which prevents them from realizing this supreme 'truth'. One can realize this supreme and only by having knowledge. The word 'knowledge' means the most palpable experience of realizing Brahman. The proper word is '*jñāna*' which really cannot be translated as knowledge. Let us illustrate the case of Brahma-realization which happened to Sri Ramakrishna as a result of most strenuous religious discipline.

The Universe was extinguished. Space itself was no more. At first the shadows of ideas floated in the obscure depths of the mind. Monotonously a feeble consciousness of the Ego went on ticking. Then that stopped too. Nothing remained but Existence. The soul was lost in Self. Dualism was blotted out. Finite and Infinite space were as one. Beyond word, beyond thought, he (Sri Ramakrishna) attained Brahman.[25]

A similar case of Brahma-realization by Vivekananda has been reported.[26] Here knowing means becoming Brahman (*Brahmavid Brahmaiva Bhavati*, i.e. the knower of Brahman himself becomes Brahman).[27] Here 'knowing' does not refer to something independent of the religious seeker. Here knowing means the realization of one's own depth,...of one's own inmost Self. Very often this Brahma-realization has been likened to the moot experience of enjoying sugar by a dumb man. The dumb man cannot talk about it, but he can express it by means of his smile and other behavioural gestures. What can we say about the Vedāntic language?

The Vedāntic language is embodied in Vedāntic philosophy, Mahāvākyas and Mantras. The function of the Vedāntic language is to awaken the seeker to re-find his own real Self.

Arise ye! awake ye!
And obtaining the desired boon understand it.[28]

The Vedāntic language is only a reminder of this eternal Truth about each and every individual person. Here *knowing*

25. Romain Rolland, *The Life of Ramakrishna*, 1930, p. 63.
26. Sri Ramakrishna: *The Great Master*, pp. 879, 917.
27. Mund. 3. 2. 9.
28. Kath. 3.14.

and becoming are one and the same thing. Hence, the function of the religious language is evocative and exhortative. Once the truth of Advaitism is realized, the philosophy of advaitism itself becomes redundant. In the state of Brahma-realization,

'the Vedas cease to be the Vedas'.[29]

This reminds one of Wittgenstein who too described his philosophy as redundant.

My propositions serve as elucidation in the following way: anyone who understands me eventually recognizes them as nonsensical, when he has used them...as steps...to climb up beyond them.
(He must so to speak, throw away the ladder after he has climbed up it.)[30]

Hence, the whole of advaitic philosophy has been likened to a ladder which is set aside as soon as one reaches the goal of Brahma-realization. Repeatedly in the advaitic literature it has been held that religious language, meditation and any form of worship has one single aim of *becoming* the Supreme Object itself. Thus, religious language is not at all descriptive, factual or empirical. Here all kinds of philosophical dialogue or reasoning is pressed into the service of *becoming* or attaining the highest end. Hence, religious language is a component of religious behaviour itself. Now we shall illustrate this in the utterances of Kabir, Sri Ramakrishna and Vivekananda.

Thou knowest me, and I know Thee
And now I am one with Thee.[31]

By meditating on Rama, my Soul has
become Rama. Since my Soul has become
Rama, to whom will I do obeisance.[32]

He who talks of Him, becomes He.[33]

29. Brahadaranyaka Upanishad IV.3.22.
30. Tractatus 6.54.
31. *The Bijak of Kabir Saheb.* Shabda 74.
32. 2 Sakhi 8 of *Kabirgranthavali.*
33. *Kabirgranthavali.* pada 328.

Let us now come to Sri Ramakrishna who demonstrated the fact of Brahma-realization.

If You meditate on an ideal you will acquire its nature. If you think of God day and night, you will acquire the nature of God.[34]

You partake of the nature of him on whom you meditate. By worshipping Shiva you acquire the nature of Shiva.[35]

If a piece of lead is kept in a lake of mercury a long time, it turns into mercury. The cockroach becomes motionless by constantly meditating on Kimura. Similarly, by constantly meditating on God the *Bhakta* loses his ego; he realizes that God is he and he is God.[36]

Similarly, Vivekananda is said to have stated,

The life of anybody who truly loves the Lord will be perfectly moulded in His pattern. Therefore, whether we truly love the Master or not will be best proved by this test.[37]

Again, the statements of Swami Vivekananda can be quoted from '*Selections from Works of Vivekananda*'.

The Hindu religion does not consist in struggles and attempts to believe a certain doctrine or dogma, but in realising... not in believing, but in being and becoming (p. 9).

For Vivekananda 'the whole religion of the Hindu is centred in realisation' (p. 12), i.e. in becoming what he meditates upon.

The Buddhist or the Jains do not depend upon God; but the whole force of their religion is directed to the great central truth in every religion, to evolve a God out of man (p. 14).

---

34. *The Gospel of Sri Ramakrishna*, p. 657.
35. *Ibid.,* p. 688.
36. *Ibid.,* p. 700.
37. *Sri Ramakrishna the Great Master*, p. 1004.

Further, Swamiji asserts that the supreme end of *bhakti* (devotion) is reached when the devotee becomes one with the object of worship. Here the lover and the Beloved become one.[38] In the same manner, Swamiji points out that the end of all religions is the realisation of God in the soul of the worshippers.[39]

Hence, religious language forms a component of religious behaviour, the end of which is to become or to imitate the object of religious adoration.

Of course, the cue is most clearly and eloquently furnished in advaitism. But even in Christianity, the end of religious behaviour is to become as perfect as the Father in Heaven is (Mt. 5.48). A Christian is exhorted to put on Christ (Gal. 3.27), so that he may become a new creature (Gal. 6.15) or a new man (Eph. 2.15; 4.23-24) or a new being (Col. 3.10). St. John in the Gospel holds that in Christ we become sons of God (St. Jn. 1.1-2; 4.14: 1 Jn. 3.1,2). Therefore, the function of religious language is not to *describe* any entity. It is a call and exhortation to *become* a thing of value. Quite naturally religious statements are not true or false. They are calculated to awaken a man into a newer and higher dimension of realization. They serve to regulate the believer's life and conduct. They are regulative of the whole man, as Kant and Wittgenstein would say. Patrick Sherry, thus states the views of Wittgenstein,

> Later on, in his Lectures on *Religious Belief* he (Wittgenstein) argued that the importance of religious beliefs does not lie in the proofs or reasoning which support them, but in the way they regulate our lives. For instance, if I believe in a Last Judgment, this is not a question of expecting a future event like a war, but of living with a certain picture before me and using this to influence my conduct. The question of evidence is irrelevant.... [40]

Religious language is an invitation 'to come and see for yourself', or 'taste the Lord and see that He is good'. In the end religious language is evocative and exhortative and living with a picture.

---

38. *The Philosophical and Religious Lectures*, p. 97.
39. *Vedanta: Voice of Freedom*, pp. 77, 78, 87.
40. *Religion, Truth and Language—Games*, p. 13.

CONCLUSION

1. Religious language is evocative with a view to deifying a believer as a thing of value, evolving him into his higher Self.

2. Religious statements cannot be assimilated to factual statements. They cannot be 'True or false or nonsense'. Hence, the attempts of A.G.N. Flew and A.J. Ayer in declaring theistic statements as vacuous or nonsense are irrelevant and off the track.

3. A religious entity is only a picture and deification of one's own ideal self into which the believer tries to mould himself.

4. Religious language of theism is really mythological, which gets constantly de-mythologized and refined in the light of changing world-view of the religious community.

Here also God is the real Self of a theist, which a believer tries to imitate and become.

CHAPTER VII

PROOFS FOR THE EXISTENCE OF GOD: THE ONTOLOGICAL ARGUMENT

INTRODUCTION

Proof may be either deductive or inductive. The deductive proof is best exemplified in a syllogism or mathematical reasoning. In both of them the conclusion follows necessarily from the premises. However, this necessity is only logical. The mathematical reasoning is purely *a priori* and consists in a consistent use of stipulated definitions of symbols. Naturally such a reasoning does not refer to any actual states of affairs. Such a necessity pertains to either tautologies or consistent use of words only. Hence, if we could establish a conclusion either syllogistically or mathematically, then this would have relevance with regard to words or definitions alone and will not have any relevance with regard to facts. Hence, if we could deductively prove the existence of God, then this conclusion will remain valid with regard to 'God' as a word or a stipulated definition of the term 'God'. But this will not establish the fact of God's existence of a personal Being.

If the existence of a personal God cannot be established deductively, then this cannot be done inductively either. (*a*) Inductive Proof starts from something observable and finally also applies to observables. But God is not an observable entity even in principle. The reason is that a God to be worshipful must be infinite and of surpassing excellence. However, an observable object can be limited to a certain span of space and time. Naturally a God who can be sensed or observed is not an infinite God of religion. Such an observable God becomes an idol. If it is so, then no inductive proof for the existence of an infinite and a personal God can be given.

(*b*) Further, if somehow we could proceed from the observable to the infinite God, then how can we establish a conclusion with regard to the existence of an infinite God from finite data? We shall find that according to the Cosmological Proof the world is *contingent* and God is a *necessary* Being. How can we prove the existence of a Necessary Being from the observed contingency of the world? The same difficulty will be raised in relation to the teleological proof for the existence of God. Of course, in the long history of religious thought many expedients have been devised. St. Thomas Aquinas is one of those religious giants who did smell the difficulty of proving an infinite God from finite data.[1] For obviating this difficulty St. Thomas Aquinas advanced the doctrine of *analogia entis*, according to which things pertaining to God can be established on the analogy of excellence found in finite things. In the estimate of competent thinkers the expedient of *analogia entis* has demonstrated more the difficulty of proving an ·infinite God from finite premises than solving it.

In recent years some powerful existential thinkers like Martin Buber (the late Jewish theologian) and Paul Tillich have shown that the world of our daily observation and science, being finite, *exhypothesis* does not contain God. Consequently no amount of observation of this world can yield any conclusion concerning God, either deductively or inductively.[2]

(c) At this stage another expedient has been advanced. It might be hazarded that God's existence is only an inductive hypothesis which can be either confirmed or disconfirmed by fresh facts.

Against this expedient of regarding God as an *inductive hypothesis*, several objections have been raised. True, Joshua on Mt. Carmel did try to establish the existence of Yahveh on the basis of an observable experiment.[3] Then even in Psalms[4] we find the statement,

'O taste and see that the Lord is good'.

---

1. Also St. Augustine was fully aware of the difficulty.
2. A. Macintyre, '*The logical status of religious belief*' in *Metaphysical Beliefs*, Edited by A. Macintyre and Ronald G. Smith, (SCM Press, 1957), pp. 195-96.
3. I. Kings, chap. 17.
4. Ps. 34:8.

But proving 'the invisible things' of God by the created things of the world[5] does not do full justice to the religious situation. If God were a hypothesis, then the religious attitude to him will be provisional. However, the belief in God is absolute and entire. The religious command is

'Thou shalt love the Lord thy God with all thy heart, with all thy soul, and with all thy mind.'[6]

Where is the room for tentativeness here? If so, then the believer will fall into the temptation of tempting the Lord.

Even if we suppose that God be taken as a hypothesis for which Laplace had no need, then how will this hypothesis be confirmed-disconfirmed? God is taken to be the creator of the whole universe; and, the universe is one. Consequently we cannot get a negative instance to disconfirm this hypothesis. The result would be that the theist and the sceptic will be resorting to the same facts within the universe. Might be that a theist would be emphasizing one set of phenomena and the sceptic quite another. But both the sets are well known to both of them. So they will be really differing not so much with regard to facts, but with regard to their *attitudes* to these facts. This will be seen most clearly in relation to the teleological argument for the existence of God. Because the theist appears to appeal to the phenomena of order, system and harmony in nature, and, the sceptic appears to show the blemishes, disorders and defects in nature, so it gives one the appearance that both of them are factually substantiating their conclusion. In reality, however, both of them are not appealing to facts, since besides this universe there is no other fact to which they can appeal. Both of them really differ in their attitude to nature. Their arguments are persuasive, but not demonstrative. Hence, in the logical sense, in the public language, they are not using any arguments at all. The appeal is to the same facts with contrasted attitudes. So the argument can never be factual. Therefore, it cannot be inductive either.

The difficulty of proving God was raised by Kierkegaard in

5. Romans 1:20.
6. St. Mt. 22:37.

the form of a dilemma. And this dilemma holds still for anybody who wants to prove the existence of God:

> The idea of demonstrating that this unknown something (God) exists, could scarcely suggest itself to the Reason. For if God does not exist it would of course be impossible to prove it; and if he does exist it would be folly to attempt it.[7]

The real strength of the dilemma lies in the fact that God exists only for the believer. And for becoming a believer a change in the person is necessary. The unbelieving eye cannot discuss God. The arguments do not establish the factuality of God directly. But they do this indirectly. They persuade the unbeliever to change his viewpoint; they help the philosophers to have an insight into the nature and aims of religious thinking and arguments. The so-called 'proofs' are really *pleas* for invoking-evoking religious bliks and attitudes. Words of Anselm (1033-1109) are still true in their existential import:

> For I do not seek to understand that I may believe, but I believe that I may understand (Credo ut intelligam).
> 'Belief' and 'seeing God' go together. Is this situation unintelligible?

Well, God is a personal Being and is believed to have created human beings with real responsibilities and free wills. Quite naturally his total situation must necessarily be fraught with actual and possible evils. Can such a personal God with our ambiguous situation be proved by philosophical arguments? There can be no experiential proof of God's existence, as was supposed to have had been provided for by Daniel's trials or Joshua's test on Mt. Carmel. If such tests were available, God will come to be accepted by the force of God's might or power.[8] Man will be subdued, silenced and hushed into the slavery of belief, but he

---

7. S. Kierkegaard, *'The Absolute Paradox'* in *'The Existence of God'*, Edited by John Hick, Problems of Philosophy Series, Macmillan, 1964, p. 211; see also J. Ballie, *Our knowledge of God*, p. 132.

8. God's 'Power' is always symbolic, theonomous and never physical or factual. *Vide* its analysis by R. Otto, 'The Idea of the Holy', chap. IV; see 2, pp. 20-22.

will not become an heir to the kingdom of God. Worse still, he might become a machine and would lose his freedom to believe in and trust a loving God. The deductive proof fares no better. In deduction the conclusion is implicitly contained in the premises, and follows from them of necessity. If there were such a proof, then there will be no unbeliever, since he has already tacitly assumed God in the premises.

Thus in this sense logic confirms what theology demands that there can be no proof of the existence of God that could be used to coerce, albeit intellectually, the unbelief into belief.[9]

We shall see that there are certain odd things about proving the existence of God. God is said to be a 'necessary being' and this is taken to be a self-contradictory phrase. 'Necessity' can be legitimately used with regard to stipulated definitions of symbols only. Again, any existing thing can be contingent only, and of anything existing we can always imagine it to be otherwise than what it is, and even the possibility of its not existing at all. If God exists, then He can also be imagined not to be existing at any time. As such 'necessary being' is a self-contradictory phrase. If He is necessary, then He is not a being and if He is a being, then He is not necessary. To say that God is a necessary being is as self-contradictory as a square circle is. However, these odd things would show themselves in our critical exposition of the different arguments for the existence of God.

There are several important arguments offered for the existence of God, namely, Ontological, Cosmological, Teleological, Moral and also some others. We shall take them one by one. We shall find that ontological argument is the nerve of all other arguments. Other arguments are so many pleas to support and supplement the conclusion of the ontological argument. The main contention of the ontological argument is that existence is

---

9. A. Macintyre, 'Difficulties in Christian Belief', SCM Press Ltd., 1959, p. 79; see also John Hick, 'Faith and Knowledge', Cornell University Press, 1957, p. 81. Here John Hick points out that if there could be any demonstrative proof, it could have hardly failed to gain general acceptance.

the very essence (Ontos) of the idea of God. This argument is *a priori*, since from the mere analysis of God-idea or the idea of perfect Being, we are deducing existence. This very contention is repeated by the Cosmological argument by adding a further step to it. It holds that the world is contingent and the contingent implies the necessary. And the idea of the necessary implies the necessary. And the idea of the necessary implies its existence. In the same way the teleological argument argues from the most complex and varied harmony in nature to the design in the mind of its Maker. Here also it is assumed that the Harmony in nature is contingent. From the contingency of infinitely complex harmony, the necessity of a designer is concluded. And again the idea of a necessary designer implies the existence of such a designer. The moral argument only adds the contingency of moral excellence to the presence of design in nature. Hence, ultimately all arguments rest their case on the efficiency of the Ontological argument according to which the idea of God carries its own existence as the very implication of the idea.

Further, the Ontological argument being *a priori* cannot establish any fact. Hence to remove this defect the Cosmological proof takes recourse to what is the most common of all the experienced characteristics of the things of the world, namely, its contingency. And from the contingency of the world, the existence of the necessary ground of the world is argued. But the contingency of the world is the most abstract quality of the worldly things and can hardly claim to be sensible. To remove this defect the Teleological argument has been advanced. This argument is based on the experienced quality of order and harmony, present everywhere in the world which meets even the most careless eye of any casual observer. The moral argument ultimately is based on the most palpably felt experience of man. Thus the empty content of the ontological argument is progressively filled up by the cosmological, teleological and moral arguments.

THE ONTOLOGICAL ARGUMENT

With these preliminaries, we can take up now the Ontological argument for the existence of God. The root of the argument is found in Plato (427-347 B.C.) and later on, more or less, in an explicit form it is found in the writings of St. Augustine (354-430 A.D.). In Plato, the 'ideas' were considered to be more important, more valuable and fundamental than the existing things. Further the idea of the Good, which for Plato is nothing less than God, was the supreme principle of reality that drew all things unto itself. Naturally, the idea of the Perfect Being carried with it its own self-validation and reality. For Plato, 'existence' was of not much value. However, for him, 'essence' was of greater worth than 'existence' and in this sense he would maintain the spirit of the Ontological argument. St. Augustine had accepted Platonism.[10] According to him doubt implies the knowledge of truth, since only for the sake of attaining truth does one doubt. Further, it belongs to the essence of truth that it is or exists. Again the being or existence of all universal truths lies in God alone in the form of ideas:

> ......in Thee abide, fixed for ever, the first courses of all things unabiding; and of all things changeable, the springs abide in Thee unchangeable: and in Thee live the eternal reasons of all things unreasoning and temporal.[11]

And of course God cannot be imagined without being. But this argument was most clearly stated by Anselm (1033-1109). Later on it was re-stated by Rene Descares (1596-1650). This argument was also accepted by G.F. Leibniz (1646-1716), by G.W.F. Hegel (1770-1831) and John Caird (1820-1898). However, there have been powerful opponents of the Ontological argument as well, namely, St. Thomas Aquinas (1225-1274) and I. Kant (1724-1804). In contemporary religious philosophy the Ontological argument has been keenly debated by Prof. A.J. Ayer, J.J.C. Smart, A.G.N. Flew, J.N. Findlay and Norman Malcolm.

ANSELM'S ARGUMENT

It is to be remembered that Anselm never meant his argument to be a demonstration from which it is not possible for the atheist to escape. He took recourse to the proof with a view to streng-

---

10. *The confessions of St. Augustine*, Pocket Books, Cardinal edition (1952), p. 120; see also pp. 240 ff. for his Platonic teaching.
11. *Ibid.*, p. 5.

thening his faith and justifying one's belief in God. For him faith is a necessary precondition of understanding God. Anselm has given his proof in two separate pieces and they have to be interpreted jointly for a correct appraisal of the argument. For him God is a Being greater than whom nothing can be thought. But such a Being can be either in thought or in fact as well as in thought.

> For it is one thing for an object to be in the understanding, and another thing to understand that it exists......But clearly that than which a greater cannot be thought cannot exist in the understanding alone. For if it is actually in the understanding alone, it can be thought of as existing also in reality, and this is greater. Therefore, if that than which is greater cannot be thought is in the understanding alone, this same thing than which a greater cannot be thought is that than which a greater can be thought. But obviously this is impossible. Without doubt, therefore, there exists, both in the understanding and in reality, something than which a greater cannot be thought.[12]

Anselm does not analytically express his arguments. What does the phrase 'existing in the understanding alone' mean? It may mean several of the following propositions:

(a) That which is imaginary.
(b) That which is purely conceptual or notional.
(c) That which is an empirical concept.
(d) That something exists in the understanding simply may mean that it is understood or grasped by the understanding.[13] In that case it will come under any one of the above-mentioned meanings.

Again, what does the phrase 'that which exists in reality' mean? 'Reality' is a very indefinite and ambiguous word: (i) it may mean that which is worthy of trust, meditation or has some

---

12. St. Anselm, '*The Ontological Argument*' in EG, p. 26.
13. Wallace, I. Matson, 'The existence of God', Cornell University Press, 1965, pp. 47-48.

such emotive significance, it may also mean an *Idea* which is real and eternal in Platonic sense, or (*ii*) it may mean that which can be sensed as an actual entity or 'that something is the case'. In the main part of the argument, Anselm uses the phrase 'existing in the understanding' in the sense of pure thoughts or concepts, i.e. in the sense of (*b*). In this sense, we can compare the two concepts, namely,

(*i*) That which can be thought in understanding only, and
(*ii*) That which can be thought both in understanding and in 'reality' in the sense of 'that something is the case'.

But here the argument is purely conceptual and there is no reference to anything which exists, for the *thought* of something existing is not the same thing as *something existing*. However, the conclusion is not about a conceptual entity only. The conclusion is that which exists both in the understanding and in reality as 'That something is the case' or as an actual entity. We can thus summarise the argument of Anselm.

God is a Being than whom nothing greater can be conceived. A Being which exists both in fact and in mind is greater than a Being which exists in mind only. Therefore, God not only exists in mind but also in fact. So God exists. In other words, actual existence is the very essence of 'a Being greater' than whom nothing can be conceived. This point has been stated more rigorously in the other statement of the Ontological argument by Anselm. Can a fool say in his heart that there is no God? Yes, it is possible if God can either be existing or non-existing. But can God be conceived even in bare thought not to be existing? No.

For no one who understands what God is can think that God does not exist even though he says these words in his heart—perhaps without any meaning, perhaps with some quite extraneous meaning. For God is that than which a greater cannot be thought, and whoever understands this rightly must understand that he exists in such a way that he cannot be non-existent even in thought. He, therefore, who understands that God thus exists cannot think of him as non-existent.[14]

In other words, Anselm holds that a Being whose non-existence is logically impossible is greater than whose non-existence is logically possible. And the non-existence of God is logically impossible because it is the highest notion.

We can analyse the main points of the Ontological argument given by Anselm in the following way.

God is an object of worship and to be worshipful God must be the highest or greater than whom nothing can be conceived. Secondly, existence is a state of the highest perfection or excellence. Hence, in some sense, existence may also be conceived as a predicate or quality like omnipotence, omniscience. Thirdly, a distinction has to be made between a contingent existence and necessary existence; God is necessary existence. Hence, the non-existence of God cannot be even thought. Therefore, the necessary existence of God is contained in the very notion of a Being greater than whom nothing can be conceived. It would be self-contradictory to deny existence of God.

According to Anselm 'existence' is some quality. This is also clear from the fact that Anselm holds, that 'a Being in thought and also in fact' is greater than a Being in thought alone. Now the term 'greater' can be legitimately used with regard to material things only; it cannot be meaningfully used with regard to two ideas belonging to different levels of language, one in fact and the other in thought. There is some meaning in saying that future teachers will be better if they be more informed than when they are not so informed. But it would be meaningless to say that future teachers will be better if they exist than when they do not exist. Hence, Gassendi appears to have anticipated Kant in objecting to Descarte's Ontological argument.

Existence is a perfection neither in God nor in anything else;..............[15]

We shall find that Anselm was also aware of the meaning of the terms 'existence' in which sense 'existence' cannot be treated

14. John Hick, *op. cit.*, p. 27
15. NEPT, pp. 51-52.

as a predicate or a quality. However, by 'existence' is meant value or worth. Hence when Anselm says that the idea of God in thought and fact is greater than the idea of God in thought alone, then by 'greater' he means 'more valuable or worthier'. This of course is also in keeping with the ordinary usage of the term. We contrast the more enduring things with transitory things. In this sense, God is said to be everlasting or even eternal and in contrast worshippers are taken to be like the grass which today is and tomorrow is cast into the oven. Hence, Anselm means that an existing God is more valuable than a non-existing God. As God is a Being greater than whom nothing can exist, so a non-existing God being less valuable cannot be an object of worship. Hence, God being an object of worship is most valuable and so can be conceived as existing only.

But it is not enough to say that God can be conceived as existing only. Existence may be either contingent or necessary. God may be conceived as a Being who happens to be existing or even to be existing everlastingly. But any object which merely happens to exist may also be imagined not to exist. Even if God be conceived to be existing everlastingly, then it means that God somehow has come or merely happens to be such. One can imagine such an everlasting God not to be existing at all. Further, God has happened to exist everlastingly, then it means that somehow God has been caused by something else or else depends on prior circumstances. However, a God to be worshipful must be infinite or unlimited. Hence, God cannot be conceived to be existing contingently. He can be conceived only as logically or necessarily existing. God is not everlasting, i.e. which contingently lasts for ever, but which is durationless or eternal or timeless. So Yahweh calls himself 'I am that I am'; He is the same today, tomorrow and for ever, i.e. He does necessarily endure. Hence, God has necessary existence.

CRITICAL COMMENTS

That a God is a Being who is worshipped and that to be worshipful. He must be infinite, eternal and perfect was never explicitly stated and so was never disputed at least by those religious thinkers who tried to refute the Ontological argument. For example,

Kant criticised the Ontological argument most thoroughly but he always presupposed that the concept of God is *ens realissimum* which is a union of a necessary being and perfection. Later on, and in quite a different context, J.S. Mill, W. James, J. Ward, J.M.E. McTaggart have advanced the view concerning the worshipfulness of a finite God. Hence, they have denied that God as an object of worship can only be infinite and perfect. But the critics of the Ontological argument have not objected to the perfection or infinitude of God. So in a critical appraisal of the Ontological argument given by Anselm, Descartes, J. Caird and Norman Malcolm we shall not raise any objection with regard to the idea of a perfect Being who alone can be considered as the legitimate object of worship. Most of the criticisms have been directed against the concept of 'God's existence' and His 'necessary Being', and, we shall take up each one of them.

First, it is pointed out that the very questions, 'Does God exist?', 'Can His existence be proved?' show that God is an entity that we know or think doesn't exist, because we ask such questions only with regard to such beings as fairies, unicorns, ghosts which ordinarily we think don't exist. We do not ask such questions with regard to familiar objects like tables or chairs. According to Thomas McPherson it is nonsense to ask: Do tables or chairs exist? So by asking the question, 'Does God exist?', according to Thomas McPherson, we bring God under the class of those things which we know don't exist. True, the notion of God is more psychologically important than that of fairies or ghosts, but logically, from the viewpoint of linguistic usage of the term 'exist', there is no distinction between Unicorn, Ghosts and God.

Of course, there are differences between God and fairies— notably that the existence of the first is maintained much more vehemently than the existence of the second; but all I want to do here is to make the general point as strongly as I can—ignoring qualifications—that the significance of 'God exists' suggests that God is the same sort of *things* as fairies and unicorns, and not the same sort of *things* as chairs and tables. We say something 'exists' when it is in another place (or 'place') from that where we are, or is unfamiliar to us (unexperienced by us); and the things that belong in these classes are pre-eminently things that *don't* exist (like fairies and unicorns).[16]

Few thinkers would accept this linguistic refutation of God's existence. Certainly we do ask questions concerning many objects which we know do exist, e.g. Are there enemies of India? Of course, we know how to verify such statements; whereas in the same way we cannot straightaway proceed to verify the question with regard to God's existence. The difference between God and fairies is not merely psychological. They belong to different languages of discourse. The linguistic usage of a concept in an ordinary language cannot be validly applied to a concept in a symbolic language, or rather to a symbol in a convictional language. This lesson has not been learnt even by Norman Malcolm who defends Ontological proof against the current analysis of the Ontological argument. In our opinion there can be no defence of the Ontological argument if we continue to talk in the language of science. This is an important statement and so a detailed criticism of the Ontological argument has to be mentioned here.

It is pointed out that the Ontological argument is highly fallacious, because it treats 'existence' as a property or predicate. Now red or green, ferocious or tame are real qualities or properties of things. We can say that a so-and-so has this or that property, e.g. we can say that this tree is green or this dog is tame. But can we say that a so-and-so has existence as its property? We can certainly classify dogs into ferocious and tame, but can we classify them into existing dogs and non-existing dogs? If non-existing dogs do not form a new species of dogs, then it shows that existence does not add anything to the meaning of a concept. An existing hundred rupee note means a note that contains hundred rupees and a non-existing hundred rupee note also means a note that contains hundred rupees. So far as the word 'a hundred rupee note' is concerned its meaning continues to be

---

16. Thomas Mcpherson, *Can the verification principle be applied to Christian doctrines* ? in *Readings in Religious Philosophy*, Edited by MacGregor and Robb, p. 367. Originally the article appeared in *Mind*, Vol. LIX, 1950,

the same whether that currency note be an actual one or an imagined one. This was pointed out by Kant and is still conceived to be a valid objection against treating 'existence' as a predicate.

> *'Being'* is obviously not a real predicate; that is, it is not a concept of something which would be added to the concept of a thing. It is merely the positing of a thing, or of certain determinations as existing in themselves. Logically it is merely the copula of a judgement. The proposition, 'God is omnipotent', contains two concepts, each of which has its object —God and omnipotence. The small word 'is' adds no new predicate, but only serves to posit the predicate *in its relation* to the subject.[17]

Therefore, 'God is' or 'God exists' does not add anything to the meaning of the concept 'God'.

The mistake arises from linguistic confusion. Because 'exist' is used in sentences in the same way as other verbs, so we think that sentences having 'exist' as a verb is of the same nature as sentences expressing attributes. 'God exists' and 'God loves' have both a noun and a verb. As they have the same grammatical form, so we take them to be of the same logical type. Now God must exist in order to love. So in the same manner the analysis of 'God exists' is God must exist in order to exist. But is it not a pure tautology? So 'God exists' is not a proper sentence, for 'being or existence' is not a predicate. As a matter of fact 'God is' is an incomplete sentence. It requires a proper predicate, e.g. 'God is omniscient or loving'.

If, on the other hand, we grant that 'existence' is a real property as 'loving', 'kind' or 'tame' is, then like all other properties it would be contingent. Just as we can think of a cow as not being either black or tame or ferocious, so we can also think of God as not having the property of 'existence'. All contingent properties can be given by experience alone and sentences containing them can be synthetic only.[18]

---

17. Immanual Kant's 'Critique of Pure Reason', translated by N.K. Smith, Abridged Edition, Macmillan & Co., 1934, p. 282.
18. *Ibid.*, p. 281.

If therefore 'existence' is a real property, then there is no contradiction in holding that God does not exist.

However, it must be conceded that Anselm too was aware that thought is not a thing, or, wishes are not objects, otherwise beggars would ride horses. Anselm grants to Gaunilo that we can conjure up the idea of an island and corresponding to this idea there may not be any island.[19] But Anselm adds that the 'idea of God' is quite different from any other idea where existence and idea may not go together. All other ideas may be conceived not to be existing. But he adds that the idea of a perfect Being is such that it carries necessary being with it. It is the idea of a Being greater than whom nothing can exist and as such it is an idea corresponding to which a being logically or necessarily exists. It has not to be equated with any other ordinary idea which has *possible* existence but not necessary existence. Keeping the distinction between necessary existence and possible or contingent existence Anselm writes:

> For although none of the things that exist can be understood not to exist, still they can all be thought of as nonexistent, except that which most fully is. For all those things and only those—which have a beginning or end or are composed of parts can be thought of as non-existent, along with anything that does not exist as a whole anywhere or at any time (as I have already said). But the only being that cannot be thought of as non-existent is that in which no thought finds beginning or end or composition of parts, but which any thought finds as a whole, always and everywhere......

So, then, it is peculiar to God to be unable to be thought of as non-existent......[20]

At this stage Norman Malcolm quotes the objection of the priest Caterus to the demonstration of Descartes according to which demonstration the existence of God follows from the very idea of a Perfect Being.

"Though it be conceded that an entity of the highest perfec-

---

19. John Hick, 'The Existence of God', pp. 27-28
20. EG, p. 29.

tion implies its existence by its very name, yet it does not follow that very existence is anything actual in the real world, but merely that the concept of existence is inseparably united with the concept of highest being. Hence you cannot infer that the existence of God is anything actual, unless you assume that that highest being actually exists; for then it will actually contain all its perfections, together with this perfection of real existence.[21]

It is pointed out that 'necessary' existence is not merely possible existence, but something quite actual. Earlier it has been stated that Anselm regards the denial of existence to necessary being as self-contradictory. However, the very phrase *necessary being*, from the time of Kant up to the present time, is considered to be self-contradictory. The reason is that 'necessary' can be legitimately used of *propositions* only and not of *things*. A proposition is said to be necessary when words employed in it are consistently used in accordance with their stipulated definitions. Whereas, any existing thing can always be imagined to be otherwise than what it is. Therefore, if a thing exists, it is merely contingent and not necessary; and, if anything is said to be necessary, it reflects only the use of words and not of things. Therefore, a being can only be contingent and not necessary. Hence, to say that a being necessarily exists is as self-contradictory as a round square.[22] This was clearly stated by Kant:

> There is already a contradiction in introducing the concept of existence—no matter under what title it may be disguised —into the concept of a thing which we profess to be thinking solely in reference to its possibility............But if, on the other hand, we admit, as every reasonable person must that

21. John Hick, 'The existence of God', p. 63.
22. This view has been accepted by a number of contemporary philosophers:
     G. Ryle, 'The Nature of Metaphysics' ed. by D.F. Pears (N.Y. 1957),
     p. 150; I.M. Crombie, 'New Essays in Philosophical Theology', Ed. A.
     Flew & Macintyre, p. 144; J.J.C. Smart, *op. cit.*, pp. 34, 38-39; K.E.M.
     Baier, 'The meaning of life', Canberra University, 1957, p. 8; J.H.
     Findlay, 'New Essays in Philosophical Theology', pp. 52-56; B. Russell,
     'A debate on the existence of God' by B. Russell and F.C. Copleston
     in *The existence of God*, ed. by John Hick, pp. 169-72.

all existential proposition are synthetic, how can we profess
to maintain that the predicate of existence cannot be rejected
without contradiction? This is a feature which is found only
in analytic propositions, and is indeed precisely what constitutes their analytic character.[23]

Norman Malcolm would not accept this criticism. He thinks
that the contention that every existential proposition is contingent, is only *a priori*; whereas, according to him, necessary existence is essential to Judaeo-Christian religious language. Hence,
according to Norman Malcolm, every existential proposition
need not be contingent.

I believe we may rightly take the existence of those religious
systems of thought in which God figures as a necessary being
to be a disproof of the dogma, affirmed by Hume and others,
that no existential proposition can be necessary.[24]

The same defence has been taken up by A.C.A. Rainer[25] and
G.E. Hughes.[26] The contention of Norman Malcolm and G.E.
Hughes has an element of truth. The element of truth is that
such a language is possible in which we can meaningfully use the
phrase 'necessary being'. But this language is religious or convictional. If we understand the phrase in the depersonalised
language of science, then it is wholly meaningless, nonsense and
self-contradictory. Norman Malcolm correctly points out that
it is meaningfully used in the religious language of Judaeo-Christian tradition; A.C.A. Rainer holds that necessary being is a
matter of Divine knowledge and religious mysticism.[27] Hughes
clearly states that the distinction of empirical and necessary is
legitimate and very valuable for scientific language, but he adds:

What I protest against is its extension—or worse still, the
conviction that it *must* be extended—beyond its natural, legi-

23. PR, p. 281.
24. John Hick, '*The existence of God*', p. 62.
25. *New Essays in Philosophical Theology*, pp. 68-69.
26. *Ibid.*, pp. 59-61.
27. *Ibid.*, pp. 68-69.

timate sphere, which is that of scientific and everyday statements about the 'natural world', to a sphere which it was
never devised to cope with.[28]

The sin of most of the defenders of the Ontological argument
and of the whole army of critics is that they treat the Ontological argument as an argument in science. In reality, this argument is in convictional language whose main aim is to evoke-
invoke the numinous experience. Judged as an argument in the
scientific language, the Ontological proof fails. By mere analysis
of the words employed, one cannot obtain factuality, which is a
matter of experience alone. By conjuring up the words 'necessary being' in the most *a priori* manner, one cannot hope to reach
any actual state of affairs. From the concept 'existent round
square', one cannot infer that there is actually a round square.[29]
It is the same thing which has been attempted in the Cosmological argument, though covertly, according to Kant. By having
the concept of *ens realissimum*, we cannot infer the existence of a
necessary being.[30] But the argument does not aim at scientifically
proving any actual being: it aims at expressing formally the un-
shakable conviction of the religious believers in God's existence.

> The religious believer finds himself unshakably convinced
> of the divine existence; his vision of the universe engages his
> imagination so powerfully that he cannot envisage the non-
> existence of God as a genuine possibility.[31]

After all Anselm is trying to justify his faith in God. His God is
an object worthy of worship, i.e. to whom the entire personality
is unreservedly surrendered—whose service is considered the
highest freedom through commitment to whom the worshipper
realises his authentic being. Quite naturally such a Being cannot
be imagined not to exist even for a moment. The *necessary* existence of God is a matter of deciding to be an authentic self. The

---

28. *Ibid.*, p. 61; also cp. Thomas Mcpherson, *op. cit.*, p. 142.
29. B. Russell in *The Existence of God*, Edited by J. Hick, p. 172.
30. PR, p. 289.
31. A. Macintyre, 'Difficulties in Christian Belief', p. 63.

necessity of God's existence is not a matter of logical necessity, but it expresses the involvement of the total personality,—it is the cry of the whole man, the highest crescendo of the chorus, 'God exists, hallelujah; God exists, hallelujah'. After all, Anselm at the very beginning of his proof wrote:

> I do not seek to understand that I may believe, but I believe that I may understand. For this too I believe, that unless I first believe I shall not understand.

Thus belief, commitment and self-involvement spell out the real significance of the ontological argument.

'The Being greater than whom nothing can be conceived to exist' is a perfect Being, a Being most worthy of being worshipped. And such a Being cannot be conceived not to exist. We must not forget that for Anselm God is interpreted as 'the truest and highest', 'the Creator', *better* than whom nothing can exist.[32] This means that Anselm is interested in God as a Being who is most worthy of worship. In this sense, that which exists in 'reality' simply means that which is most worthy of worship and trust. Naturally in this sense, 'God exists in reality' is an emotive statement or may be a prescriptive statement. In this case, God will not be an imaginary concept, nor a pure concept and certainly not an empirical concept. Any statement concerning an object which is worshipful becomes valuative or axiological. Now can we compare a God which exists in the understanding with a God which exists in reality in the sense of an object of trust and worship? Can we say that one is *greater* than another? Quite obviously we are not making a quantitative comparison. If there is any comparison at all, once again it is axiological. Stated thus the argument is not really cognitive, but axiological. Nay, the whole argument of Anselm is really symbolical. 'God' for Anselm is a Judaeo-Christian God who has revealed himself to the Patriarchs and Prophets and had become incarnate in Jesus Christ. Anselm was seized firmly by this symbol of God and this symbol so completely possessed him that he could not imagine himself to be without it. For this reason he believed that such a God cannot be imagined not to be existing even for a moment. This

---

32. EG, pp. 26-27.

indicates Anselm's existential decision and commitment to such a Being. Even Descartes, Leibniz and Spinoza have made in the end the same symbolic statement. For Anselm God who is a Being greater than whom nothing can be conceived to be existing is a necessary Being, and a necessary Being cannot but exist. This is what Descartes tried to hold by saying that existence follows from the idea of an infinite, independent, all-knowing, all-powerful Being. Just as the conclusion that all the angles of a triangle are together equal to two right angles follows from the definition of a triangle, so the existence of God follows from the very idea of Him.[33] According to Descartes, we cannot conceive God without existence, it follows that existence is inseparable from Him, and hence that He really exists. Descartes himself antici- pates an objection. It might be conceded that one cannot think of a hill without a valley, but certainly from this it does not follow that there *is* any hill in the world. Similarly it appears, not to follow, says Descartes, from his thinking of God as exis- tent that God does exist. Descartes rejects this objection. He tells us that one can think of a hill not to exist, but one cannot even think of God as non-existent.

> I am not free to think of God apart from existence (that is, of a supremely perfect being apart from the supreme perfec- tion) in the way that I can freely imagine a horse either with or without wings.[34]

But why? By 'God' is meant a substance, infinite, all-powerful and so on.

> But these properties are so great and excellent that the more attentively I consider them the less I feel persuaded that the idea I have of them owes its origin to myself alone.[35]

And thus it is absolutely necessary to conclude that God exists. It is the power of the symbol in the form of the Christian God

---

33. Meditation V, p. 103 in *Descartes*, Edited by Anscombe and Geach, Nelson, 1963.
34. *Ibid.*, p. 104.
35. *Ibid.*, p. 105.

that would not allow Descartes to think that essence and existence can be separated in God. A supremely perfect Being cannot be imagined to be devoid of existence.

Again, Leibniz was very much influenced by the Ontological
argument which is phrased like this. Each possible thing has the
right to aspire to existence in proportion to the amount of perfection it contains in germ. Since God is most perfect, therefore,
he necessarily exists. E.L. Mascall raises two objections against
this proof. First, according to Mascall there can be no common
measure of perfection by means of which the possibility of various things can be determined. Secondly, the whole of hierarchical series of Monads has a greatest number.[36] The objection appears to me just from the cognitive point of view. But a 'perfect
God' is a symbol to which Leibniz is committed. Such a perfect
God is *power* which is the source of all, also *knowledge* whose
content is the variety of the ideas, and, finally *will* which effects
changes according to the principle of the best. The same existential and symbolic interpretation is true of Spinoza's Ontological argument.

The whole argument of Spinoza is geometrical. Necessarily
this is not suited to prove any actuality of anything. The geometrical deduction is only a matter of definitions, axioms and
postulates. In the same manner if we define God in a certain
manner, then his existence too will follow necessarily. Now the
existence of God follows necessarily, if we follow Spinoza's definitions of substance and God.

> Substance, "is that which is in itself and is conceived through
> itself: I mean that, the conception of which does not depend
> on the conception of another thing from which it must be
> formed.........God I understand to be a being absolutely
> infinite, that is, a substance consisting of infinite attributes
> each of which expresses eternal and infinite essence."

Now if substance is going to be a self-contained whole, then there
can be only one substance. Again, for Spinoza, God is a substance the idea of which involves its own existence. True, here

---

36. *Existence and Analogy*, A Libra Book, 1966, p. 34.

'existence' will hardly be called a fact or 'some thing is the case'. It is purely notional. But does Spinoza mean by God a mere term to be defined according to one's convenience? No, Spinoza is a God-intoxicated mystic. For him the mind's highest good is the knowledge of God. And God does not love or hate. Therefore, he who loves God does not expect that God would reciprocate. But by our knowledge of God we know that all things follow necessarily from God and this kind of knowledge should give us delight under all vicissitudes of life. From this kind of knowledge arises, according to Spinoza, the highest possible mental acquiescence,

> ...the wise man, in so far as he is regarded as such, is scarcely at all disturbed in spirit, but, being conscious of himself, and of God, and of things, by a certain eternal necessity never ceases to be, but always possesses true acquiescence of his spirit.

Can such an equanimity of mind follow by meditation on a word 'God', can the necessity of things be merely the consequence of our use of stipulated words? The statement of Spinoza is symbolic, convictional and is an echo of his total personality surcharged with the intellectual love of God.

CHAPTER VIII

COSMOLOGICAL ARGUMENT

INTRODUCTION

If 'God' is a real proper name with his own appropriate attributes then God would be an actual entity. But if it so, then as Hume pointed out,[1] it is absured to demonstrate a matter of fact by any *a priori* argument. For this reason we can say that the Ontological argument has failed, because it is purely *a priori* and analytic. Hence, one has to take recourse to actual states of affairs, which are based on some verifiable experience. And this is what is proposed to be achieved by the Cosmological argument.

In its elementary form the Cosmological argument was first formulated by Plato (428/7 B.C. to 348/7 B.C.) in *Laws* and *Phaedrus*.[2] Later on, Aristotle (384-322 B.C.) stated it quite clearly. Afterwards it is held that St. Thomas Aquinas (1224/5-1274), regarded it as the central argument for proving God. At the present time F.C. Copleston has commented on Thomas Aquinas and in this connection, he holds that Neo-Thomists wrongly think that for Aquinas the Cosmological argument is the most important argument.[3] Nevertheless he himself has made much of the argument in the two debates concerning the existence of God.[4] Further, E.L. Mascall does take the Cosmological argument as the one single argument which underlies all the Five Ways of proving God.[5] According to Mascall 'Five Ways' call attention to the five outstanding characteristics of finite beings which at bottom can be reduced to one, namely, all finite things

---

1. David Hume, from *Dialogues Concerning Natural Religion*, in *The Existence of God*, Edited by John Hick, p. 96.
2. E.G., pp. 71-79.
3. John Hick, *op. cit.*, p. 92.
4. John Hick, 'The Existence of God', Part II (B. Russell and F.C. Copleston, 1948); and, A.J. Ayer and F.C. Copleston, 1949 in *Readings in Religious Philosophy*, Edited by MacGregor/Robb.
5. *Existence and Analogy*, Chap. IV.

have their essence distinct from existence. In such a case their existence is not self-maintaining. Hence they require a source in which essence and existence are identical, namely, God. In other words, finite beings manifest their radical dependence on God: they are effect-implying-cause.[6]

The Cosmological argument is usually expressed in two forms, namely, in the form of Causal argument and in the form of argument from Contingency. The former is not the most important form of the Cosmological argument, but this cannot be omitted since thinkers have made use of it. We shall pay a much greater attention to the argument from Contingency. At present we shall deal with the Causal form of the Cosmological argument.

CAUSAL ARGUMENT

It has the following steps:

1. Every event has a cause, and no event in the world can be without a cause.
2. Events keep on happening. The present event A is caused by the previous event B, and B in turn by C, and, C in turn by D, and so on.
3. Quite obviously the causal series is interminable. But in order to understand the whole series of cause and effect, we have to posit a First Cause which in its turn does not imply its further cause.
4. This First Cause which produces the whole series of causes and effects is the Mover only and cannot be in turn moved by anything else. This Prime Mover may be called God.
5. Hence, the world of causal series requires God to explain it. Thus God exists as its own cause and in turn as the cause of the world.

St. Thomas did not use the concept of Causality in the modern scientific sense, but in the Aristotelian sense of efficient causality with some end in view. Hence this world has to be taken as an effect of an efficient First Cause which determines means and ends for the final End. Here the concept does not mean a mere

---

6. *Ibid.*, p. 71.

mechanical antecedent of an event. Here there is the Aristotelian concept of God as an architect having some design. Hence, the effect fully reflects the nature of design fashioned out of pre-existing matter, and, the First Cause is supposed to be more perfect than the world designed by it as the Prime Mover. Hence the Cosmological Argument has to be read along with the fourth and fifth proofs for the existence of God.

The popularity of the argument really depends on a question which implies the Teleological argument. The question is: Can this world exist by itself as an accidental self-regulating system? Ordinarily, people think that the world cannot be a self-regulative system and so they search for the Maker of the world. In ancient time the mythical thinking was the rule, so naturally they looked upon the whole world as governed and controlled by a personal Being. Later on, even though much demythologising did take place with the development of scientific thinking, yet it lurked in the background sustained by the scientific postulate itself, namely, all events are intelligible and causal. So the theist thought that the scientific postulate permitted him to deny the possibility of the world being a self-regulative system. But as against the theologian as a matter of fact the causal postulate would allow that the world is a self-regulating system. Consequently, there is no logical need for assuming a First Cause. And even when we have to search for the *cause* of the world, hardly anybody today would hold that this cause is the Personal God of theism. The world is impersonal and its cause, if any, can be impersonal only.

Again, 'every event must have a cause' is only a procedural assumption of science. In itself it is neither true nor false: it is either useful or useless. This proposal has been designed to explain the series of *particular events* of the world. At the present time even this proposal has been dropped with regard to subatomic events. So this proposal cannot be universally accepted. Further, can the world be regarded as an event? It would be called an event if there is the possibility of recording the coming into and going out of being of this world. Quite obviously so far as the human beings are concerned on this earth, they have not witnessed the coming into being of this world. Naturally they cannot regard the world as an event: rather the world is the sum of all actual and possible events. Hence, the world is not an event. So the causal postulate is not applicable to the universe as a whole.

The same point was raised by Kant. According to him, the category of causality is applicable to phenomena only. The world as a whole is not a perceptible phenomenon. Naturally for Kant causality cannot be meaningfully applied to the world as a whole.[7] Reichenbach has put the same thing in the current language thus. According to him, a word is meaningful in one context, but may cease to be so in another. For example, one can meaningfully ask about the fatherhood of Ram or Shyam, but is the word 'father' meaningful in 'could there be a father who never had a child?'

> Everyone would ridicule a philosopher who regarded this question as a serious problem. The question of the cause of the first event, or of the cause of the universe as a whole, is not of a better type. The word 'cause' denotes a relation between two things and is inapplicable if only one thing is concerned. The universe as a whole has no cause, since by definition, there is nothing outside it that could be its cause. Questions of this type are empty verbalism rather than philosophic argument.[8]

Hence Russell holds that every event has a cause, but the totality need not have any. For example, he tells us that we can say that every human being has a parent, but certainly we cannot say that humanity too has a parent.[9] Causality with regard to specific events and causality concerning the universe as a totality of events, belong to two different types of statements. Prof. G. Ryle[10] would call this a 'category-mistake' which consists in using a category in one context when it actually belongs to another range of facts. Hence, the category of causality cannot be meaningfully applied to the totality of events.

---

7. P.R., pp. 255-57; and more clearly on pp. 288-89.
8. H. Reichenbach, *The Rise of Scientific Philosophy*, University of California Press, 1951, p. 280.
9. *The Existence of God*, p. 175.
10. G. Ryle, *The Concept of Mind*, Hutchinson's University Library, 1950, pp. 16f.

However, if by First Cause we understand the first member of the whole series of causes and effects, then we can always legitimately ask for the further cause of this First Cause. Under the circumstances there is no point in holding that the First Cause is without any cause. And, if the First Cause be without any further cause, then quite clearly we are holding that every event need not have a cause, at least inasmuch as the First Cause has no cause. This would be the denial of the principle of causality itself on which the Causal argument is based.

The whole argument is based on the wrong assumption that since the series is infinite it must have a beginning. The very meaning of the infinite series of causes and effects is that however remote we proceed backwards there will always be other events remoter still. It does not imply any absolute beginning. Hence, there is no point in holding that there is a First Cause of which there is no other cause. E.L. Mascall denies that the interpretation of the argument concerning the First Mover refers to infinite regress. God, according to St. Thomas, observes E.L. Mascall is not the First Cause, i.e. the first in the series of causes. God, according to Mascall, is the very source of actualization from the first moment of finite beings to their final stage. God does not merely initiate the motion, but sustains it. The term 'unmoved' mover simply indicates that the motion of finite things cannot be explained except through a being which is radically different from finite things.[11]

But really the Cosmological Argument is not merely Causal, because all causes are merely contingent. Even if we grant that heat is the cause of expansion, we can still ask the question: Why should heat expand and not contract? So now we have to explain the cosmological argument from the contingency of the world.

THE ARGUMENT FROM CONTINGENCY
The assumption of the cosmological argument from contingency is that *existence* is prior to *essence* or *idea*. Here it is maintained that essence and existence are identical. The assertion of Aquinas in this context is that the existence of God is not implied by God's essence, but that God's essence is the same as his existence.

---

11. E. L. Mascall, *Existence and Analogy*, A Libra Book, pp. 72-75.

Hence, according to this way of thinking we should not say that there must be a Perfect Being because we have an idea of Him: on the contrary, we should say that we have an idea of Him because He exists. Further, such a Being must not be a bare possibility, but an actuality. The reason is that such a Being has to explain the world as its ground and only an actuality can serve as the explanation and origin of the world, and bare possibility cannot. Both these points have been mentioned by Plato and Aristotle.

Aquinas starts with the most familiar aspect of the world, namely, things continuously come into being and pass away. Hence, there are some contingent things in the world. A thing is said to be contingent when there is nothing in the nature of the thing itself to guarantee its perpetual existence, or, more simply a thing is contingent when it does not have the ground of its own existence. It is therefore capable of non-existing, and at some time does not exist. True, the series of contingent events may continue for ever. But the point is, if a contingent event cannot exist by itself, then the world as consisting by itself, then the world as consisting of contingent events requires a Necessary Being as the ground of contingent happenings.

Here the main point of the argument is that something contingent cannot come out of Nothing. Hence something called contingent events must have come out of something which is not ultimately Nothing, but a Necessary Being. Now the fact is there are some contingent things in the world.

> But it is impossible for these always to exist, for that which is possible not to be at some time is not. Therefore, if everything is possible not to be, then at one time there could have been nothing in existence. Now if this were true, even now there would be nothing in existence, because that which does not exist only begins to exist by something already existing. Therefore, if at one time nothing was in existence, it would have been impossible for anything to have begun to exist, and thus even now nothing would be in existence—which is absurd. Therefore, not all beings are merely possible, but there must exist something the existence of which is necessary.[12]

---

12. St. Thomas Aquinas, *How God may be known through natural reason*, in

Further, Aquinas adds that this necessity is not dependent on any other being, but on itself. Hence, this necessary being is called God.

Here one can very easily see the influence of Plato according to whom there is a self-moved motion called soul which is the ground of every other motion but is itself its own ground. However, Aquinas took the help of Aristotle's notion of the Prime Mover or Pure Actuality which is its own ground and reason and is actual by virtue of its own essence.

The supreme assumption of the Cosmological argument is that the contingent world stands in need of philosophical explanatioi.. The problem therefore is: 'why things are as they are'.

But I ask why there are phenomena at all, why there is 'something' rather than 'nothing'.[13]

If this be granted to be a legitimate question, then it can be satisfactorily answered, according to Aquinas, only by positing the existence of a necessary Being. The argument of Aquinas can be more simply put into the following steps:

1. All the things of the world are contingent, that is one by one each of them at one time can pass away.
2. In the infinite series of time, all things, one by one, at one time should have ceased to exist. Therefore, at one time, by this time, there should have been nothing. Hence, there should have been a complete *Void* already by this time.
3. If there were a complete Void at any one time, then even now there should have been a Void, for out of nothing, nothing comes.
4. But there *is* something. This something, therefore, is based on *Something* which is not contingent, i.e., it is a Being which at no time can cease to be in the infinite series of time.
5. This *Something* which contains the ground of its own existence is a necessary Being. It is this necessary Being

---

Approaches to the philosophy of religion, Edited by D.J. Bronstein and H.M. Schulweis, Prentice-Hall, 1960, p. 135.
13. F.C. Copleston, 'Readings in religious philosophy', MacGregor/Robb p. 332.

which is at the basis of all contingent things (some of which exist at one time or the other), and which does not allow things in the infinite series of time to pass into nothing.
6. This necessary Being is called God.

The concluding part of the argument by Aquinas runs thus:

Therefore one cannot but postulate the existence of some being having of itself its own necessity, and not receiving it from another, but rather causing in others their necessity. This all men speak of as God.[14]

The whole argument may be syllogistically expressed thus: If anything exists, then an absolutely necessary Being exists; But, something exists; Therefore, an absolutely necessary Being exists. The fundamental contention is that the transient implies the permanent and the intellectual apprehension of contingent being as such involves an apprehension of its being related to a self-grounded reality.[15]

The second assumption of Aquinas is that an infinite time has already elapsed and that all things not capable of existing by themselves would have come to naught in this infinite series. As the passing away of an *infinite* series of time is self-contradictory, so Copleston holds that the realisation of the nothingness of all contingent things in the infinite series of time is possible.

He (Aquinas) does not say that infinite time is impossible: what he says is that if time is infinite and if all things are capable of not existing, this potentiality would inevitably be fulfilled in infinite time.[16]

But if infinite time has not already passed away, then every potentiality to be actualised in time, cannot be supposed to have been fulfilled. If time is going on, then who knows the contin-

---

14. St. Thomas Aquinas, *op. cit.*, p. 136.
15. R.L. Patterson, 'Philosophy of religion', Henry Holt, 1958, p. 126; F.C. Copleston, *op. cit.*, p. 334.
16. F.C. Copleston, *Commentary on the five Ways* in *The Existence of God.* Edited by J. Hick, p. 89.

gent would may yet come to naught. So from the mere possibility we cannot infer the *actuality* of all contingent things coming to naught, unless we accept that an infinite series of time has already passed away. But the phrase 'infinite series of time' means that the series has not terminated and can never be said to have passed away. Hence, the second assumption of Aquinas is weak. But unless we accept this, we cannot proceed further. However, the argument goes on. If all contingent things become nothing, then from nothing, nothing comes; and, even now there will be nothing. But there are things. So contingent things are grounded in a Being which is necessary or contains the ground of its own being. However, the possibility of all contingent things coming to be nothing is a bare possibility and form this it cannot be further supposed that this possibility has been realised and that actually at one time there was nothing.

Thirdly, the Cosmological argument is not merely causal. It is not merely concerned with an infinite *temporal* regress and in order to escape from it, it is not recommending us to accept a First Cause. The argument starts with the assumption that all things are dependent and the whole world consisting of contingent things may be compared to a chain of an infinite number of entities. But this chain requires as much explaining as finite things do. And this has to be explained in terms of something beyond, and other than itself.

Lastly, the Cosmological argument holds that the contingent things imply the existence of a necessary Being. Usually the term 'necessary' is used with regard to analytic necessity only. However, Aquinas assumes the priority of Being over essence or idea. So, according to him, it is the Absolute Being which is necessary. In other words, this necessity is not logical, but factual. We shall find that from the time of Hume and Kant up to Russell and Ayer, it is held that statements concerning facts can be contingent only and to say that a statement concerning an absolute Being or fact is necessary is to commit self-contradiction. Now whatever may be the criticism of the notion of a necessary Being, Aquinas, Copleston, Hick, Terence Penelhum[17] call it ontological or meta-

---

17. Terence Penelhum, *Divine Necessity*, *Mind*, Vol. LXIX, No. 274, 1960, pp. 175-86.

physical concept. As such the notion of a 'necessary being' is to be understood existentially or convictionally and not in the empirical language of science. We have already made reference to it in relation to the Ontological Argument.

CRITICAL COMMENTS

In the body of the Argument, Aquinas notes that the ultimate thing cannot be merely possible or contingent, 'but there *must* exist something the existence of which is necessary'. Hence, the assumption is that the contingent *implies* the necessary. This relation of 'contingent and necessary' is purely logical. Here the relation implied is analogous to correlation which holds between two correlates or concepts like relative-absolute, finite-infinite and so on. Hence, the necessity is purely analytic. But the argument pretends to establish the relationship between two *things* or Beings, that is, between necessary and contingent Beings. So either the necessity is analytic in which case from the contingent world God's existence cannot be proved or else this 'necessity' is factual which is self-contradictory. In other words, the 'must' of the argument fails to establish the actuality of God. It is the ambiguous use of 'must' which creates the spacious argument.

Again, the Argument assumes that the world as a whole stands in need of explanation. The question for philosophy, according to Aquinas and Copleston is: Why is there something at all? Why is this Universe at all? With regard to this assumption two difficulties have been raised: Can we legitimately or meaningfully occupy ourselves with the problem concerning the universe as a whole? Secondly, can the explanation of the world as a whole be said to be an intelligible notion? Both Russell and A.J. Ayer deny that the question concerning the universe as a whole is meaningful. According to them phenomena just happen.[18] In the language of Samuel Alexander, facts have to be noted and accepted with natural piety. Similarly, Russell[19] tells us that the universe is just there, and 'that's all'. Hence, according to them the very assumption that the world stands in need of being

18. A.J. Ayer and F.C. Copleston, 'Logical Positivism' (1949), p. 336 in *Readings in Religious Philosophy*, Edited by MacGregor/Robb.
19. B. Russell and F.C. Copleston, *A debate on the existence of God* in *The existence of God*, Edited by John Hick, p. 175.

explained is meaningless. Father Copleston would not accept this.
He would maintain that the question is not scientific or empirical
but is metaphysical.[20] Ayer and Russell maintain that the question is empirically unintelligible. Ayer would say that it is perfectly meaningful to ask with regard to any specific event: Where
do these things come from? or, What is the cause of this event?
But such a question cannot be generalised with regard to all
events taken together.

> You are then asking what event is prior to all of them. And
> clearly no event can be prior to all of them, because if it is a
> member of the class of all of them it must be included in it,
> and therefore, can't be prior to it.[21]

Most probably this question is linked up with the admissibility
of 'metaphysical explanation' of the universe. Copleston maintains that it is a fact that there are two kinds of causality and the
problem concerning the universe is not scientific. He holds that
this problem is metaphysical. Now the question is: Is metaphysical explanation of the universe intelligible?

The metaphysical explanation. according to Copleston, is an
adequate explanation, and, an adequate explanation must ultimately be a total explanation, to which nothing further can be added.[22] According to Russell, this type of *total* explanation can't
be got. The reason is that the explanation of any one thing is
another thing, which in turn is dependent on yet another thing
and this total series can't be got.[23] But can we not think it otherwise?

Ordinarily a thing is said to be explained by describing the
how between the phenomena. But this *how* is deduced from some
theory. Now do we mean by *total* explanation a super-theory or
an all-inclusive theory which should accurately describe all the
phenomena? Well at the time of Newton there were a number of
laws concerning planetary motion, formation of tides and so on.
He brought the separate and specific laws of physics and astro-

20. A.J. Ayer, *Readings*, p. 332.
21. *Ibid.*, p. 334.
22. *The Existence of God*, p. 173.
23. PR, pp. 155-57; and more clearly on pp. 288-89.

nomy under the one single law of Gravitation. This unification is no longer possible. Along with the law of gravitation, there are the laws of relativity, electromagnetism and many other laws of social sciences. Now, does 'total explanation' mean a super-theory which subsumes and unifies all the laws of every science? First, such a theory, so far has not been reached by any scientist, and even suppose that we have one, why should not one ask for a further explanation of this super-theory? This would ultimately land us in infinite regress.[24] Further, is not something inherently wrong with the notion of a total explanation which refers to *all events all at once*? A genuine explanation is compatible with one course of event and incompatible with another. However, a total explanation is compatible with all events. This makes it vacuous or empty. The thing is that *all events taken together* have not anything else from which to distinguish them. Naturally a total explanation is empty of significance because it is compatible with whatever happens in the universe.[25]

Besides, for Copleston, the ontological explanation of the universe implies the existence of a Necessary Being which alone is the ultimate ground of every contingent thing in the universe. Now such a total or ontological explanation becomes self-contradictory, since 'necessary' is validly applicable to analytic propositions only. However, analytic propositions are formal and do not apply to any actual state of affairs. Yet the ultimate explanation of the Cosmological argument is also a Being. But a Being is always contingent. So the total explanation in terms of a Necessary Being is both necessary and contingent. And this is self-contradictory.[26]

Thus, with regard to the first assumption of the Cosmological argument we can say that the universe as a whole is not a scientific problem and it can never be intelligibly discussed in the public language of science. By holding that this problem is metaphysical or ontological, we do not escape from the difficulties if we still consider such problems as cognitive, which Copleston following Aquinas maintains them to be. We think that the problem pertains to convictional language only. However, cogniti-

---

24. *The Existence of God*, p. 173.
25. MacGregor/Robb, *Readings*, pp. 336-37.
26. *Ibid.*, pp. 337, 339.

vely speaking, the universe is not a proper problem and its explanation in terms of a Necessary Being is both vacuous and self-contradictory.

We need not repeat our criticisms of the Cosmological argument concerning its second and third assumptions, because they have already been commented upon previously. With regard to all contingent things coming to be nothing in the infinite series of time, we can formulate our objection in the form of the following dilemma:

If the infinite series of time has already elapsed, then it leads to self-contradiction; and, if the series of time has not come to an end, then all the possibilities (which also includes the possibility of all contingent things to be nothing) need not be taken to have been fulfilled by this time; But either the infinite series of time has come to an end, or not.

Therefore, either it is self-contradictory or else all contingent things need be taken to have ceased to be at any one time.

Most probably few theologians would explain the Cosmological argument through the chain of infinite causes. Even Copleston holds that the argument does not propose to give any scientific explanation. Similarly, Terence Penelhum who wants to defend the religious force of the Cosmological argument tells us[27] that causal explanation leaves unanswered the several questions of 'why anything exists at all'. Further, he adds, even if one could show the whole chain of causes, one could just ask why it was that we had the sort of world which however naturally gave rise to this or that feature. As casual explanation cannot be self-explanatory, total and all-sufficient, so this kind of explanation cannot be considered adequate. Thus, we have now to pay attention to the last assumption of the Cosmological argument, namely, God exists by virtue of *factual* necessity: the Being of God is the absolute prius of everything else. It is what is said to be an *ens realissimum* and such a Being is the ground of its own existence. As such it cannot but exist.

Now Kant has something hard to say about the existence of such a Necessary Being. He tells us that the whole proof is really Ontological argument in disguise, even though Thomas Aquinas

---

27. Terence Penelhum, *Divine Necessity, Mind*, 1960, p. 176.

before presenting the Cosmological argument refuted the Ontological argument first.[28] No doubt an appeal is made to an experiential character of familiar things, namely, their contingency, yet this appeal to experience is purely seeming. In the first instance, the contingency of things is their most abstract character. Can it be said to be sensible? We can say that blue or yellow, hot or cold is really a sensible quality of a particular thing. But in comparison colouredness is much more abstract. Now 'contingency' is the most abstract quality of things, farthest removed from actual experience. So this contingency can hardly be said to be an experiential quality of things. Secondly, even this contingency of things is confined to a single step only throughout the whole argument. The real motive lies in leaping from the contingency of things to the existence of a necessary being. But mere contingency apart from other qualities of things is too abstract to be regarded an actual state of affairs. So really the argument is not *a posteriori* and therefore is not in a position to establish being or existence which can be given only by experience. What the Cosmological argument really tries to show is that the contingent things imply the existence of a Necessary Being which can never be conceived not to exist. But is this not the contention of the Ontological argument?

> For absolute necessity is an existence determined from mere concepts. If I say, the concept of the *ens realissimum* is a concept, and indeed the only concept, which is appropriate and adequate to necessary existence, I must also admit that necessary existence can be inferred from this concept. Thus the so-called cosmological proof really owes any cogency which it may have to the ontological proof from mere concepts.[29]

Hence, the Cosmological argument is at bottom Ontological and like the latter fails to establish existence from the contingency of the world.

---

28. This is what is found as a preface to the *Five Ways* of proving God, Vide *Approaches to the Philosophy of Religion*, Edited Bronstein and Schulweis, pp. 129 ff.

29. PR, p. 287.

On the other hand, if the *Necessary Being* be an actual state of affairs, a proper name of a Being who has created the world, then how can such a Being be called necessary? This was the objection raised by Hume.[30] So Kant tells us that whatever it may be that exists, nothing can prevent us from thinking its non-existence.[31] So no existing Being, not even God or *ens realissimum* can ever be taken to be necessary. This objection has been taken up by Terence Penelhum.

According to Terence Penelhum a thing must exist before it can have any quality.

A theist who saw this world naturally begins by asking the Existential question, and then try to show that the being needed to answer it is implicitly enough to answer the qualitative.[32]

Therefore, Terence Penelhum takes Kant and E.L. Mascall to task for reducing the five ways to Cosmological argument only and further to limiting the argument to 'existence' alone. According to him, Aquinas was not simply concerned with the contingency of things, but also their *manner* of being. Aquinas also referred to the grades of perfection found in things. Hence, being and the manner of being (quality) go side by side in the *Five Ways* of proving God. Terence Penelhum therefore tells us that for Aquinas the essence of finite things does not account for their existence, and also the fact of their existence does not account for their essence. In God the two, essence and existence, guarantee each other.

.........and we conclude with a being who must, by the sort of being he is, exist, and also must, by the mere fact that he exists, be the sort of being he is: one in whom essence and existence are identical.[33]

Keeping this observation before us, Terence Penelhum finds that neither the existential nor the qualitative argument would

30. EG, p. 96; R. Wollheim, *Hume on Religion*, p. 163, (Fontana Edition, 1963).
31. PR, p. 290.
32. Terence Penelhum, *Divine Necessity*, Mind, 1960, p. 177.
33. *Mind*, 1960, p. 178.

suffice. The ontological argument is fallacious, according to Terence Penelhum, because it takes 'existence' for a predicate. One can meaningfully assert a quality of a thing, but not its existence. If one says of a thing that *it is blue*, at least one means that it is visible, a coloured object and that it is not a philosophical theory or an act of Parliament. But the 'existence' of a thing gives no information about what sort a thing is.[34]

> Existence cannot vary in quantity or intensity, belóng to some members of a class and not others, or be interrupted and then resumed.[35]

The same sort of trouble, according to Terence Penelhum, besets our attempt to prove essence from existence. According to J.N. Findlay, God in order to be worshipful must possess excellences in a necessary manner, and not accidentally.[36] So 'God is good' or 'God has P', has only an analytic necessity. Of course, God may be used as a proper name and in that case 'God has P' becomes a synthetic proposition, and in this case it would mean that God merely *happens* to have P. This will not meet the religious claim of worshipfulness. God must have all excellences in an inescapable manner. This 'necessity' then can be either guaranteed by other qualities or by means of His existence. If we say that P is guaranteed by X, and X is guaranteed by Y and so on, then clearly it leads to *regressus ad infinitum*. Hence, we have to prove the essence of God through His existence alone. This shows, according to Terence Penelhum, that essence and existence are very much closer than is generally held: But can we deduce essence from existence? The Ontological argument was trying to deduce existence from essence and now we are trying to deduce essence from His existence.[37] This can be done only when we treat 'existence' as a quality or essence, which Penelhum himself would not allow. So Terence Penelhum concludes that God's existence cannot be proved. But,

---

34. *Ibid.,* pp. 179-80.
35. *Ibid.,* p. 180.
36. J.N. Findlay, *Can God's existence be disproved?* in *Philosophical Theology,* Edited by A. Flew and A. Macintyre, SCM Press, 1958, pp. 52-53·
37. T. Penelhum, *Mind,* 1960, p. 184.

he tells us, that the whole *impasse* has been due to the fact that we are using the term 'necessity' and 'contingency' with regard to propositions only. But they apply to things as well. Only we have to clarify the meanings of the terms when they are used with regard to things.

As applied to things or events, 'contingent' will mean 'dependent' or 'caused', one thing or event being contingent *upon* another; 'necessary' will mean 'not dependent on any other', and, in addition, 'having others dependent on it'. A thing is necessary if it is indispensable.[38]

Interpreted thus God is 'factually necessary'. Terence Penelhum concedes that this will not satisfy the cognitive requirement of religious belief. He therefore leaves the path of proof and takes recourse to individual confrontation with what purports to be God's self-revelation.[39]

We can conclude with Russell that any attempt to prove that God cannot not-exist will raise the question concerning the meaning of the term 'existence'.

.........and as to this, I think a subject named can never be significantly said to exist but only a subject described. And that existence, in fact, quite definitely is not a predicate.[40]

Thus the Cosmological argument has to be rejected. First, 'why should anything exist at all' is a pseudo-problem. It can be answered by the retort, 'why should it not exist'? Secondly, its solution in terms of a necessary being is equally unsatisfactory because the expression 'necessary being' is self-contradictory.

Why has the Cosmological argument failed? Because the gulf between the empirical and the unconditioned is so great that no

---

38. T. Penelhum, *Ibid.*, p. 185; See also the introductory remarks of J. Hick, 'The existence of God', p. 81; also *vide* J. Hick, 'Necessary Being, *Scottish Journal of Theology*, December 1961.
39. *Ibid.*, p. 186.
40. B. Russell & F.C. Copleston in *The Existence of God*, p. 171

argument can ever bridge it. And this is how Kant has formulated the case.[41]

> The transcendental idea of a necessary and all-sufficient being is so overwhelmingly great, so high above everything empirical, the latter being always conditioned, that it leaves us at a loss, partly because we can never find in experience material to satisfy such a concept, and partly because it is always in the sphere of the conditioned that we carry out our search, seeking there ever vainly for the unconditioned—no law of any empirical synthesis giving us an example of any such unconditioned or providing the least guidance in its pursuit.

The universe consists of contingent things only and no things of experience can have this necessity. This gulf which yawns between the empirical and the unconditioned is still more marked when we come to teleological argument.

Theists do recognise now that 'Five Ways' are not arguments so much as they are discussions concerning finite things. Contingent things do not *logically* imply the existence of God, according to Mascall. But why has the discussion been put in the form of a syllogism? The syllogistic form of the discussion helps us to apprehend God in a cognitive act.[42] The crux of the argument, says Mascall,

> "consists not in a process of logical deduction but in an apprehension, namely, the apprehension of finite beings as effect implying (or, better, manifesting) a transcendent cause;...[43]

Further, this shows that our transition from finite things (as effects-implying-cause) to the Infinite God is not unreasonable.[44] But Mascall significantly remarks that the cosmological approach declares God's existence without claiming to form a concept of

41. PR, p. 292.
42. E.L. Mascall, *Existence and Analogy*, A Libra Book, 1966, p. 80.
43. *Ibid.*, p. 89.
44. *Ibid.*, pp. 78, 90.

God. God for Mascall is 'that which exists self-existently' and that existence cannot be conceptualized.[45] If so, can we claim that our apprehension of God is cognitive? Ultimately, Mascall takes recourse to mystery.[46] What Mascall calls 'apprehensions' and I. Ramsay as 'discernment' is at bottom existential commitment and self-involvement in making theistic statements. This point will be further seen in Teleological argument.

45. *Ibid.*, pp. 88, 90.
46. *Ibid.*, p. 89.

Chapter IX

TELEOLOGICAL ARGUMENT

Exposition

The term 'teleological' has been derived from the Greek word *'telos'* which means 'end or purpose'. So the teleological argument holds that the order in nature points to a design of an infinite intelligence. Thus, it is an argument *from* the order in nature *to* a divine design. In one sense, it is simply an extension of the Cosmological argument. In the first instance, it takes recourse to the empirical features of the universe far more extensively and in a detailed manner than the Cosmological argument does. Secondly, it holds that the order in nature is contingent, since there is nothing in nature to guarantee it. Hence, the order in nature has to be grounded in a self-existing, infinite intelligence. Stated thus the argument is very old and is hinted at by Plato in *Laws*. In *Laws*, Plato tells us that the whole path and movement of heavenly bodies and of all that is therein is akin to the movement and calculation of a mind and proceeds in accordance with kindred laws. The same thought is beautifully contained in Psalm.

> The heavens are telling the glory of God; and the firmament proclaims his handiwork. Day to day pours forth speech and night to night declares knowledge.
> There is no speech, nor are there words: their voice is not heard;[1]

St. Paul repeats this poetic vision of the Psalmist[2]:

> For what can be known about God is plain to them (men), because God has shown it to them. Ever since the creation of the world his invisible nature, namely, his eternal power

---

1. Fontana Edition, Psalm 19:1-3.
2. *Ibid.*, Roman Chap., I, 19-20 Verses.

and deity, has been clearly perceived in the things that have been made. So they (men) are without excuse.......

However, in the English-speaking world, the Teleological argument was most eloquently stated by William Paley (1743-1805). In this he was preceded by the Cambridge Platonist, Henry More (1614-1687). In crossing a heath, says Paley, suppose one finds a watch. Can any one answer that it might have always been there? When one perceives its various parts so framed together as to produce movement for regulating time, one would conclude that it was made for a purpose. From the mere presence of the mechanism one would conclude that the watch must have had a maker. The same contrivance which is found in a watch is found in nature:

> With the difference, on the side of nature, of being greater and more, and that in a degree which exceeds all computation. I mean that the contrivances of nature surpass the contrivances of art, in the complexity, subtlety, and curiosity of the mechanism;.......[3]

Hence, William Paley infers that the whole contrivances of nature speak of an infinite intelligence. Paley appears to be quite ignorant of the works of Hume and Kant who had most successfully criticised this argument from design. But they were also fully aware of the popular appeal of the teleological argument from design. A purpose, an intention, a design, says Hume, strikes everywhere the most careless, the most stupid thinker, and no man can be so hardened in absurd systems, as at all times to reject it.[4] Cleanthes, the theist addresses thus:

> Look round the world: contemplate the whole and every part of it: you will find it to be nothing but one great machine, subdivided into an infinite number of lesser machines, which again admit of subdivisions, to a degree beyond what

---

3. William Paley, *'The Watch and the Watchmaker'* in *The Existence of God*, Edited by J. Hick, p, 103.

4. *Hume on Religion*, Edited by R. Wollheim, Fontana Library, 1963, p. 189.

human senses and faculties can trace and explain. All these various machines and even their most minute parts, are adjusted to each other with an accuracy, which ravishes into admiration all men, who have ever contemplated them. The curious adapting of means to ends, throughout all nature, resembles exactly, though it much exceeds, the productions of human contrivance; of human designs, thought, wisdom, and intelligence.[5]

People have always been struck by the presence of variety, order and beauty in nature. They have ever since concluded that this cannot be the product of accidence and chance. Hence, Bacon wrote:

> I had rather believed all the Fables in the legend and the Talmud and the Alcoran than that this Universal Frame is without a mind.

True, Kant has criticised this argument mercilessly, but he never lost sight of its value as a plea for faith. Hence, he observed that this proof always deserves to be mentioned with respect. According to him, it is the oldest, the clearest, and the most accordant with the common reason of mankind.[6] Kant was fully aware that no empirical evidence can be adequate enough for proving the existence of an Infinite Intelligence or the Unconditioned. Yet he never lost sight of the deep appeal of teleology found in nature.

> Reason, constantly upheld by this ever-increasing evidence, which, though empirical is yet so powerful, cannot be so depressed through doubts suggested by subtle and abstruse speculation, that it is not at once aroused from the indecision of all melancholy reflection, as from a dream by one glance at the wonders of nature and the majesty of the universe— ascending from height to height up to the all-heighest, from the conditioned to its conditions, up to the supreme and unconditioned Author (of all conditioned being).[7]

---

5. Dialogues concerning natural religion, *Ibid.*, p. 115.
6. PR, p. 293.
7. PR, p. 294.

Later theologians have simply detailed the points which have been raised by the earlier authors. For example, James Martineau (1805-1900) in *A Study of Religion* contends that the Universe is not an accidental product, but is the result of divine intention. According to him *Selection, Combination* and *Gradation* are the three marks of intention or purpose[8] and all these three are found in nature. Martineau states that the various organs of the body have been so selected out of a number of possibilities that they perform their adjustive functions in relation to the varying environmental conditions. For example, the anterior limbs of the vertebrates have some fundamental unity of plan in relation to the whole body, and yet the whole structure is flexible enough to meet an indefinite range of variations. The organs of sense have obvious reference to the conditions of life in which an organism is placed. For example, the breathing organs are well adapted in each species according to its aerial, terrestrial and oceanic conditions of living.

> The modifications in the organs of sense have, in their leading features obvious reference to the conditions on which their function is to be exercised, yet cannot have been the result of these conditions.[9]

Again, by 'combination', Martineau means 'correlation of organs', their mutual interdependence and the mutual inter-relation between the different species, even between the animal and plant life. For example, he tells us that the organs of a carnivorous animal are so made that they can work together in the most coordinated manner. Its intestines are so organised as to be adapted for digesting flesh only; its jaws are so constructed as to devour its living prey; its claws for seizing and tearing the prey; its teeth for cutting and dividing it, its organs of sense for discovering it at a distance and so on.[10] A still higher form of combination is found between one living being and another, e.g.

---

8. James Martineau, *A Study of Religion*, Vol. I, p. 247, Clarendon Press, 1900.
9. *Ibid.*, p. 271.
10. *Ibid.*, pp. 282-83.

between the mammal and its embryo. The same thing is seen in the mutual relation between the insect and the plant. Many orchids would be barren but for the services of certain moths and bees.[11]

The third mark of intention, according to Martineau, is *gradation* of arrangement

> by which a given end is attained through *a train* of independent means, *each* making provision for the next, till the series is consummated and crowned by the fulfilment.[12]

In general the *mere* life supports and sustains the higher life and all subserve ultimately conscious existence. Insects and worms are the victims of small birds; reptiles of still higher and larger birds; the smaller fish of the greater or of the marine mammalia; the carnivorous animals remain the prey of the feline order.

> Finally, it is in the chase of these, or in conflict with them, that man learns his first arts, and wins his place at the head of all terrestrial races.[13]

Hence, Martineau concludes that the design-argument is not based on mere resemblance in nature to the human contrivance, but on the special character of this resemblance.[14]

The trouble about these teleologists is that they never studied carefully the acute arguments of Hume and discerned the implications of 'The Origin of Species' (1859) which was written by Charles Darwin (1809-1882). Hume had observed that nature could be very well imagined as a self-regulating system in which a number of orders come and go. In due course, some of the uniformities in nature might have evolved through the millions of spontaneous movements taking place in nature. Afterwards, out of these uniformities came the order in which life was thrown out of them. Finally the species are as they are because of the

---

11. *Ibid.*, pp. 290-91.
12. *Ibid.*, p. 294.
13. *Ibid.*, p. 297.
14. *Ibid.*, p. 302.

fortuitous combinations, adjusting ones alone surviving and the unadjusted ones perishing in the perpetual goings-on of the universe.

> It is in vain, therefore, to insist upon the uses of the parts in animals or vegetables and their curious adjustment to each other. I would fain know how an animal could subsist, unless its parts were so adjusted? Do we not find, that it immediately perishes whenever this adjustment ceases, and that its matter corrupting tries some new form? It happens, indeed, that the parts of the world are so well adjusted, that some regular form immediately lays claim to this corrupted matter; and if it were not so, could the world subsist?[15]

As a matter of fact it was Empedocles (about 490-434 B.C.) who had hinted at the idea of fortuitous combinations of the various organs; only the favourable combinations could survive and others because of their unadapted character had to perish.[16] But it was Charles Darwin who with a wealth of staggering details had shown that the principles of natural selection alone have contributed to the survival of the fittest in the grim struggle of existence for food and mate. Changes in the members of the species mostly took place in the germ-plasm and these changes, according to Darwin, were accidental and spontaneous. Some of these changes proved favourable either as defensive weapons or attacking organs, or for procuring food (e.g. long neck in a land of trees, without low-growing shrubs or grass) or for procuring mate (e.g. attractive features as in most males of birds and animals). The variations in the germ-plasm were accidental and their adjustive features were determined most mechanically. It was this insistence on the *mechanical* selection of the successful *variant* which ruled out the possibility of the Teleological argument for the existence of a benevolent providence[17] in spite of Darwin himself.[18]

---

15. *Dialogues* in *Hume on Religion*, p. 158.
16. Gomperz, 'Greek thinkers'.
17. C.E. Raven, 'Science and Religion', p. 178.
18. Charles Darwin himself drew out a theistic conclusion towards the end of '*Origin of Species*'. "There is grandeur in this view of life, with its

At this stage, F.R. Tennant (1866-1957) who knew Hume, Kant and some of the current objections against the Teleological argument, supports it in the following way. He says that a Teleological argument based on restricted spheres of facts is precarious. He substitutes for it a comprehensive design-argument which is based on the *united* and reciprocal action of innumerable causes to produce and maintain a general order of nature. The main facts which support the Teleological argument are:

the internal adaptedness of organic beings, the fitness of the inorganic to minister to life, the aesthetic value of Nature, the world's instrumentality in the realization of moral ends, and the progressiveness in the evolutionary process culminating in the emergence of man with his rational and moral status.[19]

Of course, F. R. Tennant must have been greatly helped by the writings of Hegel and Neo-Hegelians, specially, B. Bosanquet and A. Seth Pringle Pattison. According to the British absolutists, there is the spirit of totality which presses each finite thing to transcend itself towards in all-inclusive, all-harmonious, sentient whole. In their arguments they hold that nature, though appearing to be opposed to life, in due course did prepare the way for life and when it did emerge does sustain it. In the same way life is full of grim struggle, red in tooth and claw and yet in the fulness of season it gave birth to consciousness. Life and consciousness somehow did emerge from matter in a way which

---

several powers, having been originally breathed by the Creator in a few forms or into one; and that whilst......from so simple a beginning, endless forms most beautiful and most wonderful have been, and are being evolved" (*Origin of species*, The Modern Library 1936, p. 374). Then, A.N. Whitehead wisely observes that life grows, multiplies and repairs itself and varies spontaneously. As such life is a constant revolt against the repetitiveness of matter and mechanism (Science and Modern World, Pelican Series, pp. 130-35). But the mechanical nature of Darwin's organic evolution has served the purpose of mechanising the evolutionary process, ruling out a teleological explanation of the universe.

19. F.R. Tennant, *Cosmic Teleology* in *The Existence of God*, Edited by John Hick, p. 123.

baffles conjecture and they in their turn, when the time was ripe, did pave the way for self-consciousness or spirit. Only in man the dumb nature speaks, the grim struggle of life becomes articulate and the whole process comes to self-knowledge and discernment. But man does not only conserve the past history of the whole cosmic drama before his arrival, but also contains the prophecy of all that is going to be. No doubt there might be some failures here and some back-sliding there, but the progressiveness of the onward march is clearly discernible. Are these landmarks of nature, life, spirit, the intimations of values at the heart of things, or, are the deeds of heroism, the imperishable monuments and the priceless works of art mere tales told by an idiot? As the world slowly yields its secrets, so we know that it is rational and law-abiding. Hence, the whole cosmos has some design and that appears to be the evolution of values. Teleology, after all, says F.R. Tennant, is a value-concept,[20] and the whole of nature conspires towards the evolution of values.

But is the teleological argument coercive? Can all the facts lead to the same conclusion? Or, are we not betrayir g our taste and temperament in either accepting or rejecting teleology? This is a question which strikes us when we are presented with the facts of disharmony and chaos in nature. So far as the argument goes the teleologists have onesidedly dwelt upon the facts of co-ordination, combination and gradation and all ultimately leading to values of goodness and wisdom. But if there is a design of an infinite intelligence, then why should there be so much of wastefulness in nature? Millions of eggs are laid and only a small proportion of them is allowed to give birth to young ones: and, again, out of millions only a few are allowed to survive. Does this contrivance appear to be wise? Again, if the universe has been designed by an infinitely wise deity, then why should there be so much of physical, mental and moral evil? Why should nature be ethically callous, when there is the design for the emergence of ethical characters? Why should there be famine, pestilence and calamities?

All this, Nature does with the most supercilious disregard both of mercy and of justice emptying her shafts upon the

---

20. *Ibid.*, p. 122.

best and noblest indifferently with the meanest and worst, upon those who are engaged in the highest and worthiest enterprises, and often on the direct consequence of the noblest acts; and it might almost be imagined as a punishment for them.[21]

From the above-mentioned facts, Mill concludes that there is no order in nature.

Anarchy and the Reign of Terror are overmatched in injustice, ruin and death by a hurricane and a pestilence.[22]

When opposing claims are made on the basis of the same set of facts, then the decision becomes difficult. In any case one has to carefully weigh all the facts and issues before coming to a judgement.

CRITICAL COMMENTS

Henry More and William Paley tried to apply the analogy of a machine to have had the force of the Teleological argument. Is it a good analogy? Hume has tried to draw out the various implications of this analogy with a view to showing its untenability, we need not refer to any of them here. First, the analogy of the watch and its maker shows that mechanism has been raised to the status of a key-concept for explaining the world as a whole. This key-concept is highly unsatisfactory for religion, because in religion we value freedom of will, moral worth and spiritual creativeness and mechanism is quite opposed to all of these considerations. The analogy is highly anthropomorphic, because we are thinking of the whole of reality in terms of human means and ends, nay, it goes farther than that, because only a part of that human intelligence which is confined to mechanical contrivance has become the key-notion for explaining the universe. But even if we grant that the order in nature speaks of a grand design, we fall far short of proving a creator God. At most we show that

---

21. John Stuart Mill, *Is there more evil than good in nature?* in *Approaches to the Philosophy of Religion*, Edited by Bronstein & Schulweis, p. 227.

22. *Ibid.*, p. 228.

there is a superior intelligence at work, but we do not show that such a Being is also the creator of the materials which he fashions into the orderly universe.

> The utmost, therefore, that the argument can prove is an *architect* of the world who is always very much hampered by the adaptability of the material in which he works, not a *creator* of the world to whose idea everything is subject.[23]

A God who is hampered by his materials and cannot fully control them is only a finite God. But a finite God cannot be an object of *worship*, though he can be an object of reverence or admiration.[24] If the argument had shown that God is also the creator of materials, then alone the argument will be adequate. But if the materials too come out of God, then God will become the immanent principle of nature. This is the danger of emphasizing inner teleology at the cost of external teleology. But we put the question again, Can the world as a whole be pictured as a machine? Well, one can do so if one desires, but by doing this, he cannot say that it is a faithful picture. In order to ascertain this one has to compare this picture with another universe. But are there two universes, are there two instances of similar class-membership in this case? The argument from design as an argument assumes that there are instances of similar class-membership.

> But the argument from design invites us to draw such an inference in the case of the observable universe itself, which *ex hypothesi* is not a member of a class. We have nothing to compare with the universe and therefore there is no information on which we can rely in drawing inferences about the-universe-as-a-whole.[25]

---

23. PR, p. 296. Hume also states that this reasoning at most shows that God is finite and secondly, that he is very imperfect even as a finite God (Dialogues—in *Hume on Religion*, p. 139).
24. J.N. Findlay, *New Essays in Philosophical Theology*, pp. 51, 53, Also see E. Brunner.
25. A Macintyre, *Difficulties in Christian belief*, SCM Press, 1959, p. 62; also

Because the Universe is one and as a whole is not perceptible, therefore, there can be no scientific reasoning leading to a single verifiable conclusion. But in such a case, says Hume, 'a hundred contradictory views may prove a kind of imperfect analogy; and invention has here full scope to exert itself.'[26] Because the Univere is one and the facts are the same for both the theist and atheist, the disputants rest their case on the cumulative effect of their severally inconclusive premises, viz., the theist would emphasize the data of order, harmony, correlation, gradation and so on. The atheist, on the other hand, would take recourse to the wastefulness of nature, the cruel struggle for the survival of the fittest, the callousness of nature with regard to events of pestilence, cyclones, droughts—and even the defective structure and malfunctions of the various senses of an organism. Is their reasoning empirical? This may appear to be so because each party to the dispute refers to the *facts* to support his contention.

But this is a muddle. The *dispute does not cease to be a priori because it is a matter of the cumulative effect of severally inconclusive premises.* The logic of the dispute is not that of a chain of deductive reasoning as in a mathematical calculation. But nor is it a matter of collecting from several inconclusive items of information an expectation as to something further...It has its own sort of logic and its own sort of end— the solution of the question at issue is a decision, a ruling of the judge......With the judge's choice of a name for the facts goes an attitude, and the declaration, the ruling, is an exclamation evincing that attitude.[27]

Thus we find that by means of Teleological argument one cannot proceed from conditions to conditions, till we reach the ultimate condition of the universe. We at most halt at the notion

---

see A.J. Ayer, in 'A modern introduction to philosophy', Edited Edwards and Pap, pp. 555-56; John Hick, *Faith and Logic*, pp. 134-39.

26. *Dialogues concerning natural religion* in *Hume on Religion*, p. 155.

27. John Wisdom, *Gods* in *Classical and Contemporary Readings in the Philosophy of Religion*, Edited by J. Hick, Prentice-Hall, 1964, p. 420.

of the Author of nature. Seeing that this does not satisfy the logic of worship, we argue from the contingency of the order in nature and once again from this contingency we infer the existence of an Absolutely Necessary Being.

Thus the physico-theological proof, failing in its undertaking, has in face of this difficulty suddenly fallen back upon the cosmological proof; and since the latter is only a disguised ontological proof, it has really achieved its purpose by pure reason alone—although at the start it disclaimed all kinship with pure reason and professed to establish its conclusions on convincing evidence derived from experience.[28]

Thus, the proofs have failed to establish the existence of God. The arguments had two objectives, viz., that God is an actual entity who responds to prayers, worship and adoration; and that God exists necessarily and has his attributes of Love, Wisdom, Omniscience in an inescapable manner. As existence of anything whatsoever can be given only by experience or by experienced facts, so the arguments in the last resort have to take recourse to the empirical world. So far the Teleological argument appeared to be fully empirical. But the argument, even if valid, could not establish beyond the fact that God is an *architect* of the world and not that He is its *creator*. But a finite God who merely happens to fashion the kind of world which we actually find cannot be a God to whom all knees must bow and who would induce the total self-surrender and absolute commitment of the worshipper. On the other hand, if the necessary existence of God be established through any proof whatsoever, then God ceased to be an actual entity and would turn out to be a symbol with its stipulated meaning.

We have examined all the three main arguments for the existence of God. They have failed to prove the divine existence. For Kant these three were the only possible proofs[29] and for him all of them have failed in their objective. Are they useless on that account? No. First, Kant hints that the notion of God has its

---

28. PR, p. 297.
29. PR, p. 298.

origin in *natural* inference or propensity,[30] or, that the notion of a necessary being is derived from grounds other than rational.[31] Hence, for Kant, the notion of God is a regulative ideal and is quite useful.

Thus, while for the merely speculative employment of reason the supreme being remains a mere *ideal*, it is yet *an ideal without a flaw*, a concept which completes and crowns the whole of human knowledge. Its objective reality cannot indeed be proved, but also cannot be disproved, by merely speculative reason.[32]

He further suggests that this deficiency will be made up in moral theology. Hence, it never occurred to Kant that the notion of a necessary being is self-contradictory or impossible, though his own criticisms of the various arguments could have very easily shown this to him. Further, if a statement can neither be proved nor disproved, then it is vacuous. As a matter of fact he thought that by showing this he could make God an appropriate object of faith. In contemporary philosophical theology, the notion of God is not an ideal without a flaw, but is most absurd, nonsensical and impossible. The conclusion is that the notion of God cannot even be meaningfully entertained. This has been shown both by J.N. Findlay, and A.G.N. Flew. Their view may be called Ontological atheism. According to which the very idea of God involves the logical impossibility of such a being. This has already been discussed in Chapter III.

---

30. PR, p. 290.
31. PR, p. 285.
32. PR, p. 299.

CHAPTER X

THE ARGUMENT FROM RELIGIOUS EXPERIENCE

If one has to establish the scientific factuality of God, then experience is the only final court of appeal. Now both the theologian and empiricist claim 'experience' as the cash-value of statements. They differ a good deal about the nature and kind of experience relevant for theological statements. A theist unequivocally holds that nobody can see, or smell and touch God. He, however, holds that we can have direct experience of God either through His disclosure to men (revelation), intuition, mystic trance or by the special Grace of God, by creating as if a new faculty of divination in the worshipper. Without taking up each kind of religious experience separately we shall take up the case in a general way. In general, it is claimed that everyone has a special faculty of cognising God: Some have more of it and others have less of it and a few may be devoid of it. However, here it is assumed that the capacity to become aware of God is a part of the normal human nature like the capacity to see light or to hear sound.[1] Secondly, it is claimed that the specifically religious experience called *numinous experience* is irrefutable both with regard to itself and with regard to its object in relation to which the experience takes place. In Indian tradition, as also for some Western theologians belonging to the school of mysticism, in the *numinous experience*, the experience and the object *of* which it is the experience remain inseparable. The object becomes one with the subject. *Tat tvam asi* (That art Thou) is the famous maxim of Advaitism: the knower becomes Brahman itself (*Brahmavid Brahmaiva bhavati*). As the experience itself, at least as a case of psychological occurrence has to be accepted as a fact and as it is claimed to be identical

---

1. H.H. Farmer, *Towards belief in God*, p. 40; A. E. Taylor, *The Argument from Religious Experience* in EG, p. 160. The same can be claimed for the view of Rudolf Otto with regard to *numinous experience*.

with the object of which it is the experience, so the whole of *numinous experience* is taken to be self-validating.

We have already quoted Kierkegaard earlier[2] and we can also mention two other statements of the two prominent theologians of recent times. John Baillie writes:

> Of such a Presence it must be true that to those who have never been confronted with it argument is useless, while to those who have it is superfluous[3].

In the same strain H.H. Farmer states:

> The divine reality is, by definition, unique or, in other words, we would expect that if we know the reality of God in respect of this fundamental aspect of His being at all, we shall just know that we are dealing with God, the ultimate source and disposer of all things, including ourselves, and *there will be nothing more to be said.*[4]

The argument from religious experience has two aspects; e.g., the numinous experience in which one feels the presence of God, or the healing touch of Jesus or the Mother or Rama or Kṛṣṇa. Here there are two things: (*i*) The raw experience itself, (*ii*) The experience with its interpretation by ideas. 'The Presence' is an abstract idea; 'the healing touch of Jesus' or 'The Mother' are the other two scriptural ideas. The empiricist will not dispute the fact of religious experience itself. It is as irreducible a psychological fact as the sensation of colour or touch or the affection of pain can be. If the theist believes no more than this that 'God exists' means for him the same thing as that he is having a *numinous experience,* then there will be no quarrel between the theist and the empiricist. The theist would hold that 'God' is not the name of 'numinous experience', in the same way as red is the name of a certain sensation arising from the stimulus called light-waves of 460 m.m. He would say that 'God' is the object to which his

---

2. Supra, p. 107.
3. *Ibid.,* p. 132.
4. *Ibid.,* p. 40 (Italics ours).

numinous experience is directed and in relation to which this kind of experience has arisen. Just as preceiving is a psychological act which reveals an appropriate object like a table, a rose or a chair, so the *numinous* experience reveals *mysterium tremendum* or a presence of a God of Love. Now the cognition of a table or chair, as Kant had noted, is not possible without being ultimately interpreted, through the *concepts of the understanding*. Similarly, we can say with W. Arnold Hall, that a theological statement as a cognitive enterprise is not possible without the interpretation by the thought forms, beliefs or dogmas of a specific religion of the raw feelingful awareness of the Deity called *numinous experience*.[5] Just as the psychologist maintains that there can be no bare sensation without some interpretation, so it can also be similarly held that there can be no bare religious experience without interpretation by its own specific theological concepts. If the experience be uninterpreted then it would not be distinguishable from any other experience.

Most probably theologians would not maintain that they have the bare feeling which may be called *numinous*. They would on the contrary hold that this experience is always of the deity. The very fact that they use the term 'revelation' or 'the disclosure by God of His Being' or the more dramatic concept of 'encounter', 'meeting God' shows that they want to include much more than bare awareness of a certain quality of consciousness called religious or numinous. They would hold that the uncanny experience is always *of* a deity and this *cognition* as a cognition *of the deity* is indubitable or self-validating. In order to keep the religious thought-forms in the background or in its nominal recognizable status theologians use very abstract terminology. They would not say that *numinous experience* reveals Jesus Christ or Lord Buddha or God,[6] but they would say 'a presence', 'Being of God', '*mysterium tremendum*', 'Transcendent Thou' and so on. However, it matters little whether we interpret the raw religious experience by concrete schemata or abstract ones, once we *accept* that interpretation is an undeniable process, we shall have to accept that

---

5. W. Arnold Hall, *Religious Experience as a Court of Appeal*, Hibbert Journal, Vol. 53, 1954-55, p. 367.
6. Because the concreteness and finiteness of such images are too obvious to be treated as the experience of Infinite God.

in principle theological statements are falsifiable. We shall, without any logical flaw, be in a position to find out the analysis and justification of dogmas, religious *schemata* and concepts. We can claim no immunity for theological statements from intellectual criticism.

If the theologians do not accept the corrigibleness of theological statements, then they would fall into a far greater danger than they imagine. They might utter: 'no matter what the world may say, one thing is certain I was *blind* and now I see',

> No matter what the world thinks about religious experience, the one who has it possesses the great treasure of a thing that has provided him with a source of life, meaning and beauty and that has given a new splendour to the world and to mankind. He has *pistis* and peace. Where is the *criterium* by which you could say that such a life is not legitimate, that such experience is not valid and that such *pistis* is mere illusion?[7]

Well, this experience may psychologically appear to be irrefutable, incorrigible, indubitable and self-validating, but this *feeling* of certainty is not *empirical* certainty which ensues from the intersubjective tests of an empirical statement by means of an agreed procedure containing a number of objective checks. Theologians claim empirical certainty by assimilating it to psychological certainty. Now we shall try to expose the danger of claiming psychological certainty.

Of course, the theist might say, 'I am experiencing God', feeling his presence, and I may also call it 'the Being of God'. The experience is so palpable and so convincing that the mystic may describe the whole situation as 'meeting him' or 'having encounter with him'. It is difficult indeed to analyse and clarify the concept of 'meeting God'. But this 'encounter with' or 'meeting' are concepts which are used with regard to sensible or observable persons and further such experiences are taken to be corrigible. However, apart from this linguistic difficulty with regard to concepts describing religious experience, the whole experience is

---

7. C.G. Jung, *Psychology and Religion*, p. 113.

akin to *hallucinatory* or delusional experience. This is what Russell had to say about Copleston's attempt to prove the existence of God from the mystic experience of him. People report seeing Satan in the same way as mystics report the *seeing* of God. The seeing of Satan

> seems to be an experience of the same sort as mystics' experience of God, and I don't see that from that what mystics tell us you can get any argument for God which is not equally an argument for Satan.[8]

Further, even Copleston as a good Roman Catholic did not regard mystic experience to be *immune* from discussion or criticism.[9] Quite obviously seeing a Satan is not a self-validating experience with regard to its content. In the same way the experiencing of God may be a true psychological experiencing, but the objectivity of God is not proved thereby. 'God' may be just the projection of a repressed image of one's own father, of one's infancy or of the primeval father of the primitive *horde*, as Freud would say.

Of course, there is the difference between having experience of God and a delusion of a Satan. The experiencing of God is followed by an integrative process of health, a feeling of friendliness for others,[10] a largeness of vision and a masculine vigour for all moral virtues accompanied with a peace of mind.[11] In contrast, the delusional experience of a Satan is followed by a disintegrative influence on the psychical health of the person and a deeply distressing condition which *leads* to gross maladjustment. But the *pragmatic* value of religious experience at most can vouchsafe for its desirability. For example, Paul Schmidt does not accept the objectivity of God and he denies that there can be any reasonable bridge from religious experience to the factuality of God. But he grants that religious experience is quite valuable. So one need not deny the value, worth, and the enjoyment of

8. Russell, B., 'Bertrand Russell and F. C. Copleston' in EG, p. 180.
9. EG, p. 181.
10. F.C. Copleston, *op. cit.*, p. 181.
11. W. James, *The Varieties of Religious Experience*, Longmans (1935), pp. 21, 414, 416.

religious experience, but one finds it difficult to accept the objectivity of God on the basis of *numinous experience*. Pragmatically one can prefer the seeing of God to the delusion of experiencing a devil, but on this score one cannot prove the factuality of God. Both in the last resort are deemed to be the projection of one's repressed wishes of one's infancy and being wholly psychic can lay no claim to the factuality of scientific statements. Of course, one can argue like Jung that God is an objective reality being a psychic entity. But according to his views even psychic reality has objectivity. For him it is a ridiculous prejudice to assume that existence can only be physical: Psyche is existent, it is even existence itself.[12]

'Physical' is not the only criterion of truth: there are also *psychic* truths which can neither be explained nor proved nor contested in any physical way.[13]

Again Jung tells us that God is an obvious psychic non-physical fact that can be established psychically and not physcially.[14] However, this is a departure from the usual usage of objective reality. Ordinarily the term 'objective' or 'reality' has relevance only with regard to that which can be established by the repeatable, public sense-experiences of many in a standardised way. Here Jung is confusing a psychic reality with the objectivity of public language.

One without committing any linguistic confusion can say that it seems to him that there is a star or that he is experiencing a feeling of elation. The processes are purely subjective,—they are psychological facts. We can devise tests for ascertaining their occurrence in a person. Similarly, one can claim the experiencing of God as a psychological experience. Nobody would take exception to it. Psychological health, creative love and other criteria may be accepted, for the time being for the sake of argument, as the adequate tests for verifying-falsifying the statement 'I am

---

12. C.G. Jung, *Psychology and Religion*, C.W. Vol. II, Routledge and Kegan Paul, 1958, p. 12; also *vide Modern Man in Search of a Soul*, pp. 187, 219-21; C.W. Vol. 16, p. 52.
13. C.G. Jung, *Answer to Job*, C.W. Vol. II, p. 359.
14. *Ibid.*, C.W. Vol. II, p. 464.

seeing God'. But by doing this we can at most say that A is having God-experience, a numinous experience or a religious experience belonging to a theistic tradition. The verification-falsification has nothing to do with the content of God-experience. In this context, God-statement and demon-statement have nothing to do with the objective factuality of God or demon. Here we are aware only of certain feelings, emotions, apparitions, phantoms and psychic archetypes. Here 'God exists' is just equivalent to God-experience. It stands on par with 'I have a headache'. The experience may be taken to be indubitable and if the verbal expression is carefully checked with regard to its correct use, then the statement may be taken to have a very high empirical certainty. The headache may be due to physiological reasons or due to neurotic causes, but that it is there can pass for a very high degree of certainty. It is very doubtful whether this kind of experience can be regarded as purely private and the protocol statement as wholly incorrigible.[15] But even if one concede a good deal of certitude to statement like 'I have a headache', and even if we further allow that God-statement is similar to this, it would not solve the problem of proving the existence of God from religious experience. The problem does not refer to religious experience itself, but to the object of worship which is revealed by religious experience. The dilemma may be put like this: If the experience is purely private, incommunicable, then it has all the subjective certainty which the religious man can claim for it, but it has no claim to the objectivity of the content of such an experience. And if the experience claims objectivity for its content, then it has to allow inter-subjective testing procedures. In other words, immunity can be claimed in two ways: first, by holding an analytic statement, i.e. God-experience implies God's existence. Secondly, by maintaining that one can have a purely private raw feelingfulness of God which can be enjoyed and can never be communicable through any thought-form or belief-form.

Many people argue, if there were no God, then how could any one have an experience of God? As now many theologians have become fully aware of the unconscious workings of the mind and the imaginal constructions of fictitious entities like fairies,

---

15. A. J. Ayer, 'Logical Positivism'.

centaurs and dragons so they cannot argue for the objective
existence on the basis of the theistic experience of God. Yet the
force of the analytic proposition that God's experience implies
his existence remains in the background. Hence, Copleston who
is fully alive to the problem and would not accept the analytic
proposition of God's existence from our experience of him, yet
writes:

> The actual basic experience at any rate is most easily expla-
> ined on the hypothesis that there is actually some objective
> cause of the experience.[16]

But the analytic proposition itself can assert nothing about the
actual existence of anything. The term 'experience' does not
mean more than 'the idea of God'. Both notions have only conceptual status and in themselves do not refer to any actual state
of affairs. For all practical purposes the argument that God's
existence follows from our experience of him is only another form
of the Ontological argument and, as such is open to the same
difficulties.

At one time it was thought that a sense-datum is an incorrigible entity. One couldn't be wrong with regard to it. 'I see blue'
was taken to be an incorrigible statement. It was held that one
could go wrong only when one tried to interpret it as a blue book
or blue sky or blue pen. Similarly, C.B. Martin tends to think
that a psychological statement which says nothing about a fact
or physical object can be incorrigible. For example, according
to him, 'I certainly seem to see a piece of blue paper' is incorrigible.[17] Well, if 'I experience God' were of the nature of this
psychological statement, then certainly it would be an unassaila-
ble statement. There is little doubt that John Baillie and H.H.
Farmer mean religious experience to be as incorrigible as psychological statements are: such an experience is considered to be
wholly private and incommunicable. According to J. Baillie,
argument is useless for those who never have had this experience
and is superfluous for those who have. Again, H.H. Farmer

16. EG, p. 179.
17. NEPT, p. 86.

holds that such an experience of God is impossible to communicate to persons who never have had it. But certainly both J. Baillie and H.H. Farmer do hold that such an experience of God is communicable to persons who have such an experience.

But can such an experience be communicated without some common underlying thought-forms? Not only both Baillie and Farmer are inter-communicating but are also doing so to many other Christian worshippers and thinkers. So the experience of God is after all not as private as could be claimed for it. The same is true for the same person himself. Baillie has not only the experience of God at the moment A, but he treasures it and reflects on it at subsequent moments. Naturally there is a common thought-form which remains the same for the same man under varied circumstances of recollecting the *same* experience of God. Hence, no experience can be really private. An experience which cannot be distinguished from other experiences and cannot be expressed even by the same person for his subsequent use, cannot even be noted. But if an experience can be noted, retained and subsequently used then it can be done only with the help of a language which in some sense always remains public. Even the purely psychological statement of C.B. Martin 'I feel pain' is not a purely private experience. 'I', 'feel' and 'pain' are all words of public language and a whole society of tests and check-up procedures are certainly possible with regard to the verification-falsification of 'I feel pain'. Hence, we think that there cannot be any private experience which remains communicable to others or to the experiencer himself at other subsequent moments. As 'I experience God' is a communicable statement, so it cannot be taken as an incorrigible, private and purely psychological statement. After all no truly synthetic propositions can ever be necessary.

However, Baillie, Farmer, Tillich, Buber, Otto and many others would never treat 'I experience God' as a purely subjective experience like 'I am enjoying myself' or 'I feel pain'. Only a fool will worship a fiction knowing it to be a fiction or his own state of mind, knowing it fully to be his own subjective feeling. But once we grant that there is a 'transcendent other', 'a living God', then the statement must be open to a whole society of tests and check-up procedures. And in that case the incorrigibleness and self-validatingness also disappear.

As yet we have not taken the case of mysticism which is taken to be the most acute, intense and living experience of God in its most concentrated form. The mystic claims to have the most direct and intimate experience of Divine Presence. It has a long history, but in the present century mysticism has been taken up seriously by William James, Dean W.R. Inge, R.A. Jones, Henri Bergson, Evelyn Underhill and W.T. Stace. Now we shall consider the claim of mystic experience to yield us the objective knowledge of God.

First, we shall take up the case of Theistic mysticism in which the mystic is not totally absorbed in the reality of God. Secondly, nobody is prepared to deny the value of mystic experience, but this value should not be taken as an argument for the objective reference involved in the claim of the mystic.

According to Henri Bergson, mysticism consists in the establishment of a contact and a partial coincidence with the creative Reality called God.[18] Is this contact and partial coincidence intellectual? Not purely. Then is it a matter of feeling? To some extent. It is what Bergson calls intuition. By intuition is meant intellectual sympathy by which one places oneself within the object and becomes what it is and thus knows it from within.[19] Thus mysticism is both a kind of feeling (sympathy) and also a form of knowledge. This is also the view of W. James. According to James feeling is the deeper source of religion[20] and this he calls mysticism.[21]

Along with the characteristic of ineffability, according to James, mysticism has a noetic quality by virtue of which it becomes informative of its object. He calls it a state of insight into the depth of truth unplumbed by discursive intellect.[22] Again,

---

18. I. Kant, *God as a Postulate of Practical Reason*, FG, p. 138.
19. 'An introduction to metaphysics', pp. 6, 9; 'Creative Evolution'(Macmillan, 1928), pp. 174, 186.
20. 'The will to believe and other essays' (1896), p. 116; The varieties of religious experience' (Longmans, 1935), pp. 431, 455, 501, 504; R.B. Perry, 'Thought and Character of William James', pp. 253, 255.
21. 'The varieties', p. 379.
22. *Ibid.*, p. 380.

according to James, the mystic remains wholly passive and he reports to remain "grasped and held by a superior power".[23] But what is guarantee of mystic experience to be veridical?

W. James does not accept the universal validity of mystic experience, but he grants that it is a self-validating experience for the mystic himself.

Mystical states, when well-developed, usually are, and have the right to be, absolutely authoritative over the individuals to whom they come.[24]

Again,

His (mystic's) insight into the what of life leads to results so immediately and intimately rational that the *way*, the *how*, and the *whence* of it are questions that lose all urgency.[25]

In the same strain Bergson tells us that the mystic does not directly perceive the power that moves him, but feels the indefinable presence through a symbolic vision of it.

"Then comes a boundless joy, an all-absorbing ecstasy or an enthralling rapture: God is there, and the soul is in God. Mystery is no more. Problems vanish, darkness is dispelled, everything is flooded with light."[26]

But subjective certainty no matter however intense, cannot be taken for the objective certainty of scientific truth. Both James and Bergson know this. They, therefore, advance a pragmatic and a therapeutic test for the validity of religious experience. For Bergson the truth of complete mysticism lies in making the mystics creative and energetic in all walks of life, since the reality as Elan Vital is essentially creative and is an unceasing activity. True mystics

burst a dam; they were then swept back into a vast current

---

23. 'The varieties', p. 381.
24. *Ibid.*, p. 422; *Vide* 'A Pluralistic Universe', pp. 307-08.
25. 'The will to believe', p. 136.
26. 'Two sources', p. 196.

of life; from their increased vitality there radiated an extraordinary energy, daring power of conception and realization.[27]

For James the human psyche is essentially conative and only secondarily cognitive. Consequently the primary pushes in life have to be satisfied and intellect has only an instrumental function to subserve in the services of elemental urges. The theorizing faculty, according to James,

> functions exclusively for the sake of ends that do not exist at all in the world of impressions we receive by way of our senses, but are set by our emotional and practical subjectivity altogether.[28]

However, according to James, for man there are certain problems as options for life as a whole which cannot be solved by intellectual means. These options are living because they continue to be insistent and persistent; they are forced because they haunt man day and night; they are momentous because they make a difference to the whole activity of man from the cradle to the grave. These problems are related to an unseen order which appears to a religious man to be 'coterminus and continuous' with this universe.[29] For Kant the transcendental illusions in the form of Ideals of reason arise from natural disposition. But for all their transcendental origin the objectivity of the unseen order in the form of God is illusory. For James, the living options never appear to be absurdities for the man who has them.[30] Hence, for James, when no intellectual means can decide the issues and when the issues are living, forced and momentous, then the religious man has full right to will to believe[31] in God. What are the advantages and proofs?

1. First, like Jung, James states that theistic beliefs cause regenerative changes in theists and

---

27. 'Two sources', p. 194; *vide* APR, p. 192, where R.M. Jones supports Bergson.
28. 'The will to believe', p. 117.
29. The varieties, p. 508; A pluralistic universe (Longmans, 1932), p. 307.
30. 'The will to believe', p. 29.
31. *Ibid.*, p. 11.

that which produces effects within another reality must be termed a reality itself. . . .[32]

2. Again, theistic beliefs as a result of saving experience from the unseen order adds zest in life and enhances the meaning of life. It

overcomes temperamental melancholy and imparts endurance to the subject, or a zest, or a meaning, or an enchantment and glory to the common objects of life.[33]

3. Further, William James was an ameliorist and believed that moral activity resulting in overcoming the ills of life is the supreme task of man. Materialism and agnosticism, according to James, do not support the moral nature of man. The right to believe in God is justified by the sense of adventure which it creates.

Not a victory is gained, not a deed of faithfulness or courage is done, except upon a maybe......
It is only by risking our persons from one hour to another that we live at all. And often enough our faith beforehand in an uncertified result *is the only thing that makes the result come true.*[34]

Walter Kaufmann has criticized James. Kaufmann says that James did not distinguish between legal and intellectual right to believe in an unseen order when there is no scientific evidence for its existence. However, one has no intellectual right to belief unless it is supported by sufficient evidence.[35] Again, with regard to the pragmatic argument of James, Kaufmann quotes the apt words of the poet philosopher George Santayana:

If the argument is rather that these beliefs, whether true or false, make life better in this world, the thing is simply false. To be boosted by an illusion is not to live better than to live in harmony with the truth; it is not nearly so safe, not nearly

32. 'The varieties', pp. 516, 517.
33. *Ibid.*, p. 505.
34. 'The will to believe', p. 59.
35. 'Critique of religion and philosophy', pp. 93-94.

so sweet, and not nearly so fruitful. These refusals to part with a decayed illusion are really an infection to the mind. Believe certainly; we cannot help believing; but believe rationally, holding what seems certain for certain, what seems probable for probable, what seems desirable for desirable, and what seems false for false.[36]

But apart from his metaphysical argument, Bergson offers defence concerning the cognitiveness of mystic experience and we shall take up this defence.

It has become fashionable to regard religious experience to be neurotic and Freud has called it 'patently infantile'. Bergson admits that mystics do talk of visions, ecstasies and raptures. And there may be cases of morbidity. Now if religious experience be morbid, then who will accept the deliverance of ravings to be knowledge proper?[37] In reply to this objection, Bergson as also James suggest that mystic states are not morbid but supernormal. The neurotic 'disturbance is a systematic readjustment with a view to equilibrium on a higher level'. The soul can pass from the static to the dynamic, from the closed to the open and from everyday life to mystic life only by receiving shocks and a state of disequilibrium. Here visions and ecstasies are merely incidental and take place in the state of preparation before reaching the stage of final illumination.[38] In the same strain James tells us that neurotic temperament furnishes the chief condition of receptivity of and sensitiveness to inspiration from the higher realm.[39]

As both the objection and reply to it are purely psychological and as philosophical analysis is more concerned with the context than with the origin of religious experience, so we turn now to the second objection which Bergson considers concerning mysticism. According to the second objection mystic experiences are highly individual and exceptional and are not verifiable. How can they be taken to be reliable? In reply to this Bergson points out that mystic experiences are also repeatable and verifiable if people care to undergo the same discipline to which the mystics subject themselves.

---

36. *Ibid.*, pp. 85-86.
37. 'Two sources', pp. 195, 209-10.
38. *Ibid.*, pp. 195-99.
39. 'The varieties', p. 25.

......the mystic too has gone on a journey that others can potentially, if not actually, undertake; and those who are actually capable of doing so are at least as many as those who possess the daring and energy of a Stanley setting out to find Livingstone.[40]

Again, there is another claim which Bergson maintains concerning the verifiability of mystic statements. He mentions that mystics generally agree among themselves and they mention roughly an agreed series of states. At least this is the case, according to Bergson, with regard to Christian mystics.[41] Now we shall take up claims both of unanimity and preparatory discipline.

As to unanimity, Bergson himself admits that there are God-blind people and they are utterly impervious to mystic experience.[42] So the unanimity among the mystics is a matter of a privileged class and this unanimity cannot be said to be open to public check. For this reason James holds that mystics have no right to force their verdict on the non-mystic.[43]

Thus, the unanimity among the mystics is not the same as the unanimity among the scientists with regard to the result of an experiment. Further, can the mystics claim agreement among themselves?

First, if we take a large view of mysticism in general, comprising the historical tradition of east and west, then the supposed unanimity vanishes. It is both ascetic and self-indulgent: it is dualistic in Sāṃkhya and monistic in Śaṁkarite Vedānta. It has been both theistic and pantheistic. Thus mystic unanimity is simply a matter of arbitrary selection.[44] Even Christian mysticism cannot claim any agreement. Bergson himself rejected Jewish, Greek and Indian mysticism in favour of his metaphysics of Elan Vital. W.R. Inge used mysticism to serve 'as a foundation for a modified form of Anglicanism' and Evelyn Underhill used mysticism for supporting Roman Catholicism.[45]

40. 'Two sources', p. 210.
41. *Ibid.*, p. 211.
42. *Ibid.*, p. 210.
43. 'The varieties', p. 424.
44. *Ibid.*, pp. 424-25.
45. 'The unanimity argument and the mystics', Marvin Kohl, *Hibbert Journal* Vol. LVIII, April 1960, pp. 273-74.

Hence, we reject the claim of agreement among the mystics. So there is really no verifiability with regard to mystic statements. But what about the claim of uniform preparatory discipline to have the mystic experience? Well, the discipline for having scientific experience is totally different from the discipline which the neophyte has to undergo in order to have the mystic experience. The scientist discipilnes himself to become as nearly an impersonal registering instrument for recording the data as is possible. He completely de-personalises himself with regard to the data he collects. There should be nothing by way of interests and expectations of the scientist in noting and recording the data of his experiment. In contrast, the mystic has to prepare himself psychologically to perceive what he wants to perceive.[46] If this be so, then chantings, prayers, fasting, meditations and other means of inducing mystic trance will be taken as so many means of having hallucinatory experience as a result of auto-suggestion. This is also supported by the fact that a Hindu mystic enjoys the vision of Rāma, Kṛṣṇa, Śiva and of other Hindu Gods; and a Christian mystic will report the vision of St. Mary, St. Paul or Christ. Thus the claim of mystic discipline cannot stand the test of scientific discipline and verification.

Again, mere unanimity of mystic experience will not do to establish the objectivity of God. There are numerous cases of agreement with regard to many illusions. For instance, every human subject will perceive the parallel rail lines converging towards the distance, will perceive the straight stick as bent in water and will report the seeing of water in desert and so on. In spite of agreement nobody will regard the convergence of parallel rails or the crookedness of the straight stick in water as facts. The agreement in such cases of illusions is largely due to the common nature of human sense-organs.[47] The human eyes are so constructed that they are bound to over-estimate the perpendicular and under-estimate the horizontal. Full and repeated agreement can be obtained with regard to such illusions. Hence,

---

46. Bella K. Milmed, 'Theories of religious knowledge from Kant to Jaspers', *Philosophy*, July 1954, p. 207.

47. W.T. Stace, 'Mysticism and Philosophy', Macmillan, 1960, pp. 136-46. The conclusion reached by Stace in his book is quite different from the view which has been maintained in this book.

mere agreement of the mystic report will not be very helpful in establishing the objectivity of God. As a matter of fact it was Kant who held that certain logical categories are used and must be used by human beings to explain the objectivity of scientific knowledge of phenomena. The logical constants, according to Kant, are due to the mental constitution of human beings as perceivers, thinkers and reasoners. However, the presence of transcendental illusions called paralogisms, antinomies and ideals, according to Kant, conclusively shows that no objectivity can be claimed if sense-experience is not allowed to verify and check the cognitive enterprise.

As a matter of fact, Freud too had suggested that the universal phenomenon of common myths amid varied races far removed in time and space is due to having the same proclivity towards mythical thinking. Hence, the unanimity of mystic experience may be due to the same uniform nature of mind at least in persons called the mystics. Hence, the unanimity amongst the mystics may be due to pure subjectivity and does not in itself prove the objectivity of God.

Hence, we conclude that the traditional mysticism cannot guarantee the cognitive status to theistic statements.

Therefore, God's existence cannot be proved from our experience of him. The experience of God is not a sense-experience. It is more of the nature of aesthetic experience or, better still, of an axiological nature. So let us examine the claim of establishing the existence of God from the moral experience of mankind.

CHAPTER XI

THE MORAL ARGUMENT FOR
THE EXISTENCE OF GOD

INTRODUCTION

In one sense the moral argument is the most important argument since it tries to establish the kind of entity which alone is the most worthy object of worship. What we worship is God and such a God is not bare existence (Ontological, Cosmological arguments), bare intelligence (Teleological argument) and even living spirit (argument from religious experience). He is absolutely Good and True and the Beauty which haunts the worshipper. However, the cognitiveness of the proof is much less clear here. So the empiricist does not stop to examine the moral argument by dissecting it with his technique of linguistic analysis. So we too would like to be brief.

The moral argument was first advanced in its typical form by I. Kant (1724-1804). As is well-known he had demolished all the extant arguments for the existence of God. However, in a famous statement he made the following remark:

> Two things fill the mind with ever new and increasing admiration and awe, the oftener and more steadily we reflect on them: the starry heavens above and the moral law within.

Later on John Henry Newman (1801-1890) in *A Grammar of Assent* (Longmans, Green & Co.), W.R. Sorley (1855-1935) in *Moral Values and the Idea of God* (Cambridge University Press), Hastings Rashdall (1858-1924) in *The Theory of Good and Evil* (Clarendon Press) and others like John Baillie, *The Interpretation of Religion* (T & T Clark, 1929), D.M. Baillie, *Faith in God* (T & T Clark, 1927), H.J. Paton, *The Modern Predicament* (George Allen & Unwin, 1955) have further elaborated the moral argument for the existence of God.

KANT'S MORAL ARGUMENT

In the quotation from Kant given above, it is clear that the moral argument is an expansion of the Teleological argument. In the Teleological argument the existence of God is sought to be proved from the purposive *order* in the universe. In Moral argument it is the *moral* order which is added as the decisive mark. However, for Kant the Moral argument was never taken as an intellectual argument for *proving* God. It is taken as a *postulate* and rests ultimately on *faith*. Hence, the Moral argument does not lay any claim to cognitive argument. However, in W.R. Sorley and H. Rashdall there have been attempts to give a cognitive status to the argument.

According to Kant in Moral consciousness we become aware of 'ought'. For example, we feel an obligation to speak the truth, or, we feel that we ought to return the debt we have contracted. This 'ought' implies that there are two or more alternatives: either we can speak the truth or withhold it, either we can return the debt or refuse to do it. Further, 'ought' implies that we are *free to make our choice* with regard to any alternative. This freedom in man shows that he is quite different from the phenomenal *nature* which is determined by rigorous causality or by what later on came to be known as *mechanical determinism*. Hence, to the extent man is moral he is free and therefore to that extent he is quite different from nature. As for Kant there were only two realms, namely, phenomenon and the noumenon, so if the free agent does not belong to the phenomenal nature, he must belong to the noumenal reality. Therefore, to the extent man is moral he belongs to noumenal reality. But the noumena are the ends for which the phenomena are: the appearances are the appearances of the things-in-themselves which alone form the reality. Hence, the moral agent, being a noumenal self is the reality.

However, man is not purely a moral agent. He is also an animal with desire for food and shelter, natural cravings for mate, sleep and other things. These natural desires form his phenomenal self. Man is not always directed by '*what ought to be*', his ideals, but also by '*what is*'. Man as much sleeps, eats and breathes as a thing of natural order, as he also feels an obligation of helping people in distress and of jumping into the angry waves of the Ganges to save a child from being drowned. For Kant, to the degree a man is moved by his natural cravings for food, mate and life he is a thing of nature, and by satisfying these natural cravings he obtains pleasure or happiness. However, by acting according to the demands of his Moral self, he belongs to a higher realm of *ends* or the reality. This demand of the noumenal self on the natural or phenomenal self is termed as *imperative*. This imperative Kant calls 'Categorical' or unconditional. Everybody to the degree he is moral feels an absolute obligation to help the needy, to speak the truth and so on, irrespective of reward or punishment for doing so. He expresses this absoluteness or the categorical nature of the moral obligation as the demand of the good will thus:

> "There is nothing in the world, nay, even beyond the world; nothing conceivable which can be regarded as good without qualification, saving alone a good will............A good will is good, not because of the consequences which may be frustrated by a niggardly provision of a step-motherly nature. A good will is good in itself, and like a jewel shines by its own light.

Hence, for Kant morality is autonomous and consists in having respect for the moral law alone. This *categorical imperative* as an obligation for a moral agent may be called *duty*. Therefore, Bradley calls Kant's moral theory as the theory according to which we have to perform our duties for the sake of duty. But when a person performs his duty, he may and may not get happiness. One has to perform his duty without any hope of reward or fear of punishment. After all virtue which comes from performing one's duty for duty's sake is its own reward, a good will is good in itself.

Kant emphasizes three things in his moral philosophy, namely,

1. Practical reason is higher than theoretical reason which is limited to phenomena alone. In morality we are the noumena. Therefore, the voice of the Good Will or the Categorical Imperative takes us to the very heart of the reality, the ultimate destiny of each individual. Hence, the moral life is a rational end of man.

2. Morality has a law which is not the decision of an individual or a group. It is based on a universal maxim and is binding on all persons irrespective of any caste, creed and custom.

3. Morality and scientific knowledge belong to heterogeneous realms. In the same way *Virtue* which follows the habitual performance of duty for duty's sake is quite different from *happiness* that follows from the satisfaction of natural wants. The two are quite independent of one another. The excellence or the justification of virtue comes from the respect of the moral law alone and from nothing else, e.g. neither from natural law and happiness, nor from religion. Morality is wholly autonomous. Now here Kant makes a shift towards theology.

True, happiness is ethically neutral and does not constitute moral excellence. However, happiness is also a good.

Happiness is the condition of a rational being in the world with whom *everything goes according to his wish and will*; it rests, therefore, on the harmony of physical nature with his whole end, and likewise with the essential determining principle of his will.[1]

However, the performance of duty or the attainment of virtue does not have any reference to happiness. The two are heterogeneous. Further, the practical reason impels us to promote the *summum bonum*, i.e. the highest good, which includes also happiness proportionate to virtue. As the two, happiness and virtue are heterogeneous, so it is only a postulate that two be harmonised. But how can the two be harmonised? This harmony cannot take place through the will of human beings alone: this can be achieved by a Being which is the cause of nature and is the supreme condition of causing human intelligence and will to promote *summum bonum* and the *summum bonum* includes happiness, so happiness must necessarily be connected with duty.

Nevertheless, in the practical problem of pure reason, i.e. the necessary pursuit of the *summum bonum*, such a connection is postulated as necessary: we ought to endeavour to

---

1. I. Kant, 'God as a postulate of Practical Reason', EG, p. 138.

promote the *summum bonum*, which therefore, must be possible.[2]

Hence, God who is the cause of all nature, the phenomenal and noumenal selves and who contains the ultimate principle of all connections is postulated to bring about the exact harmony of happiness with virtue. According to Kant if a judgement is *subjectively*, sufficient, but objectively insufficient, then for Kant it would be called *faith*. Hence, God as the postulate for promoting *summum bonum* is a matter of faith. Further, he wants us to be guarded against two possible errors. The duty of promoting *summum bonum* does not *promise* any happiness. Nor should we think that God's will is the reason and justification of morality. Morality is wholly autonomous and is to be judged by strict adherence to the laws prescribed by the *categorical imperative*. This is called by James Collins[3] as moral theology. God is postulated as a necessary implication of morality itself. And this implication is necessary and non-optional for the moral life.

And this need is not a merely hypothetical one for the arbitrary purposes of speculation, that we must assume something if we *wish* in speculation to carry reason to its utmost limits, but it is a need which has the force of *law* to *assume* something without which that cannot be which we must inevitably set before us as the aim of our action.[4]

The existence of God, for Kant, as shown in the proof, is not speculative and for this reason cannot be used for constructing metaphysics. It follows however from the Practical Reason as its necessary condition. In other words, we feel it our duty to promote the *summum bonum* with all our powers. This implies its possibility of being realised (i.e. the harmony of virtue and happiness in a completely holy will). And this possibility of realisation entails the existence of a Moral Judge as its necessary condition. True, the existence of God is a postulate whose exist-

---

2. EG, p. 138.
3. James Collins, 'God in modern philosophy', Routledge & Kegan Paul, 1960, p. 192.
4. Julien Benda, *Kant*, Cassell, 1948, p. 94.

ence cannot be demonstrated by Theoretical reason. That is, grant that there is morality and one will have no other option but to accept God as its necessary postulate.

> This, then, is an absolutely necessary requirement, and what it presupposes is not merely justified as an allowable hypothesis, but as a postulate in a practical point of view.[5]

At times he calls this postulate an objective foundation as it goes beyond the subjective inclination of individuals.

According to James Collins,[6] for Kant religion is an aspect of morality and is not at all the foundation of morality. As a matter of fact for Kant morality is wholly autonomous. However, Kant recognizes that morality as purely rational still requires God for energising the striving for the *summum bonum*, though not for giving it its reason. The real motive is always the *categorical imperative* out of the pure regard for the moral law. But for achieving the objective of moral striving one has to accept the postulate of God's existence. Thus the moral laws through the conception of the *summum bonum* lead to religion,

> that is, to the recognition of all duties *as divine commands, not as sanctions,............, but as essential laws of every free will in itself............*[7]

Again, Kant continues that the endeavour for the achievement of the *summum bonum* cannot be effected except through the harmony of our moral will 'with that of a holy and good Author of the world'.

> ....because it is only from a morally perfect (holy and good) and at the same time all-powerful will, and consequently only through harmony with this will that we can hope to attain the *summum bonum* which the moral law makes it our duty to take as the object of our endeavours.[8]

---

5. J. Benda, *Kant*, p. 133.
6. *Ibid.*, pp. 195-96.
7. EG, p. 141.
8. EG, p. 141.

CRITICAL COMMENTS

As was noted earlier Kant never took the Moral argument for a strict proof for the existence of God. Nevertheless there is little doubt that he regarded it more, rather than less efficacious on that account. The real implication of Kant's thought seems to be that man attains his individuality only by means of free choice of moral rightness, otherwise, man remains a mere indistinguishable existence. Further, he regarded this authenticity of individual existence as a thing of supreme value and reality. Consequently the implications of a just moral life have also to be granted their ultimate reality. According to this strain of reasoning God's existence is taken to be a necessary postulate of morality. The argument therefore is really an argument from the moral value in human experience, as A. Seth Pringle-Pattison puts it.[9] Kant himself regards the existence of a wise and a good God as an object of *faith*. Nevertheless for him it has a logical force too: God as the principle of explanation of the *summum bonum*,

> and consequently of a requirement for practical purposes, it may be called *faith*, that is to say a pure *rational faith*, since pure reason (both in its theoretical and its practical use) is the sole source from which it springs......[10]

But if God's existence is a *postulate* and is an object of faith, then no matter what we may think about the matter, it can never be warranted by logical cogency. No doubt for Kant *faith* afforded an ivory tower to religion, as a safety-vault from any attack of the sceptics. But in this case faith, being immune from logical attack delivers either meaningless or vacuous statements. Faith may serve as a hint or suggestion for any statement, but then it cannot be a substitute of any knowledge proper.

Again, Kant repeats *ad nauseam* that happiness and virtue are heterogeneous. If they are so unrelated, then how can there be any harmony between them? If virtue is not related to

---

9. A. Seth Pringle-Pattison, *The Idea of God*, Oxford University Press, 1920, Lecture II, pp. 37-38, 49-50.

10. EG, p. 140.

happiness, then it cannot be related even to happiness-worthiness. If it is maintained that their reconciliation is demanded by the moral conscience of mankind, then either grant that after all they are not unrelated or hetrogeneous, or else, they have been brought together arbitrarily by one's moral consciousness. If we hold that virtue and happiness are related then the whole of Kant's philosophy of morality and the distinction of phenomena and noumena become invalid. If we consider their union arbitrary, then the irrationality of the argument becomes too patent. If virtue and happiness are heterogeneous, then how can they be related by a third agency? By postulating God we cannot bridge the logical gulf of unrelatedness between virtue and happiness. At least the postulate of God cannot afford to do so. In the first place God is quite distinct from both of them. Happiness is the satisfaction of sentient desires and God has no sentient desires. Again, virtue is attained by performing duty for duty's sake, even in the face of temptation. And God has no temptation of any kind. His will is holy. Hence, God who has neither happiness nor morality cannot achieve the reconciliation between them. However, Kant thinks that God can achieve this union because he is 'the cause of all nature' and contains 'the principle of connection' of any type and kind. But God who connects what is connectable, cannot be supposed to reconcile what he himself has willed to be unrelated or heterogeneous. So once again either the heterogeneity of virtue and happiness is merely apparent and their reconciliation is the profounder truth or else God relates what he himself has created as unrelated. Besides, one may ask, how do we know that God has created the world? How has he been shown to be the author of human moral will and nature, according to Kant himself? Most probably this is the vital issue. Kant instead of proving this or attempting this begs the issue.

Now Kant's Moral argument can be made more effective if we would show that moral order is not contingent but belongs to the universe itself as its essential feature and further if we would show God to be the ultimate Being who is the fulfilment and realisation of the moral principle at the heart of the reality. This idealistic transformation of Kant's Moral argument takes place in the philosophy of Hastings Rashdall.

HASTINGS RASHDALL'S MORAL ARGUMENT

Rashdall according to the usual idealistic argument accepts the reality of the self and naturally also its activities which specially include duty and ideals, i.e., the facts of morality. He also grants that superficially speaking moral obligation does not appear to rest on any metaphysical commitment. But can 'true morality' be explicable without reference to a metaphysical world-view?

In the first instance, for Rashdall, the very validity of any statement whatsoever depends on its possibility of harmonising with the rest of human experience. In the context naturalism and materialism are also world-views. Can true or sound morality be consistently explained on the basis of naturalism and materialism? It cannot be explained by them, for the simple reason that they are based on the descriptive statements concerning what happens in the world. Morality, on the other hand, deals not with *what is*, but with *'what ought to be'*, not with *facts* but with *values* or *deals*. For materialism, says Rashdall, values are mere illusions. However, morality is a fact and so naturalism and materialism not being consistent with the facts of life have to be rejected.[11]

Again, the moral consciousness itself can be validly explained only when it harmonises with the moral verdicts of mankind in general. And Rashdall tells us that there is an absolute Morality, that there is something absolutely true or false independently of any number of human beings.[12]

The idea of such an unconditional objectively valid, Moral Law or ideal undoubtedly exists as a psychological fact.[13]

Granted now its being a psychological fact, how can absolute Morality be rationally justified? Now this absolute morality cannot exist in material things, says Rashdall, nor in the mind of this or that individual.[14] The absolute moral ideal can be said to be true for an absolute Mind alone. Hence, God as an absolute Mind is the only possible postulate of the absolute morality. For

11. EG, pp. 147-48.
12. Hastings Rashdall, The moral argument, taken from *The Theory of Good and Evil* in EG, p. 149.
13. *Ibid.*, p. 149.
14. *Ibid.*, p. 149.

explaining any superficial or relative morality one need not refer to the Absolute Mind, but one cannot consistently explain an 'objective' or absolute morality without postulating God as its logical presupposition, says Rashdall.

> A moral ideal can exist nowhere and nohow but in a mind; an absolute moral ideal can exist only in a Mind from which all Reality is derived. Our moral ideal can only claim objective validity in so far as it can rationally be regarded as the revelation of a Moral ideal eternally existing in the Mind of God.[15]

CRITICAL COMMENTS

The whole argument has been based on an idealistic metaphysics. As metaphysical arguments are not cognitive, so Rashdall's argument will not be regarded as logical. But apart from this general criticism, there are several features which require brief comments. Either morality is autonomous or else morality ceases to be a valid concept. According to idealism, which Rashdall accepts as the only possible *Weltanschauung* to satisfactorily explain morality, all things including human wills follow from the Absolute Mind. In this deterministic scheme of things, where is the room for free choice? Of course, W.R. Sorley advances the theory of self-limitation on the part of God to explain moral freedom in human beings. But this is not an easy concept, as we shall see for ourselves in the chapter on '*Evil and God*'. The difficulty of moral freedom does not lie with human *creatures* only, but with the possibility of *personal* God also. Personality, says Pringle-Pattison implies limitation, as we shall see in the following chapter. Thus, as in Spinoza, Hegel and Bradley, the Absolute is beyond a personal God. Hence, idealism has no place for personality without which there is no possibility of any morality whatsoever. Hence, an idealistic metaphysics cannot bear the stress and strain of the logic of moral discourse.

Further, Rashdall makes a distinction between 'morality' and 'true morality'. Where is the line to be drawn between them? True morality for Rashdall is an objective morality. But is it

---

15. *Ibid.*, p. 150.

not arguing in a circle? The problem is with regard to the objectivity of a moral ideal and can an *ideal* be objective or actual? This is a contradiction in terms. The truth-claim and objectivity are no longer admissible in the current logic of moral discourse. And Rashdall himself holds that the objective morality is 'a psychological fact'.[16] Can a psychological fact claim empirical factuality of its content? That the moral feeling is psychologically felt will be granted by all. But that is not the question when one wants to explain its objectivity. One usually refers to the moral law, Goodness or Rightness, existing independently in its own right apart from any human consciousness. Rashdall makes two self-contradictory statements here. First he tells us

that there is something absolutely true or false in ethical judgements, whether we or any number of human beings at any given time actually think so or not.[17]

And yet again he tells us

A Moral ideal can exist nowhere but in a mind...[18]

Thus the objectivity of moral law cannot be accepted in the empirical sense of science. And once we reject the claim of morality to be objective, we lose the very premise from which the conclusion was drawn with regard to the existence of God.

But most probably we are overdoing the thing by too much criticising Rashdall's proof. Rashdall himself grants that God's existence is no more than a postulate of a sound morality and that is also a *secondary* postulate of morality.[19] The moral ideal is a matter of decision by human beings in order to act in some particular way. This decision always implies the personality-involvement of the moral agents. Any argument from morality therefore has to accept this theory of personality-involvement. Consequently the moral argument has to be appraised in convictional language. However, it fails as an argument for the factuality of God in the public language of science.

16. *Ibid.*, p. 149.
17. *Ibid.*, p. 149.
18. *Ibid.*, p. 150.
19. EG, p. 150.

CONCLUDING SUMMARY OF THE ARGUMENTS

We have examined some of the most popular proofs for the existence of God. We have come to the conclusion that *necessity* and *Being* of God cannot be simultaneously maintained without making theological statements either self-contradictory or vacuous. But if we talk about God, we have to ascribe both necessity and being to God. This makes unintelligible discousre about God. We are maintaining that in the public language of science God's existence can neither be verified nor falsified. But we need not conclude that we cannot talk about God's existence. This talk is possible, however, not in the public language of science but in the convictional language of the believer. We can profitably quote here Paul Tillich:

> The arguments for the existence of God neither are arguments nor are they proof of the existence of God. They are the expressions of the *question* of God which is implied in human finitude. The question is their truth; every answer they give is untrue.[20]

The same conclusion is true with regard to *Attributes of God.*

---

20.   Systematic Theology, Vol. I. p. 205.

CHAPTER XII

THE PHILOSOPHY OF THEISM
THE ATTRIBUTES OF GOD

INTRODUCTION

We have already stated that the logic of worship implies that God must be the highest and infinite being greater than whom nothing can be conceived by the worshipper. However, he must be much more than mere being. Even the proofs concerning infinite Intelligence (Teleological proof) and Goodness (Moral Argument) would not establish the worshipfulness of God. Hence God cannot be a mere God. He must have attributes on account of which he becomes worshipful.

It is doubtful whether any substance can be without attributes: at least a God cannot be conceived without some attributes and of course, there can be no divine attributes independently of God. From the metaphysical viewpoint God has the attributes of unity, spirituality omnipotence, eternity, immutability and absoluteness. Religiously speaking God is conceived to be a person, creator, eternal, omnipotent, infinitely wise and good, transcendent-immanent and holy. For us the theological concepts concerning God's attributes are more to the point and therefore we shall try to consider some of these divine attributes.

PERSON

God has a number of attributes. But most probably from the viewpoint of worship, the person of God is the most important. For Spinoza, of course, the intellectual love of God asks for no recompense: it is unrequited and unreciprocated. It is enough for the worshipper to know that he loves God: it matters little to him whether God loves him or not. It is the love of the moth for the flame. This love is not selfish, nor unselfish, but selfless. Spinoza could maintain this, because his God is impersonal. But can a human worshipper pray to a mountain or even to a vast machine? It will be called 'raving' and not prayer. A God to whom prayers are said is a person. He may not hear the prayers at the time they are made, but in principle God must be able to hear them and in due course to answer them. A worshipper not only prays to God and loves him, but hopes that God will be responsive to him. As a matter of fact it is the love of God which awakens a man's wonder.

> What is man, that thou art mindful of him?
> and the son of man, that thou visitest him?

But if God is mindful of man and takes note of him,[1] then he is a person. A person is a self-conscious unity of cognitive, conative and affective processes, of ideals, obligation and purposes. God acts and enjoys his activity: he creates the universe and enjoys it.

> And God saw everything that he had made, and behold, it *was* very good.[2]

Not only God performs his creative acts but he knows that they are his and that they proceed from him. God is a self-conscious unity of his thinking, perceiving, willing and so on. Nay, his unity is most complete, all-comprehensive and past, present and future are all in him as an ever-present *now*. Let us illustrate this point.

Human persons are also so many integrated selves. Each person persists through his experiences of childhood, adult life and his present preoccupation as one unified self. We human persons are finite and we include very few experiences of past memories, present perceptions and future anticipations in our awareness. But we can conceive of an infinite person who sustains all the experiences in one span of self-conscious unity. In this most complete and comprehensive unity, past, present and future are integrated as one whole.

This concept of God as a person follows from the very nature of the logic of worship. He must be an infinite being with surpassing excellence. Hence, if he is a person (and as a responsive God to a theistic worshipper he cannot but be a person), then he

---

1. Psalms, 8:3-4.
2. Genesis I, 31.

must be an all-comprehensive and perfect person. His thinking, feeling and willing must be infinite and yet he must be a *unified* experience of all his acts, ideals, obligations and purposes. These requirements give rise to many theological problems. As God cannot be conceived to have senses like man, his thinking cannot be conceptual or discursive. This is what the Vedantins, Spinoza and Bradley have maintained. According to Spinoza the highest form of knowledge is of the intuitive kind in which everything seems to follow from the nature of substance, as in a flash. Hence, God may be pictured to be knowing everything in one sweep of perceptual flash. In the same way Bradley maintains that the highest experience is a post-relational whole, in which all distinctions are held up together in one sentient experience. In this sense, God is said to be *Omniscient*. As for God there can be no past and future, so the problem of foreknowledge does not arise. However, we shall find that a theist maintains that God has created free wills in the form of human beings. Now if men are free, then can God know what a free creature will do in advance? Even if we overcome the difficulty of knowing free acts in advance, then the other difficulty will be: If God knew in advance that most men will misuse their free will for producing moral evils, then why did he do so? Thus the attribute of perfect knowing is full of inopportune questionings.

As God is perfect will, he must be acting for some perfect ideal or goal. As God is perfect, he is infinitely good. Naturally he need not act for achieving any greater degree of goodness. Further, any activity as a form of conatus either contributes to greater or lesser being of the individual. But God is perfect and there can be no increase-decrease in his being. So either no activity is possible for God or else he is not perfect. Even if we override the difficulty concerning activity on the part of God, we have to ascertain the nature of this activity. A theist maintains, on pain of being an idolator otherwise, that God is *Omnipotent*. Can God perform what is logically absurd? Can he make $2+2=5$? Again, the most important activity of God is said to be his free creativity. Does God create out of something or out of nothing? Can anything be created out of nothing? These are some of the perplexing problems that arise with regard to God as a creator.

Further, what is the relation of God to the created world? Is he immanent in it or transcendent to it or somehow both?

A theist believes that God has feeling too. He is affected by what his creatures do. Now if the sufferings and triumphs of men do affect God, then he is not immutable. And if he is not affected by the vicissitudes of human life and other things of his creation, then he can hardly be said to be a person.

The problem of divine attributes follows from God as a person who is a unified experience of thinking, feeling and willing. How is this unity to be conceived? In human person the unity keeps on changing. No person remains exactly the same integrated self in youth and old age, in health and sickness, in the hours of fatigue and freshness. But God's unity is supposed to be the same. Yahweh declared himself to be the same yesterday, today and for ever: 'I am that I am'. How is this immutable, unchangeable unity to be conceived?

GOD AS IMMUTABLE AND ETERNAL

Religious man contrasts the everlastingness of God with the ephemeral existence of man and of all other created things. Man is just like the grass which today is and tomorrow is cast into the oven.[3] Nay God has been existing before the foundation of the earth and will continue to be the same even when the heavens pass away.[4]

> Before the mountains were brought forth, or ever thou hadst formed the earth and the world, even from everlasting to everlasting, thou *art* God.[5] For a thousand years in thy sight *are but* as yesterday when it is past, and *as* a watch in the night.[6]

How is this sameness or immutability of God to be understood?

Change is the mark of imperfection, for any change is either for the increase or decrease of being. God is perfect and does not have any development and he can strive for no end whatsoever.

3. Psalms, Chap. 103, V. 15-16.
4. Psalm, Chap. 102, V, 25-27.
5. Psalms, Chap. 90, V. 2.
6. Psalms 90-4.

He is the Alpha and the Omega. That is, the Omega does not *follow* the Alpha but *is* the Alpha; there is One Being, *all* at once, and complete at once.[7]

Is this immutability without change? If it is, then it is not supported by anything in human experience. 'Eternity' has been used in four senses:

1. Timelessly logical and mathematical truth.
2. Enduring through all times.
3. Time is retained and yet transcended as total simultaneity.
4. As the fulfilment of all values in the best way.

Hence, it has been maintained by some theologians that God is changeless with regard to his *essence*, but has change insofar as his accidents are concerned. In this sense, God may contain many histories but has no history of his own. This notion too is full of difficulties. Do accidents of God affect him? Are they in any sense *his* accidents? If they are his, then they do belong to him and he cannot shake them off. And if they do not affect him, then they are *not his* accidents. In any account of God's eternity time has to be retained and yet reconciled with his perfection. And these two claims are difficult to reconcile. Now we have mentioned the term 'eternity' and we have to clarify this notion too.

The concept of 'eternity' has been used in four senses.[8] It may mean that which is timeless or that which is independent of time. This is best illustrated in the axioms of logic, e.g., the law of identity or non-contradiction: A is A, or, A cannot be both B and not-B. This is supposed to be the view of St. Aquinas. According to St. Augustine, time is the characteristic feature of things creaturely and not of God. But the various quotations and references made from *Psalms* show that the Judaeo-Christian tradition conceives God as that who is everlasting or who *endures* for ever. The recurring phrase is 'God's mercy endures', 'his truth

7. Peter Anthony Bertocci, *Introduction to the Philosophy of Religion*, Prentice-Hall, 1963, p. 310.

8. *An Encyclopaedia of Religion*, Edited by Vergilius Ferm, Peter Owen, 1964; also see A. Seth Pringle-Pattison, "The Idea of God", Oxford University Press, 1920, p. 343.

endures' and 'who is from everlasting to everlasting'. God's eternity has to be understood as that which endures through the whole series of unending time. But even this concept of God as enduring from everlasting to everlasting can be understood in two senses.

We have already stated that in God past, present and future are all given at once as a single now. This is the view of the idealists like J. Royce and F.H. Bradley.

"The Absolute has no history of its own, though it contains histories without number...nothing perfect, nothing genuinely real can move. The Absolute has no seasons, but all at once bears its leaves, fruit, and blossoms".[9]

However, this view of Bradley is open to the objection which he himself levelled against time as a durationless unit. If the everlasting *now* does not change, then it is no unit of duration at all; and if the *now* does contain succession then all of time cannot be presented together. Hence, this view of time as contained in eternity contradicts the very notion of time. In the language of Bergson, time is spatialised and the succession is speciously pictured as simultaneity. Hence we come to the third view of time given by Bergson.

According to Bergson, real time is duration, eternal creativity without any beginning or end.

> Duration is the continuous progress of the past which gnaws into the future and which swells as it advances.[10]

Thus conceived for Bergson God himself is a continuity of shooting out:

> God, thus defined, has nothing of the already made; He is unceasing life, action, freedom.[11]

This view of ceaseless creativity can hardly do justice to God's immutability and everlastingness. Eternal creativity without any

---

9. F.H. Bradley, 'Appearance and Reality', pp. 499-500.
10. H. Bergson, 'Creative Evolution', Macmillan & Co., 1928 (Tr. A Mitchell), p. 5.
11. *Ibid.*, p. 362.

beginning or end has no unity of aims, purposes and ideals. A God, on the other hand, for a theist is a dependable person, a rock of ages, a shield and a sword in the face of all troubles. The ceaseless duration of Bergson is too blind and aimless creativity for the purpose of worship. Hence, in spite of Bergson's profession to the contrary, his religion tends towards mystic pantheism.

Most probably the best theistic view is that according to which eternity is interpreted not as durationless or enduring through all series of time but as an axiological state realised through time. This is the view which has been hinted at by A. Seth Pringle-Pattison in *'The idea of God'* and *'The idea of immortality'*. A work of art takes time to be planned and executed but once it becomes a thing of beauty, it is a joy for ever and it would never pass into nothingness. An appreciating eye would not be bothered by the historical dating of the work, nor will it be very much affected if it came to know that 'Mona Lisa' took twenty years or more to become a finished work of art. All that it cares to note is that it is a priceless thing of art. It will like to be absorbed, lost and melt into the splendour of its beauty. Once a work of art becomes a thing of value, it becomes independent of its being conceived in terms of time. No doubt any work of art has its beginning or end, but the real end is not the termination but the meaning of the whole work.

> The End is not the final stage which succeeds and supplants its predecessors; it is the meaning or spirit of the whole, distilled, as it were, into each individual scene or passage.[12]

Thus interpreted time is the vehicle of meaning or value. And value is an eternal thing. In this sense, God may be looked upon as the creator of values through the mutations of time. Here we look upon the ceaseless activity of God not in terms of time but in terms of his quality or value-creation.

But even this view is not free from difficulties. Do new values add to the being of God or do they not? Are all values for ever realised in God or are all values so many incidents in the life of God which make no difference to his being? Bertocci suggests

---

12. A.S. Pringle-Pattison, 'The Idea of God', p. 362.

that God is all-perfect and his activities do not add anything to him.

> To be in 'full possession' of all his potentialities, so that all he ever could be he *now is*—perfect symphony: is not such a life really eternal? Never to wax or wane, ever to remain in this perfect equilibrium of all powers enjoyed at their best: this is *the* life.[13]

Might be *the* life, but in this case the exercise of activity is a necessity which makes no difference to his being. And this is the conception of Lila or Sports in Indian Theism. The world here is either a perpetual cyclic activity or *seemingly* progressive process of Samuel Alexander. In either case, world or creativity becomes meaningless play. The full blast of this difficulty will be felt with regard to God as creator.

We can conclude now that the personality which a theist ascribes to God follows from the implication of worship. But it is bristled with difficulties. If we emphasize the unity of Gods' person then time and processes are denied; and if we emphasize the processes we lose sight of the unity of Gods' person. Now let us take the process of thinking which is involved in conceiving God as a person.

OMNISCIENCE AND FORE-KNOWLEDGE OF GOD

God is an omniscient being, for he has created all things that are. And as such how can he be ignorant of the laws that hold between them? He who made the eyes can he be ignorant of the laws of optics? God's thoughts are as much logical as is possible, since the laws are eternal and they have their basis in God. Hence, Bertocci observes[14]:

> A square circle is as contradictory to God as it is to us. God's thinking finds itself informed and permeated by the ideal of consistency. Indeed, it is our thesis that the world exemplifies logical structure, and that our created minds are guided on

---

13. P.A. Bertocci, *Ibid.*, pp. 311-12.
14. P.A. Bertocci, Introduction to the Philosophy of Religion, p. 448.

this silently operative ideal *because* God's thinking is guided by logical ideals which he can neither create nor destroy.

If God is eternal, then all his attributes are eternal and if thought is an attribute of God then its eternal laws must be characterising God's thinking or knowing. But at this stage an inopportune enquiry crops us. There are many forms of logic. Are the thoughts of God guided by two or three or many valued logics? Can we now describe the laws of logic as the laws of things? These questions cannot be easily replied to by a theist. But apart from such enquiries, God is said to know the hidden thoughts of every one of us: before whom everyone is like an open book. Jesus said to Nathanael 'when thou wast under the fig tree, I saw thee'. Hence, God is supposed to know everyone individually and completely. If it is so, then does he foreknow what a free individual person is going to do? Of course, foreknowledge to be called knowledge must be precise and accurate. Concerning God's foreknowledge two opposed views are being held by the theist. According to St. Augustine, God foreknows even the free decision of every individual in advance. However, many freewillists like Jonathan Edwards, Henri Bergson, Samuel Alexander and P.A. Bertocci deny God's foreknowledge of free decisions.

If theologians like Calvin hold that everything is predetermined and predestined from the very beginning, then like a calculator or even like an intuitive seer one can know in advance the future course of history and of human decisions. But this is not an important point of much controversy; for many of the theists do not accept the possibility of predetermination. For them an individual is indefeasibly free and a free decision for them cannot be foreknown. St. Augustine admits that an individual person is free and yet that his free decision can be known in advance. His argument is that free knowledge does not affect the nature of the act itself. Suppose somebody knows in advance that Ram would go to exile, then this foreknowledge does not prevent the exile of Ram. In the same way, St. Augustine contends 'that we will what we will' even when this is foreknown.

By the fact of his (God's) foreknowledge power (of choice) is not taken from me—a power which therefore is more cer-

tain to be because He whose foreknowledge is not deceived
has foreknown that the power will be (in the future mine).[15]

The problem of God's foreknowledge of free decisions will be
taken up again with regard to '*Evil and Suffering*'. However, the
important point is not that God's foreknowledge will predetermine
an act, but the point under dispute is, whether a free act can be
foreknown at all. A free act has nothing of the already made: it
consists in the creative throw of the new. Therefore, Bergson and
Alexander hold that the future of its very nature is unpredictable.

> Human nature is a growing thing, and with the lapse of real
> Time may throw up new characters which can only be known
> to him who experiences them.[16]

For Alexander, voluntary action is determined and yet unpredictable. We shall find that the empiricists like A.J. Ayer, A.
Flew and J.L. Mackie hold just the reverse: the willed act is free
and yet wholly foreseeable. However, for Bergson, only the repeatable is foreseeable. But human action is never reproductive only:
it is a new creation, for it swells as it advances and is influenced
by the incremental past accretions.

> But if our action be one that involves the whole of our per-
> son and is truly ours, it could not have been foreseen, even
> though its antecedents explain it when once it has been accom-
> plished.[17]

Similarly, Bertocci holds that God knows all the possible moves
on the cosmic checkboard and no action for him can be a complete surprise.

> But if John is free to choose one or the other, God cannot
> know whether John will choose A or B *until* John chooses.[18]

Hence, we find that the problem of God's Omniscience and
Foreknowledge is full of difficulties. Some of these will come up

---

15. Bronstein and Schulweis, APR, p. 297.
16. S. Alexander, 'Space, Time and Deity', Vol. II, p. 324; also see p. 329.
17. H. Bergson, *Creative Evolution*, p. 50.
18. P. A. Bertocci, *op. cit.*, p. 449.

again with regard to the problem of '*God and evil*'. On the whole
those theists who hold that God cannot foresee the free decision
of human wills, also maintain that this limitation of God has
been brought out by God himself. But how far can this self-
limitation go? Does he know what imperfection is? Does he know
what sin is? Does God know the way man knows with all his
limitations, temptations and finitude? If God, *ex hypothesi* cannot
know this, then he ceases to respond to man on the terms of man
and ceases to be a *person* for a worshipper. However, if God
knows things as human beings experience them in the form of
sins, sufferings, puzzlements and embarrassment then God ceases
to be perfect. These are some of the problems which have been
taken up by F.H. Bradley, B. Bosanquet and A.N. Whitehead.
Unless we grant that God knows through human vessels, those
difficulties are hard to be solved. And even then can they be said to
be solved at all? We shall take up the views of Bradley, Bosanquet
and Whitehead in relation to 'Hopes of immortality'. Now we
have to take up the attribute of Omnipotence which goes with
divine willing and creating.

GOD'S OMNIPOTENCE

The word Omnipotence is composed of two Latin words *omnis*
(all) and *potens* (powerful). God is supposed to be a power to do
all things. But it does not mean that God's power is to be conceived independently of other attributes of goodness, love, justice
or consistency. It is absurd to think that God can make the
square circle or that he can kill himself or commit sin.

> Indeed, the *failure to realise that the attributes of God must
> be seen in their togetherness has been the source of much mis-
> understanding and has led to the creation of false problems*.[19]

In the same way God's power can hardly be understood as a
monopolistic concentration of power. The very fact that a theist
thinks that God has created free wills, means that God has vol-
untarily delegated his powers to human beings. This sharing of
powers has serious meanings for both parties. In any case God

---

19. *Ibid.*, p. 321.

uses his powers with due regard to others and in conformity with his justice, love and goodness. In this sense Charles Hartshorne interprets omnipotence as an influence, ideal in quality, degree and scope with all things subject to its optimal (not absolute) control.

> This control is 'irresistible' in the sense that no being can simply withdraw from its reach, and that nothing can prevent it from continuing its beneficent work everlastingly.[20]

Hence, omnipotence does not mean doing all things, but the power of doing all that is worth doing.[21] However, the most important aspect of God's power is one of creation and his relation of transcendence-immanence to it. We shall, therefore, turn to this creatorship of God.

Most probably for the Judaeo-Christian theologian this is the most important attribute of an eternal, infinite and personal God. According to this tradition God is perfect and does not require anything to make his perfection any fuller. And yet God is said to be a creator. This concept is closely associated with the Hebraic notion of Yahweh who is essentially a self-revealing God. He does not require to be sought after, but who seeks one and chooses his men and nation. Yahweh used to come to Adam and Eve in the Garden of Eden; he chose Abraham, Isaac and Jacob and finally chose the Jews as his own people. God out of his own creative and suffering love sent his own beloved son to be crucified for the remission of the sins of his own chosen people. Now the concept of creation evolves out of this outgoing, redeeming and creative love of God. Naturally this intensely religious concept is hard to reconcile with the cold philosophical analysis of contemporary times. The philosophical framework cf thought at the present time is greatly influenced by physico-mathematical language and is far removed from the convictional language of Hebraic religion. So let us at first try to understand the precise meaning of God as a creator.

For a theist God must be infinite and a finite God is not a proper object of worship. Secondly, God must be distinct from his

---

20. Vergilius Ferm, *An Encyclopedia of Religion*, p. 546.
21. P.A. Bertocci, *op. cit.*, p. 322.

worshipper, otherwise worship itself will become logically impossible. Keeping these two factors in mind the term 'creation' has to be distinguished from the allied notions of 'making' and 'following or emanating'. Ordinarily a potter is said to make a pot out of pre-existing matter called clay. Here he simply fashions out a pre-existing material into a desired thing. Here the potter is not all-in-all, he has to wrestle with the refractory nature of the clay. He is limited by the materials which he moulds into a pot. God cannot be a *maker* of the universe if by it is meant that God fashions the world out of pre-existing something, call it 'matter' or 'darkness' or 'chaos' or what one wills. In this case God is reduced to the status of an *architect* who is hampered by a co-eval co-eternal and a refractory pre-existing matter. This will not be monotheism, but dualism, since besides God, matter also becomes co-existent or co-eval with God. Under the circumstance God will be limited by matter and He would cease to be an infinite and perfect Being. Such a finite God, limited by pre-existing matter will cease to be an object of worship for a Judaeo-Christian worshipper. Hence what is necessary is that God should additionally be conceived as the creator of the materials too.

However, even this phrase that God is the maker of all that is can be interpreted in different ways. Here the interpretation is either pantheistic or theistic. According to a pantheist all is God and God is all and everything comes out of God. However, according to a pantheist the world follows from or emanates from God. Plotinus and Spinoza are the two significant instances of religious pantheism. The imagery of Spinoza is Geometrical. For him the world follows from God in the same way in which all the angles of a triangle are together equal to two right angles follows from the very definition of a triangle. This Spinozistic concept is very defective and one important consideration against it is that this relation of world and God becomes as static as the relation of angles is with regard to the triangle. However, 'creation' emphasizes the *activity* of God which is absent from the pantheistic note. Plotinus fares no better. He uses the imagery of the sun and its rays. As the rays emanate from the sun, so the world emantes from God. This imagery has the advantage of showing God's creativity and the utter dependence of the world on God. However this notion suffers from a fatal defect peculiar to all forms of Pantheism, whether of Spinoza or of Plotinus or of the Absolute Idealism. Here the world and creatures become one with God. Under the circumstance God becomes responsible for all the ills of nature and evil deeds of men. Man is reduced to the status of a pipe through which the divine music rings; but no longer does he remain responsible for his own misdeeds. This is revolting to a Judaeo-Christian worshipper. For him God is holy and all-perfect and he cannot be the author of ills and evils. Any evil attributed to God takes away his Goodness and Holiness and lessens his Worship-worthiness.

The other point is that in Pantheism, God ceases to an object of worship. The worshipper and worshipped coalesce into one and so there can be no object which a worshipper can distinguish from himself to adore. Further, a Judaeo-Christian worshipper regards himself free and he thinks that the very purpose of God's creation is to have free wills who by subordinating their wills to the will of a good, gracious, co-suffering and creative Love can become fit for God's fellowship. On the other hand, Pantheism tends to rob worshippers of their freedom of will.

Hence, creation is to be distinguished from 'making' and 'emanation'. God is the absolute creator of all that is God. Nothing can exist apart from him. In order to emphasize the utter dependence of all things that are and his absolute existence a theist says that God creates the universe out of *nothing* and that he is the sustaining cause of everything in it. This nothing is nothing and not something like darkness or chaos. Hence, there is no room for an architect God or an impersonal God of Pantheism. This notion of *creation exnihilo* is full of difficulties: the difficulty of the relation of immanence and transcendence of God to the world, the difficulty of reconciling perfection with the participation of God in the suffering of men. But whatever be the difficulties in the notion of creation, a theist wants to hold that perfect God does not become less perfect or more perfect by his creation and this he tells us is possible because God creates the world out of nothing. Bertocci repeatedly tells us that the whole notion of creation is a mystery and it will be so for man for he himself is a created being.

Frankly, we do not know what is actually involved in God's

creation. But we are trying to express by this word *creation* the fact that God does bring into being what was not real either as a part of him or as a part of something independent of him. We must simply confess that we do not know *how he does it*......Perhaps we may console ourselves, at least, with the realisation that if there were anything a created mind could not be expected to understand, it would be its own creation.[22]

But is the theist paralyzed by this puzzlement? A. Jung will say 'Yes'. Yahweh does not think so. The closing chapters of the Book of Job emphasize the mystery of creation and this knowledge is calculated to instil righteousness in the hearts of men. Yahweh demands of Job:

Where wast thou when I laid the foundations of the earth? Declare, if thou hast understanding. Who hath laid the measures thereof, if thou knowest? Or who hath stretched the line upon it? Whereupon are the foundations thereof fashioned? Or who laid the cornerstone thereof;.........[23]

Let us state now the facts of creation as theist sees it, before raising philosophical issues with regard to them. God is perfect and no amount of creation can add or subtract the perfect being of God, though there can be more of beings or things as a result of divine creation. Out of his sheer creative love God creates creatures. The creation may be as much through evolutionary process as by a fiat of will. The Biblical story of creation does not speak of 'days' in the ordinary sense, since the sun and the moon were created on the fourth day and yet the three days were said to have elapsed before their creation. The sole purpose of creation for a theist is to have creatures endowed with free will and intelligence, who by overcoming temptations will become worthy of God's fellowship. This task is difficult to achieve and can be realised through much failure, pains and sweats of years by successive stages.

As we can see for ourselves dead nature was first to come forth and in due course this earth was formed with atmosphere,

---

22. P.A. Bertocci, *op. cit.*, p. 451.
23. Job, Chap. 38, verses 4-6.

light and water. Then, in fulness of time, somehow which still baffles conjecture life appeared on the surface. In the beginning it was very feeble and could hardly be distinguished from matter. But gradually and slowly it began to multiply and vary along many routes of advance. Afterwards another marvel announced its arrival, namely, consciousness and will. When and how they appeared are still in the womb of darkness, but that they did appear is undeniable. In the beginning the struggle of existence for food and mate was intense and nature was 'red in tooth and claw', but in due course in the fulness of seasons ideals dawned and began to dominate the course of history. Today human beings stand as heirs to a great fund of human heritage of goodness, beauty, heroism, truth and wisdom. Great men have become beaconlights of men: they have achieved goodness by sacrificing their joys, pleasures and comforts of life. There have been artists who have beautified life and have educated human impulses in an integrated whole; there have been scientists who wrestled long with the superstitions of ages and have laid solid foundations for the conquest of the height, depth and wildness of the universe. The story of human civilization is very incomplete and the victory achieved is yet precarious. Much has to be achieved and consolidated. But man knows that ultimately ideals will triumph; history does contain the truth of human failures of living as its recurring theme, but prophecy containing the hopes and aspirations that have brought mankind so far, contains the greater truth.

The theist feels that God has created the universe and he is also the Lord of history. He will not leave his worshipper in the midst of duped hopes and the mockery of efforts in the pursuit of values. In God all values are said to be actualised and fully embodied. In communion with him, the theist will triumph over his temptations and by the grace of God he will realise truth, beauty and goodness in his life. By living according to the will of God the worshipper may succeed so much in participating in the divine plan, that he may reflect the glory of God. This is what the Bible itself teaches, that man was made in the image of God.

I am crucified with Christ: nevertheless I live; yet not I, but Christ liveth in me.[24]

---

24. Galatians Chap. 2:20.

Again and again, St. Paul tells us that in Christ there is neither circumcision nor uncircumcision, but a new creature. By imbibing the spirit of theistic religion and by living in faith in the precepts of one's theistic belief a character is formed and a new creature emerges. Not only a worshipper feels that he has become a new creature by conquering his passions and by subduing his wild nature in the footsteps of saints and seers, but now he undertakes the task of bringing others to the kind of life which he himself lives. The creature now becomes a creator of new values.

He is not only created, he creates—even though he does not know how creation is possible. But his character is his own creation; no one else would determine it for him as he interacts with the world.[25]

This is again what Henri Bergson too says. According to him by means of mystic communion a worshipper partly identifies himself with God who is creative love, and in turn becomes as creative as the creative *Elan* itself. According to him the universe is a machine for the making of gods,[26] and the mystic with the help of God simply completes the creation of the human species. The mystic love of humanity coincides with God's love for his creation,

> its direction is exactly that of the vital impetus; it (the mystic love) is this impetus itself, communicated in its entirety to exceptional men, who in their turn would fain impart it to all humanity, and by a living contradiction change into creative effort that created thing which is a species, and turn into movement what was, by definition, a stop.[27]

Bernard Bosanquet too by appropriating the phrase of John Keats states that the world is a vale of soul-making.

Whatever may be the differences between Western theists they all agree that God is an embodiment of values and a religious life

25. P.A Bertocci, *op. cit.*, p. 455.
26. H. Bergson, *Two sources of morality and religion*, Eng. Translation by E.A. Audra and C. Brereton, Macmillan, 1935, p. 275.
27. *Ibid.*, p. 201; also see p. 202.

consists in making oneself a thing of value. In the language of Jesus, one has to recapture one's former state of sonship in the place of slavery through sins and disobedience. Only by becoming a thing of value or regaining sonship can one become worthy of God's fellowship. This appears to be the purpose of God's creation and now we are required to analyse and elucidate the religious concept of creation.

We have already stated that according to traditional Christian theism creation is a mystery. However, this much is clear that according to it the world implies the existence of God, but not *vice versa.*

> We cannot see why he creates or how he creates; we can only see that unless he did create, the world would not be here. We can see why we cannot see all this, and that must suffice us.[28]

Yet very often the work of creation has been compared to the work of an artist, of a painter, a poet or a composer. The artist creates a new character, a novel painting or an altogether new strain of music. So far as the novelty of the creative art is concerned, it may be said to represent the divine process of creation. But here the simile ends. The artist does make use of some pre-existing materials like paper-ink, canvas-paint, marble-chisel and so on. Further, he also makes use of the works of previous artists, their plans, thought-patterns, insights and so on. Besides, no artist can afford to ignore the experience of mankind in which and through which the meaning of life is portrayed. Now God does not need any pre-existing material, previous plans or even experience in his creative act. He is the sole source of all that he creates and this is expressed by saying that God creates out of nothing.

There is one thing more in the case of a human artist. The artist is greatly influenced by his own creation either for better or worse. Is God also influenced by his creation? The theist denies that the world is a part of God or that God can be identified with

---

28. E.L. Mascall, *Existence and Analogy*, Longmans Green and Co., 1949, p. 125.

God. God is under no compulsion to create the world. Thompson[29] quotes John Wild[30] in this connection:

> The first cause was under no moral necessity to create a world. Such a world could add no perfection not already contained in the divine infinity. It could add more *beings*—not more *being*.

Nowhere two opposed views have been held. According to Bertocci human sufferings, trials and spiritual triumphs do make a difference to God. However, Samuel Thompson denies it. Most probably the view of Bertocci reflects more adequately the religious thought of the worshipper than that of Thompson. But Thompson's view is more philosophical and so we shall take up his view first.

According to Thompson God is essentially non-temporal and the contingent world alone is temporal. Time itself is the creature of God. Time for Thompson is only a framework in the human mind for measuring events and as such time is in the world. Hence, following St. Augustine according to Thompson, it would be meaningless to say that the world was created at one time or that there could be anything like time before the creation of the world. It would be senseless to ask: What was God doing before the creation of the world?

> Since it is precisely the temporal character of the world that is indicative of its essence, a beginning of the world in time would imply that the world had a beginning within itself. But the fact that the world was created does not mean that it has a limit in time, it rather indicates that the world itself and consequently also time border on something which is beyond time and therefore eternal.[31]

---

29. S.M. Thompson, 'A Modern Philosophy of Religion', Henry Regnery Company, 1955, p. 447.
30. John Wild, Introduction to Realistic Philosophy, Harper and Brothers, 1948, p. 348 (Italics ours).
31. Quoted by S.M. Thompson, *Ibid.*, p. 451 from E. Frank, *Philosophical Understanding and Religious Truth*, O.U. Press, New York, 1945, p. 59.

Hence for Thompson God himself is eternal and remains unaffected by change and temporal events. He approvingly quotes Mascall in holding that God knows all that take place in time, but his knowledge is not *in* time.

> For, if God's existence is outside time it is strictly meaningless to talk about what God knows today, since God's today is eternity. It is *true today* that God knows what I shall do tomorrow but is not true that God *knows it today*;[32]

that is, the *today* of human duration. This contention of Thompson reminds one of the *a priori* synthetic unity of apperception of Kant, the relating consciousness of Green and Royce's conception of *Totum Simul*. According to Kant the knowledge of an object is built out of the discrete manifold of sensation by means of the concepts of the understanding. But in order that there may be knowledge of an object the consciousness which *apprehends* the successive parts of an object and *reproduces* some of the parts already perceived earlier and recognizes such reproduced parts to be one's own which were perceived previously must be the one and the same throughout. In other words the self which apprehends, reproduces and recognises must be the one and the same self. Green goes a step forward and holds that this relating consciousness by itself cannot be a passing event, otherwise it will not be able to hold together all the passing, discrete manifold of sensations into a unity.

> No one and no number of a series of a related event can be the consciousness of the series as related.[33]

Again, he tells us that within a relating consciousness insofar as it relates a series, there can be no change, no lapse of time however minute, no antecedence or consequence.[34] No doubt the knowledge of a theorem is acquired in time, but our knowledge of it as a piece of scientific truth is timeless. In the same way

---

32. S.M. Thompson, *Ibid.*, p. 459 from E.L. Mascall, '*He who is*', Longmans, New York, 1948, p. 119.
33. T.H. Green, *Prolegomena to Ethics*, S. 16, p. 20.
34. *Ibid.*, S. 57, p. 62.

God is eternal though it takes cognizance of temporal things. However, most probably the theory of Josiah Royce and his illustrations of the theory have influenced the views of both Bertocci and Thompson. According to Royce in our own consciousness we have the analogue of the eternal consciousness.

> Listen to any musical phrase or rhythm, and grasp it as a whole, and you thereupon have present in you the image, so to speak, of the divine knowledge of the temporal order. To view all the course of time just as you then and there view the whole of that sequence,—this is to be possessed of an eternal type of insight.[35]

This one span in which the successive notes are apprehended together as a whole is very limited so far as human beings are concerned. But it can be pictured to be an infinite span in which all the temporal, successive events can be apprehended together in one now. In this one single span successive units remain successive, but they are all *present* in this divine consciousness: present past, present perceived present and present future. Thus God is conscious, not *in* time, but of time and of all that is in infinite time. In the divine span of consciousness the temporal process completely falls and is present all at once. The past and future are at once present. This view of Royce, according to which all the successive temporal events are wholly contained in God's eternal now has been adopted by Thompson in the following manner.

At the time of experiencing an event its successive parts as past, present and future can be distinguished from one another. But afterwards when we recall it in our memory, then we can recall it either from its inception to its end or from the end to its beginning. The important point is that all its successive parts are held together in one span of attention. Secondly, even when all parts are united together in one span or focus of consciousness, the differentiated parts continue to remain distinct and unique in relation to other antecedent and consequent parts. Why can we not imagine that in God this span of attention or focus of con-

---

35. J. Royce, 'The world and the individual', Vol. II, p. 145.

sciousness is stretched to infinity so as to include all temporal events? Further, in the manner in which the unity of self-consciousness of Kant does not change or the relating consciousness of Green is not an item of the series of changing events or again the absolute of Bradley which contains many histories but has no history of its own or the eternal God of Royce contains all the temporal events completely in one eternal now. So also Thompson holdst that God includes the temporal without himself becoming temporal. Thompson hastens to explain this difficult notion by means of an illustration.

A novelist writes a story and many things happen in this story. But the novelist does not exist in the time of his drama or fiction. Similarly, Thompson tells us that God creates the temporal events, but he remains unaffected by them.

> God can be aware of the temporal in an awareness which is not temporal, for past and future are themselves present in God's awareness.[36]

This view of Royce and Thompson is full of difficulties. Both of them hold that eternal consciousness contains the temporal order as a whole with their distinguishable successive events in their uniqueness.

> He (God) is aware of the whole events of nature. He knows every episode, but he knows it in its place in the whole event of nature.........yet in knowing the whole event of nature He differentiates every part from every other part.[37]

Is it psychologically or logically defensible? First, human beings experience events *in* time and for them events are successive. Is there any meaning of holding that events are *successive* in an eternal consciousness? If the eternal consciousness contains succession or change, then how can it be said to be timeless? If on the other hand, the eternal consciousness is timeless, then it cannot contain succession. Ordinarily several items can be held together in their uniqueness severally? When we attend to one item in its

---

36. S. M. Thompson, *op. cit.*, p. 458.
37. *Ibid.*, p. 456.

uniqueness, then others are there in the background. We know no experience in which the past, present and future are all held up together in their differentiated and distinguishable features in one ever present 'now'. This would justly be called the reduction of succession to simultaneity, temporal flow to spatial co-existence. We must not ignore the fact that the notion of eternal consciousness has its root in Kant's synthetic unity of apperception and this notion for Kant was purely logical. A logical category is timeless, but God's eternity is the never-ending duration. The two notions are hard to reconcile.

The thing is that God is conceived to be eternally perfect, above all change and yet he is taken to be the creator of the changing temporal world. How can the finite, imperfect and changing world follow from eternal God? The view of Royce and Thompson is only a clever expedient which has been devised to give us the specious reconciliation. Really the world is denied. It is given a fictional status. Thompson clearly says that God remains as unaffected by the temporal flow of the world as the novelist remains untouched by the dramatic time. In other words the world becomes a fiction, a sport or lila of God which the Indian thinkers have been maintaining for such a long time. However, if God remains unaffected by the world, then is there any room for the individual's prayers or worship? Such a God is hardly distinguishable from an impersonal reality. And this is the charge which has been brought against the Absolutist notwithstanding their protests to the contrary. Most probably some light has been thrown by A.N. Whitehead on the relation between the temporal world and eternal God and we shall make a passing reference to his view.

Whitehead's philosophy in the baldest outline is a synthesis of Platonic ideas and of Leibniz's Monadology through the Einsteinian mathematical physics. According to him there is a world of constant flux constituted by actual entities or occasions. An actual event is the ultimate unit of natural occurrence. It perishes the moment it is born. It has no external adventure, but only the internal adventure of becoming. Its birth is its end.[38] Actual entities are always interrelated through prehension (i.e. grasping

---

38. A.N. Whitehead, *Process and Reality*, Cambridge University Press, 1929, p. 111.

together), positive and negative. Prehended actual entities give rise to concrescence.

> Concrescence is the name for the process in which the universe of many things acquires an individual entity in a determinate relegation of each item of the 'many' to its subordination in the constitution of the novel one.[39]

However, this concrete creativity of natural occurrences due to another factor called by Whitehead as 'eternal objects' which roughly correspond to the 'ideas' of Plato. Eternal objects like the ideas of Plato and 'forms' of Aristotle are abstract and are incomprehensible without reference to some one particular occasion of experience. Their nature becomes exemplified through their ingression into prehended actual entities on the occasion of the concresence of new events.

> Thus an eternal object is to be compounded by acquaintance with (i) its particular individuality, (ii) its general relationships with other eternal objects as apt for realization in actual occasions, and (iii) the general principle which expresses its ingressing in particular occasions.[40]

Hence, actual entities by prehending and being prehended by preexisting actual entities are for ever freshly synthesized for the ingression of eternal objects which are the forms into which the world-creativity is cast.

From the above account it might appear the Whitehead like his contemporary Samuel Alexander tries to explain the emergence or concrescence of new entities as a self-regulative process. This is not so. For Whitehead God is the ultimate principle that decides as to which of the infinite possible forms should ingress into any specific concrescence. He is, therefore, the creator and principle of concretion.[41] Is God also in process?

God is that non-tempered actual entity, according to White-

---

39. *Ibid.*, p. 299.
40. A.N. Whitehead 'Science and the Modern World', Pelican Book, pp. 228-29.
41. Science and the Modern World, Chapter X.

head, which enters into every creative phase and yet is above change. If change be allowed, then, according to Whitehead, God would internally become inconsistent, which is a note of evil. God, being actual includes a synthesis of the total universe. God includes in himself the realm of eternal objects as qualified by the world, and the world as qualified by the eternal forms.[42] Thus God has two kinds of nature, namely, a primordial and a consequent nature. In his *primordial* nature God is constituted by his conceptual experience of eternal objects, which nature is not limited by actuality. In this aspect God is free, complete, eternal, unconsious and deficient in actuality. The consequent nature of God originates with the physical experience derived from the temporal world, and acquires integration with his primordial aspect. In this aspect of his consequent nature God is incomplete, 'everlasting' (not eternal), fully actual and conscious. It is not true, says Whitehead, that God is infinite in all respects. If he were, he would be evil as well as good. He is complete in the sense that his vision determines every possibility of value. God is the complete conceptual realization of the realm of ideal forms.[43]

Like any eternal object, God is inseparable from the world. God in his consequent nature completes the deficiency of his mere conceptual reality. God's conceptual or primordial nature is unchanged, but his consequent nature is derived from the creative thrust of nature. Each temporal occasion embodies God, and is embodied in God. In God's nature, permanence is primordial and flux is derivative from the world; in World's nature, flux is primordial and permanence is derivative from God. Creation achieves the reconciliation of permanence and flux when it has reached its final term which is everlastingness.[44]

It is true to say that God creates the World, as that the World creates God. God and the World are contrasted opposites in terms of which creativity achieves its supreme task of transforming disjoined multiplicity, with its diversities in opposition, into concrescent unity, with its diversities in contrast.[45]

---

42. A.N. Whitehead, 'Religion in the making', Macmillan, 1926, pp. 98-99.
43. Religion in the making, p. 154.
44. Process and Reality, p. 529.
45. *Ibid.*, p. 52.

Most probably it will be unfair to Whitehead's philosophy if we were to criticise it after giving such a perfunctory exposition of it. But it appears that Whitehead has not succeeded in reconciling the non-temporal and temporal character at once in his concept of God. One gets the impression that 'the primordial nature of God' corresponds to the 'infinite and inexhaustible potentialities in the life of the Absolute' of Absolute Idealism. In the manner of Hegel and Hegelians according to whom God actualises his infinite potentialities through nature, life and mind. Whitehead appears to hold that the primordial nature of God gets exemplified and concretised through the World. But in this case the God of potentialities becomes too abstract and too 'thin' for the purposes of worship. The description of God in terms of paradoxes betrays the shaky hold on many rebellious thoughts which have been brought together in the vast and challenging system by a master mind:

> It is as true to say that God is permanent, and the world fluent, as that the world is permanent and God is fluent......It is as true to say that God transcends the World, as that the World transcends God. It is as true to say that God creates the World, as that the World creates.[46]

Following in the footsteps of Whitehead, Charles Hartshorne states that there is no being which in all respects is absolutely perfect, but that there is a being in some respect or respects perfect and in some other surpassable.[47] But is the being of God divisible into two such parts? This notion is open to the same criticism which F.H. Bradley has levelled against the concept of an 'essential self'. Is the part which is perfect related to the imperfect parts or not? If they are not related, then they do not belong to the same entity. In that case the two natures primordial and consequent end in a dualism, in a bifurcation against which Whitehead so vigorously protests. However, if they are related, as obviously

---

46. Process and Reality, p. 492.
47. Charles Hartshorne, 'Man's vision of God', Clark & Co., Chicago, 1941, p. 15. See the illuminating article, Edward H. Madden and Peter H. Hare, *Evil and Unlimited Power* in the *Review of Metaphysics*, December 1966.

they are, then even the non-temporal primordial nature of God begins to be clothed in the vicissitudes of change and becoming. So the temporal creation of God and the eternal God unaffected by the temporal flow of the world cannot be reconciled. If, on the other hand, we accept that God is affected by the sufferings of his own creatures, then let us see whether this notion of Bertocci fares any better.

According to Bertocci the omnipotent God, above all vicissitudes of his creations, unaffected by the miseries and adoration of his creatures cannot be called a friend of his worshippers. The sublime dignity of such an impassive God does not induce the all-out commitment of his worshippers to him. For him a God who suffers with his creatures even when they abuse his redeeming love is the most potent object of religious worship and adoration.

> God the Suffering Father is as powerful as God the creator, and certainly he is more worthy of absolute devotion than God the impassive person whose eternal bliss is not to be marred by the plight of his creatures.[48]

For him, therefore, sin, suffering, penitence, self-surrender and triumph over sin do qualify the emotional quality of God's life and being. Does this admission mean that God is infected with change, according to Bertocci No, so far as his real nature is concerned. According to Bertocci the existence, moral goodness and wisdom of God remain unaffected by sin and the ingratitude of men. Nothing can prevent God from realizing the best possible thing for all in every situation.[49] But God yet remains profoundly influenced by the doings of men. God suffers most and most innocently. He suffers to redeem men of their sins and he suffers again due to the ingratitude and ignorance of men for whom He has limited himself by the creation of the world. This redemptive suffering and suffering because of extreme goodness comes out most clearly in the death of Jesus. We can therefore turn to the death of Jesus for clarifying the notion of divine suffering.

---

48. P.A. Bertocci, *op. cit.,* p. 461.
49. *Ibid.,* p 461.

THE MEANING OF THE CROSS

For the author every form of religion, specially theocentric faith is expressed in the 'language of myth and symbol'. So is Christ the crucified. But it is a potent symbol for seeing what is divine. Now what is the most significant utterance of Jesus from the Cross? This is his prayer for forgiveness of those persons who were responsible for putting him to the death of the Cross.

"Father, forgive them; for they know not what they do"[50] Why is it so? It means that no amount of evil can take away the goodness of God, God who is in search of sinners, of notions to convict them of their sins and to redeem them of their condemnation. No prodigal can ever dry up the fountain of redeeming forgiveness of God. It is very difficult to fully interpret the fourth and fifth utterances[51] from the Cross. But it might be interpreted as the travail of goodness in the face of overwhelming weight of ingratitude, denials and blindness of men towards the Love of God. The sixth and the seventh sayings of Jesus mark the triumph of the suffering Love of God. It is the assurance that sins and sufferings have been turned into the joy of victorious death,...... a surrender and a final dedication of life to the assuring Love of God.

> And when Jesus had cried with a loud voice he said, Father, into thy hands I commend my spirit, and having said thus, he gave up the ghost. Now when the Centurion saw what was done, he glorified God, saying, certainly this was a righteous man.[52]

Only in this sense we can say that God's goodness remains undiminished by the sins of men and unaugmented even by the triumph of the cross by his own son who remained obedient to him till his death. Yet the life of Jesus dedicated to the Gospel of the redeeming love of God was momentous creation of God,......a second Adam raised from the sin of the first into the reclamation of the sonship of God. The creative, outgoing love of God is fully

---

50. St. Luke, 23-24.
51. (4th) My God, my God, why hast thou forsaken me', and (5) 'I thirst'.
52. St. Luke, Chapter 23, Verses 46-47.

active, leavening his creation with his goodness and blissful living.

However, the very function of a symbol is to convey a message. The moment we interpret it literally we rob it of its meaning. Certainly sins, ingratitude of a Judas, the death of a friend (Lazarus) and physical sufferings of men and even their hunger and thirst did powerfully move Jesus. If Jesus reveals the nature of God, then a Christian theist ought to say that God is infected with change and is affected by his own creation. It is difficult to see as to how a being having personality can ever be called eternal and for ever unchangeably perfect. A Jesus was made perfect through suffering, even through the death of the Cross. This same question is raised in the form of transcendence and immanence of God. Does God remain transcendent to his created world or does he remain immanent in it?

TRANSCENDENCE AND IMMANENCE OF GOD

Transcendence and immanence have been satisfactorily dealt with by Samuel Alexander[53] and so let us follow his account. A transcendent God is one who exists outside the material world and his creatures. Deism is that religious system in which God's transcendence is most exclusively emphasized. In theism, however, God is both transcendent of and immanent in the world. For Alexander, immanence means much more than Gods' entry into the world of his creation. For him an immanent God pervades the whole of nature and is exhausted in it. He contrasts immanence of God with his Omnipresence. For him, to be present *at* a thing is not the same as to exist *in* it.[54] Most probably the notion of immanence is best illustrated in the doctrine of Aristotle's *horme*. For example, the tendency in an egg to become a chick is said to be its horme. It is wholly within the egg as its very indwelling essence. It is the presence of this hormic tendency within the egg which forms it into the chick. But certainly this formative principle cannot be said to exist also outside the egg. So if God be held to be immanent in the world, then, according

---

53. S. Alexander, *Theism and Pantheism* in *Philosophical and Literary Pieces*, Edited by J. Laird, Macmillan, 1939.
54. *Ibid.*, pp. 320-23.

to Samuel Alexander, God cannot logically be maintained to be transcendent also.

The theory of an immanent God is best illustrated in the pantheism of Spinoza. Of course in the Spinozistic pantheism God is the indwelling spirit of the world as *nature naturans* and is also *natura naturata*. Nothing is outside of God and God also does not exist beyond the world. In his system there is no room for real freedom of will, though man may illusorily think that he is responsible for his own acts. If God does everything and creates all that is, then he is also the author of every evil in the world. Nay, God becomes no more than an abstract principle like the hormic tendency in an egg to become a chick. Such a tendency can hardly be credited with personality or will. Spinoza is not afraid of holding the impersonal character of his God. The *amor intellectualis dei* of Spinoza does not require the responsive love of God. Here man loves God, but God can take no note of it.

However, sublime and exalted may be the religious fervour of *amor intellectualis dei*, a theist finds it unsuitable for his purpose. For a theist God is a person who has created this universe for the emergence of a responsible creature endowed with freedom of will and creative of values. Man, for such a conception is a copartner and co-creator of the universe. God, therefore, has to respond to the adoration of man and to the prayers of a contrite and bruised heart. Further, man as a co-creator with God has to be responsible for his acts and is to be praised for his good acts and blamed for wrongful ones. As such a purely immanent God, as was held by Spinozistic pantheism, is not acceptable to a theist.

But mere rejection of immanentism is not enough, since there are a few important points in it which have to be included in any satisfactory form of theism. According to Judaeo-Christian theism man has been made in the image of God and so He is present in each man. For this reason St. Paul held that God is nearer than our hands and feet or that in him we live and move and have our being. It is because there is the spirit of God in each one of us that man turns to God and worships him. Besides, God can reveal himself to man only when the latter has been endowed with the capacity of recognizing and cognizing Him. This means that there is some kinship of nature between God and his creatures. If this is so, then the worshipper is quite naturally drawn in adoration towards God. Now immanentism emphasizes this nearness of kinship between God and man. Besides, the immanence of God means that he continues to be the sustaining ground of the universe.

Again, a transcendent God does preserve the individuality, freedom and co-creatorship of his worshippers. God too can be personal and responsive to the prayers, adoration and love of his worshippers. However, the trouble is that a transcendent God, as in deism, has no reason to take note of his own creation. After creating his world, he can be imagined to have retired from the world. As a matter of fact deism did picture God as an absentee Landlord. Since a transcendent God does not need the world to add to His perfection, the concern of God for his creatures is hard to explain.

> When I consider thy heavens, the work of thy fingers, the moon and the stars, which thou has ordained; what is man, that thou art mindful of him? and the son of man, that thou visitest him?[55]

Therefore, S. Alexander showing the inadequacy of Transcendentism succinctly put down:

> God does indeed need man, but as man needs man. The unification of God and man remains artificial.[56]

It seems obvious that both the transcendence and immanence of God have to be reconciled and yet the two are difficult to reconcile. This difficulty is most keenly felt with regard to the doctrine of creation. A transcendent God remains distinct from the materials out of which he might be said to create. But we have seen that in this case he becomes an artificer or an architect of the world. On the other, if the materials are created by God, then we have to maintain that the world comes out of nothing. But the meaning of creation *ex nihilo* is that it comes from God himself since 'nothing' is nothing apart from the being of God. In this case the real language is that the world follows

55. Psalm, Chap. 8, pp. 3-4.
56. *Ibid.*, p. 326.

from God either in the form of emanation or as the modification of God. In any case the term 'creation' becomes inapplicable since in creation God becomes *distinct* from the world. However, what we say that God creates out of nothing, then He becomes identified with the world. For this reason Bertocci and other Christian theologians regard the act of creation as a mystery. But clearly the use of the term 'mystery' means that the fact of creation cannot be made intelligible.

COMMENTS ON THE ATTRIBUTES OF GOD

If we treat the attributes as descriptive of a Being called God, then we are bound to fall into contradictions and errors. The linguistic confusion which is found with regard to the arguments concerning the existence of God seems to beset every discourse about the divine attributes as well. When we start talking about Omnipotence, Omniscience Creation, Infinitude and Perfection of God, then our statements become empty or vacuous. And the reason is the same. God is all-inclusive and naturally there can be nothing to count against any assertion concerning the divine attribute. We maintain God's eternity and when the facts of the world seem to count against it, we at once deny that God's eternity can ever be touched by it. When God's goodness remains unaffected by sins and sufferings of men and we find that such a Being is not worshipful enough, then we at once shift our stand and hold that God is a mystery and his creation cannot be fully explicable. What is the net result?

> If God is perfect then nothing *could* count as evidence against his rightness. If anything *could* count as evidence against his rightness, then the justification of ethical statements in terms of God's will is not absolute.[57]

Should we conclude that any religious discourse about God's attributes is meaningless? Well, if religious statements be taken to be descriptive or cognitive, then this charge of linguistic confusion, vacuity and circularity cannot be set aside. For us religious language is convictional the sole purpose of which is to create truth in one's own self and in all other things through this.

57. C. B. Martin, '*The Perfect Good*' in NEPT, p. 215.

Flew concedes this much too, since for him creation apart from holding the absolute dependence of the world on God and the rejection of any possible dualism of God and pre-existing matter carries "the suggestion of certain conduct and attitudes as appropriate".[58]

D.M. Mackinnon fully agrees with Flew.[59] According to him this doctrine of creation follows from an imaginative vision of the world, which induces an attitude of trust and cheerful exploration of the world by exorcising the fear of malignant powers from men.[60] The religious view, says Mackinnon, is fertile and illuminating which invites 'a posture for men under the sun that vindicates itself'. What made the writers of the Epistles and the Gospels adventure into the language as they did adopt and speak the mysteries of creation, says Mackinnon, 'was more perhaps the riddle of a life lived and a death died than any sort of arguments'.[61]

Quite obviously the story of this life lived has been said so that we may emulate it and also in due course to prepare ourselves for the kind of death narrated in the Epistles and the Gospels. Well, if the kind of life lived and the death died makes one committed to it by being convinced of its adequacy and efficacy, then it is the religious truth for the person concerned. Afterwards, if by following in the footsteps of the Master one can murmur in one's last breath :

the time of my departure is at hand. I have fought a good fight, I have finished my course, I have kept the faith,[62]

then it would be said to be conclusively verified for the believer. It will be true for others, when they can also be infected with his example. Therefore, religious truth concerning a good life, for becoming gold fit for heaven, is not given but is made true and is proved to be so by having others as the witness of the earnestness of the life lived and of a cheerful resignation to the

58. A. Flew and D.M. Mackinnon, 'Creation' in NEPT, p. 173.
59. *Ibid.*, p. 179.
60. *Ibid.*, p. 175-76.
61. *Ibid.*, pp. 183.
62. Timothy II, Chapter 4:7.

inevitableness of death. The important thing about the language of creation is that men may become things of value and finally gods and creators of values.

But theologians try to explain the reality of God in terms of personality and a perfect Being. What is the result of this kind of thinking? Nothing but confusion. If God is all-powerful, all-good then why is there any evil at all?·Theologians amongst whom some of the best minds can be found, have in vain racked their brains. As long as we interpret God as an objective entity concerning whom descriptive statements can be made, we shall fall into endless contradictions and unedifying puzzles. So now let us take up the problem of evil which has vexed and perplexed the theist from the very beginning. The very failure of the theologians will at least prepare the mind of other religious thinkers by seriously modifying, and, might be by rejecting the traditional approach for a view which may hold the prospect of some light 'in the encircling gloom'.

CHAPTER XIII

THE PROBLEM OF EVIL

PROBLEM STATED

According to Plantinga[1] theism maintains the following five propositions:

(a) God exists, (b) God is omnipotent, (c) God is infinitely good, (d) God is omniscient, and (e) evil exists. On the whole the empiricists like J.L. Mackie, A.G.N. Flew and H.J. McCloskey contend that the fact of evil negates (b) and (c). Out of the five propositions necessary for a theist, stated at the beginning of the chapter, Mackie thinks that the following three will do for his[2] purpose.

1. God is omnipotent.
2. God is good.
3. There is evil.

Of course, here good and evil are taken to be opposed: good eliminates evil and *vice versa*. If so then if any two be true, then the third would be false. From this it follows that the fact of evil is completely incompatible with the actuality of an omnipotent and a good God.[3] This is a very discomforting situation for a theist. If God be not omnipotent or infinitely good, then for a theist he will not be worshipful enough. Therefore, the important problem for a theist is, 'how can a just, omnipotent and an infinitely good God create evil or permit evil?

Some thinkers have sacrificed the omnipotence of God in favour of His Goodness (J.S. Mill, William James, J.M.E. Mc-Taggart and E.S. Brightman); others have regarded evil as mere appearance (F.H. Bradley, B. Bosanquet, Absolutists and Advai-

---

1. Alvin Plantinga, '*The free will defence*' in *Philosophy in America*, Edited by Max Black, George Allen, 1965, p. 205.
2. And not like the Absolutist evil is taken to be good in the wrong place or lesser good and so forth.
3. J. L. MacKie, *Ibid.*, p. 201; A Flew, *God and Philosophy*, Sect. 2.42.

tins); some others hold that evil is partially good inasmuch as it is instrumental to some higher good (G.W. Leibniz, R.A. Tsanoff). Still others hold that natural and moral evils are inevitable incidents in a morally purposed world (F.R. Tennant and Mark Pontifex). For a theist however the presence of evil poses the dilemma:

> Epicurus' old questions are still unanswered. Is deity willing to prevent evil, but not able? Then he is impotent. Is he able but not willing? Then he is malevolent. Is he both able and willing? Whence then is evil?

Thinkers have tried to escape from the dilemma in various ways.[4]

1. The evil, when looked at rightly, may be really good. According to McTaggart, this refusal to see evil as evil runs counter to facts. We can refuse to see evil only on the basis of complete moral scepticism, according to which human beings are incapable of determining the rightness and wrongness of human conduct. Otherwise, McTaggart would hold how can anybody deny the fact of physical and moral evil when it is the clearest deliverance of human judgement? If human beings cannot be sure of evil then how can they be credited in judging right or good aright?

There is another expedient to deal with the problem of evil, which is similar to (1).

2. According to St. Augustine and Leibniz, whatever exists is good, when it is viewed in a total perspective. Pain and sin appear to be evil from a partial viewpoint.

McTaggart himself does not name and person or the system with regard to (2). However, we know that apart from St. Augustine and Leibniz, the Gradationist and Absolutist hold the view that pain and sin are evil only in appearance. From the viewpoint of the whole universe there is nothing which can be said to be wholly evil. Against this view McTaggart holds that (2) can be supported by a metaphysical argument of a somewhat abstruse and elaborate nature. Further, he adds,

---

4. J.M.E. McTaggart, 'Why God must be finite' in APR, pp. 278-79.

Supposing that it could be proved that all that we think evil was in reality good, the fact would still remain that we think it evil. This may be called a delusion or a mistake. But a delusion or a mistake is as real as anything else.[5]

3. Pain and sin, if they existed, would be bad. But it is maintained that they do not really exist. In its most pronounced form this view is attributed to Christian Science in America. However, the view of Christian Science is so unrealistic, that it may be omitted from discussion.

As noted above the fact of evil cannot be ignored on the plea of its being treated as a delusion. McTaggart continuing his criticism writes:

If, again, the existence of the delusion is pronounced to be a delusion, then this second delusion, which would be admitted to be real, must be pronounced evil, since it is now this delusion which deceives us about the true nature of reality, and hides its goodness from us.[6]

Under the same head we can list the view of a number of Indian thinkers according to whom evil is only an illusion and does not really affect the soul. We may further also include here the view that evil is the privation of good. This solution of the problem is only verbal. Even if evil be regarded as the absence of good, we may still ask, 'why is there absence of good'? We can also refer here to the doctrine of the 'relative' God of Whitehead and Charles Hartshorne.

'RELATIVE' GOD[7]

Unlike Mill, A.N. Whitehead and Charles Hartshorne have advanced the theory of a 'relative God'. By this concept, they mean to keep the notion of an infinite God intact and yet in certain respects hold him to be limited. God is said to be relative

---

5. APR, p. 278.
6. APR, pp. 278-79.
7. For a fuller discussion the reader is invited to an article by Edward H. Madden and Peter H. Hare, 'Evil and Unlimited Power', *The Review of Metaphysics*, December 1966.

to the past which he cannot annul, to the freedom of actual occasions which he cannot control, to the concretion of the physical world which he does not, theistically speaking, create. This relative God of Whitehead has two distinct natures, Primordial and Consequent. Now God is unlimited because he encompasses all logical possibilities (Primordial Nature); because of 'admirability', i.e. unlimited sensitivity to the feelings of other being[8]; because of his ability in conserving and harmonising all values; because of his 'reliability' of intention to preserve and harmonise he is absolute. However, can the two attributes of 'relative' and 'unlimited' be consistently applied to God? And, again, can this complex nature of God solve the problem of evil?

True, the natural events do not thwart God but serve as occasions for his creative activity. However, this is also a fact, according to the authors, that God neither creates nor controls the flow of actual occasions. He at most takes advantage of their happenings with a view to actualising eternal objects as the principle of concretion. This means that God is quite at home in the materials with which he works. But does he not become as limited as the concept of an architect is taken to be? For all practical purposes God becomes an artificer, but not a creator. And as the principle of concretion how can he assure the triumph of Good over the evil if he does not create the flow of natural events?

Secondly, God as an entity or a principle of concretion cannot be said to be a personal being of theism. The principle of conceretion, for Whitehead, is 'Aristotle's God as Prime Mover'.[9] If it is so, then the Good or Evil under discussion is hardly relevant to a Principle. Good or Evil has meaning only in relation to a Personal Being with Will and Intellect. Whitehead leaves us in doubt concerning this point. For him moral values are not primary. They have to be subordinated to the aesthetic value.

As order is therefore aesthetic order; and the moral order is merely certain aspects of aesthetic order.[10]

---

8. Charles Hartshorne. *The Divine Relativity*, New Haven, 1964, pp. 22-24.
9. A.N. Whitehead, Science and the modern world, Pelican.
10. A.N. Whitehead, Religion in the making, NY, 1926, p. 105.

And the aesthetic order does include a good deal of apparent evil. For Whitehead the world is good when it is beautiful, but it does not explain the presence of evil in the mode or proportion in which we actually find it. So either we say that the world is the best possible world with all its evils or else we say that evil is really no evil or finally we can say that in God's order the presence of evil has to be mysteriously 'enjoyed'. How do we get away from the difficulty which the presence of evil offers to us?

Hence, we conclude that the distinction of 'relative' and 'limited' is more verbal than real; God Becomes more of an entity or a principle than the personal being of theism; and, the moral evil is silenced in the massiveness of aesthetic feeling. Therefore, instead of facing the problem the very concepts of unlimited power, God and moral evil are distorted.

Hence, we cannot explain away the fact of evil by calling it 'good in disguise' or 'delusion' or 'privation' or 'as a partial good' or by explaining away the moral evil by merging it in the aesthetic order. Therefore, St. Augustine admits the reality of evil.

Therefore either is that evil which we fear, or else evil is that we fear.[11]

Of course, theologians may under the guise of piety eschew the problem of evil on the ground of God's inscrutable ways.

Shall moral man be more just than God? Shall a man be more pure than his matter?[12]

Yet the presence of evil does militate against the goodness of an Omnipotent creator. St. Augustine too feels the weight of the fact of evil.

Either God cannot abolish evil or he will not: If he cannot then he is not all-powerful, if he will not then he is not all-good.

---

11. APR, p. 236.
12. Job 4:17.

St. Thomas Aquinas too was aware of the proplem and has raised it with same poignancy with which Hume expressed it later on. Aquinas would ask: God is infinitely good and powerful, since whence is evil?

> If one of two contraries be infinite, then the other is excluded absolutely. But the idea of God is that of an infinite good. Therefore if God should exist, then there would be no evil. But evil exists. Consequently God does not.[13]

However, it must be confessed that the Weltanschauung of the Middle Ages would not allow Aquinas to entertain any serious doubt concerning God's existence. Only in contemporary times the presence of evil is interpreted as the real refutation of an Omnipotent and infinitely good God. This has been most clearly stated by R. Puccetti.

God in order to be worshipful has to be conceived as omnipotent, omniscient and perfectly good. These *a priori* requirements should also interpret power, knowledge and goodness in terms of ordinary use and usage. These attributes not only describe God but also describe his relation to the world of human experience. The human experience shows that there is innocent suffering in the world.

> ......we would not say of a man who knowingly tolerated innocent pain which he could prevent that he is good unless there were mitigating circumstances or he had plausible reasons for doing this, (6) in the case of God there can be no mitigating circumstances and we know of no possible reasons, therefore, (7) this world is not consistent with the concept of God and therefore (8) God does not exist.[14]

The spirit of this argument has been elaborated by the empiricists at a great length to which we shall refer very shortly.

---

13. Quoted by P. M. Farrell, 'Evil and Omnipotence' in *Mind*, 1958, Vol. LXVII, p. 399.
14. R. Puccetti, *The Concept of God* in Philosophical Quarterly, Vol. 14, July 1964, p. 244.

Out of the many solutions which the Christian apologetics have offered, most probably two of them stand out, namely, (*a*) Instrumentalist view of evil in a graded universe and (*b*) Free-willist Defence. As the instrumentalist defence has been most powerfully advanced by F.R. Tennant, so we shall now present its brief exposition.

I. INSTRUMENTALIST VIEW OF EVIL

For F.R. Tennant the world is essentially evolutionary, giving rise to an hierarchical order of graded things. In this scheme of things, according to him, physical and moral evils are inevitable concomitants of 'the best possible world'. For him, all things work together for good. By 'all' is not meant 'each and everything', but a sum of all things taken together. Tennant agrees with Paley and others that evil is prophylactic, i.e. it serves as a warning against danger (e.g., the burning of fingers by fire) or that at times it is punitive and purgatorial.[15] But even this conclusion, for Tennant, holds good only when we view the universe as a whole and not in a universe taken in piece-meal. Tennant does not want to minimise the problem concerning physical suffering of the sentient world. For him, however, the following is the real task:

> It must be shown that pain is either a necessary by-product of an order of things requisite for the emergence of the higher goods, or an essential instrument to organic evolution, or both. Short of this, we cannot refute the charge that the world is a clumsy arrangement or an imperfectly adjusted mechanism.[16]

Suffering, for Tennant, is necessarily incidental to the evolution of moral excellence. Much of suffering follows from the regularity and uniformity in the workings of Nature. For example, fire uniformly burns the finger and certain diseases would follow if we do not take precautionary measures. But certainly

---

15. "Remember, I pray thee, who ever perished being innocent? Or where were the righteous cut off ?" (Job 4:7).

16. F.R. Tennant, 'That evil is necessary' in APE, p. 255; See also p. 256.

uniformity and regularity are conducive to the emergence of morality and the evolution of the latent capacities of men.

> Without such regularity in physical phenomena there could be no probability to guide us: no prediction, no prudence, no accumulation of ordered experience, no pursuit of premeditated ends, no formation of habits, no possibility of character or of culture. Our intellectual faculties could not have developed.[17]

As the formation of character and the pursuit of worthy ends are moral, so much of physical suffering may be taken as a challenge for their emergence and sustenance.

REDUCTIONISM AND McCLOSKEY

H.J. McCloskey rejects the thesis of instrumentalism. According to him, the fact of physical evils creates a number of distinct problems which are not reducible to the problem of moral evil.[18] Whatever may be the merit of McCloskey's contention, unless physical evil be also at the same time moral evil, it cannot militate against God's goodness. Hence, physical evil has to be reduced to moral evil and it has to be shown that physical evil is utterly pointless and absolutely unredeeming. It is because of this fact that physical handicaps result into moral aberrations that Marxian tirade against the bourgeoise-society gains weight for the have-nots of the world. It is because of this that the instances of cruelty so vividly described by Feodor Dostoevsky[19] are cited as relevant against the infinite goodness of God. Hence, a theist correctly sees physical evil as an instance of moral evil. Indeed McCloskey himself notes that physical evil in the form of moral evil constitutes an acute problem for the theist. Hence, most probably a theist is essentially on a sound footing in reducing physical evil to moral evil. But the problem in this case is, Is the reductionist-defence sound?

---

17. *Ibid.*, p. 256.
18. H.J. McCloskey, *God and Evil* in *God and Evil*, Edited by Nelson Pike, Prentice-Hall, 1964, pp. 61-62, 74.
19. F. Dostoevsky, *Rebellion in GE.*

CRITICISM OF INSTRUMENTALISM

J.S. Mill (1806-1873) has advanced acute criticism of instrument-alism in *'Three essays on religion'*. According to him, the facts of Nature show that it is callous and non-ethical and has no moral purpose to serve. Nature, says Mill, commits every day those very crimes for which men are hanged.

> Nature impales men, breaks them as if on the wheel, casts them to be devoured by wild beasts, burns them to death, crushes them with stones like the first Christian martyr, starves them with hunger, freezes them with cold....All this, Nature does with the most supercilious disregard both of mercy and of justice emptying her shafts upon the best and noblest indifferently with the meanest and worst; upon those who are engaged in the highest and worthiest enterprises, and often as the direct consequence of the noblest acts;.......[20]

Of course, the argument of Mill is wholly irrelevant. Nobody takes nature to be moral: Nature is wholly non-moral. What is contended by a theist is that nature indirectly helps the emergence of morality in due course. As a matter of fact the cruel blows of nature challenges the faculties of man to rise above their source. However, Mill would retort, Is it always the case that evil subserves the good? When a child or a youth in the full promise of a noble life dies, then whose good is achieved? Here the theist would say, unless we know what happens in the inmost recess of the sufferer and about his ultimate destiny in the life to come, we can say nothing decisively. But this reply from ignorance cannot answer the charge. Mill would say: granted that human skill, fortitude, prudence etc., might have followed from animal and human suffering, and, we might even grant that martyrdom has been achieved from tyranny and persecution;

> Yet whatever incidental and unexpected benefits may result from crimes, they are crimes nevertheless. In the second place, if good frequently comes out of evil, the converse fact, evil coming out of good, is equally common.[21]

20.　J.S. Mill, *'Is there more evil than good in nature?'* in APR, p. 227.
21.　*Ibid.*, p. 230.

Besides, often evil produces its own kind. For example, bodily illness produces greater susceptibilities for other illnesses, causes incapacity for physical work and dampens mental proclivities for hard work. Mill further adds that poverty is the parent of a thousand ills; and frequent oppression lowers the whole tone of human character.[22] If creation were just and the creator omnipotent, then suffering and happiness would be proportionately distributed. Is it so?, asks Mill. Even Kant had to admit that virtue is not rewarded. Here Flew would join hands with Mill in holding that men get paltry sum of good in exchange for enormous sacrifices.[23]

> To call such a being, ruthlessly paying an enormous price in evil means to attain his good ends, himself good is merely flattery: 'worthy only of those whose slavish fears make them offer the homage of lies to a Being who, they profess to think, is incapable of being deceived and holds all falsehood in abomination.[24]

If providence were just, then happiness should be distributed evenly, even if virtue be not rewarded. As against this, happiness and misery seem to depend much on the accident of one's birth, and on the faults of one's parents, society and other circumstances beyond the control of individuals. Hence, according to Mill, all things do not conspire towards moral goodness. If God were just and omnipotent,

> Wherefore do the wicked live, become old, yea, are mighty in power?
> Their seed is established in their sight with them, and their offspring before their eyes. Their houses are safe from fear, neither *is* the rod of God upon them..........[25]

Besides, even if it be admitted that evil is a necessary concomitant of good, who can determine the proper measure of

---

22. *Ibid.*, p. 231.
23. A.G.N. Flew, *Divine Omnipotence and human freedom* in NEPT, p. 147.
24. Mill, J. S., 'Three Essays on Religion', Longmans, 1874, p. 52.
25. Job 21 : 7-9.

evil, just sufficient to produce the maximum of good? How can one further determine whether the computed amount of suffering could be the proper evidence of a beneficent providence?[26] The whole argument of the theist, says John Laird, is dubious, because it is wholly indeterminate. But one wonders whether any philosophical argument can ever be conclusive. Why should Mill, Laird, Mackie and McCloskey demand the impossible?

Further, McCloskey tells us that the view that evil is instrumental to good is not only inconclusive, but also vicious. If evil is necessary to goodness, then it follows that to maximise the good, the evil too has to be increased in the same proportion.[27] This objection is as old as Christianity itself. St. Paul tells us that some slanderously report that the doctrine of Grace is 'Let us do evil, that good may come'.[28]

McCloskey forgets that, according to a theist, evil is not something positive. It is a privation of good. Hence, according to the traditionalist, evil serving the cause of good ultimately disappears or is transformed into the good. Similarly, Spinoza pointed out that the saint and the wicked both serve the purpose of God, but the wicked in fulfilling the divine purpose perish in the act. If McCloskey had seriously attended to the case of the traditionalist, then he would not irrelevantly state that the discovery of the use of anaesthetics or of Salk's anti-polic vaccines is a matter of regret for a theist.[29]

At this point, Mackie raises another objection. If God, according to Mackie, works with the help of means, then he ceases to be omnipotent. This criticism was made by Kant in connection with the physico-theological argument. According to Kant, if God has to make use of means, then he is reduced to the status of an artificer. The same point is raised by Mackie. He holds that only by resorting to a causal law that one can say that one uses a certain means for achieving a certain end. If God makes use of evil to produce good, then says Mackie, God in a sense subordinates himself to a principle.[30]

---

26. J. Laird, '*Evidence against a providential God*' in APR, p. 266; J.H. McCloskey, *Ibid.*, p. 71; J.L. Mackie, *Mind*, 1955, p. 205.
27. H.J. McCloskey, *Ibid.*, pp. 72, 74-75.
28. Romans 3:8.
29. *Ibid.*, p. 75.
30. J.L. Mackie, *Mind*, 1955, p, 205.

A traditionalist would not accept the contention of Mackie. Working according to a law does not take away God's omnipotence. So there are two opposed views concerning omnipotence to which we shall make reference a little later on. Now we find that two other objections have been made against the instrumental theory of evil. If evil is a means to good, then evil cannot be said to be totally opposed to good, for instrumentalism holds that evil somehow promotes the good. And how can this be possible if evil is totally opposed to good? Secondly, the instrumentalist can also hold the view that evil is really lesser good or it is a foil to the good with a view to enhancing the aesthetic appeal of the good. Both these versions of instrumentalism have been advanced with regard to Freewillist Defence of evil. So we shall turn now to it.

II. FREEWILLIST DEFENCE

A traditionalist maintains that God is both infinitely good and omnipotent. However, omnipotence for him is the power of doing everything which is logically possible. According to Aquinas, "...nothing that implies a contradiction falls under the scope of God's omnipotence".[31] Secondly, the traditionalist holds that with free will goes the possibility of doing either good or evil. It is no limitation on the part of God if he cannot make free persons always choose the right. Combining these two stipulations of omnipotence and free will the theistic doctrine is as follows:

Out of his abundance of creative love God has made creatures with a view to helping them to become worthy of his fellowship. For achieving this man has to become a holy will with the result of always choosing the right freely by overcoming the temptation of doing wrong. This desideratum of the capacity of overcoming the evil is attended with the real risk of choosing the evil. Hence, if moral agents have to evolve as the supreme end of the universe, then the possibility of sin or moral evil has to be conceded. For God the creation of good and holy wills far outweighs the possibilities of sins. God, therefore, according to the traditionalist is not responsible for moral evils: Man alone is responsible for moral evils for he alone creates them by his wrong choice. Logi-

---

31. Summa Theologica, Part I, Question 25, article 4,

cally, for the freewillist defence, it is impossible to be both free and yet not to have the power of doing evil. Professors J.L. Mackie and A.G.N. Flew who wrote parallel papers, independently of each other, have also refined this doctrine before subjecting it to their linguistic attack.

For Mackie and Flew, certain higher virtues like forgiveness or fortitude, presuppose not only free will, but also the actual occurrence of certain evils.

Thus what we might call the second-order goods of sympathetic feeling and action logically could not occur without (at least the appearance of) the first-order evils of suffering or misfortune. And the moral good of forgiveness presupposes the prior occurrence of (at least the appearance of) some lower-order evil to be forgiven. This may be already a second-order moral evil such as callousness, thus making the forgiveness a third-order good.[32]

This view may be thus schematized:

First-order Good
1. Goodness of health goes with the evil of pain or disease.

First-order Evil

Second-order Good
2. Sympathies, benevolence, skills of doctors, arising from cornering the first-order evil.

Give rise to

Second-order Evil
Malevolence, Cruelty, Callousness.

Third-order Good
3. Greater benevolence, forgiveness and fortitude to overcome the second-order evils.

Here the second-order evil is largely due to the wrong exercise of free will. Hence,

---

32. A.G. Flew, '*Divine Omnipotence and human freedom*' in *New Essays in Philosophical Theology*, Edited by A. Flew and A. Macintyer, SCM Press, 1958, p. 146.

it is being assumed that second order evils, such as cruelty, are logically necessary accompaniments of freedom, just as pain is a logically necessary precondition of sympathy.[33]

Thus according to A. Flew and J. Mackie, even if the second and third orders of evil be explained in terms of the misuse of free will, the first order evil remains unexplained.[34] Again, according to them, second and third orders of goodness remain subservient to evils and further, any excessive amount of evil as means to goodness is self-defeating.[35] We shall examine the thesis of A. Flew and J. Mackie by analysing the two key-notions of Free will and Evil.

FREE WILL

The contention of Mackie and Flew has reference to the analysis of the term 'free will'. According to the traditionalist free will cannot be completely caused by God without involving us in self-contradiction. Empiricists like Mackie, Flew, McCloskey, Ayer and Nowell-Smith hold, on the contrary, that free will is fully compatible with causal determinism. Hence, Mackie observes

> ...why could he (God) not have made men such that they always freely chose the good? If there is no logical impossibility in a man's freely choosing the good on one, or on several occasions there cannot be a logical impossibility in his freely choosing the good on every occasion.[36]

In the same way Flew holds that there is no contradiction involved in saying that God might have made people so as to always choose the right.[37] This linguistic analysis should be distinguished from a similar view of McTaggart. McTaggart thinks that omnipotence is compatible with doing the logically impossible. Therefore, an Omnipotent God can fully control free will.

---

33. J.L. Mackie, *Evil and Omnipotence, Mind*, 1955, p. 208.
34. NEPT, p. 146-147; J. L. Mackie, *Ibid.*, p. 207.
35. J.L. Mackie, *Ibid.*, p. 208; NEPT, p. 147; God and Philosophy, 2.54.
36. J.L. Mackie, *Ibid.*, p. 208-09.
37. A.G.N. Flew, NEPT, p. 149.

...it is quite evident that a God who cannot create a universe in which all men have free will, and which is at the time free from evil, is not an omnipotent God, since there is one thing which he cannot do.[38]

Mackie and Flew would agree that omnipotence is not compatible with the logically impossible. But they do maintain, against the traditionalist, that causal determinism is compatible with free will.

FREE WILL AND CAUSAL DETERMINISM
From the days of Locke and Hume the empiricists have maintained that a free act may be causally determined. Locke in his own way declares free will to be illusory. Only a substance can have an attribute, says Locke; but an attribute cannot have another attribute. 'Will' is an attribute of man and therefore will cannot be said to possess any attribute like 'free'.[39] However, Hume has advanced a more acceptable analysis of free will:

For what is meant by liberty when applied to voluntary actions? We surely cannot mean that actions have so little connection with motives, inclinations and circumstances, that one does not follow with a certain degree of uniformity from the other.[40]

Hence, Hume maintains that a free act is *determined* by motives, inclinations and circumstances. Freedom can legitimately be denied only when there is an external or internal constraint.[41] For example, a person put in chains or in a jail is said to be not free. Hence, a Humean empiricist makes three statements about free will.

1. Every act not determined by external or internal compulsions or restraints is free.

38. J.M.E. McTaggart, *Why God must be finite* in APR, pp. 283-84.
39. John Locke, *'Essays on human understanding'*, BK II, Chap. 21, 14.
40. 'David Hume on human nature and the understanding' Edited by C. Briton and Paul Edwards, Collier Classics, 1962, p. 104; also see p. 105.
41. *Ibid.*, p. 107.

2. Human behaviour being determined by psychical determinants or by social and other causal factors makes no difference to the freedom of will.
3. Hence, a voluntary action is both free and fully determined.

Prof. A.J. Ayer agrees with Hume that a free act is compatible with causal determinism.

> For it is not *causality* that freedom is to be contrasted with, but *constraint*...from the fact that my action is causally determined it does not necessarily follow that I am constrained to do it.[42]

The reason is that free act is not a chance act, but is a caused act. So causal determinism is compatible with free act. Cranston quotes Ayer again.

> To say that I could have acted otherwise is to say, first, that I could have acted otherwise if I had so chosen; secondly, that my action was voluntary in the sense in which actions say of the kleptomaniacs are not; and thirdly, that nobody compelled me to choose as I did: and these three conditions may very well be fulfilled. When they are fulfilled I may be said to have acted freely.[43]

The same empiricist point has been more persuasively explained by Nowell-Smith in 1949. He puts the query: 'Are all men's decisions subject to or free from scientific laws?' Now an action is said to be not free if it is *forced* by external constraints, but it is always determined by scientific laws, psychological, social, economical and so on. And scientific laws do not compel. Therefore, an action regulated by non-compelling scientific laws is free.

---

42. Maurice Cranston, 'Is there a problem of the Freedom of Will?' Hibbert Journal, Vol. 51, 1952-53, p. 49.
43. M. Cranston, *Ibid.*, pp. 49-59, Quoted from A. J. Ayer, Prolemics 5.

Anyone who knows me well enough can predict how I will vote if there is a general election this week; but he does not thereby *compel* me to vote, in this way. The fact of our action being compelled and the fact of its being predictable are two quite different facts; and we only confuse them because we use this metaphor of governing, obedience and compulsion in our talk about scientific laws.[44]

We shall find that the contention of Mackie, Flew and Nowell-Smith is not correct. There are two sets of facts which are mentioned with regard to a voluntary act.

1. There are motives, causes and past habitual decisions in the form of sentiments and character with the help of which a free choice is made.
2. However, the choice is exercised by the ego itself. And, according to T.H. Green this ego, is eternal; it never began, because it never was not.[45] We may not agree with Green, but the traditionalist would not include the free choice in (1).

The explanation of the voluntary action of Mackie, Flew and Nowell-Smith is relevant to (1) only. But this has no relevance with regard to (2). And yet any satisfactory account of a voluntary action relates to the free exercise of the ego itself. The anti-freewillist contends that because a voluntary action is determined by (1), therefore, it is *wholly* determined. He totally ignores the second factor, and, yet the nerve of the freewillist lies in the second factor. As we see it, it is not a matter of linguistic convention alone,[46] but is also an empirical question which in principle is verifiable by psychology. Because the empiricist exclusively

---

44. M. Cranston, H. J. 1952-53, p. 53.
45. T.H. Green, Prolegomena to Ethics, Sec. 114, p. 119.
46. Even if we treat the controversy concerning free will to be linguistic, then why should we accept the convention of the empiricist and not of the traditionalist ? As a matter of fact the traditional view is very near the commonsense usage. Hence, it is the empiricist who violates the linguistic convention (A. Plantinga, 'Philosophy in America, pp. 207-208).

confines himself to (1), so for him the denial of free will means the denial of any constraint, which would mean randomness. However, the freewillist does not deny the factors of character, sentiments, dispositions and so on. For him they are the economising agencies through which the free choice of the ego works. At least this is the view of W. McDougall, J.A. Hadfield, Watts and others. But J.L. Mackie maintains that a voluntary act is totally determined by one's character.

> If it is replied that this objection is absurd that the making of some wrong choices is logically necessary for freedom, it would seem that 'freedom' must here mean complete randomness or indeterminancy, including randomness with regard to the alternatives good and evil, in other words that men's choices and consequent actions can be 'free' only if they are not determined by their characters.[47]

Certainly the possibility of wrong choice is a logical implication of a free act, though not the actual making of it. But it is quite wide of the mark to hold that the denial of *total* determinism is tantamount to the acceptance of randomness. The traditionalist of course maintains that it is God's purpose to have moral agents endowed with holy wills who will always freely choose the good. But such a holy will is a matter of emergence and self-creation, though once again by the Grace of God. But let us take up the thread of the empirical explanation of free will before subjecting it to criticism.

For Flew a free act is at the same time a determined or caused action. Take a paradigm case in which Murdo is said to marry Mairi quite freely. It means that there was no social or parental pressure on Murdo in freely choosing to marry Mairi. Yet again this has to be conceded that a team of psychologists and physiologists *in principle* are 'able to predict a person's behaviour far more completely and successfully than even his best friends now can, even up to one hundred per cent completely and successfully'.[48] Even then the act will be called 'free', because, says Flew,

---

47. J.L. Mackie, *Mind*, 1955, p. 209.
48. NEPT, p. 150.

Murdo chooses between alternatives, decides for himself that alternative which appeals to him, without any pressure from outside. To maintain in this case that Murdo could have acted otherwise than what he actually does, does not mean, according to Flew, that it was unpredictable or uncaused.

> It is to say that *if* he had chosen to do otherwise he would have been able to do so; that there were alternatives, within the capacities of one of his physical strength, of his I.Q., with his knowledge, and open to a person in his situation.[49]

Hence, for Flew a free act is predictable, completely determined, explicable and foreknowable in terms of caused causes. Now, if a voluntary act would be fully determined, then it can be held

> . . . that Omnipotence might have, could without contradiction be said to have created people who would always as a matter of fact freely have chosen to do the right thing.[50]

Again, God is the creator and man is his creature. If the free act of the man be said to be fully determined, then he hardly differs much from an automaton. For example, in a psychological experiment a subject is hypnotised and in this state he is instructed to carry out certain acts in a specific order. It is found that in the post-hypnotic state the subject carries out the instructions in the minutest details. Yet the subject in the performance of the act feels fully free and on being challenged he would furnish reasons for the details of the act. If God the creator be said to determine the free act of man, then man would carry out the act exactly as the subject of the psychological experiment does in accordance with the instruction imparted to him during the hypnotic trance. In other words, the voluntary actions of man would become wholly predestined. But even the fully predestined act, according to Flew may be called 'free'. Not only a free act is compatible with pre-destination, but, according to Flew, this is the most consistent view to take in relation to an omnipotent creator. The theist, according to Flew, maintains

---

49. A.G.N. Flew, *op. cit.*, p. 150.
50. *Ibid.*, p. 152.

that all power is in God's hands all the time, that every move, every thought of his creatures depends on him for its initiation and conservation, and presumably therefore that he could change the heart of any man at any time if he wanted to reverse his wants.[51]

Hence the notion of a creator God, for Flew is

of the Great Hypnotist whose commands all his creatures carry out, usually unknowingly. To fail to appreciate this is to fail to take the theological doctrine of creation seriously.[52]

We shall shortly take up the question of free will, but the whole question arises in the context of God's omnipotence. What, if this very notion be vicious?

We might argue that the whole notion of an omnipotent creator God is logically vicious. If this is so the problem of evil cannot arise, since the notions of God as either all-powerful, or all-good or as even existing at all will all be equally vicious. This is a position to which the present writer is very much inclined.[53]

Of course, Flew does refer to this problem again in Chapter IX of *New Essays*. But it is J.L. Mackie who dwells on this in detail and so we now shall give an exposition of his view concerning the fallacious nature of the notion of omnipotence.

THE PARADOX OF OMNIPOTENCE

Can we say that God is omnipotent, but he cannot control created free wills? Or, can an omnipotent being make rules which bind him or create things which he cannot subsequently control?

If we answer 'Yes', it follows that if God actually makes

51. NEPT, p. 167.
52. NEPT, p. 168; In *'God and Philosophy'*, Flew further contends that by *'creation'* is meant that God can be either a supreme puppet-master or the great hypnotist (2.35).
53. NEPT, p. 165.

things which he cannot control, or makes rules which bind himself, he is not omnipotent once he has made them: there are *then* things which he cannot do. But if we answer 'No' we are immediately asserting that there are things which he cannot do that is to say that he is already not omnipotent.[54]

This sort of paradox is not for the freewillist alone says Mackie, but equally applies to the determinist. Let God be omnipotent for a determinist.

And since God is omniscient, and since his creation of things is total, he both determines and foresees the ways in which his creatures will act . . . . The question is not whether God *originally* determined the future actions of his creatures, but whether he can *subsequently* control their actions, or whether he was able in his original creation to put things beyond his subsequent control. Even on determinist principles the answer 'Yes' and 'No' are equally irreconcilable with God's omnipotence.[55]

Mackie illustrates this dilemma with the help of a similar paradox of the sovereignty of the British Parliament. British Parliament has sovereignty of enacting laws concerning things other than itself. But apart from this sovereignty No. 1, it can also enact laws about its own powers. This may be called sovereignty No. 2. Now the Parliament has unlimited powers with regard to both sovereignties Nos. 1 and 2.

If we say that parliament is sovereign we might mean that any parliament at any time has sovereignty (1), or we might mean that parliament has both sovereignty (1) and sovereignty (2) at present, but we cannot without contradiction mean both that the present parliament has sovereignty (2) and that every parliament at every time has sovereignty (1), for if the present parliament has sovereignty (2) it may use it to take away the sovereignty (1) of later parliaments.[56] What the

54. J.L. Mackie, *Mind*, 1955, p. 210.
55. *Ibid.*, p. 211.
56. For example, S may legislate that in future parliament can nationalise the private industries, then this legislation will seriously curtail the power of S.

paradox shows is that we cannot ascribe to any continuing institution legal sovereignty in an inclusive sense.[57]

Suppose now that in like fashion God has omnipotence P_1 and P_2, with regard to created things and himself respectively. If God has P_1 at all times, then no created beings can act independently of God.

Or we could say that God at one time had omnipotence (2), and used it to assign independent powers to act to certain things, so that God thereafter did not have omnipotence (1); But what the paradox shows is that we cannot consistently ascribe to any continuing being omnipotence in an inclusive sense.[58]

If the above-mentioned reasoning is valid then the paradox of omnipotence shows that unqualified omnipotence cannot be ascribed to any being that continues in time. Of course, one may argue that God is non-temporal. However, in this case, says Mackie, we cannot meaningfully ascribe omnipotence to him. Thus Mackie concludes that the freewillist defence of evil cannot be reconciled with God's omnipotence.

CRITICAL COMMENTS

The empiricist holds a free act can be fully determined or completely controlled. Might be that Nowell-Smith and others might not directly subscribe to the thesis of Flew. However, they would also hold that even a fully predestined act can be said to be free in a certain human context. The freewillist need not deny this. But on the whole, traditionalist would hold that *a fully determined act*, in the usual and commonsense usage will not be called free. He would quote Spinoza, and, Freud adhering to the doctrine of psychic determinism declared that the freedom of will is a pleasing illusion.[59] This point is made all the more clear by Moore's clari-

---

57. *Ibid.*, p. 212.
58. *Ibid.*, p. 212.
59. Introductory Lectures on Psychoanalysis (English translation, 1923), pp. 21, 38, 87-88; W.D. Hudson, 'An attempt to defend theism' in *Philosophy*, Jan. 1964, pp. 20-21.

fication of the term 'free' in relation to the objection raised by
Garnett with regard to Moore's use of the term.

According to Garnett, Moore holds that moral responsibility
of an agent means:

> that he could have done differently *if* he had chosen, with-
> out implying that he *could* have chosen differently. But our
> examination of the terms 'voluntary' and 'involuntary' seems
> to show that the difference between them implies also that
> there is a stage in voluntary action when one is able either to
> choose or not to choose to perform a certain act.........it is
> commonly believed that only voluntary actions are such that
> the agent is able to choose either to do or not to do, and that
> only to such actions do ethical qualities belong.[60]

Moore agreed much with Garnett:

> I now think it is *certainly* not sufficient and that one reason
> why it is not is that a *necessary* condition for its being true
> that his action was morally wrong is, that he should have
> been *able to choose* some other action instead. If he *could not*
> have chosen any other action than the one he did choose,
> then his action cannot have been morally wrong......There is
> *some* sense of 'could have chosen', and *the* sense in which we
> naturally use it in this context, in which the proposition that
> an action was morally wrong, and, more generally, the pro-
> position that the agent was morally responsible for it, cer-
> tainly *entails* that the agent could have made a different choice
> from the one he did make.[61]

If Moore is right then if an action cannot be otherwise than
what it is, if the agent could not have chosen the action other
than the one he did choose, then the action is not voluntary or
free. Hence if an act is wholly and completely determined, then
according to the well-established convention, it cannot be called
'free'.

---

60. The philosophy of G.E. Moore, Edited by P.A. Schilpp, The Library of living philosophers, 1952, p. 181.

61. Moore's Reply, *Ibid.*, p. 624.

Again, does the denial of complete *determinism* mean random-ness, as Mackie suggests? No, The effectiveness of character, sentiments, dispositions has not been denied. What the tradi-tionalist denies that these are the *only factors* involved in volun-tary actions. The free choice, according to the traditionalist, is a matter of the ego or self. Hence, the Hegelians have always regarded a voluntary act as a 'self-determined act'. A voluntary action is said to be determined by the free ego after balancing the conflicting forces at work and by resolving the conflict in favour of an alternative against the rest, by taking the help of organised self, character, self-regarding sentiments and other sentiments. At least this is so explained by R.H. Thouless, Shand, W. McDougall and other psychologists. This is so for the classical thinker T.H. Green. For Green, a voluntary act proceeds from an ego which by distinguishing itself from the various com-peting desires, freely chooses any one of them.

> This constitutes an act of will; which is thus always free, not in the sense of being undetermined by a motive, but in the sense that the motive lies in the man himself, that he makes it and is aware of doing so....[62]

Again, Maurice Cranston states the problem very precisely by pointing out that it is *choice* and not action that we praise or blame. Only in a derivative sense, an action is said to be caused uncaused.[63] Further, he tells us that the choice is determined by *rational* principles,[64] and not by past causes (as Freud and others would hold). Here Cranston quotes Bowen:

> An advocate of free will must admit that a volition is deter-mined without a *cause*; but he does not need to assert that it is determined without a reason. Now motives are reasons and the relation between a reason and its consequent is...entirely distinct from that between a cause and its effect.[65]

---

62. T.H. Green, Prolegomena to Ethics, Sec. 102, p. 106.
63. M. Cranston, 'Is there a problem of the freedom of the will?' H.J., 1952-53, pp. 47-54.
64. Principles like 'lying is wrong' or 'it is better to give than to receive'.
65. *Ibid.*, p. 51.

From the foregoing discussion, one can easily discern that here the claim of Flew and Mackie in favour of their own usage of 'free will' is not decisive. There is also another convention of the theist, according to which even an omnipotent creator cannot create a free will which will always choose the right. And this convention is much better established than that of the empiricist. Further, the whole controversy between the empiricist and the theist is not one of facts, but of two contrasted attitudes to life. In other words, the problem of free will is wholly metaphysical. It cannot be established by means of cognitive arguments. At the end of this chapter we shall try to ascertain the metaphysical significance of the problem. We can take up this issue again only by further clarifying the notion of 'omnipotence' and 'evil' with which the issue is associated.

OMNIPOTENCE AND FREE WILL

The traditional freewillist advances two points with regard to evil. For him, the world is 'a vale of soul-making', or, the supreme end of the universe is to transform creatures into co-creators with God. This can be achieved only when the free will is made holy through obedience to the will of God even in the face of all temptations for disobedience. This end of God requires that there be creatures endowed with freedom of will, and with the freedom of will the possibility of choosing evil goes necessarily. However, the supreme end of having co-creators is so much desirable that no price is too high for its realisation. Hence, moral evil, which results from the abuse of wrong choice, has to be permitted. Even an omnipotent God, for the freewillist, cannot cause a free will always choose the right. For him the very notion of causal determination of a free choice is self-contradictory. Thus, S.A. Grave correctly observes that the point of the theist's reply is that moral evils are not necessary, but necessarily possible consequences of freedom.[66] Secondly, the freewillist holds that foreknowledge of a free act is self-contradictory. True, St. Augustine did not note this self-contradiction and as a result of which in the churches even now it is read that God is one 'in

---

66. S.A. Grave, 'On evil and omnipotence', *Mind*, Vol. LXV, 1956, p. 259; Mark Pontifex, 'The question of evil' in *Prospects for Metaphysics*, p. 131.

whose eyes all hearts are open, all desires known, and from whom no secrets are hid'. But Bergson and Samuel Alexander, who have occupied themselves exclusively with free creation, deny the possibility of foreknowing the free creative act. According to Bergson, each act is simple and productive of a new form. For him even a superhuman intelligence cannot foresee the simple, indivisible free act.

> For to foresee consists of projecting into the future what has been perceived in the past........But that which has never been perceived, and which is at the same time simple, is necessarily unforeseeable.[67]

In the same way, Samuel Alexander also holds that the creative future cannot be foreknown even by God.

> The only meaning which can rationally be attached to the notion that God can predict the whole future is that the future will be what it will be.[68]

Hence, a theist concludes that a free act cannot be foreknown.[69]

> We can accept the following statement of Flew: If an act is foreknown, then it must be treated as completely determined; But a free act is not completely determined.

Therefore, a free act cannot be foreknown.

If a free act cannot be foreknown, then much of the objection of McCloskey loses its force. McCloskey states that God is omniscient and he foreknows that many would-be sin. Therefore, his foreknowledge and infinite goodness could have prevented the creation of such free wills.

> He is said not to choose to do this. Instead, at the cost of the sacrifice of the many, He is said to have ordered things so

---

67. H. Bergson, 'Creative Evolution', Eng. Tr. Macmillan, 1928, pp. 6-7.
68. S. Alexander, 'Space, Time and Deity', Vol. II, Macmillan, 1927, p. 329.
69. *Supra*, pp. 226-27.

as to allow fewer men to attain the higher virtue and higher beatitude.........[70]

Even if God cannot foreknow a free choice, then certainly he cannot be said to favour a few saints at the cost of many sinners. According to Indian Theism even the sinners will be ultimately redeemed as is illustrated in the case of Ahalya, Ravana and many other Rakshasas. Let us come to omnipotence. Mackie holds that 'omnipotence' becomes a self-contradictory notion if it is ascribed to a *continuing* being. He illustrates this with regard to the sovereignty of the British Parliament. Has Mackie proved his point? The whole contention will gain weight if it is granted that omnipotence is compatible with doing the self-contradictory. A God, according to a theist, cannot destroy himself, cannot become finite and so on. If it is so, then omnipotence cannot also achieve the self-contradictory result of a fully determined free will. Hence, the paradox of Mackie does not have the same agreed consequence.

Can an omnipotent God control free creatures who of their very nature cannot always be controlled?

This may sound a valid paradox for Mackie, but is nonsense and self-contradictory for a theist. A fully controlled free will is the same as *necessarily* free. Again, *necessity*, as the empiricist himself would maintain is validly applicable only to propositions, so it cannot be legitimately applied to a free act or any actual event. A proposition concerning an actual, voluntary act can only be contingent. Hence, Mackie's paradox can be resolved by saying that an omnipotent creator has created beings some of whom would freely and contingently always choose the right.[71] In other words, this world is a vale of creating holy wills. Once such wills emerge, they by their own free choice would always act rightly.

Again, Mackie's paradox stands on par with liar's paradox and its solution lies in Russell's theory of description or types.

70. H.J. McCloskey, *op. cit.*, p. 82.
71. S.A. Grave, *op. cit.*, p. 261.

According to this, the statement which is devised to explicate the meaning of other statements of lower generality cannot be reflexively applicable to it. Now God's omnipotence is postulated to explain the limitations of creatures. Therefore, God's omnipotence, which has been used as a limiting principle cannot be applicable to God's omnipotence itself. Hence, consistently speaking, God cannot undertake any step to limit himself. This could be self-contradictory. Once again, we can quote P.M. Farrell to the effect that for a traditional theist omnipotence means,

> the power to effect everything possible, i.e. everything which could in the nature of it, be.[72]

For a theist, therefore, a finite creature by his nature is contingent and his voluntary acts cannot be necessary. If it is so, then God's omnipotence could not have created a free will and a contingent being who would always as a matter of fact necessarily choose the right.

Now we turn to the second key-notion of 'evil' involved in the empiricist attack on the freewillist defence of evil.

A SUMMARY OF FREE WILL

1. Free will means a choice of one alternative out of several possible options. Every alternative is caused and determined. But the *choice* of one alternative by discarding others is free and not controlled. This is the standard use of 'free will'. A completely controlled action is not said to be free. Hence the use of the term 'free' in relation to a completely determined act by Mackie and Flew and others is not commonly permitted.

> God cannot cause Smith to refrain from performing A, while allowing him to be free with respect to A; and therefore whether or not Smith does A will be entirely up to Smith: it will be a matter of free choice for him.[73]

---

72. P.M. Farrell, *Evil and Omnipotence* in *Mind*, 1958, Vol. LXVII, p. 401.

73. Alvin Plantinga, *The Free Will Defence* in *The Philosophy of Religion*, by B. Mitchell, p. 113.

2. God can create beings who will always at all times do the right. Angels are said to be such creatures. They are always good and never bad. But God has also created free men who can either choose the good or evil, at various times.

According to theists God has created free wills who through obedience to God and by His Grace will successfully always choose the good. Jesus Christ for the Christians and Sri Ramakrishna for the Ramakrishnaites are those free men who have succeeded in doing always what is right. Such persons having free will for choosing either good or evil, have always chosen the good, are said to be much superior to angels.

Ordinarily however free men can either choose the good or evil. By repentance for the evil acts and prayers for becoming holy, free men can approach the end of becoming saints. The world is truly a vale of soul-making.

Hence, if God brings about that the men He creates always do what is right, then *they* do not do what is right freely, but God does this. Hence God cannot create *free* men who will always do what is right. Holy will cannot be created, because it is a matter of realisation and attainment by overcoming the evil.

THE NATURE OF EVIL

So far as the problem of evil is concerned much of the arguments of the atheist, empiricist and analyst somehow takes evil to be a positive thing which frustrates or limits the omnipotence of God. For example, Mill after citing the many instances of blemishes in nature, concludes that God is not omnipotent but is infinitely good.

> The only admissible moral theory of creation is that the Principle of Good *cannot* at once and altogether subdue the powers of evil, either physical or moral;.........[74]

Here 'evil' has been taken to be a positive quality. But traditionally evil is the privation of good, i.e. the absence of good from persons where it is intended to be. Privation is to be distinguished from negation. Negation indirectly asserts the existence of

---

74. APR, p. 233.

something positive. For example, when we say this tree is not green, we indirectly imply that it has some colour other than green. It might be brown or yellow by virtue of which the term 'green' cannot be applied to it. In contrast, privation means the present absence of a quality of thing, e.g. this man is blind. Of course, this man at the present time cannot see, but in future the man can be endowed with vision. In other words, privation of a thing can be replaced by a positive quality. Now if evil be the privation of good, then, it means that in due course it will be replaced by the good.[75] Hence, even a Nero or a Judas in the fulness of time will become angels of heaven. Thus, evil is pure nothing and nothing cannot limit anything.

For instance the people brought a man to the Master who was born blind, and, seeing him the disciples asked:

> Master, who did sin, this man, or his parents, that he was born blind? Jesus answered, Neither hath this man sinned, nor his parents: but the works of God should be made manifest in him.[76]

Here evil has been taken to be the privation of the good. The evil of being born blind was later replaced by the glory of God. It isn't such a notoriously hard saying, as Flew have us believe.[77] The statement of McCloskey is equally wide of the mark. He seems to think that in prinicple the instrumentalist is committed to the view that evil in the total context contributes to increasing the total ultimate good,

> so equally, it will hold that good in the total context may increase the ultimate evil. Thus if the principle of the argument

---

75. F.H. Bradley would not accept this explanation of privation, since for him even privation implies affirmation. However, a close scrutiny would show that Bradley has seriously erred on this point because of his prepossession. As a result of his absolutism he had to show that ultimately everything has the positive core of the absolute reality. To get one convinced of Bradley's untenability one has to read the explanation of Bradley concerning the judgment, 'This stone is blind', (Principles of Logic, pp. 118-19).
76. St. John 9:2-3.
77. A.G.N. Flew, NEPT, pp. 156-57; also God and Philosophy, 2.45.

were sound, we could never know whether evil is really evil, or good really good.[78]

A FURTHER COMMENT ON MCCLOSKEY'S VIEW

For the purpose of the book we have shown that the arguments of Flew and Mackie are not as victorious as they suppose. But McCloskey claims that the account of moral evil in terms of free will breaks down on more obvious and less disputable grounds than those indicated by J.L. Mackie.[79] Hence, we pay now a special attention to his criticism of the freewillist defence.

The freewillist defence, according to McCloskey, makes two assumptions:

1. Free will even with moral lapses is better than a universe in which there are fully determined and completely pre-destined creatures or automata who would always choose the right and do the right thing.
2. Free will with the possibility of moral evil alone provides the basis of the emergence of holy wills. This assumption is rather inaccurately stated by McCloskey thus:
   What all these have in common is the claim that the good consequences of free will provide a justification of the bad consequences of free will, namely moral evil.[80]

I. We need not dwell on the first kind of defence by the theist in the form in which McCloskey understands it, for its statement by McCloskey has unnecessarily been distorted. According to him a theist would allow

that it is logically possible on the free will hypothesis that all men should always will what is evil, and that even so, a universe of completely evil men possessing free will is better than one in which men are predestined to virtuous living.[81]

---

78. H.J. McCloskey, GE, p. 72; also J.L. Mackie, *op. cit.*, 208.
79. GE, p. 762.
80. *God and evil*, in *God and Evil*, Edited by Nelson Pike, Contemporary Perspectives in Philosophy series, Prentice-Hall, 1964, p. 78.
81. *Ibid.*, p. 78.

First, 'to be predestined' and 'virtuous living' are self-contradictory statements, according to the traditionalist. If McCloskey chooses, as Flew and Mackie do, that according to his stipulated convention 'free will' and 'predestined will' are compatible then this will not be binding on the traditionalist. A theist thinks that virtuous living is possible only for free wills who freely choose the action according to the wishes of God. Who can decide between these two opposed linguistic conventions?

Secondly, logically speaking, it must be conceded that free will hypothesis is compatible with the possibility of *all* men *always* choosing the evil. But does a theist who believes in the omniscience and infinite goodness of God accept this possibility? Elijah also thought so, but Yahweh informed him that there were at least seven hundred men who had not worshipped Baal.[82] The theist believes that God knows that there would be sinners and prodigals, but in His divine dispensation He has so arranged things even from the beginning of creation that sinners and prodigals, at least a good number of them, would become penitent and return to God. So what is possible for McCloskey is not compossible for the theist. Even in the Gita, God is pictured not to allow the possibility of the triumph of the evil.

> When righteousness is weak and faints and unrighteousness exults in pride, then my Spirit arises on earth.
> For the salvation of those who are good, for the destruction of evil in men, for the fulfilment of the kingdom of righteousness, I come to this world in the ages that pass.[83]

Hence, for the theist free will and the total moral evil are not compossible; it matters little to him if they are so for Mr. H.J. McCloskey.

In the same strain, it is logically possible that all men always choose the good. Unfortunately the theist knows this that free will and total moral goodness are not compossible on this earth, purely as a matter of fact.

---

82. I King 19:14, 18.
83. Chap. IV, verses 7-8.

Because straight is the gate, and narrow is the way, which leadeth unto life, and few there be that find it.[84]

But a theist does admit and fervently hopes that few there are who do enter into the kingdom of God through the narrow and straight way.

We may condone the slip of 'rational automata' on the part of McCloskey, but how can we concede to him the logical validity of his decision with regard to two opposed proposals? He states his proposals thus:

However, no matter how we resolve the linguistic point, the question remains—which is more desirable, free will and moral evil and the physical evil to which free will gives rise, or this special free will or pseudo-free[85] will which goes with absolute goodness? I suggest that the latter is clearly preferable.[86]

Not only, it is a matter of decision between two proposals, for which some reasons can be advanced by way of justification: but the preference shown by McCloskey ignores many points of the theist. The theist assumes that the beatitude of the saint is of infinite value and cannot be exchanged for any commodity of lower value. Secondly, the theist also believes that ultimately evil will be purged. McCloskey and others of his way of thinking make too much of popular eschatological beliefs concerning heaven and hell. However, a theist need not indulge too much in eschatological hopes and fears. Indian theism does not accept the fact of heaven and hell as eternal and ultimate, and Christian theism is more concerned with redeeming and reclaiming the sinners than with their eternal damnation. A theist is prevented from making any final conclusion concerning evil in the face of God's omnipotence and infinite goodness because,

we can never see all of the picture. Two things at least are

---

84. St. Mattew 7:14.
85. A rational agent predestined by God always to make virtuous 'decisions'.
86. *Ibid.*, pp. 79-80.

hidden from us; what goes on in the recess of the personality of the sufferer, and what shall happen hereafter.[87]

True, this is not a convincing argument, but any argument against theistic stand has to take a fuller picture of the theistic discourse. Now we come to the second objection by McCloskey against the freewillist defence. Most probably McCloskey holds this to be his special argument and an improvement on Mackie's criticism of the freewillist defence. The nerve of the criticism is that the presence of any pointless and superfluous evil is fatal to God's goodness. And McCloskey mentions three points to show that some moral evil is entirely superfluous.

(i) God could intervene to prevent some and perhaps all moral evil, as He is believed to do in a few cases in answer to prayers.

(ii) God could have made man with *less* bias towards evil, thereby preventing some evils at least.

(iii) An omnipotent God could have so ordered the world that fewer chances of evil might have been possible.

In what respects these three points in principle differ from the contention of Mackie according to whom free will is compatible with absolute determinism is a matter for McCloskey's cool reflections. We shall confine ourselves to a few observations only. Intervention in answer to prayers is quite different from God's intervention on His own initiative. As a matter of fact prayers for the forgiveness of sins or for preventing one from falling into the evil of temptation or for overcoming the temptation is the right use of free will for becoming gold fit for heaven. God's intervention at His own initiative in all cases is tantamount to holding free will to be compatible with absolute foreknowledge, prediction and control. Further, how can anybody purely on a human level and hold *a priori* that some cases of evil are superfluous? This is the very point which McCloskey and others of his kind cannot establish. His other contention that men could have been created with less bias to evil or complete bias for good, or that actual

---

87. I.M. Crombie, '*Theology and falsification*' in *New Essays in Philosophical Theology*, Edited by A. Flew and A, Macintyre, SCM Press, 1958, pp. 124-25.

circumstances could have been created for the exercise of good only are thin disguise of Mackie's observation that free will is compatible with absolute goodness. As the latter is not tenable, so McCloskey's case too is equally untenable. Besides nobody can fail to note the strong note of anthropomorphism in relation to McCloskey's concept of God.

II. Most probably the second defence of the freewillist is more important. According to this defence final beatitude or moral virtue attained after a hard struggle with real risk of evil is incomparatively higher than one without any such struggle and risk. This defence does not imply that one should court temptation as McCloskey would have us believe. As a matter of fact the prayer of the theist is to save him from temptation. This means that the path of moral struggle is through the vale of sorrow and suffering. For a theist temptation and struggle are necessarily contingent for finite creatures and cannot be set aside from a contingently and finitely created universe. Temptations arise in such a world and are not put in the way of man by God. This is what is meant by saying that God does not will evil, so it would not be quite correct to say that God *puts* temptation in the way of man. According to McCloskey God becomes immoral because he allows the possibility of moral struggle and fall.

> To put severe temptation in the way of the many, knowing that many perhaps even most will succumb to the temptation, for the sake of the higher virtue of the few, would be blatant immorality; and would be immoral whether or not those who yielded to the temptation possessed free will.[88]

The contention of McCloskey rests on many assumptions. He is not taking the graded universe as a whole on which a theist like F.R. Tennant would insist. Then McCloskey ignores one very important assumption of the theist. The theist maintains that the emergence of the holy will is the end and anything less than this would not serve the purpose of God's creation. For a theist the alternatives suggested by McCloskey offers the husk rather than the kernel of moral attainment. McCloskey submits the following alternatives:

---

88. *Ibid.*, p. 82.

(i) The higher virtue of some and the evil of many others
     (due to the abuse of free choice),

Or

(ii) The lesser virtue of many more, and the evil of many
      fewer (due to God's intervention or due to creation of
      a universe which will be comparatively freer from temp-
      tations).

Most probably McCloskey does not realise that the comparison between the two states differing in *kind* cannot be logically
made and any choice between these two or more such alternatives
is not a matter of logic but of free decisions: the alternatives
under discussion relate to an absolutely holy will and to virtuous
automata. Further, unless people be told the meaning of 'rational automata' who are completely predestined always to do the
right, one can hardly make any sense of the suggestion made by
McCloskey. According to him, an omnipotent God could have
created 'rational' agents predestined always 'to choose' the right
things for the right reasons.[89] At this stage the observation of
Ninian Smart is worth studying.

Flew, Mackie and McCloskey make much of the possibility
of free will compatible with absolute goodness. Ninian Smart
contends[90] that the concept 'good' has meaning only in relation
to temptation, courage, self-interest, self-sacrifice and so on.
Good apart from the possibility of real struggle and risk has no
meaning at all. So Smart by means of various constructions of
utopias shows that the concept 'good' would have no clear meaning if by means of divine intervention the possibility of evil be
completely brushed aside.

Thus the abstract possibility that men might have been
created wholly good loses its clarity as soon as we begin to
imagine alternative possible universes. If then the Utopia
Thesis is quite unclear, it cannot assert anything intelligible
about God. And so it cannot serve as part of antitheistic
argument.[91]

---

89. *Ibid.*, p. 83.
90. *Omnipotence, Evil and Supermen* in *God and Evil*.
91. *Ibid.*, p. 112.

The point of Ninian Smart can be put a little differently thus. The ethical statement that a certain 'X' is good has meaning only when there are circumstances in which it can be falsified. A statement concerning good which can never be otherwise than good, is ethically vacuous. It would simply mean that 'a good act is good' or more simply 'good is good'. However, linguistically speaking, 'Men are good' is a synthetic statement. Once again by reducing free men to rational automata who will always do the right, we are proposing a state of affairs in which 'ought' is reduced to 'is', the ideal is reduced to the actual. In such a state of affairs, the moral distinction altogether disappears.

Therefore, we conclude that McCloskey has not improved upon the argument of Flew and Mackie.

Now we have tried to clarify the notions of evil, Omnipotence and free will and we can interpret them in the convictional language in the following way.

CONVICTIONAL INTERPRETATION OF EVIL
A. Macintyre states that a religion 'is always concerned with how men are to live and with what their fundamental attitudes to life are to be'.[92]

Hence religious interest is not primarily theoretical. A worshipper does not seek to prove or know God primarily: he wants to praise Him. Our religious concern with God is not speculative: a worshipper seeks to enter into personal relationship with Him.[93] As knowing and thinking are subordinate to the task of living, so arguments and reasonings remain subservient to the religious end of soul-making. Now any belief and practice which in the course of a religious tradition has stood the test of time and which is borne out by the personal experience of worshipper assumes the form of an article of faith. This article of faith is not a cognitive achievement so much as it is a matter of personal decision and commitment.

A life led according to religious beliefs and practices of a religion in the ultimate analysis is the truth of that religion. For doing this the believer learns the language of the religious community to which he belongs, shares his life with other members

---

92. Metaphysical Beliefs, p. 201.
93. I.M. Crombie, 'Theology and Falsification' in NEPT, p. 124.

of the community and realizes a certain inwardness through prayers, fastings, rituals, hymn-singing and praising God and so on. Once the worshipper feels that he is shaping himself in the direction in which his God wants him to be moulded, he becomes thoroughly convinced of his beliefs and practices. The more he feels the peace of mind, the more convinced he becomes of his belief. A steadfast progress in the direction of the religious truth is the evidence of his belief. This kind of truth is more to be judged by the believer himself. If he finds as a result of his religious beliefs and practices the enlargement and enrichment of his personality and a deeper flow of the current of his life, then whatever others have to say about his religious beliefs, for him they form the very pearl of his life; they contribute to the meaning of his existence. He does not need any other proof of the truth of his belief.

Inward conviction is reflected in outward acts. Naturally the religious truth inwardly realised issues in social acts. Very often they issue forth in selfless service and a broad compassion for the whole humanity. A complete person in his both inward realisation and outward acts is the truth of the religious statement. Hence, religious truth is made or created. Each religious man is a challenge to others. Others may accept him if they are convicted in their hearts of the truth which he portrays in his life and conduct, or they may reject him as unacceptable to them. Now the meaning of 'evil and omnipotence' for a theist is gleaned from his belief and practices.

For a theist evil is there to be assimilated into his life by overcoming its distracting influence. The attitude of Job in the face of calamities is a point:

'Naked came out of my mother's womb, and naked shall I return thither: the Lord gave, and the Lord hath taken away; blessed be the name of the Lord'.[94]

This utterance of Job is in a certain religious context of a Transcendent God who was worshipped more for his power than for his moral character. For this reason A. Macintyre[95] and I.M.

---

94. Job 1:21.
95. Difficulties in Christian Belief, pp. 79, 85-86; Metaphysical Beliefs, p. 202.

Crombie[96] maintain that religious statements are meaningful 'in faith' and not 'outside faith'. For a Christian theist evil is there to be overcome and no amount of evil can ever separate a believer from the God of Love:

> Who shall separate us from the love of Christ? Shall tribulation, or distress, or persecution, or famine, or nakedness, or peril, or sword?
>
> ....
>
> For I am persuaded, that neither death nor life, nor angels, nor principalities, nor powers, nor things present, nor things to come. Nor height, nor depth, nor any other creature, shall be able to separate us from the love of God, which is in Christ Jesus our Lord.[97]

A theist is not a double-thinker in relation to evil. The evil for Indian thinkers is most patent and Lord Buddha has taught the reality of evil so vividly and so cogently that Buddhism and Indian thought have been dubbed 'pessimistic'. But the teaching is for the purpose of withdrawing men from ephemeral pleasures and of inducing them to a life of spiritual bliss. Hence, for Indian thinking the endless chain of births and rebirths has the sole purpose of realising the eternal state of Nirvana or Moksha. Hence, evil is there to be overcome: it is not allowed to be the last word about the universe.

For a Judaeo-Christian theist the fact of evil is central for his belief. Christianity is a religion which preaches the reclamation of sinners and redemption of sins. Hence, Patterson Brown[98] tells us that Christianity would become void in a morally perfect universe, 'a religion of salvation would be senseless in Paradise'. So the reality of evil is not an argument against, but an argument for a Judaeo-Christian God.

Evil is the most palpable reality for a theist. The allurement of sin is taken to be very great. Once a person becomes a slave to sin he becomes blind to the redeeming love of God. At least this is the interpretation of the crucifixion of Jesus. A Christian

---

96. NEPT, p. 130.
97. Romans 8:35, 38:39.
98. Patterson Brown, *Religious Morality, Mind,* 1963, Vol. LXXII, p. 235.

theist believes that Jesus as a divine light came into the world, which was darkened by sin and 'the darkness comprehended it not'. Nay, some theists belonging to Judaeo-Christian traditions, believe that persons darkened by sins are likely to lose irredeemably and irrevocably the chance of becoming co-creators with God.

The Omnipotence of God is also a convictional concept. This is attributed to God with a view to inducing a shuddering dread in the worshipper. Most probably this has been best clarified by Rudolph Otto and we shall therefore follow his suggestion. According to Otto, God is felt numinously as '*Mysterium Tremendum*' and he is felt as aweful with holy dread. He is apprehended as exalted and overpowering majesty. The wrath of God is a terrible thing indeed.

> 'Wrath' here is the 'ideogram' of a unique emotional movement in religious experience, a moment whose singularly *daunting* and awe-inspiring character must be gravely disturbing to those persons who will recognize nothing in the divine nature but goodness, gentleness, love and a sort of confidential intimacy, in a word, only those aspects of God which turn towards the world of men.[99]

Of course, for Otto, this overpowering might and the wrath of God are not intellectual concepts. And this is our view too. The purpose of these non-rational ideograms is to evoke religious feeling. At least this point is clearly illustrated in the Book of Job where God thunders forth his might and Job submits himself to him.

> I have heard of thee by the hearing of the ear: but now mine eye seeth thee[100] wherefore I abhor myself, and repent in dust and ashes.[101]

Job knew fully well that God was not just to him and yet he submits himself to God for none else can save him.

---

99. R. Otto, 'The idea of the holy', Oxford Bookshelf, 1936, p. 19.
100. In other words, he has now the most favoured vision of God.
101. Job 42:5-6.

Thou knowest that I am not guilty; and *there* is none that can deliver out of thine hand.[102]

For God is not a man and the ultimate judgement lies with him. Job does not reason out the thing. He surrenders himself to God, since for Job man cannot be more just than his creator. The Lord said to Job:

Shall he that contendeth with the Almighty instruct *him*? he that reproveth God, let him answer it.
Then Job answered the Lord and said, Behold, I am vile; what shall I answer thee? 'I shall lay mine hand upon my mouth'.[103]

The omnipotence of God is not an intellectual concept and so discussion about God's creating free wills who will always choose the right is not in the context of religious meaning. The image of God is there with the attributes of Omnipotence, wrath, majesty, awefulness and of course of goodness and love and so forth. If a worshipper remains dumb with holy dread, then the function of religious concept is over.

Hence, for us, the empiricists are as much in the wrong as are the theologians who take religious statements to be assertions. Our account of the quasi-descriptiveness of religious statements is essentially sound. But its soundness will be further fortified if we could further exhibit the part which the image or ideogram of God or deity plays in our psychological life. A psychological account of religious concepts and images would successfully explain the quasi-descriptive nature of religious statements.

---

102. Job 10:7.
103. Job 40:2-4.

CHAPTER XIV

THE PROBLEM OF IMMORTALITY

INTRODUCTION

There are many senses in which the term 'immortality' has been used. The sense in which the problem is important for the theist means the endless duration of the personal existence of the individual with the prospect of infinite enrichment of the personality. This means that the individual personality with its present memory and purpose is conceived to continue; and, secondly, this infinite duration offers opportunities of better realising the higher purposes of man. However, the term 'immortality' stands for various kinds of immortality, which have to be distinguished from one another.

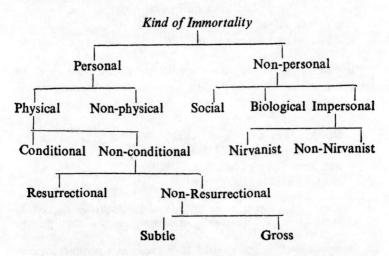

Kind of Immortality

In the first instance, immortality means either the survival of the personality of the individual with his continuing memory and purpose, or, the survival of the individual in some form without the continuity of his memory, purpose, reason and self-consciousness. For example when the chemical elements of the individual's body are reabsorbed in the cosmic matter, then in some sense the individual's body does continue to exist. But then it would not mean the survival of the personality of the individual.

PERSONAL IMMORTALITY

Even personal immortality has been variously conceived. It may mean that a human individual is composed of two distinct factors, Puruṣa and Prakṛiti, body and soul. What remains immortal is the soul or Atman and not the body. This is the predominant conception in Indian philosophy and it was also held by Plato. As the soul is eternal, so it is not subject to decay:

> Dehi nityam avadhyo 'Yam
> dehe sarvasya Bharata
> tasmat servani bhutani
> na tvam sochitum arhasi[1]

> Na jayate Mriyate va kadacin
> na 'yam bhutva bhavita va na bhuyah
> Ajo nithah śāśvato 'yam purano
> na hanyate hanyamane śarire[2]

Even though the body does not belong to the Soul, yet the final discriminative wisdom continues with the released soul. At least this appears to be the substance of Sankyha philosophy.[3]

> Dṛasta Maye' tuypekṣaka ekah,
> dṛaṣṭa 'hamityupara Matyanya
> Sati Sam Yoge' pi tayoh
> Prayojanam Nasti Sargasya[4]

---

1. Bhagavadgita, Chap. II, Verse 30. That which dwells in the body of everyone is eternal and can never be slain: therefore, thou shouldst not grieve for any creature.
2. Bhagavadgita Chap. II, Verse 20. It is never born nor dies; nor once in existence can it ever cease. It is eternal, everlasting and Primeval. It is not killed when the body is destroyed.
   See verses from the 18th to the 30th of Chap. II.
3. S.S. Suryanarayana Sastri, The Samkhya Karika, Madras University 1930, Verses 57-68.
4. *Ibid.*, Verse 66.

So there can be personal immortality even in the released soul. In other systems of Indian thought there are various other fates of the released soul to which we need not refer in this context of 'personal immortality'.

However, in the West in popular religious thought the hope of immortality is entertained in the form of the continued existence of quasi-body also. This survival of the body after death may be held to be universal or it may be entertained for the chosen few only. The view that only some will attain immortality to the exclusion of the rest is called the doctrine of *conditional immortality*. Many Christian theists do not regard the Biblical teaching of eternal damnation for life of torment consistent with the conception of the loving God of Christianity. So they advance the doctrine of conditional immortality, according to which only the righteous deserve to live everlastingly. Indeed, many passages from the Bible can be quoted in support of this view.

> In the way of righteousness *is* life: and *in* the pathway *thereof there is* no death[5]
> And fear not them which kill the body, but are not able to kill the soul: but rather fear him which is able to destroy both soul and body in hell[6]
> For God so loved the world that He gave his only begotten Son, that whosoever believeth in him should not perish, but have everlasting life[7]

Even when Universalism is held, according to which view, all individuals will survive death and according to their deeds will go either to hell or heaven, there are two possible doctrines. According to one view, the soul will continue to live in purgatory, till the day of Judgement. After that the believers will enter heaven everlastingly and the sinners will enter hell where they will

---

"'She has been by me' says one and indifferent; 'I have been seen', says the other and ceases to evolve further in spite of the conjunction."
5. Proverb 12:28.
6. Mat 10:28.
7. St. John 3:16.

lead the life of unceasing torment for ever. Most probably this speculation was very much influenced by Plato's parable of the Line and by other Greco-Roman sources. The other view is that the soul will return to God or will even cease to be on the death of the individual. However, on the day of judgement the trumpet will be sounded and the souls will be re-created along with their earthly bodies. The righteous will enter heaven and the sinners will go to hell. After this there will be no second death. St. Paul who shared the belief with other Pharisees that there can be no soul without the body and that without the continuation of this body in some form there can be no personal immortality also held that the corruptible body has to be transformed into some incorruptible form:

> Litsen, and I will tell you a secret. We shall not all die, suddenly in the twinkling of an eye, *everyone* of us will be changed as the trumpet sounds. The trumpet will sound and the dead shall be raised beyond the reach of corruption, and we who are still alive shall suddenly be utterly changed. For this perishable nature of ours must be wrapped in imperishability, these bodies which are mortal must be wrapped in immortality.[8]

Again, the non-resurrectional immortality may be conceived either in the form of gross body or in the form of subtle body. In Indian thought the jivas are conceived to exist in subtle etheral forms. In contrast, the Psychical Research Society conceives the survival of the individual in some sensible existence.

NON-PERSONAL IMMORTALITY

Many thinkers have advanced the theory that there is no personal immortality and that there can be no survival of man after the dissolution of the body. Still they advance the theory of immortality.

1. Though an individual dies, he yet lives in his progeny. This may be termed biological immortality. Anybody can see that this is highly unsatisfactory. Though children resemble their

---

8. I. Corinth 15:51-53 (Fontana Books).

parents and grandparents, yet they also vastly differ. Unless the individual himself survives with his memory there is hardly any psychological satisfaction in the prospect of biological survival. Further, this cannot bring any consolation to the unmarried and childless.

2. Yet again is the doctrine of *social immortality*. Though Plato left behind his mortal remains, yet his thoughts are still living with us, and they still powerfully influence our thoughts and lives. No doubt, the prospect of social immortality is a powerful incentive for adding to the sum of human values, yet it is only a poor substitute of personal immortality. Very few can ever hope to inherit this kind of social immortality and even then it cannot last for ever.

3. There is a type of immortality which may be called Nirvana. Here the personality is dissolved through the efforts of Samadhi. The ego is completely dissolved and a state is reached 'beyond perception and non-perception'. It has reached the state of perfection and once that state has been reached it becomes immortal. This conception is of a certain life of value and quality and not of quantity. Here the deathless life is not measured in terms of years lived but in terms of works done and values achieved.

> It is not growing like a tree
> In bulk, doth make men better be;
> Or standing long an oak three hundred years,
> To fall a log at last, dry, bald, and sere;
> A lily of a day, Is fairer far in May,
> Although it fall and die that night;
> It was the plant and flower of light.
> In small proportions we just beauties see;
> And in short measures life may perfect be.[9]

Why? Because the lily of a day in the words of Keats is a thing of beauty and is a joy for ever:

'Its loveliness increases; it will never pass into nothingness'.

---

9. Ben Jonson, 'It is not growing like a tree'.

4. Monistic or *Pantheistic Immortality*. The third is to be distinguished from the second, because in the second the immortality consists of continued social influence. But in the third kind there is the qualitative or axiological immortality of having attained perfection or of putting on immortality even in this earthly frame (jivanmukti). Here the individual becomes eternal even if there is nobody to take cognizance of it. This has to be sharply distinguished from the pantheistic kind of immortality according to which the individuality is lost, merged and absorbed in the Absolute Reality:

> I give Thee back the life I owe,
> That in Thine ocean-depths its flow
> May richer, fuller be.[10]

Here the river is said to be preserved even when it is lost in the ocean, or the drop of water is said to be conserved even when it melts into the river.

We shall dwell more on this kind of Advaitin immortality or the immortality of the Absolutist in the West, a little later. So we shall confine ourselves to the kind of immortality which is theistically sound and important.

IMMORTALITY FOR THEISM

Seldom theism has been held without some accompanying doctrine of immortality. For example, St. Paul believing in the resurrection of the dead and everlasting life thereafter wrote:

> And if Christ be not raised, your faith *is* vain; Ye are yet in your sins. Then they also which are fallen asleep in Christ are perished. If in this life only we have hope in Christ, we are of all men most miserable.[11]

For St. Paul, of course, death is the wages of sin and redemption and righteousness mean unending life. Here we find that in a subtle way personal immortality has been combined with qualita-

---

10.   A Church hymn by George Matheson.
11.   I Corinth 15:17-19.

tive or axiological significance. The persuasiveness of the theistic argument is derived from its insistence on the high quality of life hoped for. But the quality insisted on is quite independent of everlastingness. Here the *eternity* of truth, beauty and goodness is confused with the enduringness of the body. Thus, theism holds that the life of faith, obedient to God until death, a life of virtue and righteousness will be conserved to the end. There are places where a certain kind of qualitative life is called immortal, excluding the idea of physical existence.

In the Johnnine Gospel the immortality of a qualitative kind of life is most clearly emphasized. Whosoever believes on Jesus Christ as the only begotten Son of God shall not perish, but will have an everlasting life.[12] Then, again,

> verily, verily, I say unto you, He that heareth my word, and believeth on him that sent me, hath everlasting life, and shall not come into condemnation; but is passed from death unto life. Verily, verily, I say unto you, The hour is coming *and now is*, when the dead shall hear the voice of the Son of God: and they that hear shall live.[13]

Then there is the famous utterance of Jesus:

> I am the resurrection, and the life: he that believeth in me, though he were dead, yet shall he live:
> And whosoever liveth and believeth in me shall never die.[14]

Even in St. Paul's writings, the immortal life consists in living Christ and this means the becoming of a new creature. From all these considerations, A. Seth Pringle-Pattison gathers that eternal life taught in the New Testament is not a state of existence to follow upon physical death, but is an all-absorbing state of experiencing the love of God in Christ.[15] Hence, Pringle-Pattison approvingly quotes the wise words of Schleiemacher:[16]

---

12. St. John 3:16.
13. *Ibid.*, 5:24-25 (Italics ours).
14. *Ibid.*, 11:25-26.
15. Eternal life in APR, p. 497.
16. *Ibid.*, pp. 489-90.

The goal and the character of the religious life is not the immortality desired and believed in by many...... It is not the immortality that is outside of time, behind it or rather after it, and which still is in time. It is the immortality which we can have now in this temporal life. In the midst of finitude to be one with the Infinite, and in every moment to be eternal, that is the immortality of religion.

This view will be fully endorsed both by the Vedantin and Nirvanist. But will a Christian theist accept this pale consolation of an eternal life as a substitute of everlasting physical existence?

A. Seth Pringle-Pattison himself in his earlier writings[17] has written in favour of the conservation of individuals as substantive beings. According to him, the relative independence of human personalities and the existence of God as a living Being are bound up together.[18] The argument of the theist can be stated briefly thus. The creater God out of the abundance of his outgoing and creative love has created the whole universe with a view to giving rise to creatures who ultimately would be moulded into souls. Only such souls can be the fit persons deserving the fellowship of a holy God. Now if we look back at the history of the evolutionary scheme of this universe, then we shall find that the making of souls is the sole aim of the universe. But does the path of making souls run smooth? No. After a good deal of preparation life emerged on the earth. In the beginning it was feeble and could hardly be distinguished from the dead matter from which it had sprung. But it began to multiply along divergent lines of evolution. Many routes proved dead ends and many species became extinct. Along a few of these routes life made a successful ascent into homoids and anthropoids. Here also there were many gropings and many failures and then at last man emerged with conscious will and ideals. After a good deal of struggles civilized existence has become possible and even this is so superficial that it stands in a precarious state of being swamped away every now and then.

---

17. A. Seth Pringle-Pattison, 'The Idea of God', Lectures XIV and XV and Note D; see also Proceedings of the Aristotelian Society, 1917-18.
18. The Idea of God, p. 427.

However, after many sacrifices, appalling failures, much tears
and sweats and blunderings a few persons emerge as real souls in
the form of saints, seers, scientists, leaders of history and so on.
Now if the universe be rational and its aim be, as we can
see through a vast landscape of history, the making of souls,
then should they be allowed to perish after they have once
emerged? Should the trials and failures of millions of lives
through billions of years be treated so perfunctorily? The
question is deepened by two further considerations. First, no
person however great and successful in his career can ever say
that his purposeful activity has no more grounds to cover. As
soon as one step is covered, another looms ahead to be mastered.
A Newton, a Darwin, an Einstein, a Wittgenstein, a Kant have
ample rooms for purposeful activity. Why should their lives be
snapped for ever? Secondly, the creator of this universe is
supremely good and infinite intelligence. How can He allow a
saint, a seer, a scientist or any person of value to perish? In
other words, the task is infinite and the time allowed on this
earth is extremely finite. If after making a good start they are
swept away into utter annihilation, then such a creator can
hardly be credited either with intelligence or goodness. Without
the conservation of these saints and seers God would be a sort
of divine playboy or an abortive artist.[19] Therefore, Pringle-
Pattison concludes that God lives in the perpetual giving of himself in his finite creatures, and, if this perpetual creative act is
not a child's play then finite persons somehow must be preserved.[20]
Now the question is, 'is personal immortality possible'?

According to Flew[21] that which lends 'huge human interest'
and harbours 'the logically unique expectation' is the belief in
the physical continuance of the departed in the next life after
death. Secondly, unless 'you' or 'I' survive in the next life, the
talk of immortality will cease to have any interest for human
beings. About the second point raised, Flew holds that ordinarily
person-words like 'I' or 'you' refer to beings with bodies with
their special constellations and functions. And if 'death' means

19. G. MacGregor, 'Introduction to religious Philosophy', Houghton
    Mifflin, Boston, 1959, p. 206.
20. *Ibid.*, p. 411.
21. *Death* in NEPT.

the dissolution of bodies, then how can we meaningfully talk of survival? Here D.M. Mackinnon also agrees with Flew. He also tells us that we can talk of surviving catastrophe, but we cannot meaningfully speak of surviving death.[22] However, Flew does not press this point of linguistic appropriateness with regard to 'you' or 'I surviving death'. For the time being it might not be self-contradictory to hold the survival after death if person-words be allowed to have 'a contingent and not a necessary reference to ostensible objects'.[23] Therefore, the real point of issue it that immortality is a matter of factual claim. Now if it is so, can we plot the experience of which it is the expression? In the usual way Flew implies that no verifiable or communicable experience is possible on the vast value of personal immortality. So the unique hope of survival has no solid basis in experience. He approvingly quotes the words of Wittgenstein:

> When we are dead nothing is experienced, not even emptiness: for there is no one to experience. For each of us 'the world in death does not change, but ceases'.[24]

The linguistic refutation of Flew is not valid, for the *hope* of immortality is not a factual claim; it is not a scientific theory which can be either confirmed or falsified by experience. The hope is expressed in terms of religious teachings and grammar. But even here facts, logic and commonsense have to support and sustain the hope. So let us picture the hope of survival in the endless next lives to come.

The unique expectation of endless survival includes not only the survival of memory but also the prospect of the pursuit of the same earthly aims and purposes for their better realisation. But can a person continue to be persuing the same purposeful activities of a poet, a scientist, a sage, a social worker without the continuance of the same earthly situations, hopes and fears in the same socio-economic enterprises? If the continuance of the earthly circumstances are necessary ingredients of survival, then are they involved in the unique expectation? Well, religious

---

22. NEPT, p. 261.
23. NEPT, p. 269.
24. NEPT, p. 272.

hopes of survival in a paradise are entertained without the earthly circumstances. They refer to a state where the weary are at rest and the wicked cease from troubling and where there are no tears and no sorrows. But without the fear of defeat and the possibility of failures there can be no inducement for energetic activities, enterprise, adventures and risky undertakings. We have already seen that for becoming a soul an individual has to be free and freedom has no meaning unless there is also the possibility of choosing the wrong. Hence if the survival-theory demands the discontinuance of the earthly circumstance then this also implies the loss of personality and the cessation of the path of perfection. But what if the unique expectation involves the continuation of earthly circumstances?

If the survival-theory includes the endless continuance of the earthly circumstances, then it is demanding for the endless repetitive cycles.

And the prospect of awakening again among houses and trees, among children and dotards, among wars and rumours of wars, still fettered to one personality and one accidental past, still uncertain of the future, is not this prospect wearisome and deeply repulsive?[25]

Where is the room for betterment? For this reason Indian thinkers talked of release from the chain of endless births and rebirths. For them the endless chain means imperfection and the continuance of sorrow rather than of hope.

Punarapi rajani punarapi divasah
Punarapi pakshah punarapi masah
Punarapyayanam punarapi varsham
Tadapi na munchtyasha marṣam

(Again the night and day, again the fortnight and the month, again the half year and the year and yet the jealousy and desire do not depart.)
Therefore, Shankaracharya prays to God Shiva to help him

---

25. G. Santayana, 'Ideal Immortality' in APR, p. 509.

across the ocean of endless birth and rebirth.[26] Hence the case of personal survival is not supported by the fact and logic of discourse on 'immortality'.

A theist like D.M. Mackinnon does see the difficulty of believing in personal immortality and yet somehow thinks that it should be made possible. He thinks that the anguish of human spirit at the time of bereavement is not an emotional outburst for a pinchbeck survival, but is a matter of

> the place of man in the world that is at issue. Almost we would beg the world that it does not treat our agonies as nothings.[27]

And yet he gives away the case of personal survival.

> Christian theology, which did so much to transform men's attitude to the after-life, speaks less of immortality than of resurrection, less of personal survival than of the life of the world to come.[28]

The thing is that the hope of personal immortality can be maintained only by a belief in a perfect, benevolent and a creator God. The whole consideration rests on accepting the theory that a perfect God creates creatures who would ultimately grow into beings capable of fellowship with God. Once they emerge, how can God allow such beings to perish? If the saints of old are mere dust, then says MacGregor,[29] theism will be emptied of its meaning. The same point with the greater emphasis has been mentioned by Bertocci:[30]

> Any God who allows value-possibilities, who allows value-making and value-realising beings to cease for *no good reason*, is guilty of a crime whose monstrosity defies expression. Indeed, one can readily see why persons who would find no reason for immortality might well disbelieve in God.

---

26. *Stotraratnavali*, pp. 304-305, Verses 8-9 of Charpataman Javikastotrani.
27. NEPT, p. 265.
28. *Ibid.*, p. 265.
29. G. MacGregor, 'Introduction of Religious Philosphy', p. 206.
30. P.A. Bertocci, *op. cit.*, p. 527.

But what, if the case of the existence of a personal God itself comes to be doubted ? We have already seen that it would be not quite appropriate to insist too much on the existence of a personal God. Naturally the case of personal immortality will be considerably weakened. The philosophical argument has been advanced more for the *eternal* life of values than for the survival of personal immortality. For this reason D.M. Mackinnon talks more of the life to come than of personal survival. Even Bertocci talks of 'eternal life' and 'practising death' towards the end of the last chapter of his book:[31]

> That is, at critical steps in growth some cherished value, literally 'impossible' to give up, has to be jeopardised for the sake of a greater value which lies ahead, remote and uncertain.

Should we not maintain then that the question of immortality deals less with personal immortality than with the conservation and progressive realisation of values? This is clearly envisaged by the classical writing of Plato put into the mouth of Socrates at the time of his death.

> The difficulty, my friends, is not to avoid death, but to avoid unrighteousness; for that runs faster than death.[32]

This consideration for Socrates was absolutely true, even when for him the problem of personal survival was wholly insoluble and riddled with uncertainties. His last words on the subject were:

> The hour of departure has arrived, and we go our ways—I to die, and you to live. Which is better God only knows.[33]

But even when the problem of immortality is one of eternal values, it may mean the eternity which is timeless, above the risk of change, or it may mean an eternity which has been realised through and in time by an adventure of creative thrust into open

31. *Ibid.*, p. 549.
32. Thoughts on the death of Socrates, APR, p. 476.
33. APR, p. 478.

possibilities. The former may be called a non-Nirvanist eternity and the latter may be called Nirvanist eternity. As non-temporal eternity has largely been maintained by metaphysics, so this may also be called metaphysical eternity; and as Nirvanist eternity is also a matter of a life committed to a conviction, so this may also be called convictional. We shall take up the case of metaphysical immortality first.

METAPHYSICAL OR NON-NIRVANIST IMMORTALITY

Plato gave many arguments in favour of the eternity of the soul. Most of these arguments are purely *a priori*: they tend to prove the eternity of the soul by means of the definition of the term involved. For example, Plato tells us, that soul is *simple*. A simple is that which cannot be decomposed, and if it cannot be decomposed, then it is eternal. Hence, soul being simple is eternal. Again, Plato tells us that soul is *self-moved*. Only that thing will come to rest to which motion is imparted from outside. As coming to rest is said to be death and as the self-moved soul can never come to rest, so soul is eternal. But how do we know that the soul is either simple or self-moved? They are so, per definition. If so, then the statement 'the soul is simple', or, 'the soul is self-moved' is purely analytic and has nothing to say about any actual state of affairs. Again, according to Plato, soul cannot be destroyed even by its specifically opposite malady. If anything can be destroyed, urges Plato, then it can be destroyed by a malady or evil which is specific to its nature. Now the specific malady of soul is injustice or wickedness. But wickedness does not destroy the soul. On the contrary, we find that the wicked live long and thrive most. This argument of Plato suffers again from its being *a priori*. Why should we posit that a thing can be destroyed by an internal cause alone? Further, how do we know that wickedness is the specific malady of soul? The eternity of soul has nothing to do with the shortness or longevity of life on this earth, then the long life of wicked people, even if empirically true, has nothing to do with the life to come. Again says Plato, Ideas are eternal and only an eternal soul can know the eternal ideas. Now this proof presupposes the doctrine of pre-existence of souls, recollection and the eternity of ideas. If a person does not accept such metaphysical doctrines, then, he is not likely to accept the contention of Plato.

The whole difficulty of Plato is that he conceives the soul wholly apart from the body or 'matter', whereas the soul we know of is always an embodied soul. How can we determine the existence of a disembodied soul from our experience of embodied souls? The whole proof therefore, is one of abstractionism. Again, he talks of non-empirical soul, so whatever proof he offers is wholly *a priori* and no *a priori* proof can be descriptive of an actual state of affairs called a soul. Apart from Plato, other proofs based on the considerations of mind-body relationships and pragmatic utility has been advanced.

For example, it is pointed out that if the body can influence the mind, then why should we not think it possible that the mind can also influence the body? It is pointed out that in the state of willing the cause is mental and the activity is bodily. Again, on many occasions people by a mere fiat of will do resist the bodily desires. Further, thinking is supposed to cause the utterance or writing of words. Nay, it is held that mental processes can go on independently of the bodily movements. For example, the most important things about thinking is its meaning and the same meaning can be mediated through the most varied bodily movements. For example, the beauty of the sunset can be described by the most varied expressions of many languages. Now the meaning is the same though the verbal expressions are most varied. This shows that meaning is independent of its verbal clothings.

The whole argument is full of confusion. If we suppose the mind-body dualism to be valid, then *ipso facto* the reality of the mind is presupposed by it. But why are we committed to hold to dualism? Why should we not think of mind as a function of the nervous system? When legs perform a certain kind of movement, then this movement may be called 'dance'. But is there any point in holding that 'dance' can exist independently of the bodily movement? It is true for us to set aside any talk of 'mind' as a ghost in the body. Again, nothing can be inferred from the fact that the meaning can be mediated through a number of varied expressions. As a matter of fact the sameness of meaning can be questioned. Any translator knows that in translating one word of one language into another word of another language does not convey exactly the same sense. If it were not so a good translation of *Shakuntalam* into English will dispense with the original. But we know that it is not a fact. Secondly, all that we can conclude is that approximately the same meaning can be mediated through a number of alternative bodily expressions; but not that it can be independent of any bodily expressions. Any fact of existence can be guaranteed by experience alone, and can never be established by means of conceptual arguments alone. Unless soul or mind can be empirically established by means of communicable and repeatable experiences, its existence in independence of the body cannot be legitimately held. So far as experience goes mind is always experienced as a function of the body and, empirically speaking, we cannot hold to a conclusion in which mind is said to be existing apart from the body. Thus the phenomenon of the mind-body relationship does not support the thesis of the independent existence of the mind.

Most probably the pragmatic arguments in favour of the eternal mind are much weaker. It is held that the effects of believing in immortality are so salutary that they may be taken as evidence for the truth of the belief. This is no argument. The fiction of 'Pilgrim's Progress' by John Bunyan is highly beneficial, but nobody would conclude that it is a true description of an actual pilgrimage. Besides, the effects of believing in eternity may be followed by the slackening of efforts for improving the world in which one lives. As a matter of fact Indian thought generally takes the soul to be eternal and yet this thought, says Schweitzer tends to make people world-and-life-negating. Hence the belief in eternity need not be followed by salutary effects. So the pragmatic argument is too weak to prove the eternity of the soul.

Again, it is held by the idealist specially that the whole universe is rational. Now the whole universe has been working for the emergence of rational creatures. It would be too irrational to suppose that after rational creatures have emerged they be allowed to perish. The whole argument is too complex to put into a few words. We shall include much that we consider valuable in the idealistic argument. However, from the phenomenon of human rationality we cannot argue for the reality of cosmic rationality.

In any case metaphysical arguments no matter however forceful can never be conclusive. We trust that the nerve of the argument for immortality lies in convictional language and therefore we shall turn now to the Nirvanist Immortality.

THE NIRVANIST IMMORTALITY

The state of Nirvana is attained by a person in this earthly frame. But once the Nirvana is attained, the person becomes secure from the risk of change, i.e. from the endless chain of enduring states of births and deaths. This timelessness has been attained in time through the vicissitudes of temporal flow. Hence, in this kind of eternity time is retained and yet transcended. For example, any great work of art, like the *Madonna* or Venus of Milo or Paris, must have taken time in which it was produced. But once the work has been accomplished, it becomes a thing of beauty. One stands for hours contemplating the beauty enshrined in it and one asks no question about the time taken in its production. As a work of art it transcends its age, race and person and becomes an eternal thing of enjoyment. The same is true for a person who makes himself a thing of value, a co-creator with God of valueworthiness.

A Leonardo, a Galileo, an Einstein, a Shankara, a Gandhi no doubt are born at a certain epoch and imbibe all that is best in their time. They not only draw heavily on the common fund of human heritage, but also enrich it in their turn. A Newton not only fully assimilated the findings of Galileo and Kepler, but by advancing the theory of gravitation greatly enriched the scientific knowledge of his time. Here is a theory which no doubt took time in which it was matured, but once it became established it remained timelessly true. This is true of every scientific discovery and every logical or mathematical invention. In the case of Newton and Einstein we abstract their discovery from their personalities. Yet we know that a man in flesh and blood called Newton by becoming a mathematician alone would have established what he in fact did establish. But mankind knows this much as any theologian does. However, it also correctly holds that which made Newton immortal was his discovery and not the fact that he lived at a certain time and place. The important thing is that this house of clay became the habitation of timeless mathematical and scientific discoveries. The house of clay called Newton became an important vehicle of scientific truths and without this vehicle the scientific truth could not have been imparted. England will remain proud of her Newton, but the world would pay homage to Newtonian discoveries as things of all ages, of the whole mankind, and would regard his time, white colour of his skin and his being an Englishman as mere accidents. Now we ask, what is eternal? The accidents of his birth, nationality and race? Or, the scientific discoveries which will stand the test of time?

Comparatively the discoveries of science, for the sake of convenience, can be separated from the scientist. The reason is that a scientist has to train himself to look at things most objectively, by carefully and assiduously preventing his personality from being involved into what he observes, notes and reports. People do not note that the scientific language of disinterested objectivity and descriptiveness is as much convictional as religious assertions undoubtedly are; the difference is that in scientific assertions the scientist convictionally practices de-personalisation and in purely convictional assertions the personality is thrown into the assertions. In purely convictional assertions man can hardly be distinguished from what he asserts. In the case of a moralist and a religious person, the man making the assertion himself becomes a thing of value, because assertions cannot be distinguished from the man who makes the assertion. It is claimed that he who knows the Brahman himself becomes the Brahman (*Brahmvid Brahmaiva bhavati*). Christ felt that he was the very thing he was asserting: 'I am the Way, the Truth, the Bread of life, the Life Eternal'. St. John truly saw that Jesus was the Logos or the Word,

'and the Word was with God, and the Word was God'.

The assertion of Jesus is religiously or convictionally true, 'My father and I are one', 'He who has seen me, has seen the father'. So in things spiritual the maker of religious truths, becomes himself timelessly true, beyond the accidents of time and the ever-vanishing moments of change. This is what happens in the case of prophets, seers and sages.

By contemplating on things changeless and timeless one tends to become oneself a timeless existence. This is what is exemplified in Spinozistic *amor intellectualis dei.* According to Spinoza by setting our affection on things which do not change, we are delivered from the disturbances of passions. By constantly viewing things *sub specie aeternitatis* we are filled with that love with which God loves himself. This love is not selfish nor unselfish, but selfless. It goes beyond the personality and becomes a thing of eternity.

That which lifts a passing moment from momentariness to the plane of eternity is the ideal. The ideal which unites two or more passing events into a series cannot be itself a passing event. Hence, by idealising the passing moments of our lives we pass from the realm of time into the kingdom of eternity. As noted earlier this is what happens in the work of art, where beauty confers eternity, as Keats would hold. Similarly Schopenhauer held that through contemplation of the works of art we attain to the eternity and universality of Platonic Ideas. No doubt the Venus of Milo has many parts and exists in a spatio-temporal framework. But it comes to represent beauty which is timeless: in contemplating on it time stops, relations vanish, the Idea of beauty as an eternal object alone remains.

In the life of moral earnestness and religious commitment the transforming influence of the ideal of Goodness is most marked. Either by the gentle influence of a Jesus or a Gandhi or by a deliberate 'imitation of Christ' our lives are transformed. By the influence of Jesus, the insignificant Galileans became the gallant men of history: they transformed the whole of the ancient world. Peter who denied his master thrice became the pillar of a new kingdom. Not only the ideal serves as the leavening force, but the leavened man himself begins to leaven others in turn. The more the man leads an idealised life, the more ideal he himself becomes to enjoy double immortality: first, the idealised life confers on him the eternity of the ideal he tries to embody, and, secondly, to the extent his idealised life becomes a beaconlight to others, he becomes concretised reincarnated in the lives of his followers. This is what is exemplified in the theory of Bodhisattvas. A Bodhisattva not only becomes eternal, but in turn he tries to rescue the whole humanity from destruction. In his case the fine statement of Santayana[34] is most appropriately applicable:

> By becoming the spectator and confessor of his own death and of universal mutation, he will have identified himself with what is spiritual in all spirits and masterful in all apprehension; and so conceiving himself, he may truly feel and know that he is eternal.

What we are stating here is that an idealised life serving as an ideal attains to the eternity of Platonic Ideas. Individuals, no matter however great are not conserved in their physical frame. It is enough that they appreciated beauty, goodness and truth and appropriated them in their lives. The humanity will remain grateful to them. These immortal climbers will be remembered to posterity, but we must also remember that there are many other heights and many other unchartered seas and oceans still unexplored. They too have to be brought within the ken of humanity. Bosanquet has expressed this in what he calls as the adjectival view of individuality.

> While we serve as units, to speak the language of appearance the Absolute lives in us a little, and for a little time; when its life demands our existence no longer, we yet blend with it as the pervading features or characters, which we were needed for a passing moment to emphasize and in which our reality enriches the universe.[35]

Of course, there is no finished reality anywhere and the reality of the Absolute does not arise for us. Religious truths are made true. The life of eternal values has to be won and attained here and now in this earthly frame, by one's free decision and commitment to it. No one can confer Nirvana on anyone. It has to be attained by one's own ceaseless efforts and by one's own light. 'Appo Dipo Bhava' were the last words of Lord Buddha on the subject.

---

34. G. Santayana, *Ideal Immortality* in APR, p. 518.
35. B. Bosanquet, *Proceedings of Aristotelian Society*, 1917-18, p. 506.

'Be a light unto yourself and seek your salvation with diligence'. Once the eternity of Nirvana is attained, it transcends perception and even non-perception. This Nirvana is neither selfish nor unselfish but selfless in the most literal sense of the term.

Chapter XV

THE ENCOUNTER OF RELIGIONS

Introduction

In most cases religion, according to Carlyle, is a thing what a man does practically lay to heart, and know for certain, concerning his vital relations to the mysterious Universe, his duty and destiny there, that is in all cases the primary thing for him, and creatively determines the rest. Very often, according to him, man does not assert the content of his beliefs to himself, much less to others. This might be the case with the majority of believers, but a theology does more. Whilst religion is the sphere of rituals, symbols and worship, theology is an attempt to formulate the concepts, to elucidate the articles of faith and to offer apologetics in the event of misunderstanding and attack on the beliefs. Theology in comparison with religion is an intellectual attempt to interpret what a man practically believes. But a theologian remains wedded to his religion. He tries to understand the articles of faith, beliefs and practices of his religion as an involved man. He looks upon his religious beliefs and practices with passion, fear and love. 'The basic attitude of the theologian is commitment to the content he expounds.'[1] In principle, there are as many theologies as are religions. Hence, there are Christian, Muslim, Buddhist, Jewish and other theologies. At times under the same religion there are several theologies corresponding to its different sects, e.g. Christianity and Buddhism.

If we had remained confined to theologies alone, most probably interreligious dialogue would have become difficult if not impossible. However, the intellectual content of different theologies do not remain esoteric. The very nature of a concept is that it should be shareable and communicable. Secondly, theological concepts are largely grounded in the intellectual climate and weather of the age in which they are formulated. For exam-

---

1. Paul Tillich, *Systematic Theology*, p. 23.

ple, Christian theology was at first formulated in terms of Greek thought and is now articulated in existential terms. Therefore, by virtue of their conceptual contents theologies come to be studied together in what is known today as the comparative study of religion. A comparative study of religion is not concerned with anyone religion in particular. It has to offer a certain conceptual framework in which different theologies can be grasped, but the framework has to be constituted in the spirit of religion, i.e. with wide sympathies, understanding and mutual involvement in the lives of religious men belonging to different races and creeds. This is an important point to keep in mind, since a mere desire to study different religions is not religious and the tolerance for the peaceful existence of all faiths is likely to degenerate into mutual indifference. Much of the anthropological, sociological and even psychological study has been too intellectual which has paved the way for secularism or irreligion. Secularism is the belief which confines itself to finite goods of this worldly existence by denying any connection of man to his supernatural or spiritual concern. But we cannot make men entirely non-religious. After all the history of man has been the history of his religion. If man forsakes God he is likely to be possessed of demons. Lessons of Nazism and other forms of fascism cannot be so easily forgotten. Further, even communism and democracy for some people in all essentials are also forms of religion. Man therefore cannot live in spiritual vacuum. As a result of his knowledge of history he knows that his religion divides ¡as much as it unites. But he is also deeply conscious of the desideratum that religion should unite all men severally and collectively. Man has desired the unity of all religions at all times. The Indian tradition of wide tolerance for all religions almost from the time of the Vedas up to the time of Mahatma Gandhi and Radhakrishnan is so rich that it does not require any special mention. But even the western thought has not been wanting in such similar observations.

According to the New Testament the Word of God is the light which lightens every man (Jn. 1:9), and that God has not left himself without witness to all nations (Acts 14:17) and that in the Father's house there are many mansions and that there are many sheep which do not belong to one fold only and that the laws of God are written in the hearts of men (Rom 2:14-15). Finally, there is the utterance of St. Paul: "Gentiles? Yes, of the Gentiles also" (Rom 3:29). Again, according to the Christian tradition, the Greek thinkers are said to be the instructors who as schoolmasters have led men to Christ. Hence, Justin, the philosopher-martyr said:

All who have lived according to the Logos are Christians even if they are generally accounted as atheists, like Socrates and Heraclitus among the Greeks.

St. Augustine shared the same belief and Heiler quotes the following utterance of Nicholas of Cusa (1453):

God is sought in various ways and called by various names in the various religions, that he has sent various porphets and teachers in various ages to the various peoples.[2]

In the same way Heiler reminds us the following eloquent witness of Joseph Görres:

One Godhead alone is at work in the Universe, *one* religion alone prevails in it, *one* worship, *one* fundamental natural order, *one* law and *one* bible in all. All prophets are *one*; they have spoken on *one* common ground in *one* language, though in different dialects.[3]

If the unity of all religions is to be achieved and if religions are accepted as valid, then we have to determine the various grounds of such a unity. At least the following four positions have been taken up in this regard.

    I. Only one religion is true and all others are false.
    II. Though all other religions are not false, yet there is only one religion which contains religious truth in such a comprehensive or superior manner that in comparison with it all other religions can be safely ignored.

---

2. Friedrich Heiler, How can Christian and non-Christian religions co-operate? *Hibbert Journal*, Vol. 52, 1953-54, p. 109.
3. *Ibid.*, p. 111.

III. All religions are at bottom one: differences between them are local and accidental. The different religions can be described to be the different dialects of one and the same religion.

IV. The plurality and relativity of religions are absolute and religions have to learn from each other by incorporating the various insights through mutual participation.

V. From the fact of plurality and relativity of religions it might be concluded that no religion is true and that traditional religions should be discarded and that Secularism, Marxism and Humanism should be substituted in their place. However, the last position refers more to the future of religions than their unity, and, so here we shall not discuss the issue raised in this position. Now we shall take up each position one by one.

I. ONLY ONE RELIGION IS TRUE AND ALL OTHERS ARE FALSE

The monopolistic and exclusive claim of religious truth in favour of one single religion draws its inspiration mainly from two considerations. First, tacitly it assumes that there are the same basic religious needs in all men. For this reason, Ferre talks of 'one common human nature' and 'one common world'.[4] Secondly, the monist, monolithic and monopolist think that the object of religious concern is an absolute object which underlies all religions. In our opinion both the assumptions are false. There is nothing like one common human nature. Men differ by virtue of their types, functions and mentality. They are either extraverts-introverts, intellectualist-intuitionist, tenderminded-toughminded and so on. If men are not the same basically in the concrete, then their worlds will also be as various as they are.

The facts belie the monopolistic theory of religion. The fact is that there are many religions with their respective saints and religious values. As such they cannot be branded as so many aberrations of demonic possession. As a matter of fact if one religion be true and others false, then it would mean that religion is not a universal phenomenon of mankind. This will cut at the root of religion itself. The monopolistic theory of religion is

---

4. N.F.S. Ferre, *Reason in religion*, chap. XV, p. 290.

based on the further assumption that the object of religion is absolute and that this can be intellectually determined. However, this assumption is false, not because as yet no such absolute object has been found out, but because it does not do full justice to religion itself. The object of religion is not an object of detached, disinterested and neutral objectivity. It is a matter of our infinite passion and ultimate concern (Kierkegaard, Paul Tillich). The object is most real and gripping when we are most involved in the object of our infinite concern. If the total personality of the believer is involved in apprehending the object of the ultimate concern, then the religious object will appear as diverse and varied as the personalities of the different believers. Hence, we cannot maintain that there is only one asbolute object of religion and corresponding to it there is only one true religion.

There is yet another difficulty. If Christianity, Islam, Buddhism, Judaism and the rest of other religions start making the same claim, then how can there be any arbitration between them? Ferre rightly holds that there can be no judge of religions.[5] Western theologians, however, even some of the best of them, hold a view akin to the monopolistic claim. Their theory may best be called monolithic.

II. The monolithic theory does not deny the value of other religions. But, according to it, all other religions are relative and partial and in comparison with all of them only one religion contains the religious truth in the most pre-eminent and superior manner.

F.S. Ferre is a profound religious thinker and is far above superficial sentimentality. He maintains that there is a universal commonness of faith at the centre of all religions and along with this secondary but important differences which characterize each religion[6]. Further, according to him, there is a common life with diversity in response to a common God within common basic need as foundational to concrete religions.[7] But along with this observation he also holds that the life of Jesus is the normative event for the whole mankind.

---

5. *Ibid.*, pp. 30-31: also see, Huston Smith, *The religions of man,* Harper & Row, pp. 310-12.
6. N.F.S. Ferre, *op. cit.*, p. 301.
7. *Ibid.*, p. 308.

The highest arrival of meaningfulness in human history, I suggest, is the life, teaching, death and resurrection of Jesus Christ. The highest I have found is the love of God as lived and taught by Jesus. I cannot see how anything can be higher than the all-inclusive, unconditional and eternal love that was at least conclusively suggested by Jesus' life and instructions.[8]

So for Ferre, Christianity built on the faith in the universal God of love is the final standard for all religions.[9] This is all the more remarkable for a thinker who considers Hinduism, Buddhism and other great religions as universal options of mankind.

W.E. Hocking is yet another noble thinker whose wide sympathies can never be questioned and yet he also takes Christianity to be the universal religion of mankind. He is fully aware of the danger in holding a particular religion to be the universal religion. A universal religion, it might be contended, must be free from provincialism and relativities. However, Christianity has to include within it the history and person of the founder. Against this objection, Hocking holds that religion in the abstract can hardly be a religion at all. The universal itself is too abstract to have any concrete import for religious life. Hence, the universal love of God as the creative source of all wills to create love through suffering has to be most suitably exemplified. And this, according to Hocking, has been exemplified in the life, teaching and death of Jesus. However, Hocking does not rule out the constant need of refashioning the historical irrationalities, changing conditions of life, current demands, concepts and techniques for the elucidation and realisation of the generalities of religious imperatives.

Is Christianity, then, as a whole, universal? My answer is that it is on the way to become universal, and that its travail through the western passes of modernity has qualified it, and requires it, to take a certain leadership in meeting the religious problems of the coming civilization;....[10]

8. *Ibid.*, p. 67.
9. *Ibid.*, p. 332.
10. W.E. Hocking, 'Christianity and the faith of the coming civilization', *Hibbert Journal,* Vol. 54, 1955-56, p. 346.

Interestingly enough, he adds, that even matured Christianity will require the spiritual iron of the East contained in the doctrine of universal karma. Thus the future universal religion of mankind will be the amalgam of Hinduism and Christianity.

But if Jumna and Ganges run together, shall the united lower stream be called Ganges or Jumna? Is it neither? Is it both? Or is it that one whose symbol men freely find compacted with the sense of both, holding in an historic life and deed, for which there can be no repetition and no substitute, a prophetic answer to man's eternal need?[11]

For Hocking in the last analysis, the historic life of Jesus for which there can be no repetition and no substitute, purified and universalized by the spiritual iron of the East is the final answer for the future civilization.

In the same way Friedrich Heiler who opened his article with a number of quotations in favour of a universal religion,[12] ultimately regards Christiantity as a universal religion. According to him, in a microcosm it contains all the essentials of a universal religion. Heiler, quoting Rudolph Otto holds Christianity to be superior to all other religions:

It (Christianity) is superior, not as truth is to falsehood, but as Plato is to Aristotle; not as the master to his slave, but as the eldest son to his brothers.[13]

Even Indian tradition is not averse to the monolithic theory. As a matter of fact it passes to monolatry by holding fast to monolithic theory. According to it, very often it is held that there may be many popular religions for the masses, but there is only one true religion from the esoteric point of view. Nothing can be said about the Gita without qualifications, since it is too complex to be characterised as monism, mysticism, theism or pantheism. However, the Gita too has elements of the monolithic theory.

---

11. W.E. Hocking, *Ibid.*, p. 349.
12. F. Heiler, *op. cit.*, p. 111.
13. *Ibid.*, p. 115.

Even those who are devotees of other gods, worship them with faith, they also sacrifice to Me alone, Son of Kunti, though not according to the true law. (IX:23)
Worshippers of the gods go to the gods, worshippers of the manes go to the manes, sacrifices of the spirits go to the spirits and those who sacrifice to Me come to Me. (IX:25).

Most probably verses (chap. IV: 11, VI: 30-31, VII: 20-23) can be interpreted in the same way. Then the verse IX: 34 leaves us in no doubt that the worship of Lord Krishna is considered to be the highest religion which fulfils all other religions.

Abandoning all duties, come to Me alone for shelter. Be not grieved, for I shall release thee from all sins. (XVIII: 66)

However, on the whole the Indian tradition is more pantheistic, monistic and monolatrous than monolithic. In contrast, western thinkers appear to be incorrigibly monolithic.

The monolithic theory is open to the same difficulties with which the monopolistic theory is beset. If all religions begin to make the same claim of pre-eminence, then who is going to be the arbiter between them? This battle of claims and counter-claims instead of promoting understanding and sympathies would lead to disharmony and even irreligion. The element of truth contained in the theory is that every religion has to universalize its claims for an all-inclusive world-membership in a spirit of humble co-partnership with all other religions. Unless a religious man feels his religion to be universal, with its claim for the whole humanity, even for the erring ones, there can be no true religious commitments. A religion which promotes ill-will, hatred, war and is against scientific advance and socio-economic plan is not a real religion. So every religion in order to be religion must vie with all other religions in respect to its maturity, modernity, reasonableness and all-inclusive membership. However, in making any claim for whatsoever good it may contain it has to make others its judge, because by virtue of the infinite passion and commitment each religionist cannot help thinking of his religion as the universal religion. In the last analysis, it has to be conceded that religious truth is many-tongued and no one tongue can claim precedence over the rest.

III. THE ESSENTIALIST VIEW OF RELIGIONS

So far the claim of universality has been made in favour of a religion, but the same claim can be made for religion in the abstract. For example, according to Radhakrishnan, there is one religion of the Supreme Spirit: all other religions are so many dialects of the same religion of the Supreme Spirit.[14] Though the view of Bhagavan Das is less philosophical than that of Radhakrishnan, yet it is as much essentialist in its intention. Let us take the essentialist version of Bhagavan Das first.

According to Bhagavan Das, no particular form of religion is indispensable. From this fact two conclusions can be drawn, namely,

(a) Rejection of all religions, or
(b) Acceptance of all religions.

But both are impracticable steps, according to Bhagavan Das.[15] Hence, according to him, the only practical and wise course is to sift out the elements of *Essential Religion* from the non-essential forms.[16] The essential elements can be obtained by the method of majority-rule, i.e., by receiving not only the greatest number, but also unanimous votes from the living religions.[17] These elements would constitute universal religion. Bhagavan Das extensively quotes from the Quran, Sufism, Upanishads, Shiva-Mahima Shruti and many other religious texts to show that there is one Truth, one Religion and one God. One of the typical quotations is:

Veda and Sankhya, Yoga, Shaiva-view,
And Vaishnava, and many others such,
Men follow as they variously incline!

---

14. S. Radhakrishnan, *Eastern religion and Western thought*, pp. 306, 308, 319, 320, 327.
15. Bhagavan Das, 'The Essential Unity of all religions', 1947, p. 49.
16. *Ibid.*, p. 49.
17. *Ibid.*, pp. 48, 51-52.

Some thinking this is best; some others, that;
Yet thou art the One Goal of all these ways,
Some straight and easy, others crooked, rough,
As of the countless streams, the one great sea.[18]

Again, he quotes the following from the Quran:

Teachers are sent to each race that they may Teach it in its
own tongue, so there may be No doubt as to the meaning in
its mind.[19]

From all such quotations Bhagavan Das concludes that certain
essentials are common to all religions:

Truth is universal and not the monopoly of any race or teacher; that non-essentials vary with time, place, and circumstance; that the same fundamental truths have been revealed
by God in different scriptures, in different languages, through
different persons born in different nations.[20]

Dr. Bhagavan Das was moved by the noble motive of uniting
the rival claims of all religions. But his statements do not stand
up to philosophical precision. He never enumerates the essential
elements. Quotations have been taken indifferently. The oneness
of which he talks has been indifferently taken to be abstract (upanishads), mystical (sufism) of an undefined goal, of a God with
and without attributes, of Truth and, so on. For the sake
of philosophical purpose this oneness should have been stated
precisely. Again, according to Bhagavan Das no particular
religion is indispensable.[21] But if no paths are indispensable then
the goal too is equally not indispensable. The metaphor of the
'goal' is highly misleading. The goal of religious striving is not
something external to the worshipper: it means an inner change
and an integration of the total personality as a result of religious
beliefs and practices. So the goal cannot be divorced from the

18. *Ibid.*, p. 53, Quoted from Shiva-Mahima Shruti.
19. *Ibid.*, p. 56.
20. *Ibid.*, p. 56.
21. *Ibid.*, p. 49.

specific paths of the various religions. Therefore, once we grant the variety of paths, we will have to grant the differences of the goal too. We cannot take a generalised view of the goal and the particularised view of the paths. Other implications of the essentialist stand will be taken up in the sequel.

The theory of many pathways leading to one common top of the mountain need not commit itself to an essentialist view of religion. It may mean that all religions are relatively true in an absolute way. It may mean that each worshipper by accepting a religion with full devotion and total commitment reaches his own goal.

Even when morality becomes autonomous, it requires some stories (R.B. Baithwaite), some myths, legends and history behind each form of religious morality. Kant was the most important thinker who maintained the autonomy of morality. But he knew fully well that very often men know what their duties are, and, yet they may fail to perform them. They require some sort of psychological booster to aid them in performing their duties. Hence Kant recommended that duties be regarded as divine commands. It is the presence of such myths and stories which make religious morality different from one another.

Hence it is not enough to say that all religions teach about God. The concept of God is not the same in all religions. Christians teach that God is essentially forgiving and transforming love; Islam teaches that Allah is essentially compassionate judge of man's doings. The concept of God is not the same even for Shankara and Rāmānuja.

Therefore to underlining the essential similarities in moral teaching and in worshipping a similar God is not enough. Differences are as important as the similarities. As Bhagavan Das ignores differences, his theory of essential unity of all religions fails us. So let us now turn to Radhakrishnan who also teaches the essentialist view of religions.

Radhakrishnan is essentially a Vedāntin. According to the Shankarite Vedānta there are lower and higher standpoints. From the lower standpoint we worship Iśvara and take him to be a creator, sustainer and destroyer of the world. However, the worship of Iśvara has to be ultimately transcended on attaining the higher standpoint of the absolute Brahman. The absolute, however, is beyond all qualifications and description: it is pure light and essence and in comparison with it all other lesser lights are impurities.[22] However, the worship of any god, at the lower level is an indispensable means of reaching the final goal. Radhakrishnan quotes here from Maitri Upanishad to pin down his point of view:

> Some contemplate one name and some another. Which of these is the best? All are eminent clues to the transcendent, immortal, unembodied Brahman; these names are to be contemplated, lauded and at last denied. For by them one rises higher and higher in these worlds; but where all comes to its end, there he attains to the unity of the Person.[23]

Again, whilst commenting on verse 11, Chapter III of the *Gītā*, Radhakrishnan regards all forms of worship as aids for becoming aware of our deepest self.[24] Thus all religions are relatively true and yet in the final attainment of the absolute truth they are false and have to be finally denied.

Radhakrishnan is very eloquent in holding that all religions are true and does not explicitly state that in the final analysis they are all false. If he had emphasized the latter, then the difficulty of his stand would have become apparent. But unless he denies the ultimate truth of all religions, he cannot say that only one religion of the Supreme Spirit is true. Tactical expediency however should not blind us to the philosophical difficulties inherent in the essentialist view of the universal religion. Further, he can deny the ultimate validity of all religions on the basis of his metaphysics of non-dualistic Vedānta. Now whatever be the strength of his brand of metaphysics, in the contemporary temper of philosophizing, it will not be considered to be a strong case for any religious theory.

Apart from his metaphysical stand, is the religion of the Supreme Spirit religion at all? If the religion of the supreme spirit be a religion, then like all other religions it will be infected with

---

22. S. Radhakrishnan, 'Fragment of a confession' in *The Philosophy of Sarvepalli Radhakrishnan*, 1952, p. 79.
23. *Ibid.*, p. 78.
24. S. Radhakrishnan, *The Bhagavadgita*, p. 158.

relativity. But it might be retorted, it is not *a* religion amongst other religions, it is *the* religion which underlies all other religions as their essence and ground. In this case, the religion of the supreme spirit is a philosophy of religion, — some sort of meta-theology. True, one may hold one's meta-theology with passion and conviction, but we would be unjustifiably taking the philosophy of religion for theology and still worse if we take it for a religion. The religion of the supreme spirit may contain the essence, the barest common denominator underlying all religions, but this abstraction cannot be taken to be a form of concrete religion. Previous to Radhakrishnan, other Indian thinkers have called the advaitic theory of religion as super-religion and not as religion.

At times Radhakrishnan emphasizes less the fact of one religion and dwells more on the spirit of loyalty to all religions. In this context, he recommends the spirit of fellowship in the place of their amalgam, fusion or their sublation.

> The different religious traditions clothe the one Reality in various images and their visions could embrace and fertilise each other so as to give mankind a many-sided perfection, the spiritual radiance of Hinduism, the faithful obedience of Judaism, the life of beauty of Greek Paganism, the noble compassion of Buddhism, the vision of divine love of Christianity, and the spirit of resignation to the sovereign lord of Islam.[25]

This is a good rhetoric and sounds so convincing. But is it feasible? Can we accept the resignation to the sovereign will of Allah, the suffering love of Christianity and the Buddhistic compassion for the suffering humanity in the same breath? If we allow the differences which characterise each religion, then we cannot bring them together under one class except through the device of syncretism; and, if we do not allow for the differences, then we shall be denying each religion. If we deny the birth, teaching, life and death of Jesus along with the whole of Christian history and tradition, then will there be anything of Christianity left? And if each religion be allowed their distinctive features, then they cannot be

---

25. S. Radhakrishnan, *Fragments*, p. 76.

consistently held together. Can the Muslim claim concerning the prophet Muhammed as the final seal of the prophets, the Jewish hope for the futuristic Messiah, the Buddhistic doctrine of Anattavada, the suffering love of God of Christianity be consistently reconciled?

However, one cannot easily brush aside the Catholic spirit of Radhakrishnan's theory of the Supreme Spirit. It is a philosophical attempt to bring together all theologies for their mutual understanding. Unless we are intellectually convinced of this stand, we cannot proceed further for mutual participation. For turning the wise counsel of Radhakrishnan into actual practice we have to accept the fourth stand. We have to combine the intellectual love for all religions into love and respect for all religions. As a matter of fact Radhakrishnan himself observed that we must understand the experience of people whose thoughts elude our familiar categories, and this cannot be achieved by doing away their distinctive features. Further, he added that the new world society requires to be based on respect for different cultural traditions.[26] In the end, Radhakrishnan confesses that the absoluteness of truth implies the relativity of all formulations of it.[27] Truth, for Radhakrishnan, wears many vestures and speaks in many tongues. Hence, it appears that he would have gladly accepted the fourth stand had he been not possessed of the vedantic monism.

IV. The Plurality and Relativity of Religions are Absolute
Men differ widely from one another and correspondingly their religions too differ. Each can see the religious truth as he perceives it and by following the light wherever it may lead him he fulfils his destiny. Here we are reminded of the last words of Lord Buddha 'Appo dipobhava' (Be a light unto yourself and seek your salvation with diligence and there is no other refuge for you). Here there will be as many lights or religions as are the types of men; and, each religion is relative to the mental constitution of the worshipper. Here we have to face an important objection. It might be contended that the admission of plurality and relativity would cut at the very root of inter-religious dialogue. If

26. S. Radhakrishnan, *Fragments*, p. 73; *Easten Religion*, p. 32.
27. The Philosophy of S. Radhakrishnan: *Reply*, p. 811.

differences are fundamental, then how can there be any mutual participation?

We grant that there is a common colourless screen on which religious objects are projected, and, if it satisfies the critics, then we can also grant the presence of an undifferentiated numinous experience as the common underlying element behind all religions. Let us elaborate the points concerning the commonness of the *object* and the *subjectively felt experience*. Tall figures of Shankara, Aquinas and Tillich have given us all the information which we can possibly have about the common object of religious experience. All the three thinkers tell us that we can describe this absolute object only negatively. Ultimately, according to Shankara, the absolute may be described as *Sachchidananda*. But this positive form is misleading. According to Shankara all that we can say is that which is not the absolute sat (existence or being) if not Brahman, that which is not absolute consciousness is not brahman and so on. Hence, we cannot go beyond the language of neti (not this, not this).

Similarly Aquinas holds that we cannot say what God is: we can say what he is not. True, God has the transcendentals of being, thing, unity, distinction, true and good. But these transcendentals really describe nothing. They ultimately state only this much that he is what he is, or, in the biblical phrase 'I am that I am'. Lastly, Paul Tillich holds that God is being-itself and beyond this statement anything we say of God is symbolical. All the three agree in holding that we know *that* God is, but not *what* he is. Is there any point in stating that we know the barest of existence or even the being of God without his quality? But this is all that can be asserted about the absolute object of religious experience. We hold that underlying all religions there is a common blank screen of this colourless, qualityless Brahman or the Ultimate Transcendent on which all religious symbols are projected. From the viewpoint of a worshipper the symbol is what he cares for. But the plurality and the relativity of the symbols should teach us the lesson that no symbol is ultimate. Hence, all religious utterances require to be constantly purified in the light of the collective experience of religious men, belonging to various traditions and cultures.

What is true of the object is also true of the subjective experience of worshippers. Religious experience is as varied as men are. If we try to find out the common denominator underlying all kinds of religious experience, then at most we can say that it is *mysterium tremendum et fascinosum*. Such an experience, according to Otto, cannot be fully conceptualised: it can only be evoked. Can we state anything intelligible about it? Further analysis has shown that it is holistic, highly intense or stirring, total, all-consuming, shaking and integrative. But this is as much true of religious as also of non-religious experience. Does not a communist or secularist feel the same? Hence, any attempt to isolate the object or the experience as the essence of religion fails. We have to take into account the distinctiveness and differences of religions too to explain the numinous experience.

Further, people may object that the admission of plurality and relativity of religions will destroy the truth of religion. According to the objector, there is some truth about religion, and, if religions be regarded as relative then the element of this truth will be destroyed. However, this wide-spread view is wholly untenable. Religious 'truth' is not factual: it is existential. The religious truth is not discovered but is made true in one's life and death. The lives of saints exemplify and bear witness to the truth of the God they worship. If we are stirred and shaken up by such lives and hold them to be the exemplification and fulfilment of a true life, then that by which they live is also true. Hence, religious truth is not a matter of correspondence or comparison with an object out there, but is a matter of authentic existence through the adventure of faith in an object of devotion with its capacity to evoke the same sort of response on a wide scale. But that alone is religiously true which can click light in the individual. This infectiousness depends as much on the light as also on the psychological determination of the individual. There will be as many religious insights as the kinds of worshippers are. The mental constitution of a worshipper depends on his psychological endowments and the peculiarities of the historical or biographical accidents of his life. The task therefore before us is to overcome the fatality of our psycho-socio-cultural determinants in such a way that the minds may become supple enough for mutual accommodation and participation.

It is useless to talk of any fusion of religions with a view to having an amalgamated world religion for all mankind. The fusion can be effected only by the regimentation of thought, but as against this, history has shown that heresies can never be entirely stopped. We have to allow the historic identity of each religion with its visions and genius. Here the words of Mahatma Gandhi can be quoted with advantage:

> I believe in the Bible as I believe in the Gita. I regard all the great faiths of the world as equally true with my own. It hurts me to see anyone of them caricatured as they are today by their own followers.[28]

The only point is that the various insights of the different religions must cross-fertilise the visions of one another. This requires a good deal of understanding of the various religious commitments and means an attempt to be co-involved in the mutual commitments of men. What does an *understanding* of other religions mean? One should take full cognizance of the conviction, commitment and existential decisions involved in the practice and beliefs of each religion. To understand this kind of commitment we require a high degree of disciplined imagination by virtue of which we place ourselves into the very inside of the religious man we want to understand. This may be styled as the kathenotheistic or henotheistic endeavour to enter into the religious commitments of people different from ourselves. This requires us:

> to step ourselves into the other fellow's shoes; and this again, as everyone realizes, also implies the capacity to take our own shoes off first.[29]

In other words, even a student of comparative religion has his besetting ideals, his commitment and his existential decision. Nobody can study with a clean slate. His conviction makes him peculiarly responsive to the matters of his own religion and renders him comparatively insensitive to verdicts issuing forth

---

28. Eastern Religion, p. 313.
29. R.J. Zwi Werblowsky, On the role of comparative religion in promoting mutual understanding, *Hibbert Journal*, Vol. 58, 1959-60, p. 33.

from other existential decisions. We are all engaged men and without involvement one cannot be religious. The knowledge of this indispensable element in being religious will deliver us from intellectual intolerance of faiths other than our own. Nay, the study of comparative religion requires that we should make an effort to enter, metaphorically speaking, into the shoes of other religionists by putting off our own. This would mean that a Christian should imaginatively try to live and feel as a Buddhist if he wants to understand Buddhism, and, the same prescription is true for understanding any other religion. For most of us the experiment is too difficult. But a few religious geniuses have not only imaginatively but also literally entered into the shoes of other religionists. The example of Ramakrishna Paramhansa readily comes to our mind. So the students of comaparative study of religions can practise wide sympathies for other religions by means of disciplined imagination. At least by making determined efforts to pass into the commitments of other faiths, specially those lying near to our range, our minds would become supple enough to grasp them: at least such efforts will breed respect and love for other faiths. In the end there will dawn a desire to listen to other faiths even if we think that ours contains all that is worth in religion.[30] Listening will lead to understanding and co-involvement in the spiritual enterprise of men belonging to various creeds and races. After all Ganga and Jamuna remain distinct at their confluence even at the time of their holy embrace. This implies an ecumenical movement of all religions with a view to achieving accommodation, mutual participation and co-involvement in the human enterprise of living at our depths and full potentials.

RAMAKRISHNA'S UNITY OF RELIGIONS

Ramakrishna saw things which human beings are not permitted to see, and, described and spoke about things which is not lawful for any mortals to utter. For him the purpose of life is to realize God.[31] But he also knew very well that apart from various sects of

---

30. Huston Smith, *The Religions of Man*, 1958, p. 312.
31. *The Gospel of Sri Ramakrishna* by M. Hence, M stands for this book. M. 104, 273, 331.

Hinduism, there are other religions too like Islam and Christianity. So he attempted to establish a unity of religions.[32] RK* desired something infinitely greater than the reconciliation of warring creeds. He wanted that man as a whole should understand, sympathise with and love the rest of mankind. In one word, each religious man should identify himself with the life of humanity.[33] Nay more. At the point of deep spiritual realisation,

You realise that all things live, like your own Self, in God. You become the will-power and the conscience of all that is. Your will becomes that of the whole universe.[34]

RK was a Sādhaka who put faith above reason (M. 130). Nonetheless his points can be jotted down which unmistakably show the basis of his solution to be Vedāntic. One is not quite sure whether he was Advaitic or Viśiṣṭādvatic.

1. RK's first important point is that God or the absolute religious entity is both with and without forms (M 32, 128, 175, 191, 217, 218 and so on).

The Primordial Power is ever at play. He is creating, preserving, and destroying in play, as it were. The Power is called Kali. Kali is verily Brahman, and Brahman is verily Kali. It is one and the same reality. When we think of it as inactive, that is to say, not engaged in the act of creation, preservation, and destruction then we call It Brahman. But when It engages in these activities, then we call It Kālī or Śakti. The Reality is one and the same, the difference is in name and form.[35]

---

32. M., 39.

33. Romain Rolland, *The Life of Ramakrishna*, Almorah, 1930, p. 206.

34. *Ibid.*, p. 247.

35. M., 134-35. This is the tenor of RK's view about Brahman. This view of RK is largely *Viśiṣṭādvaitic*, for according to Rāmānuja, Brahman in the state of *pralaya* remains in a subtle state which may be regarded as *nirguṇa*. However, in the manifest state, Brahman is *saguṇa*.

Again,

> ....the true religions teachers of all times and ages are
> like so many lamps through which is emitted the life of the
> spirit, flowing constantly from one source............the Lord
> Almighty.[36]
> The Avatāra is always one and the same. Plunging into the
> ocean of life, He rises up in one place and is known as
> Krishna; diving again and rising elsewhere, He is known as
> Christ.
> On the tree of Satchidananda grow innumerable fruits such
> as Rama, Krishna, Christ and others............[37]

The difference between one deity and another is one of name
and form. For example, gold is one, but it can assume many
forms in different kinds of ornaments.[38] The same chameleon can
assume different colours.[39] In this context the following statement
cannot be taken otherwise than what has been mentioned above.

> It is like water, called in different languages by different
> names, such as 'jala', 'pani', and so forth............All three
> denote one and the same thing, the difference being in the
> name only. In the same way, some address the Reality as
> 'Allah', some as 'God', and some as 'Brahman', some as
> 'Kālī' and others by such names as 'Rama', 'Jesus', 'Durga',
> 'Hari'.[40]

2. Again, RK holds that God is all-pervading spirit. He
exists in all beings, even in the ant.[41]

> O Mother, Thou art verily Brahman, and Thou art verily
> Shakti. Thou art Purusha and Thou art Prakriti. Thou art
> Virāṭ. Thou art the Absolute, and Thou dost manifest Thy-

---

36. T., 184.
37. T., 126-27.
38. T., 691.
39. T., 687.
40. M., 135.
41. M., 104.

Self as Relative. Thou art verily the twenty-four cosmic principles.[42]

In the light of the above-mentioned statement Riencourt thinks that RK's theology is pantheistic.[43] Rolland states that according to RK, the Lord moves under a diversity of forms.........pious, hypocrite and even the criminal.

> I say: 'Narayana in the pious man, Narayana in the hypocrite, Narayana in the criminal and the libertine'.[44]

Again,

> I believe in my God the wicked, my God the miserable, my God the poor of all races.[45]
>
> ....it is God who manifests Himself as the atheist and the believer, the good and the bad, the real and the unreal; that it is He who is present in waking and in sleep; and that He is beyond all these.[46]

Though God is manifested in all, it is not so not in the same degree. Spinoza too held that God is in all things but not in the same degree. There is more of God in an angel than in the mouse. RK also holds that the manifestations of God are different with different things. God is more manifest in some than in others,[47] more in man than in the stone[48] and certainly more in the heart of His devotees than elsewhere,[49] the more in the holy than in the wicked.[50]

As God is manifest in everything, so He is present in idols as

---

42. M., 123.
43. Romain Rolland, *op. cit.*, 229.
44. *Ibid.*, p. 101.
45. *Ibid.*, p. 279.
46. M., 236.
47. M., 319, 320, 342.
48. M., 321.
49. M., 320
50. M., 181.

much as in His attributes. So even idol-worship is valid and help-ful for the beginners.[51]

> God is with form and without form. Images and other sym-bols are just as valid as your attributes. And these attributes are not different from idolatry, but are merely hard and petrified forms of it.[52]

3. As all deities are valid, so sincerity and earnestness of faith are necessary for reaching God.

> To be sure, God exists in all beings
> God can be realized through all paths. All religions are true.
> The important thing is to reach the roof. You can reach it by stone stairs or by wooden stairs or by bamboo steps or by a rope. You can also climb up by a bamboo pole.[53]
> The Christians, the Brahmos, the Hindus, the Mussalmans all say, 'My religion alone is true'. But, Mother, the fact is that nobody's watch is right. Who can truly understand Thee? But if a man prays to Thee with a yearning heart, he can reach Thee, through Thy grace, by any path.[54]

Thus RK renouncing the narrow path of the monopolist and fanatic held that through earnestness and yearning all lovers of God will reach the same goal.[55] If a man has faith, then RK states that it does not matter whom he worships.[56] Hence, RK concludes.

> All religions and all paths call upon their followers to pray to one and the same God. Therefore, one should not show disrespect to any religion or religious opinion. It is God alone who is called Satchidananda Brahman in the Vedas, Satchi-

---

51. Romain Rolland, *op. cit.*, p. 198.
52. *Ibid.*, p. 182.
53. M., 111.
54. M., 93.
55. M., 304-05.
56. M., 289.

dananda Krishna in the Puranas, and Satchidananda Shiva in the Tantras. It is one and the same Satchidananda.[57]

4. Different creeds are but different paths to reach the Almighty. Diverse are the means by which this Kâlī temple may be reached......some come here in boats, some in carriages, some on foot. Similarly, different people attain God by following different creeds.[58]

If all gods and all paths.are true, then which one deity should one follow? Also one should realize that men differ in their taste and temperament,[59] and trees in the garden are of different kinds.[60] Under the following conditions RK advises us thus:

I should say, 'Fix your attention on that form which appeals to you most; but know for certain that all forms are the forms of one God alone.[61]

Knowing that all paths lead to the same Truth, we should not despise other Deities, but maintain an attitude of respect towards other religions.[62] The Lord has provided different forms of worship to suit different men with different capacities and with different stages of spiritual development.[63] As God has many aspects, so God is described according to the particular aspect in which He appears to his particular worshipper.[64]

.........the Lord of the universe, though one manifests Himself differently according to the different likings of His worshippers and each one of these has his own view of God which he values most. To some He is a kind master or a devoted friend.[65]

---

57. M., 306.
58. Teachings T. 696.
59. M., 188-89.
60. M., 211.
61. M., 184.
62. F. Max Muller, *Ramakrishna*, Sayings, 250, 251.
63. Teachings, 697.
64. *Ibid.*, 17.
65. *Ibid.*, 13.

Hence, one should know that only through 'ignorance one harbours sectarian views and quarrels'.[66] If one knows that men differ in their types, temperament and spiritual development, so their objects of worship have to differ and God reveals Himself to different men differently to suit their requirements. Two things have been emphasized by RK. First, sincerity, earnestness and faith in worship of any deity whatsoever; secondly, belief in one God.

Whoever performs devotional exercises, with the belief that there is but one God, is bound to attain Him, no matter in what aspect, name, or manner He is worshipped.[67]

In order that earnestness and seriousness for one's own religion may not degenerate into fanaticism, RK enjoins the believer to have belief in one God, as ultimate referent underlying all religious faiths. RK states:

Remain always strong and steadfast in thy own faith, but eschew all bigotry and intolerance.[68]

Again,

.........one may have that single-minded devotion to one's own religion, but one should not on that account hate other faiths. On the contrary, one should have a friendly attitude toward them.[39]

RK did not stop there, but advised that one should practise other faiths for a time.[70]

I had to practise each religion for a time.........Hinduism, Islam, Christianity. Furthermore, I followed the paths of

---

66. *Ibid.*, 698.
67. *Ibid.*, 695.
68. *Sayings*, 247; *vide Sayings*, 250, 251, 272.
69. M., 225; *vide* Teachings, 683, where respect for all religions has been recommended.
70. M., 128.

Shaktas, Vaiṣṇavas, Vedāntists. I realized that there is only one God toward whom all are travelling; but the paths are different.[71]

For this purpose RK took to Islam and uttered the name of Allah in 1866. Similarly in November, 1874 RK took to Christianity. In a vision Christ whispered to him thus:

> Behold the Christ, who shed his heart's blood for the redemption of the world, who suffered a sea of anguish for love of men. It is He, the master Yogin, who is in eternal union with God. It is Jesus, Love incarnate.[72]

AN APPRAISAL

It is a matter of wonder that a man so intoxicated with God could ever walk on this earth. Hence, his followers regard him as an Incarnation. Whatever he said was experienced by him most palpably. His doctrine of 'Unity of religions' is not to be criticized, but is to be humbly followed and duly acknowledged. But it is the verdict of a mystic who never left behind his intoxication. We humble men can only show our difficulties in relation to his verdict.

1. There is little doubt that RK was a Hindu of Hindus[73] but not narrow and local. It is Hinduism at its best which also means the highest point reached of an uninterrupted tradition which was nourished by Indian seers at last throughout three thousand years. He worshipped Shiva, Kālī, Rama and Krishna, and, yet meditated and realized formless Brahman. He taught and has epitomized the paradoxical aspects of idol-worship and the worship of one God. He was wholly soaked in Rama, Krishna, Chaitanya, Kālī without deviating from Brhma-realization. He was a Hindu without any nomenclature and a sect. His spirit hovers over India and mingles with the spirit of the world.

2. In Indian thought different religions are taken to be so many paths that lead to the same mountain top, or, the many rivers that lose themselves in the sea. But God-realization is not

---

71. M., 129.
72. Romain Rolland, *op. cit.*, p. 87; also M., 34.
73. M., 45.

a place, but is a matter of becoming. The Master himself noted that Bhakti leads to the service of the Lord, and, *Jñāna-Mārga* leads to mergence into Brahman. This mergence does not mean extinction but perfection. Hence, all paths do not lead to God-realization, certainly not the five-fold *Makari* principle. He himself noted that some paths may be devious.[74]

We also know that some deities like ghosts, devils and Satan (*Gītā* 17.4-6) are not to be worshipped. The God-intoxicated mystic was too saintly a man to overlook these difficulties.

3. True, the Master recommended worshipping any deity with the awareness that this will lead to God-realization. But the *Gītā* itself observes that the worshippers may be mistaken in this regard (7.24). No doubt, the Master very often took to pantheism to include all kinds of deity, standing for wickedness and criminality. But he also has emphasized the higher and lower manifestation of God. Lower deities will pull down the worshipper towards, e.g., worldliness. Mammon and sex are also deities. Matter bereft of spiritualism is also an object of adoration. In one's enthusiasm for establishing harmony of religions one should not overlook the lower forms of worship.

4. The most important concept is of a Reality which is both with and without forms.

Apparently this is self-contradictory. The Master himself states the following in this context:

> He who is attributeless also has attributes. He who is Brahman is also Shakti. When thought of as the Creator, Preserver, and Destroyer, He is called the Primordial Energy, Kālī. Brahman and Shakti are identical, like the fire and its power to burn.[75]

Again,

> ....Brahman and Shakti are identical..........you cannot think of the milk without whiteness, and again, you cannot think of the (milk) whiteness without the milk.[76]

---

74. M., 98.
75. M., 107-08.
76. M., 134.

Conceptual framework cannot be stretched to include Kālī (representing forms) and Brahman (formless) in any consistent manner. The illustration refers to a concept of substance-attribute relationship. But Kālī and Brahman are both substances and the two substances cannot be identical.

Besides, RK thinks that Kālī and Brahman are two modes or aspects for *thought*, but are they also apart from our (human) thinking? The two aspects of the Supreme Reality cannot be entertained in the same thought, but in two separate thoughts taken up successively.

Again, Rāmānuja has tried to reconcile multiplicity with unity in his own way. For him, Brahman is qualified with *cit* and *acit* as his body, but Brahman is one body-spirit complex. In the state of *pralaya*, the body aspect of *cit* and *acit* remains in a very subtle form, scarcely to be differentiated. Hence, in subtle state Brahman may be called *nirguṇa* and in gross manifested form, He is *saguṇa*. But even in the state of *pralaya*, Brahman really remains nascently qualified.

The Master has taken many illustrations, but none of them can remove this inconsistency. The distinction for RK is a matter of his *samādhi*. In *savikalpaka* samādhi and also in *premabhakti* the Reality appears as personal and with attributes. However, the same object of love in *nirvikalpaka* samādhi melts into ineffable ocean which remains without any distinction. In this sense the Master has truly said that Divine Mother is none other than the Absolute. Really even for RK, Brahman is more important, for only on this basis he has been able to establish harmony of religions. On the whole, the worship of *Saguṇa Brahma* is the primary stage of worship[77] and it matures into *Nirguṇa Brahma*. Or, as Rolland puts it:

Dualism, 'qualified Monism', and absolute Monism, are stages on the way to supreme truth. They are not contradictory, but rather are complementary One to the other.[78]

5. Taking to Islam or Christianity must not to be taken seriously. These were not cases of *true conversion*. Whether a Muslim

77. M. 127.
78. Romain Rolland, *op. cit.*, p. 198.

is a Muslim, or, a Christian is a Christian can be known not only
by the whole life lived, but also by one's death. He was fully convinced that every deity ultimately merges into Brahman. Every
worshipper at first becomes what he worships and finally merges
into Brahman. Hence, by taking to Islam, he himself became a
Muslim saint, and, by taking to Christianity, he became Christ
himself. But as such he failed to become Brahman himself.

6. RK laid down the maxim, *jiva is Shiva*[79] and regarded the
service to man as the worship of God.[80] But he was not interested in the improvement of social life, even though he decried
caste.[81] He said once:

> 'Suppose God appears before you then will you ask Him to
> build hospitals and dispensaries for you?.........A lover of
> God never says that. He would rather ask for a place at
> His Lotus Feet'.[82]

He wanted people to love God and the more one loves God,
the less active one becomes.[83] Hence, his message grew more
powerful with Vivekananda who lost himself, in social service
and improvement.

Finally, it must be confessed that RK's doctrine of 'The Unity
of Religion' has been backed by a teacher of rare spiritual attainment, and, is a sacred Trust bequeathed to Indians.

ADVAITIC UNITY OF RELIGIONS
According to Shankara, Brahman alone is the Supreme Reality
which has to be realized. Is there no Īśvara? Of course, Shankara admitted the reality of Īśvara and recommended devotional
method as an aid for realizing Brahma.

Nor do we wish to contend against the devotional approach

---

79. M., 315.
80. M., 36.
81. M., 243-44, 309, 336.
82. M., 143.
83. M., 108, 114, 138, 151-52, 308, 314, 315, 335.

and the unceasing one-pointed meditation on God; for this has been recommended both by *Shruti* and *Smṛti*.[84]

Not only this, but Shankara also admits that Iśvara is in proximity to Brahman[85] and Vs. 3.3.39 suggests that the qualified Brahman (i.e., Iśvara) is fundamentally one with the unqualified (*nirguṇa*) Brahman.

Shankara further holds that the worship of Iśvara also pertains to liberation through successive stages (*Kramamukti*).

And as those also who rely on the knowledge of the qualified Brahman in the end have recourse to that (*nirvāṇa*), it follows that they also do not return (*Vs.* IV.4.22).

The final absorption of the *bhaktas* in *Nirguṇa Brahman* occurs at the time of periodic *pralaya* (*Vs.* IV.3.10).

But it must be confessed that Shankara did not explain the relationship between Iśvara and Brahman logically. It was left for Kabir and Sri Ramakrishna to point out the inseparable relationship between Iśvara (*saguṇa*) and Brahman (*nirguṇa*). According to Kabir, Iśvara and Brahman, *saguṇa* and *nirguṇa* are inseparable.

संतौ घोखा कासू कहियें ।
गुण में निरगुण में निरगुण गुण है,
बाट छांड़ि क्यूं बहियें ॥

(But Kabir also states that without going beyond the worship of the qualities, the worshipper will not reach his ultimate goal).

ग्राकार की ग्रोट ग्राकार नहीं ऊबरें,
सिव विरंचि ग्ररु विष्णु तांई ।
जास का सेवक तास कौं पाइहैं,
इ꣠ठ को छांड़ि ग्रावो न जांहीं ॥

(*K.G.* pada 199)

---

84. Vedānta-Sūtra. II. 2.42.
85. *Ibid.*, IV. 3.9.

(The finite cannot obtain liberation by the worship of the finite. He can obtain the limited gain by his devotion of his deity).

Finally, Kabir states the following:

हद चले सो मानवा, बेहद चले सो साध,
हद बेहद दोऊ तजैं, ताकर मता अगाध ॥

(Bijak, Sākhi 189).

(Ordinary men follow the limited, the saints follow the unlimited. But the deeper minds go beyond both of them).

Indirectly it means that the worship of the qualified deity is the primary stage. Going beyond and through it is the realization of the unqualified. But in the final realization one goes beyond both. This point has been further elucidated by Sri Ramakrishna.

For Sri Ramakrishna Brahman is both with forms *(Saguṇa,* like Rama, Krishna) and without form *(nirguṇa).*

Well, it seems to me that both the formless deity and God with form are real.[86]

When the Godhead is thought of as creating, preserving, and destroying, It is known as Personal God, *Saguṇa* Brahman, or the Primal Energy, Ādyashakti. Again, when It is thought as beyond the three guṇas, then It is called Attributeless Reality, Nirguṇa Brahman, beyond speech and thought; this is the Supreme Brahman, Parabrahman.[87]

Both *Saguṇa* and *nirguṇa* aspects of Brahman are inseparable, but for the seeker God with form is the primary stage and the formless Brahman is the final stage.[88]

That which is the Absolute has also its relative aspect, and that which is the Relative has also its absolute aspect. You cannot set aside the Absolute and understand just the Relative. And it is only because there is the Relative that you can transcend it step by step and reach the Absolute.[89]

86. The Gospel of Sri Ramakrishna by M., p. 217.
87. The Gospel, M., pp. 218, 321; also see pages 567, 608, 634, 635, 734, 802.
88. *Ibid.,* p. 127.
89. *Ibid.,* p. 851.

The natural question is, 'which one of the deities with forms should be the starting-point for the theistic believer. This choice depends on the psychological proclivities of the seeker, or, as it is said on the *Saṁskāra* of the seeker.

> If you asked me which form of God you should I meditate upon, I should say: Fix your attention on that form which appeals to you most; but know for certain that all forms are the forms of one God alone.[90]

One should not run away with the idea that Brahma-realization is a matter of intellectual understanding. It is a matter of strenuous religious discipline and is reached ordinarily after a long period of earnest quest. When it comes, it shakes the very foundation of the personality of the seeker.

> It is like a huge elephant entering a small hut. The house shakes to its foundation. Perhaps it falls to pieces.[91]

The state of Brahma-realization of Sri Ramakrishna has been beautifully described by Rǿmain Rolland,

> The Universe was extinguished. Space itself was no more. At first the shadows of ideals floated in the obscure depths of the mind. Monotonously a feeble consciousness of the Ego went on ticking. Then that stoṭ ꝑeᶦ too. Nothing remained but Existence. The soul was lost in Self. Dualism was blotted out. Finite and Infinite space were as one. Beyond word, beyond thought, he (Ramakrishna) attained Brahman.[92]

Hence, the Advaitic religion of Brahma-realization is not mere philosophy, but a matter of spiritual attainment. But what do we mean by 'Brahma or Brahman' in this context?

---

90. *Ibid.*, p. 184.
91. *Ibid.*, p. 747.
92. Romain Rolland, *The Life of Ramakrishna*, 1930, p. 63; for a similar state of Brahma-realization of Vivekananda, *The Great Master*, pp. 879, 917.

Brahman is completely undifferentiated, without any internal and external relation and difference. It has been described as a state of dreamless sleep. The stage of Brahma-realization has been beautifully described by the *Bṛhadāraṇyaka* Upanishad.

There a father becomes not a father; a mother, not a mother; the worlds, not the worlds............a *Cāṇḍāla* is not a *Cāṇḍāla* (B.U. IV. 3.22).

The Chhāndogya tells us that a *Brahma-jñāni* sees even a *Cāṇḍāla* as Brahman. The *Muṇḍaka* informs us that Brahman has no caste (I.1.6). In the same way the Gītā states that the Lord observes no distinction between the lowly born, women and the Śūdras (IX. 32). Further, the Gītā (V.18) observes that sages look at the learned brahmin, a cow, an elephant and even a dog and an outcaste in the same distinctionless way.

This religion of Brahma-realization is the absolute criterion of the spiritual attainment in any theistic form of worship. Advaitism, from Shankara to Sri Ramakrishna through Kabir, holds that one can start on a spiritual pilgrimage from any starting-point available to him according to his upbringing or *saṁskāras*. A Krishnite can easily adopt the worship of Krishna as his deity. Similarly, a Christian can adopt Christ as his deity, and so on. But what is the standard by which will they measure their own attainments?

The standard has been provided by the statement of Brahma-realization. One has to reach a state where all distinctions of caste, creed and nationalities are obliterated. Shankara states this thus:

.........the aim of the Śastras is to discard all distinctions fictitiously created by Nescience.　　　(Vs. I. 1.4)

In the same way, the Bible says,

Be ye therefore perfect, even as your Father which is in heaven is perfect.　　　(Mt. V. 48)

For he maketh his sun to rise on the evil and on the good, and sendeth rain on the just and on the unjust.　　　(Mt. V. 45)

One has to start with a religion in which he is born or the religion which appeals to him most. But he has to practise with full devotion till he reaches a state in which he overcomes all differences. Thus, the advaitic recognizes the claims of particular forms of relgions, but does not recognize their absoluteness with their particularities. It does not recommend the ecclecticism of Bhagvan Das or the fusion-theory of Radhakrishnan. But it lays down the absolute standard which every religion has to attain. This absolute standard underlies every form of religion which holds out the prospect of uniting all religions. Here lies the confluence of relative and particular religions and of the Absolute standard of Advaitism. This is the amalgam of Jamuna and Ganga. Let us illustrate.

Let a Christian starts with the worship of Jesus Christ as his God. He should worship with a view to reaching the stage of loving his Christian brethren. At the next stage he should make no distinction between a Bihari, Bengali and Keralite. Then next, he should overgrow the distinction between Protestants, Catholics and other Christians belonging to other denominations and races. Then he should realize his oneness with other followers of various other religions. Lastly he has to reach a state when all distinctions fall away, and, he and Christ become one: This is the way in which a Hindu or Muslim has to ascend step by step till at last all distinctions are lost and merged in the deity of his worship. Not mergence so much is emphasized here as the realization of distinctionlessness.

CONVERSION OR PROSELYTIZATION

When one religion comes in contact with another, then a number of results follow. At times there is clash which happened between the Christians and Muslims, between the Parsis and Christians, and so on. But by coming in contact with another religion, a religion may also be deepened and enriched, and there may be cross-fertilization of religions. When Christianity came in contact with Hinduism, then a good deal of reformation took place in Hinduism, as a result of which Brahmo-Samaj, Neo-Vedantism, Arya Samaj and Prarthana Sabha came into being. At the same time, Paul Tillich, one of the foremost theologians and R. Otto included much in their theory the influence of Hinduism. However, in the first phase, missionaries of Christian religion could not fully understand the depth of Shankara and Rāmānuja. They thought that it was their religious duty to convert the Hindus into Christianity. Certainly number of Indians were converted into Christianity. Here two words are used inter-changeably, namely, conversion and proselytization. However, there is a subtle distinction between them.

Conversion means to change from an irreligious to a holy life; to change by spiritual experience, from one spiritual life to another. But a proselyte is one who has come over from one religion to another. This kind of change may be due to temptation, terrorization and other means. This may or may not be due to spiritual change of heart and will. For instance, many Śūdras were converted into Islam and Christianity to escape from social tyranny and humiliation. Dr. J.N. Sarcar writes that a great many Shudras embraced Islam and welcomed the Muslim conquerors as their liberators.[93] Gandhiji called such Christian converts as 'rice Christians'.

Judaism, Islam and Christianity favour conversion which in many cases are really proselytization. As against these Semitic religions, Hinduism does not favour conversion. There are a number of reasons for Hinduism in not favouring conversion.

1. First reason is that that for Hinduism (rather Brahminism), the Vedas are eternal and they contain pure form of religion. Any departure from Vedism is to accept an impure form of religion.

As against this, Semitic religions accept in the progressive and gradual revelation of God when the time is ripe for the higher form of religion.[94] Kierkegaard regards that the disciple at the second hand is superior to the older and earlier disciples, because he knows much more about the historical development, needs and enlightenment through the ages. Hence, Semitic religions regard Brahminism as earlier and naturally an incomplete revelation.

Christianity thinks that it has gone through the test of moder-

---

93. J.N. Sarcar, *Islam in Bengal*, Calcutta, 1972, p. 23.
94. Mahayana Buddhism also favours this progressive form of revelation by the Buddha.

nity which other religions have not yet faced. So it is in a position to offer better religious insights than either Hindu conservatism or Muslim Fundamentalism. Hence, Christianity is most given to conversion.

2. Brahminism accepts *Karmavāda*, according to which the present state of a Hindu depends on his previous karmas, specially the caste into which he is born. Even the Gītā favours caste-determinism.

> The fourfold caste was made by me, in accordance with guṇas and karmas. (*Gītā* IV.13)

Again,

> Better one's own defective dharma, than others' Dharma, well-performed; Better is death in one's own Dharma; Another's Dharma's fraught with fear. (*Gītā* III.55)

Further,

> Better one's Dharma incomplete, than others' Dharma well-performed; By acting as our nature calls, We do not any sin incur. (*Gītā* XVII.47)

The whole caste-system ends in the exploitation of the Śūdras in social economics and humiliation in the society. Naturally Christianity has picked up the Adivasis and scheduled castes for conversion.

3. Any religion which denounces caste as Buddhism, arouses the anger of Brahmins, for they alone enjoy a very privileged position in social and political life. This has been the case from the time of Chankya, Peshavas up to the present Indian political life. Hence, conversion and consequent liquidation of the scheduled caste would take away a big vote reserve of the Brahmins. We will raise this point again when we come to deal with the political use of religion.

But now we will take up the view of Radhakrishnan who has spoken most vehemently against conversion.

RADHAKRISHNAN ON CONVERSION

1. First, for Radhakrishnan every religion is true for the person who believes in it, for every form of religion appeals to its devotee with the same inner certitude and devotion.[95]

We have already criticized this subjectivity, which is not the essence of religion and Radhakrishnan himself could not subscribe to it. Besides, every form of religion is not equally right, even according to the *Gītā* (XVII.3-6), for many men of no understanding worship the manifest form, not knowing the Absolute form of Brahman (*Gītā* VII.24).

2. No individual can live without his personal and traditional memory. If we tear up the individual from his traditional roots, he becomes abstract and aberrant.

> History is something organic, a phase of man's terrestrial destiny as essential for him as memory is for personal identity ....To forget our social past is to forget our descent.[96]

Certainly the past history serves as a guide and lesson, and, at times a source of inspiration. But to remain chained to the past is fraught with dangers. One must not make an idol and fetish of the past. Living on the glories of the past without making efforts to improve the present is detrimental to progress. One does not live in the past alone. The past has to be made living and vibrant in relation to the needs and challenges of the present. Hence, the past has to be reviewed and renewed in the light of the present and future. To be glued to the past makes a nation unfit in the struggle of existence. The past has to be used for meeting present emergencies and future challenges.

Besides, the past history of India has brought untold miseries for the teeming millions of Śūdras and adivasis. Would these people like to remain wedded to their past? They would like to shake off their past chains and would like to jump into the main stream of Indian national life. For the vast number of Śūdras and Adivasis, the past history contains nothing but their exploitation.

---

95. *Eastern Religion*, p. 327; *vide* M., 328, 329, 345.
96. *Eastern Religion*, p. 328.

Again, the world history has become conscious of itself. It is changing the world picture of the past. It is moving in the direction of one world, one people and one parliament. Regional histories have to be pressed into this world ecumenical movement.

Further, when one talks of history, then one should not ignore the fact that at present in India there are Aryans, Tamilians, other races and tribes. Even Syrian Christians have been in India for the last two thousand years, and Muslims have made India their permanent home. Should all races and tribes continue their differences! All races and tribes have to bring their flowers on the alter of Mother India so that she be the home of one integrated people. Of course, the depth of Advaitic philosophy cannot be ignored for bringing unity between the rival claims of all religions. This is the view of the author already discussed before.

Thus, there is no one history of India. There are histories. And a convert only exchanges one history for another. When the Śūdras of Bengal were converted into Islam, then they simply exchanged their history of exploitation and humiliation into another history of pan-Islamic brotherhood. Hence, it would be too dogmatic to hold that Śūdras and others converted into Islam and Christianity have become 'abstract and aberrant'. Who can deny the benefits of Christianity enforced on the head-hunters of Khasi-hills and other aboriginals of India? In this connection, Radhakrishnan makes another point against conversion.

3. As a means of creative religion the native cult has an absolute advantage over any imported religion, for a convert to a new religion feels like an illegitimate child with no heritage, no link with the men who preceded him............There is no inner development or natural progress to the new religion.[97]

True, mere copying Western Christianity has not resulted in any new religious upheaval in Indian Christians. Many Western dogmas about Virgin birth of Jesus, Resurrection of Jesus, His

---

97. *Eastern Religion*, p. 328; *vide Recovery of Faith*, p. 199.

second coming etc., have not pulverized Indian spiritual think-ing. As a matter of fact, negligence of Bhakti and advaitic mysti-cism has resulted in the poverty of Indian Christian theology. But there is no reason why Indian Christianity cannot have an Indian Christian theology. This criticism of Indian Christianity is not true of Indian Islam which even now is contributing much to Islam.

4. Radhakrishnan makes an important plea for the preserva-tion of many religions, for the cross-fertilization of ideas.[98] And it has to be conceded that in most cases missionary zeal for con-version is based on the depreciation and contempt of other religions.[99]

It is a recognized psychological fact that men differ from one another with regard to their psychological proclivities and up-bringing, called *Samskāra*. For this reason no one religion can claim to be the universal religion of the world. Knowing this Shankara recommends *Karmayoga* for the Kshatriyas and *Jñānayoga* for the Brahmins. Hence, different types of religion are bound to continue at least in the near future. That the people belong to different types, have been taught by the *Gītā* and in modern times by C.G. Jung and others. Hence, missionary enter-prise will help people to choose that kind of religion which fits most into their psychological requirements. Further, missionary enterprise is helpful to mankind in finding one's spiritual anchor-age. But is it a fact that missionary enterprise relating to con-version is based on the depreciation and contempt of other religions.

Missionaries sacrifice a lot of their comforts and even useful pursuits of their life, as was certainly the case with Albert Sch-weitzer. Best missionaries have been those people who were first converted into a religion. Afterwards their spiritual experience is so valuable to them that they want to share it with other men. Here, we are reminded of Ramakrishna. He was a great Vedāntic mystic and enjoyed his vision as of inestimable worth and not liking to enjoy it alone, he kept on preaching it to all people.[100] If

---

98. *Ibid.*, p. 330.
99. *Fragments of a Confession*, p. 74.
100. *Teachings of Sri Ramakrishna*, Verse 149.

a missionary is a theist, then he feels that he has been commissioned by God to preach his gospel to the world.[101] Again, the venerable Guru noted:

> There are some who, after eating a mango, will wipe their lips clean, lest others should know, but there are also some who, receiving a mango, will call others to share it with them. So there are some who, realising the Divine Bliss, cannot rest without seeking to make others also realise it.[102]

Hence, missionary enterprise is motivated by compassion for others for sharing Godly living. This was the case with Lord Buddha, Shankaracharya and many other world preachers. Hence, the view of Radhakrishnan is highly distorted.

In this context, Radhakrishnan makes another important statement:

> Our aim should be not to make converts, Christians into Buddhists or Buddhists into Christians, but enable both Buddhists and Christians to rediscover the basic principles of their own religions and live up to them.[103]

As a matter of fact the discovery of the supreme end of Brahma-realization is known as the point of departure from the ordinary men of life and religious practice. This is really a birth into a new Being. In the real sense this is the valid meaning of coversion in which a religious man is changed into a holy man. This is well illustrated in the life of Balmiki, Tulsidas and some-Alvārs. In Christianity, Saul was changed into St. Paul, and Peter the fisherman became a fisher of men.

Nobody can really speak against conversion in which there is not only a change *in* will, but *of* will for a New Being or a God-centred Being. But it is proselytization against which Radhakrishnan is so much concerned. A proselyte is one who leaving one religion, adopts another, without necessarily a change of heart

---

101. *Ibid.*, Verses 172, 715.
102. *Ibid.*, Verse 714.
103. *Fragments of a Confession*, p. 74.

and will. But proselytization is a historical process from time immemorial, in India, and, all over the world.

Many races have entered India and made India their home. The Yavanas, the Schythians, the Parthians, the Sakas and Hunas have entered India and have been absorbed into Hinduism as a result of proselytization. Similarly, when the Buddhists fell on hard times many of them made their way into India and were absorbed into Hinduism. Kabir-pantha, Gorakh Pantha have their base in Buddhism. Similarly, when the Muslims entered India, they succeeded in proselytizing many Shudras and even high caste Hindus into Islam. The same thing happened in the case of Christianity when it entered on its mission of evangelising India. Why is Radhakrishnan so much against it when the history of India records many cases of proselytization? Then why is there so much hue and cry? The whole issue is political, for votes go by communal consideration. Conversion and proselytization mean fewer Hindu votes. The people against conversion are not sincere, for their cry against conversion goes against the secular character of Indian Constitution. Does not secularism mean 'equal respect for all religions'? Does not the Constitution grant equal right to all religions to preach and propagate their faith?

Of course, Radhakrishnan has expressed his view on the basis of Hindu conservatism. This is inherent in the Vedic claim that the Vedas are eternal, and they alone contain the supreme truth. Hence, in the interest of religious truth no departure from Hindu beliefs and practices can be permitted. According to the Vedic claim, pure religious truth prevailed only in the *Satyayuga*, and, then this truth got successively through *Tretā*, *Dvāpara* and *Kaliyuga*. But do the moderners accept this?

One thing is certain that Hinduism itself records spiritual growth and progressive deepening of spiritual enrichment and attainment. In the Ṛgvedic tradition, *svargaprāpti* was deemed to be the highest goal of human existence. In the Upanishads, the abode in heaven was regarded as ephemeral. Instead the highest goal was regarded as the attainment of Brahman.

Shankara, following the Upanishads, has emphasized the goal of Brahma-realization and the attainment of heavenly abode was deemed to be inferior and ephemeral in comparison with it.

There is little doubt that Shankara was a devout theist and an avowed monist. How can these two elements be consistently harmonized? No doubt, Shankara too has united these two ends, but it was left for Ramakrishna to have harmonized theism and monism, *bhakti* and *jñāna, sagunopāsanā* and *nirguna-prāpti.* Ramakrishna held that bhakti is suited to the majority of people. But it is only a first stage in the spiritual ascent of a few aspirants of *Brahmajñāna* and Brahma-realization.

Hence, spiritual realization is a matter of growth and ever-deepening of insight. Let us open our windows and doors of the heart so that the light may enter through them. What is needed is conversion of the heart and will. Various names and forms will finally fall away in the state of final spiritual attainment where a father, is not a father; where a mother, is not a mother; a Muslim, is not a Muslim; a Christian, is not a Christian. Here Jesus, Vishnu, Shiva all will take us to a region where there are no separate temples, mosques and churches, but only light and peace. This is supreme goal of a Hindu, a Sufi and a Christian. Let us all be converted to this Faith of Man.

SECULARISM

When democracy has to be firmly established in a country with a large number of rival religions, then it has to define its relation with religion. Usually there are three kinds of relationship in which religion stands in a democratic country.

1. Co-existence of all religions, or, equal respect for all religions.
2. Neutrality with regard to religion.
3. Denial of religions in running the country and in its preservation, progress and future aspirations.

Of course, there can be a democracy with one religion as its centre. For example, Pakistan is said to be an Islamic State, and, the same is said to be about Bangladesh. This kind of theocentric democratic government has not been recognized in the West, even though in most of the Western States Christianity is the ruling religion, why?

The reason is that by making a State a theocratic State, the religious priests or the ecclesiastic authorities begin to interfere in the matter of Government decisions and law-making. What is wrong with it? Well, most of the religions have arisen in a pre-scientific age, and, the modern States are given to science and technology and international relationships. For this reason the Government comes in clash with religion even when it is professed by a vast majority of the citizens. For example, when a government finds that it cannot provide food, jobs and other necessities of life, then it legislates birth-control. This is not liked by Roman Catholic Christians. Hence, there issues out conflict between the Government and religion. Hence, purely as a result of historical development, in the Western States religion has not been recognized as a partner of democracy. This does not mean that religion is not made a weapon for winning election. Till John Kennedy no Roman Catholic could ever be elected as the President of U.S.A. Even now in Germany Christian Demo-crates form an important political party. But in general a government is said to be Secular. What does Secularism mean in the West?

Secularism in the West means the cultivation of a scientific at-titude in life, and specially towards religious claims in the light of a scientific world-view. Hence, it means the full exploitation of the resources of one's country with the help of science and technology in utter disregard of super-naturalism. Therefore, secularism is this-worldly and religion is other-worldly. In this sense, Secularism is not anti-religious but quite indifferent to religion. Religion is kept apart from all public activities—social, economic and political. For example, for facing drought science and technocraft are used, and, not mass prayers. Religion is relegated to man's personal life only. This is best seen in John Dewey's Naturalism. Can this meaning of Secularism be adopted in India?

No, there are many reasons for not adopting this sense of secularism. First, as yet most Indians have not developed a scientific attitude to life. Even a scientist thinks of bathing in a sacred river when he is asked to observe the Solar eclipse. A team of doctors postponed the hour of surgical operation for witnessing Mahabharata scene on the T.V. (dated 27-11-1988).

Most of the Hindu ministers in the morning do not see visitors because of their hour of Puja. And one can find a vast mass of men on the occasion of *Kumbha* and other Melas. Hence, in India Secularism means respect for all types of prevailing religions in India. Even the Prime Minister of India makes it a point to visit as many temples, shrines, gurdwaras, mosques as is possible. Religious orthodoxy in its dazzling colour is maintained on the T.V. for winning elections. Religious holidays have been declared public holidays. Hence, Secularism in the preamble of Indian Constitution means 'co-existence of all religions', or, 'equal respect of all religions'. This is what Gandhiji has maintained.

I believe in the Bible as I believe in the Gita. I regard all the great faiths of the world as equally true with my own. It hurts me to see any one of them caricatured as they are today by their own followers.

Thus, in India secularism is a religious and not a political concept. One should remember that for Gandhiji, political activity was taken as a religious activity. Unfortunately people do not also record the view of Mahatma about the kind of religion he had in mind.

This religion transcends Hinduism, Islam, Christianity etc. It does not supersede them. It harmonises them and gives them reality.[104]

But can this kind of concept work on the Indian scene?

Nehru was a western man. No doubt in his mind 'secularism' meant this-worldly pursuit with the help of science and technology, for taking India forward from her backwardness. Why did he succumb to the confused view of secularism as equal respects for all religions? Nehru advised people not to mix up religion and politics in the government of the State, but encouraged respect for all religions. Thus, Indian secularist partly took from the Mahatma his very personal way of taking political life as a

---

104. *Harijan*, 10-2-1940.

form of religious activity, and, Nehru-Mahatma view of having
equal respects for all religions. Indian politicians have disregard-
ed the very special meaning of religion which Mahatma had in
his mind, and, Nehru's advice not to mix up politics and religion
in the affairs of the State. Thus, the confused meaning of secularism has been on the Indian scene, in spite of Mahatmaji and
Nehru. But Nehru realized that Hindus and Muslims are religious people and their wish in favour of religion has to be res-
pected. Secondly, partition of India was followed by a great
deal of Hindu-Muslim rioting. Both Muslims and Hindus have
to be persuaded to live together in peace by securing for them
religious co-existence. Nehru granted this concession as a political weapon for restoring Hindu-Muslim peaceful existence in
Indian democracy. He hoped that in the long run the Indian
politicians will outgrow their religious passion with the growth
of industrial growth and spread of science-education. There is
little doubt that Nehru laid down the foundation of scientific
pursuits and industrial development. Hence, Nehru allowed
'secular state' to respect all religions equally. Has it worked on
the Indian scene?

1. The result of the interpretation of secularism as equal
respect for all religions has made Muslim more fundamentalist
and the Hindu intolerant. The Kashmiri Muslims pelt stones on
the Indian team when it wins against the Pakistan team. A Hindu
is as keen to pit against the Muslim. Hindus in most of the States
in India have succeeded in banning cow-slaughter. The result is
that with the least provocation Hindu-Muslim riots take place.
There can be no peace as long as religions lay claim to their
exclusive claim for spiritual excellence. Religions make opposed
claims. For example, Christians claim that 'God is Jesus' which
for the Muslims is blasphemy. A Hindu every morning turns to
the rising Sun and most non-Hindu religionists regard this to be
an idolatry. Jains and Buddhists in principle are atheistic and, in
contrast, the prophetic religions are theistic. How can people live
in peace, when they profess opposed religious ideologies?

As a matter of fact, a fairly large number of Indians are
Hindus. In Cinema shows, T.V. programmes there is bound to
be far greater weightage given to Hinduism, than to other religions. How can then religious neutrality be maintained? On this

basis of Indian kind of Secularism certain problems are bound to create a good deal of headache to Indian government. The problem of Babri Masjid is a case of this nature.

It is altogether false to say that Hindus have remained most tolerant in religious matters. Shaivites have killed the Jainas and have always fought against the Vaiṣṇavas. The Hindus never developed that cohesiveness which Muslims have. Caste is a divisive factor. For this reason, the Hindus could never succeed against the Muslims. No doubt, Maharattas and Rajputs as local Hindu forces did arise against Muslims. But in Bengal, a large number of Shudras became Muslim and welcomed the Muslim conquerors as their great liberators. Even now the Hindus are divided into the untouchables or scheduled caste, backward Hindus and Hindus of the higher order. All India Hindu Movement has not caught the fire. Once all Hindus become one, there will be more intolerance and riots. Thus, the theory of co-existence of all religions has not worked and is not likely to work.

2. With the interpretation of secularism as equal respects for all religions has worked well with Congress political party. It has granted as much lattitude and protection to Muslims as is possible. Muslim vote bank has favoured the Congress. Again, the Brahmin leadership of the party succeeds in catching the Hindu votes too. And the Harijans with their reservations have made them insensitive to the humiliation and atrocities in their everyday life. But has this worked for nationalism?

Some Indian leaders think that 1857 revolt against the Britishers was really the first beginning of Indian Nationalism. When even after forty-one years of Independence Indians have not become nationalist, then how can it be hoped that in the past in 1857 they were really nationalist? Because the leaders have to get votes, so most of the political leaders of the Hindus are really caste leaders. Hindus are really not Hindus, but are Brahmins, Rajputs, Bhumiharas, Kayasthas, and so on. Because Hinduism means acceptance of caste with Brahmins as the supreme caste, so Hindu religion in political election simply means the acceptance of Hindu fundamentalism.*

---

* The whole political life of Bihar is caste-based, as is clear from the statements in Indian dailies. Suhail Haleem writes under the caption *Booth-capturing* in Times of India, March 9, 1990 Politics in our country, still

The same is true of the Muslims. As political party consisting of Hindus works on the basis of caste, so it also works on the basis of Muslim voters. As there are only a few pockets of full Muslim majority, so the Muslim leaders choose that Muslim constituency where party Hindus will help them elected. This is true for most of the Congress Muslim leaders. But these Congress Muslim leaders can get their Muslim votes for owing full allegiance to Islamic fundamentalism.

Hence, Indian secularism makes a Hindu more of a Hindu, and, a Muslim more of a fundamentalist Muslim. The result? There is no political fight on any principle. Even the communists in Bihar are dominated by the privileged Hindu caste people. For lack of any principle, there is brain drain, unemployment, over-population. No post and no award is possible without the caste and communal backing. Every form of corruption is protected by the caste leadership of the party. Every politician knows that family-planning by legislation is a must. But it is not presented because of losing Muslim votes.

By defining Secularism as 'respect for all religions', religion has entered into the political life of the country as a cankerous growth within it. The sooner this definition of secularism is given up, the better it is. Secularism need not be anti-religion as it was in Russia at the beginning of communist revolution. The reason is that religion is also a force and many an Indian will do his duties towards his country as his God's command. But the Government should remain religion-neutral. Secularism means exploitation of the natural resources of one's country with the help of science and technology with a view to even distribution of resources and jobs for all its citizens. No religion can be higher than the service, defence and furtherance of the future good of the State. Man was not made for religion, but religion was made for man. The ideal man and God are one and the same. The urge to be an ideal citizen by developing one's capacities and abilities to the full in active co-operation with the rest, is most

---

being strictly caste-based". Similarly 'The Times of India News Service' reports on March 22, 1990:

"Another feature which seems to have become a State-wide phenomenon was the utter disregard for party loyalty with only caste considerations as the guiding factor".

sacred and most in line with the evolutionary *nisus* within man. What man has been in the past is nothing in comparison with what man can be in the future, with the help of science, technology and other modern equipment of mankind. No religion has any right to curtail the happiness of other fellowmen.

Hence, we conclude that secularism can mean that the State should remain indifferent to religion in its drive to make the State, industrialized and fully self-sufficient. In the State, religion can be allowed as a private affair of an individual. The West has reached this conclusion after a good deal of experience.

TOLERATION

There might be hesitation in holding that there is one universal religion of the Supreme Spirit. However, it can be stated that there is one common referrent involved in every religion and that there is an absolute standard of reaching a state of differenceless in the final practice of every form of religion. But along this absolute standard of reaching the goal in which all differences are blurred and lost, all forms of religion are infected with relativity, even though there are degrees of being higher and lower. The higher form of relative religions is that which consciously and deliberately adopts this standard of differencelessness. The lower forms of relative religions are those which are not aware of the absolute standard of reaching the state of differencelessness. Besides, the lower forms suffer more from anthropomorphism than the higher forms that keep on refining and purifying their religious concepts to escape from gross anthropomorphism. But one has to realise that every form of religion is relative and as such cannot claim the sole monopoly of religious insight. As such each form of religion should exercise toleration. Toleration means refraining from persecuting the followers of religions other than one's own. It means intellectual breadth and charity which comes not only from a humanitarian consideration, but from the realization that every form of religion is relative. As such, we should try to learn from other religions and deepen our own religious sensitivity by appropriating something and some insight valuable in other religions. Hence, the most important point to realize is that every form of religion is relative, including one's own. This realization logically would entail toleration. Let us summarise the reasons for holding all religions to be relative.

I. First, we have maintained that the Supreme Reality cannot but be unknown and unknowable (*Bṛhadāraṇyaka Up.* II. 4.14; *Maitri* VI.7; Kant's theory of Synthetic unity of Apperception; Wittgenstein's theory of keeping silence about God).

But we have also maintained that religion is psychologically embedded in our mental constitution. So we must search after our highest concern of Brahma-realization. Thus man is condemned to know the unknowable, what can man do?

II. He draws a picture of the unknowable Brahman, according to one's intellectual reaches and world-view. In the primitive stage the picture is most anthropormorphic and with the progress of knowledge and a higher form of world-view the picture gets more refined. For instance, the God of Jews at first demanded animal sacrifice and later as a result of increase in religious sensitivity, the same God demanded a contrite heart, humbly following the commands of the Lord. Thus the picture in any religion whatsoever cannot but be relative, for it is bound to change in the light of increase in knowledge, world-view and deeper sensitivity towards the unknown reality.

III. Thirdly, we have already drawn attention to the fact that in the growth of personality, everyone has a notion of an ideal self which he projects on the wider screen in the form of one's god. As men differ in their types, function and mental constitution, so their ideal Self and God are bound to differ with persons in their various cultural upbringing.

IV. The same point has been raised in Indian systems. Men differ in their temperamental constitution, depending on the proportion of *Sattva, rajas* and *tamas,* and past Karmas. Hence, as men are, so are their gods (*Gita* XVII.4-6). Hence, religions are bound to differ and be relative.

V. Religion is not Science. A statement in science can be true or false, but religious statements cannot be assimilated to factual statements. So religious statements cannot be true or false, as L. Wittgenstein and his followers hold now. However, religious statements can be genuine or fake, authentic or inauthentic for the believers.

Therefore, from the viewpoint of religious philosophy there

is no room for religious intolerance. Further, one should realize that in India there has been a history of religious toleration. Ashoka's edict engraved on the rocks advises us to honour every form of religious faith. The root of this toleration is to reverence one's own faith and never to revile that of others. It rebounds to the glory of India that a parliament of religions was held by the most enlightened emperor Akbar. He allowed free discussions of all faiths and established an ecclectic religion of Din-Ilahi. In our own day Mahatma Gandhi has clearly stated:

I believe in the Bible as I believe in the Gita. I regard all the great faiths of the world as equally true with my own. It hurts me to see any one of them caricatured as they are today by their own followers.[105]

The Greeks on account of their intellectual breadth and syncretism had held wide Toleration. But even Islam advises toleration.

Unto each nation have we given sacred rites which they are to perform; so let them not dispute with thee of the matter, but summon thou unto the Lord. (*Surah* XXII.67)

Allah will judge between you on the Day of Resurrection concerning that wherein ye used to differ. (*Surah* XXII.69)

Again,

'Let there be no compulsion in religion'.

Hence, forcible conversion has been condemned in Islam. Hence, in Modern India every faith is allowed to exist and to practise, and even to propagate its own faith. But why is the country not free from caste and religious tumult and tension? The reason is the political use of religion.

RELIGION AND POLITICS
Secularism as a form of philosophy means a revolt against a theocentric State, and, separates religion from political life.

---

105. Radhakrishnan, S., *Eastern Religion*, p. 313.

Nehru has advised us not to mix up politics and religion in the affairs of the State. However, he hoped that people professing different religions will co-operate, with the government and will not disturb the peace of the citizens. So he advised people to respect all religions. However, in practice the Prime Minister of India on various occasions have been visiting shrines, mosques, gurdwaras, thereby encouraging religions. Many religious festivals have been converted into national holidays. Hence, the political practice is to encourage religion, whereas it is the duty of the secular state of India to weaken the hold of religion. What is wrong with the Secular State of India to encourage religions for obtaining the votes of the masses?

The reason is that the State and Religion are opposed in their nature, aims and methodology. Religion is other-worldly, and, the State is this-worldly. Religion relies on *revelation*, largely stored up in scriptures in conducting the lives of its followers. As against this the State relies on science and technology for exploiting the natural resources and even distribution of goods and services to its citizens. There is no limit to the progress of science and technology. Hence, the State seeks control over nature for making progress in lengthening the life, good health and prosperity of its citizens. The State honours the scientists, technocraft and all those citizens who make this-worldly life as happy and prosperous as is possible. As against this aim and the claim of progressiveness, religion is conservative. Religions had their rise before the rise of science. Naturally they hearken back to the past. Hinduism believes in the eternity of the Vedas, the Christians in the Bible which was written over two thousand years ago. Thus, religion accepts that all that people are required to know is to have faith in what was taught in the ancient past. Most of the religions believe that this world is only a temporary abode of men and their eternal life is in the heaven. Hence, religions are conservative and other-worldly.

If religion and the State are so much opposed to each other, then how can they co-operate? Well, by respecting each other. Religion has to be relegated to the claim of the private life of each citizen, and, the State has not to interfere with the personal faith of the people. In like manner, the State is not to recognize the claim of religion in its activities and affairs of the State.

Religion as a private affair and the State as the public affair of the people should not interfere with each other, since the Ten Commandments of the Bible, and, the *Pañca-Mahāvrata* of Indian religions are the oldest laws of the State. Religion as the private faith of the citizens will help them in due discharge of their duties in the State, and, the State will ensure freedom to its citizens in the practice of their religion. However, this happy division of religion and the State often comes to be disturbed.

Very often religion claims this-worldly power in the furtherance of its practice. Judaism, Islam and Sikhism claim a share in the affairs of the State in the interest of their religion. According to both Judaism and Islam, religion makes the nation. This seriously collides with the State of India. In India there are two major religions, namely, Hinduism and Islam. Hence, according to Islamic claim, India is the home of two nationalities, namely, the Hindus and Muslims. But it does not require any deep knowledge of history that this is an untenable claim. Many of the Muslims of India were once Hindus. So the two are not separate races and people. Besides, it is not true even in Islamic countries, namely, there are Arabs, Turks, Iranians and many other nationalities. In the same manner, Jews may be religious minority, but they owe their citizen rights of the country which they own as their homeland. Hence, religion cannot make a nation, even though on the basis of religion, the Indian sub-continent has been partitioned into Pakistan and Hindusthan. But what about Sikhism?

Sikhism is a purely Indian religion and in the beginning it was just a sect of Hinduism like Kabir panth, Gorakhnath panth. For Guru Nanak three vows were necessary for a Sikh, namely,

Kirt Karnā (singing hymns), *Waṇḍ Chhakanā* (earning one's livelihood and sharing it with others) and *nām japnā* (muttering the name of Guru).

However, Guru Hargobind assumed two swords called '*piri* and *miri*'. *Miri* was there to defend and pursue political end; *piri* was to be used for safeguarding spiritual end. But it was Guru Gobind Singh (1675-1708) who changed the whole complexion of Sikhism. He transformed the peace-loving Sikhs into soldiers. *Bhakti* and *Shakti* were interfused and a Sikh now is a saint-soldier, rolled into one. Guru Hargobind emphasized the primacy of allegiance to truth and moral virtues, and, not to submit to the exclusive claims of a secular State. Guru Gobind Singh conferred spiritual power to Guru Granth Saheb which has been installed in the Golden Temple. The temporal sovereignty lay in Akal Takht, and, these two were expected to work in co-ordination. Thus, religion and politics are inseparably blended in Sikhism. How did this kind of religion work in the Brithish time?

True, Guru Gobind Singh had established the identity symbol by introducing the observances of five *Kakars* (i.e., comb, Kesh, Kara, etc.). But these five *Kakars* were inseparably blended with the politico-spiritual pursuits of the purest of Sikhs, known as *Khalsa*. Britishers fully used the Khalsa by including and recruiting them in the Indian army. The Khalsa Sikh were not only distinguished from the Hindus, but also from *Sahajdhari* Sikhs, Namdari Sikhs and the Udāsis. Being called the military class of India, the Khalsa Sikhs sought an independent Khalistan at the time of handing over the power to the Indians: But the number of the Khalsa Sikhs did not justify the creation of an independent Khalistan. What happened then?

The Indian Government continued the policy of recruiting the Sikhs in the army out of all proportion, with the result that they form the sword of India. Indeed it worked well in 1967 and 1971 war with Pakistan. Why do the Sikhs want an independent Khalistan is not very clear, seeing that they have transformed Punjab into the granary of India, and, into an industrial State of India? Per capita income of a Sikh is higher than that of any Indian in any other State of India. Three points are relevant in this context.

1. Religion and Politics came to be mixed up in the religion of the Khalsa.

2. Secondly, their great prosperity, both at home and abroad gave them the feeling to be the superior class of men. And yet they could hardly dominate Indian government.

3. Thirdly, the inimical foreign powers could instigate the Indian Sikhs through foreign Sikh settlers. Certainly Pakistan

has been training and arming the Sikhs, may be through direct or indirect connivance of powers unfriendly to India. What can India do? Should it use superior force to overcome the Khalistanis by helping other Sikhs loyal to India? But the great lesson which the Government of India has to learn that religious hold over the people has to be weakened by becoming really secular. Secondly, Akal Takht has to be used for political purpose under the democratic set-up of the Government of India. Are the Sikhs really anti-Hindu?

Personally we do not think so. We have already held that Sikhs are Hindus, in the wider sense of 'the Hindus', though Guru Granth Saheb does not favour Brahminism with its caste and idol-worship. Sikhs are killing more Sikhs than Hindus. This shows that their political motivation is against anybody who does not support Khalistan. In any case, the secular government of India has to give up the slogan, 'Equal respect for all religions'. Let us take up the case of the Muslims.

Muslims came to India about a thousand years ago and ruled over the vast part of the country for over five and a half hundred years. Muslims never combined as a whole against the Hindus, and, Hindus too never combined against the Muslims. In certain pockets Maharattas, Rajputs and Sikhs established themselves against the Muslim rule. But the Hindus never combined themselves against the Muslims during pre-British days. However, under the subjugation of India under one British rule, there could be the possibility of Hindus unifying themselves under one umbrella, and, in like manner the Muslims could have combined. But the British rulers were too shrewd. They introduced the principle of 'divide and rule' and adhered to it very carefully. Sikhs were separated from the Hindus and the Rajputs and Maharattas from one another. Yet they could use the Hindus against the Muslims, and, the Muslims against the Hindus.

Under Mahatma Gandhi's leadership to a great extent Hindus and Muslims combined to fight the Britishers. But somehow due to mutual suspicion of each other, Muslims and Hindus separated with the result that Pakistan was created out of India. The years 1946 and 1947 saw great killings, of Hindus by the Muslims, and, of Muslims by the Hindus. Till today the Hindus and Muslims maintain their separate existence. Tolerating each other as a matter of convenience. Least points of disagreement lead to communal riots between the two communities. The tension between the two communities is largely political and not religious. Take the instance of Babri Masjid. Muslim leaders raise hue and cry to catch Muslim votes and, the Hindu leaders do the same to secure Hindu votes. Can the Congress Government not solve the issue?

Surprisingly enough the nationalist Muslims have no place either amongst the Congress or the Muslim League. The more communal you are, the more popular you are in the community to which you belong.* With this communal tendency, how can one afford to escape from communal riots? The Congress Government and party has very great advantage in this regard.

First, under the leadership of Mahatma Gandhi some outstanding Muslim leaders worked on the platform of the Congress. Secondly, Mahatma Gandhi himself met his martyrdom in protecting the lives of the Muslims. Naturally, the Congress Party, has been siding with the Muslims and championing the cause of their security, religious worship and even Urdu and some employment. In the State of Bihar Urdu is a second officials language. The Congress Government has established 'Minority Cell' which is for redressing some of their outstanding grievances. Yes, so far the Congress Party has succeeded in winning the Muslim votes. But is it a step towards secularism where religions have to be weakened?

Muslims are more fundamentalists in India than even what they are in Pakistan, Egypt, Iran and Turkey with regard to the matter of divorce, or, some such personal laws of the Muslims. One must not ignore the fact that the Congress Party lost at the poll because the Muslims did not vote for the Congress in 1977.

---

* *Vide*, Ajay Kumar, *VP's Minority Platform*, The Times of India, March 30, 1990. It is told there is no place for Secular Muslims since the Khilafat movement in 1920. Mr. Kumar maintains that there has been preference for the orthodox bearded Muslims.

"Seven decades later, similer political compulsions still hold good for Mr. V.P. Singh. To gain and secure the support of the Muslims, particularly in the crucial Hindi heartland, he finds it necessary to strike a deal with the bearded power-brokers."

Mr. Kumar also mentions, on the authority of *The Illustrated Weekly of India* that Mr. Singh has made a written agreement with Shahi Imam.

The issue was one of family planning. But can India become a welfare State with regard to food, employment, health-services and so on, in the situation of our present population explosion? And no community in India is prepared for family planning. Here, we are making a political issue under the guise of religion. In a democracy votes count, and, smaller the number of votes fewer are the chances that the community will get its due at the hands of the majority.

Here, by making political use of religion, the country is made poor and backward, and religion too gets vulgarised. By assuming religious liberty, retaining Urdu, and, by encouraging the Muslims to retain their personal law regarding divorce, and full freedom not to observe family planning, the Muslims are segregated from the rest of the Indian nationals. Segregation keeps the tension between the Hindus and Muslims alive, resulting at times in communal riots. But it suits the Congress Party, for segregation from the other Indian nationals and by the promise of extending all kinds of security for the Muslims, the Congress Party gets the support of the Muslim mass. The political use of Hinduism is most direct and this again keeps the country disunited, weak and backward.

The Hindus are divided into caste. The political leaders are really caste leaders. This is as much true of the Congress Party as of any political party. Each candidate at the time of election appeals to his caste men and may make pact with other castes for the purpose of election. Hence, Hindu nationalism has not grown up even now. Thus, there is really caste-federation in the legislative assemblies. The result?

Formerly, the slogan used to be socialism and secularism for election purposes. Now at present (1988) 'socialism' remains only in the Constitution and on paper, it is not even mentioned in the speeches of political leaders. Thus, the economic exploitation of the poorer castes goes unchecked. In spite of repeated assurances to the poor sections the programme of raising their economic standard remains unimplemented. Rising inflation, population explosion and corrupt practices add to the woe of the poor castes. Thus, the country remains poor by making direct use of caste-religion for the Hindus.

Secondly, in the British days, there were hardly any caste

riots. But by making caste as the basis of election, castes remain in tension, and, in the State of Bihar at present there are caste riots. The reason for this is both economic and political. In the oppression of the scheduled castes by the Zamindars belonging to the higher castes, the economic consideration plays as much part as political factor. Thus, the political use of caste results in caste riots.

Thirdly, corruption in the States goes unchecked. There are several causes of corruption, but one cause is certainly caste leadership. Any person belonging to the higher caste may indulge in corrupt practices. He can always rely on his caste-leadership in the political field if he falls into trouble for committing economic and other crimes.

Political parties try to enforce and perpetuate reservation for the scheduled castes and tribes. True, a few people have profited from reservation in the services, legislative assemblies and councils, admission into educational institutions. But reservation has not raised the scheduled castes as a whole either socially, economically or politically. Even now after 41 years of Independence they continue to be the object of humiliation, exploitation and mass violence.

Thus, the political use of religion neither serves the State nor religion. The State remains economically, socially and politically poor and backward. Religion gets polluted because of constant riots in the name of religion. Politically the country becomes unstable on account of the Separatist tendency based on religion. The political use of religion by the communalist and casteist is highly dishonest and politically is unethical and unpatriotic. But alas! in near future there is no hope to get out of cast or communal consideration.

Religion may not teach to hate one's fellowmen, but politics does. Political use of religion is not in the service of democracy. But will the political leaders learn this lesson?

INDEX